CONTENTS

PREFACE 1
CAST OF CHARACTERS 3
A FUNERAL 7
PART ONE - THE FLIMSIEST OF FOUNDATIONS 9
PART TWO - UNDER THE RADAR 101
PART THREE - STEALING A PARTY 169
PART FOUR - OCTOBER SURPRISES 288
ABOUT THE AUTHOR 475

PREFACE

The manuscript for this book was written in 2013 and the political context - the seizure of the Labour leadership by a radical insurgency - seemed almost absurdly far-fetched. Now there's the opposite danger; the risk that life has imitated fiction (if not art) a little too early for comfort. But the book attempts to describe not just the ease with which a perfectly legal take-over can be mounted in UK politics but the corrosive effect of ambition on relationships and the difficult transition to a period when in terms of the private lives of politicians and what is acceptable all bets appear to be off.

The story of Raphael Sinclair and his political ascent unfolds through the eyes of three participants; Helen Mitchison, an old friend and colleague, writing her political memoirs years later; Ned Warren, one of the group of young insurgents which sees Sinclair as its route to the top, writing, emailing and then texting his brother in Australia; and Barrie Jones, Sinclair's long-term aid, confiding his thoughts and fears about the man he loves but knows too well, to a secret diary, never to be published. TV bulletins and a media commentator complete the narration.

I am indebted to four people: to my friends, Martin Bailey, Gareth Williams and Stephen Clark who have waded through the text, made genuinely helpful and pertinent suggestions and broadly encouraged me in a venture which takes me far out of my current comfort zone, which is writing and talking about European politics. The fourth is my partner, Jean Schons, who helped me in the transition from the typed text (which he saved on a number of occasions) to a form presentable for e-publication. The book is dedicated to him.

But all four are absolved from any responsibility for all which follows and which, for better or worse, is my own work.

Any resemblance of any character to any person living or dead is coincidental for the most part.

AUTHOR'S NOTE; For the sake of clarity, each of the extracts of the three 'narrators' is published on a separate and sometimes very short page. The media comments (excerpts from broadcasts, commentaries etc.) are in italics.

"What a story. Everything but the bloodhounds snappin' at her rear end!"

Bridie, from 'All About Eve'

CAST OF CHARACTERS

The politicians

The MPs

Raphael Sinclair

Helen Mitchison

Hattie Reynolds

Maudie Hinton

Paul Howkins

Louise Marchant

The cabinet ministers

Derek Jamieson

Brian Dawkins

Rory McBain

Marsha Worthington

Bradley Mortimer

Arthur Rillington

Ted & Mary

Two Prime Ministers

The Peers

Lorna, Baroness Horrocks of Risborough

'The Lord Snake'

The other parties

Tim..., the leader of the Conservatives

Andrew..., the leader of the Liberal Democrats

The economics spokesmen of the opposition parties

The backroom boys and girls

Bill Sampson

Bob Hatchway

MariLisa Ngowo

JoBoy Miles

Gwilym Rhys

The chairperson of the TUC

The brats

Ned Warren

Angus Buchanan

Rashida Hussein

Rupert Dennison

Aidan Richards

Staffers & Officials

Barrie Jones

Nigel Bolton

Marjorie Delaney

Elaine Chayter

Miranda Fawcett

Bo Sampson

Eddie Smith, the driver

The Foreign Office

Dame Cynthia Montcalm

Sir Clarence Montague and 'Lady Penelope'

Dame Elizabeth Jones-Wright

Helen Chandler

The body guards

Bud Mitchell

Kevin

The Mayberry connection

Tom Carter, local party chair

Rodney Wills, local party agent

Friends and Family

Digby

Martin Warren

Ted

Nicholas, an ex

Marie-Claude Bolton

Marie-France, hotelier

And Jose Durrao Pinto, who brings nothing but trouble

The media

The political editor of the BBC

A tabloid reporter

J C Dunnett, prize-winning commentator

A FUNERAL

That Tuesday it was raining so hard at the North London Crematorium the raindrops bounced back to a height at which they seemed to double up with their successors. The only thing exceptional about the event for any unfortunate passer-by was the phalanx of soaked photographers unable to keep their lenses dry, as if enveloped in a lachrymose film. A procession of black cars moved in. The little family first. Then several more, with the Prime Minister getting out of his alone, in a black raincoat, collar up, his face concealed from the media. Four cars back, after security, more of the 'New Left celebrities', some faces still unknown to the general public, and in any case scarcely recognisable in their rush to avoid the drenching.

Half an hour later, with the downpour continuing, no worse, no better, the leader emerged first, the goodbyes to the family having been said inside in the dry. Again he moved too quickly for any of the crews to get usable shots. The car sped away with the Prime Minister sitting on the side furthest from spectators, looking away to avoid a clean shot.

Quite a few cars back, Helen Mitchison, her fairish hair bedraggled despite the black scarf she had prudently brought with her to the office that morning, sat next to Barrie Jones. Helen's face was unremarkable: middle-aged, pleasant, a little careworn, a small nose slightly upturned and a complexion which needed just a little more make-up than it received. On most days she was dressed sensibly - even a little too much so - but in a way she deemed suitable for a professional woman shortly turning fifty. Today of course as required she wore a black skirt, just below the knee, a black jacket, and a slate grey blouse with a high neck. In any case all was hidden by a black trenchcoat, done up to the top button.

Barrie Jones sat on the side furthest from the building's gates and even in the space of the few seconds longer to get to the right-hand car door had managed to get his black suit wet through, so that everything seemed to stick to his small body, once so wiry, now fleshing out quite unflatteringly, his shirt front buttons beginning to strain. His dark curly hair, streaked now with flecks of grey, somehow picked up the lights from the flashing car lamps.

They had known each other for ten years but when they finally spoke a few words after a silence which was less dutiful and more a moment of reflection about the darkest time of the extraordinary season they had just lived through, his pleasant, slightly lilting voice reminded her of how attractive in an entirely asexual way she had found him when they had met first. Despite all the emotional strain he retained a chirpiness which more than any physical attribute was the essence of his charm. Some very bright men seem to retain a restless youthful energy which belies their years. He was bright, a bit of a chatter-box, with quick movements - he trotted when you walked beside him - deeply loyal, constantly turning to look at you with his overwhelming desire to please.

****

In the end, for Barrie Jones, any prolonged silence was uncomfortable so he asked a question he had often pondered, "Are you writing all this down?" he asked. "I see you scribbling away at meetings."

"Yes, Barrie. A sort of history of the time we've been through - a personal one. But please don't tell anyone, and I mean anyone."

A few moments later she asked, "And you, are you writing something?"

"Well, I keep a diary- not every day of course. I don't have the time and I'm too knackered in the evening, but I catch up on Sundays before everything gets too blurred. Have done for years. Dunno if it's usable or not."

"This story?"

A few miles on, after another natural silence, she came back to the subject. "I suppose we'll need someone's permission; who can give authorisation? The cabinet secretary?"

"Well it depends when you want to publish it, but the old rules have been pretty much eroded away by all the previous lot. No, the one we should all watch out for is Ned; all the immediate stuff. The blogs. The tweets, even during cabinet..."

"Ah yes", she said "but Ned has licence from on high."

PART ONE - THE FLIMSIEST OF FOUNDATIONS

HELEN'S STORY

(Extracts from 'Insurgency-the Inside Story' by the Rt. Hon. Helen Mitchison)

I first met Raphael Sinclair at the Freshers' Fair, all the university societies and clubs touting for new members among the first-years. I went with two other girls from St Hilda's whom I had met two days before, but we split up as soon as we got into the hall when I made a bee-line for the Labour Club stall (not much choice really with my father being a Labour MP[1], and mother chairing our ward party) but clearly the Labour Party was the last thing on the minds of my two fellow freshers.

And there he was, tall, collar-length jet black hair swept back directly from his forehead, with a Clark Gable moustache, very dark brown expressive eyes which could fix on you as if you were his only interest in the world giving him the cover to think about something else, and the deep chocolate voice which projected but not too obviously - everything harnessed to please and charm. Even then, with a tatty blazer, worn shiny through overuse, jeans which were neither faded nor particularly clean, a green check shirt which clashed with the jacket and was one size too small, and shoes which hadn't been cleaned since purchase, he projected a kind of charismatic glamour. It turned out that he was a fresher too and that he had been left in charge of the stall by two second-years in search of a sandwich. When he was freed from his task he took me for coffee in the Turl[2], where he talked mostly about himself and his ambitions and we arranged to meet up at the first Labour Club event of the term (to listen to the first in the series of second-rate former ministers who were now in the market for any old meeting).

Within weeks I was a Sinclair groupie - Labour Club meetings, the Europe Society, the Fabians, and the Union. And we climbed the ladder together, but with me always in his wake. For a long time I think I saw him every day. We got into the habit of meeting up in the Bodleian[3], going for coffee or a snack lunch, planning his next political move, with him graciously allowing me a place on the various 'tickets' he led, and going to parties together some evenings, where we danced, where he stole all the limelight and after which he sometimes walked me back to the college when nothing, absolutely nothing, happened. I worked hard,

---

[1] Graham Mitchison, MP for Dewsbury, 1964-1983
[2] A street in Oxford well-known for cafes and bars
[3] The University Library

but once prelims[4] were out the way he took the view that reading the Economist, the Guardian, the Times and the political weeklies would see him through which, irritatingly, it did.

My hopes were momentarily raised when I was invited the first time to Mayberry during the long vac[5] to stay with his parents. The Sinclairs had a pleasant semi-detached house with a well-tended garden. I got on well with his parents, both I think secretly relieved to see Raphael showing a bit of interest in a girl. His father was headmaster at the largest local comprehensive, disappearing behind clouds of fairly foul-smelling pipe tobacco, but while looking his years retained such a beautiful clear voice and excellent diction that you might have taken him for a Shakespearian actor. He certainly had a way with words. Mrs Sinclair, who must have been stunning in her youth with those dark eyes, short black hair and the way she rather dazzled with bright blouses and skirts, taught French at a neighbouring school, and supplemented her income doing commercial translations for local companies. I had not been surprised when I learned that Raphael was their only child, but the extent to which they lived through him by proxy was almost shocking.

At the start of the second year, Elaine turned up. Elaine Chayter's reputation had galloped before her: the glamour, the clothes, the father a successful novelist, the mother presenting 'lifestyle' shows on the BBC. She stood out from even the smarter Lady Margaret Hall crowd with her wavy light brown hair, her 'been there, done that' expression, her way of walking into a room, sniffing out the most likely coming man, latching on to him, and more often than not going back to his place. Other women were at best minor obstacles to be trampled over. Labour was beginning to come back from the grave, so Labour it was. The only man of any interest in the Labour Club was its new chairman, Raphael Sinclair. So it was in that direction that her hat was flung. I didn't stand a chance. Within a week it was, "Elaine thinks this...Elaine says I should do this...Elaine had a great idea" - an idea always involving Elaine of course. Hard-working Yorkshire dowdiness versus Southern Belle was no contest. Elaine's parents had a cottage outside Ludlow, with a grass tennis court, and Raphael started being a regular weekend guest. By the next summer the two of them were holidaying at Portofino, in her uncle's villa.

---

[4] Preliminary examinations, taken after two or three terms in the first year
[5] Vacation

Between us, we carried off most of the glittering prizes (more like semi-precious ones in my case). I succeeded Raphael at the Labour Club and managed to be elected as Secretary of the Union during Raphael's term as President, when he pulled off the triumph of getting both living former Prime Ministers and the US Vice-President to speak in debates. Elaine also managed the double in his wake but it was clear that they were no longer 'a couple'. And he took me to the May ball at his college just after finals. I was quite nervous; would this finally be it? But no, it was as if he was partnering all the other guests, the centre of attention, the rising star around whom all others revolve. He did not completely ignore me, of course, but we only danced a few times, and never, I noticed, to a slow tune.

With my good upper second, I managed to scrape into the BBC as a trainee. Elaine just flew in. While I was in the management stream, holding meetings with surly shop stewards for the removals men, and sitting on recruitment boards travelling from one tedious provincial hotel to another interviewing potential secretaries, Elaine was hoisted into news, soon presenting London regional bulletins before going national.

Raphael had got the same degree as me but seemed quite happy to take a job with the main teachers' union, working his way up the political department. At his suggestion we shared a flat in Southwark, although I had to veto the idea of Elaine making it a threesome. Throughout our twenties we both stuck at our jobs, and both made our way. And we both got on the Labour Party's approved candidates list and started getting called to selection conferences. Suddenly, at the age of just 30 he was selected for the one safe Labour seat in Mayberry where his parents lived, just beyond the constituency boundary. I missed out on getting picked for father's old seat at Dewsbury, but, surprisingly, was selected for Derby North, a more marginal seat but still one with a long Labour tradition.

There was some press interest in 'the rising star couple', 'the candidates who live together' on which we made no comment one way or another. The moment it dawned on me how convenient all this was, was the night after we had both become brand new Labour MPs at the age of 32. We had a bottle of champagne, reminisced a lot about the quirks of the campaign and I led him to my bedroom. I got him to lie on the bed, slowly started kissing him but after a few minutes while I waited for the next step (which never materialised) he just said quietly, almost pathetically, "Why don't we just have a nice cuppa?"

After thirteen years I finally understood that it was just never going to happen.

EXTRACTS FROM THE DIARIES OF BARRIE JONES

(never published)...

I see this advert in the New Statesman, 'Shadow Minister seeks research assistant...' The salary is lousy, but I telephone. A nice woman with a warm kindly voice, not young I guess, answers, "Raphael Sinclair's office. Marjorie Delaney speaking. How can I help?" I introduce myself, she asks me to send in my CV, end of conversation.

****

I had almost forgotten that call I made for the job with Sinclair, the shadow higher education minister but this week the 'phone rings and that same warm voice is saying, "I do apologise for the delay". My heart sank - he's obviously chosen someone else. "Mr Sinclair would like to meet you if you're still interested in the position. He's seeing three people. Would next Wednesday afternoon suit you?"

****

I arrive early just to cope with security. I meet Marjorie under the clock, as arranged. She's just what I imagined, smaller perhaps, with a kind, open almost concerned face, but not submissive or shy. She has no trace of accent; acknowledges everyone on the way up some back stairs to Sinclair's office; wears no makeup, and is wearing flat sandals without stockings.

I go into the small room, just a double desk, four work chairs, no armchair, quite dark, with only a tiny window, too high up to afford any view except of the leaden sky. His side of the desk is strewn with papers, her half in perfect order. He rises, bigger than he appears on the screen, tall but also heavier - heavy bones I should think. Good looking alright, but not immediately sexy, dressed in a rumpled corduroy jacket, with trousers just half an inch too short for those long and rather sturdy legs, black hair swept back but not with any brylcream or anything as far as I could see. About 35: strong handshake and direct penetrating gaze, giving nothing away.

Impeccably polite, with a really good 'political voice' displaying authority but also some warmth; he puts me in a seat, offers tea and says, "Now, Mr Jones, tell me about yourself". (Rather formal by the standards of

Labour comradeship I'd say – or is this the first sign of ministerial airs and graces?).

I had decided not to lie, and go into my prepared spiel – trying not to gabble, "I was born in Aberdare twenty-seven years ago. My father's head of the Transport Department at Cardiff City Council. My mother teaches part time at the local primary. They're both in the Party. As you may have seen in the CV, I got a first in history at Cambridge. I was in the college choir and rose to the dizzying heights of membership secretary at the Labour Club" (this brought an indulgent smile).

"I took the Foreign Office exams, and passed. My first foreign posting was Madrid as third secretary. Then at the beginning of the year I decided I did not want to carry on lying about myself. So I told Personnel that I was gay, despite the dissembling when I had first been vetted. They were actually nice about it, sought various outplacements but that didn't work. So by agreement, I resigned and they gave me the good references which I sent along with the CV." He nods. "Since then I've been applying to think tanks, charity management jobs, and now this."

There was a long pause before he says, deadpan,

"Shame about Cambridge but otherwise a very good CV."

We then have more of a conversation than an interview, and talk for ages about my political views, NATO, the Middle East, and Europe.

I say, "I'm afraid I know nothing about your area apart from just thinking generally that Education is important."

He replies, "Actually I'm looking for a move myself and Foreign Affairs is what I want in the long run. Well, as Marjorie will have told you we still have someone else to see this afternoon, so we won't hold you up any longer."

I get up to leave, and he escorts me to the door, but just before opening it he takes my elbow – just a shade familiar - and says as an afterthought, "Look, could you hang around downstairs for about an hour. Marjorie will then come and fetch you back and we can continue our chat."

It was a long hour, and then he comes himself, sits me down in one of the alcoves designed for plotting or assignation, and says,

"Can you start on Monday? The salary's lousy but our allowances should be going up next year."

****

And so it's started. It feels like there's going to be a pre-Sinclair and a Sinclair period to my life! The three of us, the boss, Marjorie and I, are crammed into the one office. It seems to me that the restless intelligence and political imagination of Raphael has a perfect counterpoint in Marjorie's quiet efficiency. As for me I've been immediately thrown into drafting, researching, and batting ideas across the table in the crowded room. Raphael smokes (which shocked me a bit) but most of the time goes out to the small door near the roof of the tower, in deference to a distaste which Marjorie and I make obvious without daring openly to express it.

****

I've worked with him now for four months. I like and admire him hugely. Do I fancy him? I don't think so. He's got great looks of course but he is terribly tall and I like small guys – is that so I don't feel threatened? But I do want to spend more time with him. So I finally screw up my courage and yesterday, after Marjorie had finally left the office, I say, "Come on, let me take you for a drink." He looks a bit taken aback, then says, "Why not?" and off we go to a pub just ten minutes away off Victoria Street. We chat amiably for nearly an hour, had a couple of beers when he said, "Better get back home. Helen's preparing something and invited round a couple of friends."

****

After a year working with Raphael I now see the whole Helen thing doesn't add up. They behave like an old married couple but I know they don't go on holiday together. Each year he heads south - Greece, Spain, Portugal - 'for a bit of golf', with unspecified friends, and comes back looking happy, relaxed and rested, with his almost-but-not-quite movie star looks restored.

From time to time in the office there'll be, "Barrie, why don't you take Marjorie for a coffee?" with my cheeky reply, "Because we've just had one" followed by his "That wasn't a suggestion" to close matters followed by my rejoinder "And how long do you suggest we take drinking our coffee?" which earns me a surly look.

A few months ago he contrived to take 6 trips to Italy in quick succession - easier to justify now that he's the party's spokesperson on Europe, and it was the Italian presidency of the EU, but in July and August when the whole of Europe is at the beach?

While I was opening the mail this morning, with Marjorie recuperating from her broken right arm, a photo falls out of an envelope, a rather posed picture of a beautiful young man, with long sleek black hair, stretched out, with a white speedo which just about covered the prominent essentials. And on the back, 'Gianni XXX'.

****

Last night it was intimate confessions time. I'd gone to the house in Battersea he shares with Helen to drop off some papers he needed for a Midlands business conference on trade with Europe the next day. Helen had gone off to Bristol for some regional party event. The house is on one of those nondescript old railway estate terraces, 2 up, 2 down, but nicely furnished (by Helen I assume) with comfortable sofas in light pastels and more airy than one would expect coming in from the street. And there is a pretty patio where Helen has placed lots of pots with different bushes to offer flowers in rotation to give a little dash of colour for most months of the year. I think they bought it cheap and will be surprised at what they'll get if ever they sell.

We worked for an hour and had a couple of drinks. I had taken my jacket and shoes off as usual and strewn papers round the floor. He sat on the sofa, I was kneeling on the floor. Stupidly I sat back with my head leaning against his left knee. I stayed put. I could feel him tense up. A minute passed and I removed my head, turned and could see tears welling up.

The floodgates opened. He blurted out that he'd fancied me rotten, the first time he'd seen me (which rather explained the touch on the elbow!). At least he had the good manners not to say that that was how I got the job. He'd loved the late night calls, the dropping in and out of Battersea, and the sheer proximity at the office. But somewhere along the line, he said, the desire had turned into 'the deepest friendship two men could have in an unconsummated relationship' and which itself was a sort of barrier to going the whole way. This sounded a little bit like rationalisation – either he didn't want to push me because he was afraid of rejection (though, in reality, would I have rejected him at that moment?) – something Raphael certainly isn't used to; or because I'm already too useful to him and too visible to others to risk a failed affair.

Whatever, there was more to come, "I've started having relationships abroad. It's the same pattern…" He went upstairs for a moment and came down with a selection of his 'holiday snaps'- quite the Mediterranean grand tour, the Greek, the soulful Italian (the one with the white speedos in the photo, I assume), a Spaniard and, by way of a detour, the almost regulation Brazilian he'd met in Italy, near the Spanish steps and who had picked him up quite shamelessly, taking his hand openly, and more or less dragging him back to his hotel just a couple of doors away from Keats' House. They were an impressive gallery, all dark, except curiously the Greek, all young but not kids either and all with the same searching needy eyes.

"Each time it ends in tears. They each want to come here, want me to meet their families, then to be introduced to my friends. They each want to settle down, and that of course can't happen because it would bring down the curtain on everything here. So I start to disengage, but I do it clumsily and don't end things neatly. So recriminations, upset all round, and bad feelings which I could have avoided if I hadn't led them on in the first place. Now there's an election coming all these shenanigans have to stop. You and I, Barrie, it could have been the one real thing but at least I've got the best and truest friend I could ever hope for."

Sad really.

HELEN

We had moved to Battersea in our own version of 'Keeping Up Appearances'. I realised that this meant nothing for our relationship. We shared a house, a kitchen and a bathroom; when neither of us had something else planned we snacked together and watched a rented video. I thought he might be seeing Elaine again; she telephoned often, rather later in the evening than elementary courtesy might indicate but then I saw a diary piece about her and a theatre director.

Raphael took on Barrie Jones in his office. I liked him hugely; he was like a little garrulous friendly teenager, with his short curly hair and twinkly eyes. He always brightened you up when he came round to the house, which was nearly all the time - and sometimes he followed his boss to Mayberry whenever there was more than routine 'surgery' work. It was obvious to me that Barrie was smitten, infatuated, possibly in love; and at first Raphael spoke constantly about his 'brilliant, clever' assistant of such great integrity, such excellent drafting skills, like the best civil service appraisal report for someone the boss wants promoting.

But they did not go on holiday together. Barrie was still at the 'seeing the world' stage; every year a new continent while for Raphael holidaying meant the sun and golf and, with hindsight I now assume, sex; and always somewhere along the Mediterranean coast.

One evening after a couple of his trips to Greece, the telephone rang at home. A young man with a strong accent was asking where Raphael was. His English being poor, I spoke to him as Joyce Grenfell used to lecture those children in her class, informed him that 'Mr Sinclair' was away and that I would give him a message if he would give me his name. He became quite insistent so I gave him Raphael's office number. He rang back six times that evening, his voice progressing from tremulous to lachrymose.

After I had unplugged the telephone I sat down as I began to take in the blindingly obvious: after fifteen years of hoping against hope, of stratagems to corner my prey, of subjugating my needs and desires to fit in with his wishes, I now knew that the only man I had ever loved was not the slightest bit interested in women. He was polite, courteous, and friendly with women. He genuinely liked working with them, enjoyed their company. They felt valued in his presence. But it had been hopeless from the start because he just preferred men. It was as simple as that. I was not angry. He had never lied or 'led' me on, although clearly our arrangement had provided convenient cover. I sat there numb, the realisation of my stupidity and myopia making me inert, listless and empty.

However, life goes on. The next day the election was called. We both held our seats easily as Labour cruised to victory. By late Friday afternoon, Raphael Sinclair was Minister of State for Europe at the Foreign and Commonwealth Office, on the edge but not inside the cabinet; and I had become Minister of State at Education, responsible for Higher Education, ironically Raphael's old portfolio. There was no time to mope, we had a world to change.

THE UNPUBLISHED CORRESPONDENCE OF NED WARREN TO HIS OLDER BROTHER MARTIN,

emigrated to Adelaide, Australia in the mid nineties

Dear Mart,

You'll have had mum and dad on the 'phone so you'll know. Result!

I was in bed, seriously hung-over, the same state I've been in since Lorraine dumped me; the words 'fat', 'git', 'drunken', 'slob', 'stinking', 'groping' and 'scum bag' being the essence of the last things she said to me. Dad came into my bedroom (unusually without knocking), all of a quiver and holding 'the letter'. The dean of Balliol, my new best friend, was writing to tell me that I was now an Exhibitioner (no coarse remarks, please; not an exhibitionist or an exhibit) - to read PPE (that's politics, philosophy and economics to you, mate, and sounds to me like a lot more reading than pleasure would dictate). I have to 'go up' (get the vocab right) end of September so quite a few more nights to be spent at the Rising Sun. I'll get a grant and a room in college for the first two years.

Dad goes downstairs, in tears, shouting like a lunatic at mum and the dog, "He's in! He's in!" The whole Matlock fraternity comes round; much refilling of teapot and patting of my sore head. Me constantly feeling faintly sick and wondering whether to make a run for the loo, but quite enjoying the adulation for Matlock's representative of the 'jeunesse dorée'.

When we go the next day to the new hyper-hyper-hyper market at Mayberry (to buy me a new suit for college which shows you which century mum's still in) there's this geezer in the car park, on a soapbox, shouting the odds through a loudspeaker, rubbishing the Tories. He's quite good really, spoke directly to you, not like some of the more robotic New Labour people. Quite left as well. Turns out he's the local Labour MP, Raphael Sinclair (very Labour name, I don't think). He's already got a majority of 7,234 - not that I'm some kind of political nerd. When he's finished, before I can stop her, mum goes over, preening, and says, "Mr Sinclair, can I introduce you to my son, Edward, who's going to Oxford in the autumn."

He shook my hand. Smart looking bloke, a bit different from the others, he looked me straight in the eye. "Well done, which college?" "Balliol, sir" (yes I know grovel, grovel!) and he says, "Better and better. Mind you join the Labour Club, and then you can invite me to speak."

He's bound to win. Dad says all his mates at the Postal Union are working flat out for Labour this time, even if some of them don't buy the whole New Labour stuff. So this guy Sinclair will be a minister by the time you read this.

Hope you and Lill and the girls are OK. Must be midwinter down there, can't be much worse than High Summer here.

A little bit of respect in the future.

Your luvving bruvver,

Ned

EXTRACT FROM 'A POLITICAL OBSERVER:

An Anthology of the JC Dunnett articles in 'The London Gazette', (199- to 201-)'

For nearly twenty years JC Dunnett has been writing the finest articles about British politics for 'The London Gazette'. His scepticism, wit, insights and independence of spirit have made his commentaries the most widely read in the political world. We are proud to be publishing this anthology, and we start with a piece he wrote shortly after joining the magazine in 199-..

"I've never voted in an election or joined a political party. Every time I've been tempted to stray from the independent course I'd set, or been momentarily seduced by the apparent cogency of an argument or the clarity of its advocacy, I've poured myself a large scotch, sat in my favourite armchair and given myself a little time for thought. This election offered just such a moment of febrility. This young man offering to the lead the country does have a freshness about him. He speaks well. His programme, such as it is, appears irreproachably moderate.

And the country has tired a little of the Tories after eighteen years, even if the ousting of the Iron Lady shifted the music from Wagnerian climaxes to the kind of easy listening which featured so prominently on the wireless in the 1950s. New Labour offers us something a little more modern, pop music but sufficiently middle of the road to reassure us. No-one in this band is going to smash their guitars on stage or wreck the hotel furniture during their tours.

But as I dig a little deeper all my innate hesitancy returns. What exactly do they stand for? I've read their pledges, so helpfully reduced to five slogans on a loyalty card, and found myself wondering who on earth could oppose that? But if it's as easy as that, why has it not been done before?

And if the winsome champion of 'the new politics' (does anyone except your humble scribbler hanker after 'the old politics'?) has his own appeal to the upwardly mobile and the Mondeo-driving residents of Worcester, what has he to say about all the global challenges facing us? How do we protect the planet if we remain so friendly towards the automobile? How do we place ourselves 'at the heart of Europe' when we intend postponing joining the new currency our continental friends are about to launch? How do we pay for a free health service, the national totem, when financing our ageing population's needs for care will one day consume all the nation's budget? If we remain in such a compromising proximity to the current American regime, what price will we have to pay to ingratiate ourselves with its possibly less congenial successor?

I've spent many an hour searching the deathly prose of the new great Helmsman, and his somewhat forbidding chancellor, and I find these questions never raised let alone answered. Indeed, the only thing of interest to be found in the speeches of our young Prime Minister is their scant reverence for syntax and what my parents used to describe as 'proper English'. But I do rather doubt whether this reveals a revolutionary intent, rather a capitulation to the hordes of communications advisers, now swarming Downing Street, all at the taxpayer's expense, and counselling against completing grammatically constructed sentences as likely to dull 'the message'.

There is talent on the Commons' benches behind him and in the junior ranks of his government. But they will be forced to take sides as the cosy diarchy the Prime Minister has established with his Chancellor begins to fall apart."

NED

Dear Mart,

Got here on Tuesday, just a couple of days early to get acclimatised before term starts. Mum and Dad drove me with all my stuff, conveniently forgetting my drums, we had a look round and saw the room. It's on what they call back quad (courtyard to you, quadrangle, geddit?), staircase XV (never 15, remember that when you write, not exactly a daily occurrence). The room seemed to shrink by the time all my stuff had been brought up. It's got a couple of windows on to the quad, with mum pointing out, "They don't seem to have heard of double glazing in these parts. It'll be parky in winter, can get very cold in this area. You should have brought that Xmas jumper your aunt Sybil knitted" (remember the reindeers gambolling on a puce background - all the rage here I'm sure!). There was a 2-bar fire - this part of the college not being linked into the central heating system, which only works in the new staircases where they put the Yanks and any other fee-paying sucker from the big wide world. The furniture is basic, a single bed (a fairly accurate prediction for my sex life the next few years, I'd say), a sink and mirror, presumably for throwing up in and then seeing how green you look, a desk for all that studying I'll be doing, one chair there and a couple of armchairs, last upholstered in the late 1940s. Oh, and a coffee table with more cup and glass stains than clean spaces; and a couple of cupboards that are not only not fitted, they look like they might keel over at any moment, especially since they've had my stuff put in them. So this is how young gentlemen live!

By the time I'd got my gear in, and fitted up my stereo (every day dicing with death with the wiring here), it was time for some grub, so I waddled over to hall, climbed the steep steps and grabbed some pretty dire food from the buffet, sat on one of the plain wood benches and gobbled it down; there being a kind of race to see how quickly you can polish off this revolting stuff and get on with your life. After this feast I went over to the JCR (that's Junior Common Room, for oiks) to loll around on the heavily damaged Styrofoam sofas (difficult to rise from them with my customary elegance of movement) and see if there was any local talent. Two girls come in, look at me and beat a hasty retreat. I was going to try some of the pubs and went back towards my room to pick up an anorak - the only one which still fits.

Just as I was entering into the dark hall (bulb gone and term not even started) I bump into this tall guy with fairish hair well over his collar, deep grey blue eyes, slim but you'd know he was there. He took me in with one quick gaze, held out his hand, unsmiling, and said, "Hi there, my name's Angus Buchanan".

Turns out he's doing PPE too but with rather more economics than I'd care for. Already after 12 hours there he seems to know everything about college and university life. He immediately made it clear he was very left-wing Labour; told me how to sign up to the Labour Club, the Fabians, the anti-racist groups, every left-wing cause you could mention. He'd done it all 'on-line' (I'll explain one day since computers have probably not reached South Australia yet) from Aberdeen. He warned me off the Union ("bunch of self-regarding elitist prima donna careerists, and that's just the women"). He told me to drop into his room in two days' time at 5 o'clock (note the precision) and we could get to know some other people in our political studies 'set'.

By the time I went downstairs to answer this summons I'd had my first run in with my scout (they're called 'college servants' but actually they are spies for the proctors - fancy name for the local gestapo - sent to terrorise students), who told me to clear up 'this disgusting mess' (I thought that was his job, just like it used to be mum's), and met my tutors, one of whom looked pityingly at me when he asked me what I had been reading in the summer, and where I rattled off the list of all those detective novels.

In Angus' room, neater, and I'm sure bigger than mine, he introduced me as "Folks this is my neighbour, Ned Warren, from the beautiful city of Matlock". There was a really pretty Pakistani girl, Rashida Hussein, pale, cool, discreetly dressed, there's clearly money in her family. Angus has obviously got the hots for her, and I don't blame him. And there were two other blokes: a posh, fair pretty boy type called Rupert Dennison, with a hoity-toity accent, from St Paul's (the poshest school in London); very, very sure of himself, well dressed - in this connoisseur's view. Of course he has the kind of voice that he manages to raise just a pitch above any of the others to command silence. If Angus had mugged up on the political clubs, Rupert knew everything about the social customs of our new tribe, the restaurants to be seen in, the going rate for bribing scouts, and had already wangled himself a room upgrade at the expense of some unsuspecting comprehensive kid from Rotherham. He'd simply frightened the kid off with tales of rat infestations.

The last of this quartet is called Aidan Richards. He's got feral black hair, the style of which he seems to change every day, and a beard which comes and goes as if painted on in the mornings as to order. He's middling height, speaks with a kind of unplaceable estuary accent (that's

Thames not Humber!) and is dressed not in the flash way of Rupert but with a kind of style. He's a bright comprehensive kid (like me), with a bit of menace about him (not like me) but with I guess a lot of sex appeal (so not so unlike me after all). His eyes tell you he's done everything with anything which walks.

When Rashida went up to the attic loo I asked as nonchalantly as possible, "Where does one pick up local talent?" Rupert replied "Tradition says it's got to be the Bodleian, soulful eyes meeting over piles of books, and a confident but not quite arrogant 'how about a cup of coffee?'"

Aidan took over, "Not for the sort of blokes I'm into. I want older men, so I'll just have to work my way through the tutors, though if I stick to the SCR here it will be three years of celibacy for me. Perhaps a trawl through other faculties further afield will yield more promising results."

Oh dear. I think Angus was as stunned as I was. The first 'out and proud' gay man we'd ever met in the flesh as it were.

Angus quickly moved on to the safer subject of organising a takeover of the Labour Club and ousting what he described as the "social fascists and careerists". The means appear to be bullying, intimidation and then once successful - authoritarian control. Sounds quite fun really.

Sorry to hear about little Jen's fall. Hope she'll soon be back in the saddle.

Love from your little brother,

Ned

HELEN

After his boss the Foreign Secretary[6] had the stroke, Raphael ended up doing everything at the Foreign Office: all FCO questions in the House, all the EU Council meetings, all the visiting dignitaries, even having to go with the Queen on her first visit to South Korea. He had tried to get out of it but the Prime Minister had insisted, trilling on about "South Korea being a new strategic partner of huge importance". I was worried about the strain which was starting to show on Raphael's face.

Of course, Rory's stroke had barely hit the news headlines before speculation about his successor became rampant. Various favourites of the PM and the Chancellor were the subject of endless commentaries; few journalists thought that anyone outside the inner circles of the warlords of New Labour could conceivably get the job. But in the end the aplomb with which Raphael acquitted himself, particularly in a sticky Commons debate on the Balkans[7], and all the time that he had deputised during the lengthy artificial prolongation of Rory's life made his succession almost inevitable when the plugs were finally pulled.

After his appointment there were several profiles with Raphael as 'the coming man', 'above the melee', 'joining the small group of possible successors'. Several papers had got hold of photos of the pair of us (with me looking particularly dowdy, and him stellar) and referred to us as Labour's new power couple, speculating on my possible promotion to the cabinet in the next reshuffle; at least two referred to us as 'husband and wife'. I was upset, Raphael not at all. He never mentioned foreign dalliances and I supposed that that had all come to an end once he had got into office.

Then, as the drumbeat for war grew louder, things turned sour. I only saw Raphael occasionally at rushed breakfasts very early in the morning - he had turned down the official London flat, which was snapped up by a senior colleague, and even declined to use the country house at weekends. He was clearly burdened with doubt about the war, bottled up his reservations except, it seemed, in cabinet, where he demanded legal advice about going in without a new UN resolution. When he circulated the FCO legal advice, which was crystal clear (he showed it me), he earned a reprimand from the PM in cabinet, along the lines "so

---

[6] Rt Hon Rory McBain
[7] In March 200-

it's the FCO which now gives us legal advice, well, the next time I'm in need of a Middle East Peace Plan I'll ask the Department of Transport".

Raphael felt increasingly shut out of decision-making. The Americans were quite brazen about wanting him replaced. And, as if to call, parts of the press started with snide stuff about the FCO "not being on side" or "soft on dictatorships and the causes of dictatorships", and Sinclair being "more French than the French". "After all", as one particularly venomous piece had it, "his mother is a French teacher." All of this bile was clearly inspired by Downing Street, either No 10 or No 11. Throughout Raphael kept his head down, was loyal in public and deeply unhappy.

BARRIE

My love for Raphael knows no bounds! He really dug his heels in this week and insisted I be his special adviser, despite the residual 'security risk'. When his Private Secretary, the ferocious Ms Cynthia Montcalm with her sharp features and piercing cut-glass accent, tried to put me in some cupboard at the end of the corridor, he just raised his voice a notch and said "If necessary he sits in my office. He knows more about foreign policy than most of the people in this building put together".

I know we can do good stuff on Europe. And of course having Marjorie with us helps no end (though I note that there were no FCO objections to her coming along, just to me!) The visits to Battersea and the odd trip to Mayberry seem likely to continue, and our intimacy unimpaired.

****

The PM finally announced today that Raphael is Rory's successor. He died last night. Odd atmosphere in the place as we moved all our stuff over. But it'll be a great team; Marjorie, La Montcalm, with whom I get on well enough these days: the kind of middle-aged hard-nosed battle-axe every minister needs but she and I occasionally share a laugh about some of Raphael's more outlandish ideas. And then there's Nigel Bolton, an FCO professional they've made official spokesman. He's about my age, as taciturn as I am chatty - odd for our main communicator - but he writes like a dream, is very media savvy and seems thrilled to be with us. Last week I went to his place for dinner, spellbound by the small house in Pimlico and by his beautiful French wife, Marie-Claire, who obviously has the money (her parents have vineyards in the Medoc) and wears the trousers. An odd contrast: he - a little dumpy, with rather babyish features, and not particularly well turned out, she - with that effortless French grooming. They'd invited Raphael for dinner the previous week (her initiative) and of course for our Francophile boss, it was inevitably amour at first sight.

Nigel's already earned his keep with some masterclass drafting on the prospects for conflict, just this side of loyalty but giving a clever dose of the need for restraint and reflection.

****

If anything I'm seeing more of Raphael outside the office than ever. I quite often head back with him to Battersea, just to plan the days ahead, but last night he finally comes round and has supper with Digby and me in our Fulham pad. It was the first time he's met my better half, and it doesn't go that brilliantly. If I didn't know better I'd say that Raphael was showing off (as if!), lording it over my poor chubby, short-sighted little Digby who is tongue-tied at table and then retires to the kitchen to clear up.

Digby puts on Radio 3 quite loud and has shut the kitchen door so that we can talk freely. I am still smarting from the serial slights he had meted out to my significant other and start off with, "You behaved overbearingly. I think you're almost a bit jealous".

He gives a barking loud false laugh and said, "Nonsense. I like the man. What exactly does he do for a living?"

"He's a clerk at the DWP and before you say anything sneering he's very cultured, reads more widely than either of us, loves ballet - and is a loyal party member."

Thus rebuked Raphael quickly returned to his favourite subject - himself – and went into a long moan venting all his frustrations about being side-lined, his anger at the No 10 machine and the hostile briefings, and his fear that the decision to go to war had in fact already been taken. He also intimates that he is just feeling a bit lonely.

When Digby brings in the coffee, he is then the focus of Raphael's 1000 watt charm. I feel sick!

When we go to bed, Digby asks again if I had ever slept with him "because it sure feels that way to me". I have managed to make the two men I care about most a little bit jealous – quite cheering really!

****

For once I blame Marjorie. She was the one who told Raphael about the persistent phone calls from this very polite young Scotsman asking him to speak to the Oxford Labour Club, how he was from the same college, how the chair, the secretary and all the other officers were also from Balliol; she was the one who persuaded him not to cancel at the last moment when he realised at the beginning of a lousy week that he had agreed to go to Oxford on a wet Monday in November, "they'll be ever so disappointed; a real blow to them." She was the one who persuaded him not to come back late that night but to stay at the Master's Lodge. So he took the 5 p.m. train to Oxford and started the journey which looks to me like it leads to disaster.

NED

Dear Mart,

You must be over the moon about the girls' exam results. Mum's been boasting about her clever offspring in the corner shop, probably irritating half the street.

High jinks here too, I can tell you. I guess even in Adelaide word has reached about this stupid criminal war which a Labour government is going to commit us to. Well, Angus pulls off a star guest for our last meeting of term: none other than the man of the moment, our Foreign Secretary, Raphael Sinclair (Mayberry Central, majority 14,746 from memory). Packed house guaranteed. Brings in our star performer, looking pretty haggard although he's only just forty; but he makes a good speech, no notes, covers the ground - ethical approach, excellent on the Middle East and Europe, a bit wobbly on the Russians, sceptical about the Turks joining the EU (a new one on me from a Labour minister). By now he's perked up, bats all the questions, even a complicated one from Rashida about talking to Hamas, and a typically smart-arsed effort from Rupe about the Tory press. Then right at the end comes the killer from Aide, sitting at the back, dressed in a long black coat, hair all over the place, like a louche version of Che Guevara. He uncoils himself, stands and asks,

"On the war, you've said that a second UN resolution is what you're looking for. Why? Is it necessary under international law?"

Long pause. "The position of the government is that a second resolution would give us a basis for intervention under international law." He sits down, looks pleadingly at Angus, as if to say, "I'm dog tired. Get me outta here."

But Angus then says to Aide, "Does that answer satisfy you, Aidan?"

"No, of course not; let me help Mr Sinclair by asking it another way. If you don't get the second resolution and therefore don't have a basis under international law, but the US and our PM decide to go ahead anyway, what would you do?"

"That as the cliché goes is a hypothetical question."

Aidan persists, "Answer it, please. Would you resign if you aren't satisfied that what we are doing is compatible with international law?" There was now some stirring in the hall and scattered applause.

Sinclair pauses and then says, "Under those circumstances, yes." Every one stands cheering.

Wow, history is made. I get to make the vote of thanks and the guy from the Oxford BBC owes me one, because I let him in to record it on his little machine even though the Foreign Office guy had phoned specially that morning to tell us 'no press'.

It gets better. Angus has already fixed for him to come back to his rooms for a couple of drinks before retiring to the Master's Lodge. As we pass the porter's Lodge by which time our guest has finished off two fags, he sees who's in the retinue apart from our Scottish wunderkind, Rashida, me, Rupe and his tormentor, Aide, looking both sullen and self-satisfied at the same time - as only he can.

The night porter rushes out of the lodge and says to our guest, "Excuse me sir but we've been having a lot of calls from the No 10 switchboard. Could you possibly give them a ring back?"

"Oh, nothing that can't wait until tomorrow, I expect. Thank you, anyway." And so we continue living the dream.

HM's Foreign Secretary seems all amiable and relaxed, and helps us finish off the best part of a bottle of Sainsbury's finest malt. By this time Aide has disappeared without even saying goodbye and shortly after exchanging email addresses (a private one in his case and telling Rupe to give it to the absent Aide) and suggesting we all come and visit his office during the Christmas vac he heads off down the stairs and across the quad to his billet.

Anyway by the time I get down to the quad, ten minutes later and after heavy hints from Rashida, I come across Aide and Rupe having a right old barney, with Aide saying that Rupe had ruined everything. When I asked what exactly had been ruined, Aide turns to me and says charmingly, "shut it". Rupe then proceeds to enlighten me at his most sneering: "The sudden absence of our esteemed scholar here was to allow him to loiter in the shadows, waiting for our guest to come downstairs so that he could be propositioned for 'something a little stronger.' (This is the language Rupe always speaks - I think it's called 'Oxford smartarse').

"Fortunately for the future security of the realm I was soon on hand to discourage the minister from succumbing to any temptation. He made a flustered exit, thanked Aidan here for his help - help with what? Unzipping his fly? - one might ask - and then was quivering so much he could hardly get his key in the lock. Which must be a metaphor for something".

"I'd have had him, you know, if you hadn't come along you little shit." He then hit Rupe quite hard in the stomach, made him wince, put his arm round him and took him back to his room, doubtless for some of that 'something stronger'. I was left to my own devices.

Yesterday, all over the press, 'Minister to resign', 'Minister carpeted'. We all get summoned to Angus' rooms for the post-mortem which as usual is a good excuse for a monologue. "He's really good. He's got what it takes. If he goes now, he could be the front man for all real socialists. He's not one of us of course, just an old-style right-wing social democrat. But for our current purposes he'll do." (By which he means he'll do to get us all on the road.) We all more or less agreed with only Rashida holding back, as if there was something she didn't really like about him. But she's not one of nature's enthusiasts anyway; in fact, bro, she's one hell of a calculating bitch but where Angus is concerned she's part of the package.

Later on I picked up Jean who's a history second year at Oriel, had a few drinks, went a bit too far with her in the lane outside and got a good slap for my pains. Back to the drawing board.

In haste,

Ned

PS If you want breaking news as it happens from the epicentre of the western world, you're going to have to give me your email address.

BARRIE

Oxford's been the turning point. Raphael took the milk train back to Paddington, got into the office shortly after 8.30 by which time Downing Street had called 10 times shouting at either Nigel, Marjorie or me, with messages escalating from "What exactly did the Foreign Secretary say last night?" to "What the fuck's going on?" to, finally, "The Prime Minister will see the Foreign Secretary at 11 a.m."

He puts on a front of insouciance, "All I did was to repeat government policy."

"But" I ask "did you say you'd resign?"

"Well, I did say I'd resign if we were breaking international law…"

Nigel, practicality quickly overcoming his irritation, says, "I think we should have a complete black-out for a few days. And I suggest you get into No 10 the back way. And remember you've got Foreign Office questions on Thursday."

Raphael replies, "That's a lifetime away. Remember, Nigel, most MPs have the attention span of cabbage white butterflies. They'll be on to something else by then."

He reports back after his summons to the PM who of course hates personal confrontations just as much as he does. The boss had said that it was he who decided policy and that ministers shouldn't wing it: Raphael countered by asking him what precisely the conditions for intervention were.

"Of course we want a second resolution, as a belt and braces operation. But if it's in any case going to be sabotaged by the French using their veto, we can't allow that to stop us. The US will go ahead anyway and we want them to keep on board with our efforts in the Middle East. Now please, Raphael, just keep your head down and it will all blow over."

Back at the office he seems to return to routine but I can tell he's agitated. At 6 he calls me in and says, "I'm all in. I need to talk. Let's go to your place and ask Diggers to rustle up some of his excellent pasta and then disappear into the kitchen. It's important." Of course Digby's furious, not least because he then had to flog on a couple of tickets for Covent Garden, all to act as chef by appointment to someone he still doesn't trust. But he usually does what I tell him.

When we get home, and with Digby shut off in the kitchen, it all comes out. How he'd been hijacked by these very clever kids, the set up at the end of the meeting, the BBC there conveniently to record the event. But there's something else, and he's bursting to tell me.

"The kid who asked me the question, this Aidan, he just blew me away. You know, dark, soulful, dangerous. While he was asking the question he was undressing me. Then of course when we went back to the Scots guy's rooms, he said nothing and left early, without saying a word. I wanted out anyway, but I knew he'd be waiting for me. So I made my excuses and sure enough he was hanging around in the yard, barely visible, under a light with the bulb not replaced, with that old fetid smell of rotting sycamore leaves; him propped up against the wall in this ankle-length dark coat, with one leg bent to the wall to balance.

"He was smoking, otherwise I might have missed him, but he knew I was coming. He offers me a fag, lights it in his own mouth from his own, and I swear as he passes it to me I can see a shaft of light reflected in a filament of saliva. We smoke for a moment, saying nothing, just staring at each other, me scared that my heart is about to give out.

"He then says, 'Come up to my room and you'll get something stronger.' I tell you I was going to accept: then along pops the clever dick public schoolboy, Rupert, who says archly, 'So that's what you two are up to; shame we don't have bicycle sheds'. All I can think to do is mutter some thanks to Aidan 'for his help', muster a shred of dignity by twittering on about my early start, walk a little unsteadily to the Master's Lodge, fumble with the keys to unlock the front door, all the while the two of them enjoying the spectacle.

"As I get inside I can hear, first, some laughter and then perhaps a scuffle, certainly a slap but I don't look back. Of course I can't sleep a wink, and they've put me in the room which gives out to the brightest lights on the Broad. And I couldn't and I can't get him out of my head. I'm thinking of him all the time. If that other little show-off hadn't have turned up, God knows how it would have ended."

He pauses and I say coldly, "Well thank Christ for the little show off. It was probably all a set-up. You'd have done some drugs, whatever, and had sex. He'd then have boasted about it all over the city, and for him you'd just be another little notch on his bedpost. The next thing would have been the headlines, 'The Minister and the Student; our night of sex and drugs.' Great for the man on the moral high ground. And what a gift for the No 10 machine, 'The PM has to take no lessons in ethics from Raphael Sinclair.'"

"You're right but I've got to get in touch with him, in safer conditions perhaps."

"No you haven't" by now I'm almost shouting. "You're entering the most important few weeks of your life. You owe it to your whole purpose in politics to put this behind you. You owe it to Marjorie. To Nigel. You owe it to me."

I think he got the point.

NED

>>>>>>>>>>>>>>>>>>>>>>>>>>>>>>>>>>>>>>>

From: ned.warren.1982@hotmail.com

To: martin.warren.78@hotmail.au

>>>>>>>>>>>>>>>>>>>>>>>>>>>>>>>>>>>>>>>

What a day! The regal treatment at King Charles Street. We all arrive (minus Aide, more of this later) on time, all spruced up, particularly Rupe who looked as if he's taken up modelling for his career, Rashida smart in a pastel grey trench coat, Angus has a long dark coat which made him seem even taller. I was - how can I put it? - a bit more colourful, that green anorak mum gave me for Christmas, my blue trousers which I'd pressed myself that morning, and the red jacket you laughed at when you were all over at Christmas.

We are met at the gate by the boss' factotum, a small Welsh lad, curly top, very friendly and obviously bright. Talks all the time. After security it's straight up to the boss' office. Remember the head's study at school - well multiply by ten, half the National Gallery on the walls and really big armchairs you fall into and then find difficult to get out of; and the desk big enough for ten US presidents to sit around each getting pleasured by willing interns. Relaxed and charming he gives us forty-five minutes, talks about the party, the big issue of the moment where he's a bit on his guard, and seems in no hurry to shove us out.

One little jarring note: at the end he asks where Aidan is. Barrie, the Welshman, said flatly but surprisingly emphatically as if closing off conversation on this point, "You didn't have his address, minister." Barrie took us out, gave us the quick tour, the Locarno Room and the new atrium, then it was off to the Refectory for a light lunch (a bit too light for my liking - and just mineral water!).

Boy can this Welsh geezer talk! He gives us a long string of anecdotes about protocol mishaps, usually involving his boss, funny but loyal.

As we are on our way out Rupe hands Barrie a piece of paper with Aidan's address, email and telephone numbers, "so that your boss can get hold of him whenever he wants - maybe even get a personal tour! He'll be really sorry to have missed out on this". Snide bastard.

Thanks for the tie and the shirt, which will fit when I lose a few pounds (New Year's resolution).

Love to all,

Ned

BARRIE

What I described to him as his 'Balliol pick-ups' came today and did the tour. Of course I had omitted to remind him that he hadn't handed over any contact details for Aidan Richards (the one who nearly buggered his career in two different ways, all in one evening). I don't want him within a hundred miles of Raphael. I meet them at the gate: the smart serious Pakistani girl, Rashida Hussein, who says little and thinks a lot; Angus Buchanan, even taller than Raphael, with beautiful grey-blue eyes, fairish hair swept back to reveal a high forehead, cerebral but very chilly; Rupert Dennison, archetypal upper middle class cutie, bright twinkly blue eyes, perfectly shaped face everything in balance, shortish blond curly hair, clever of course but with mischief seeping through every pore. And then 'the fat kid' (Raphael's description), Ned Warren, the predictable total mess, with the colour combination from hell (makes Digby look like George Clooney) but funny, and not nearly as daft as he looks. He has this brush-cut hair which everyone wants to pat, but the small piggy eyes show that he's not missing much.

Raphael was obviously annoyed about the absentee but hid his disappointment from them, was courteous, answered all their questions and graciously brought it all to a close on time but leaving them with the feeling that he would far prefer to spend the whole day with them. Lunch is pleasant apart from some clever little digs from Rupert wanting to know exactly what my job was; some intelligent questions from Angus and Rashida who each give me their mobile phone numbers. Ned filled in any gaps with soppy good-natured jokes. As they were leaving Rupert hands me a piece of paper with all Aidan Richards' contact details. "Be sure to give it to the Foreign Secretary, he'll probably want to give Aidan a very personal tour. Aidan will be very upset when he learns he's missed out". During all this the tone swerves from arch to menacing.

Immediately they turn the corner, I bin the paper.

Raphael seemed a bit cool with me for the rest of the day, but says nothing!

NEWSFLASH: BBC NEWS

12.15 pm WEDNESDAY MARCH 8

It has just been announced from Downing Street that the Foreign Secretary, Raphael Sinclair, has resigned. His resignation letter, also just released, says that the resignation had 'become inevitable when it was decided to intervene militarily without the explicit authorisation of the UN Security Council which I judge to be indispensable if the war is to be compatible with international law.' The Prime Minister's reply thanked Mr Sinclair for his excellent service in the government for over five years. Helen Mitchison, the Universities' minister, who lives with Mr Sinclair, has also resigned. More junior ministerial resignations are expected later in the day.

HELEN

We timed the resignations for just after he had left what would be his final cabinet meeting. He knew he was going to be in a minority of one, no-one else being prepared to challenge the official view of the Attorney-General. My letter arrived at Downing Street just 15 minutes after his, so we were both on the news bulletins, with the inevitable sub-text about the former 'golden couple' setting off into the wilderness together.

Over the next 24 hours, seven other junior ministers went, including Hattie Reynolds[8] and Maudie Hinton[9], both ministers of state, one at Housing, the other at Work & Pensions. These would not have been my first choice as companions to accompany me into the jungle. Each on her own was just about bearable - the buxom brunette Hattie who was already finishing with her third husband, the brassy life and soul of any party, known for dancing on tables as after-hours entertainment during trade union conferences. She had a kind of cheap glamour which bizarrely seemed to appeal to Raphael, who liked being pawed in public (of course only in public), but on her own she could be kind and reflective.

Maudie was not stupid, but hard as nails, thin as a rake with peroxided spiked hair, eyelashes laden with black make-up and a mouth with its default mode set at sour. She must have had some dreadful times with men because she would snarl whenever anyone tried it on, and was bitchy about all women including, and especially, me, but not Hattie of course.

Together they were lethal, a stream of venom whenever anyone came into the room, running us all down behind our backs and playing up to their image as 'the last two working class women left in the Labour Party' that some in the press liked to project. They were certainly more of a political loss to the PM than me; and they both seemed genuinely fond of Raphael.

He was as good as his word about going to ground after the resignations, no press interviews, not even a Commons statement, "We mustn't rock the boat now that our men and women in uniform are at war". It was pure calculation, of course.

---

[8] MP for East Rotherham, 1992-
[9] MP for Stoke Newington, 1992-

Two days later he convened the refuseniks to meet at our place in Battersea in the early evening. He explained his personal approach, advised against continuing the battle in the Parliamentary party or at party conference, but said they should all keep in touch. We were all, even Maudie, a bit emotional as they left.

He and I then went to the local Thai at the top of the hill on Battersea Park Road. I had decided to tell him my news.

'Raphael, this may not be a good time but I want to move on too. I've met someone. Ted, he's a chartered accountant, nothing to do with politics but he's kind, loving and he's there for me. He's divorced with two teenage boys who live with their mother, although she was the one who walked out. He's got this nice house in Parson's Green, and I think I'll move in this weekend. I expect we'll get a good price for the house here.

"Raphael, you've got to get a life for yourself too. You need someone's head on the pillow next to you in the morning, and preferably not a different one each time." I was being very brave.

There was a long pause. Then he said, "You're right, Helen." He looked away, and I did wonder whether he might even cry or whether this was for purely theatrical effect. He then went on, "I was thinking the day we resigned together, our relationship has been the most important in my life so far. But I also have to live a little bit more outside politics, face up to things and accept that having a relationship requires commitment."

We actually held hands all the way downhill, had a long hug before going up to our separate rooms. The next morning I started packing.

EXTRACT FROM 'THE JC DUNNETT ANTHOLOGY (199- to 201-)'

The resignation of a Foreign Secretary on a matter of principle, and in this case the committal of British troops to a distant theatre of war, is a rarity in our politics. The Lord Carrington fell on his sword twenty years ago because public opinion demanded a blood sacrifice when the defenders of a tiny remote outpost of our Empire appeared to be asleep on their watch. Before the last World War, the then Mr Eden resigned not in protest against military action but against our appeasement of a foreign threat.

So Mr Raphael Sinclair has walked away from the office he inherited through the untimely demise of his predecessor. The unpopularity of the war and its probably messy aftermath will tempt some into believing that unwittingly or not this intelligent politician, only just turned forty, may have positioned himself rather conveniently to appeal to the thousands of Labour Party members who have been shocked to find so mercilessly revealed what they touchingly still appear to believe to be 'their' government entering into a war whose legal and moral underpinnings are so fragile.

But Mr Sinclair has determined that his own exit should be without fanfare because he seems to understand that criticising the belligerent posture of a government in wartime runs counter to the instincts of the British people, who rally round the nearest flag at the first volley of gunfire. The Labour Party in the country and the trade unions who detest the war will not move against the cabinet as long as the war ends quickly, the body bags are not too numerous, and the government retains a healthy lead in the opinion polls.

Mr Sinclair will have looked over his shoulder and counted the number of ministers who followed his lead, and will have noted his isolation in the cabinet and the anonymity of the junior supporters from the front bench who accompany him into the wilderness. He may well be rueing the day last autumn when he made a rather rash promise to students at his old university about resigning in the absence of support from the United Nations about military action. He may even be irritated that this pledge was given at what he imagined to be a private meeting but which one or two of my colleagues had managed, indeed had been encouraged, to infiltrate and record.

He will be the hero of the hour - but just for one hour - to many students and anti-war protesters, unused to principle playing any role in our political game-playing. But in the bigger scheme of things, by which I mean the oncoming Downing Street wars between the Prime Minister and his sore-headed neighbour, the departure of Mr Sinclair will seem to confirm the views of some that the member for Mayberry is a dilettante condemned to an ephemeral part in the epic struggles ahead, albeit now assured of having his own footnote in the saga.

Many assume that Mr Sinclair will draw the conclusion that the lucrative lecture circuit and - why not? - his own television series on, for example, his adored Mediterranean will in the end prove more rewarding than building patiently the kind of base in the party and among his parliamentary colleagues which alone could make him a factor with which to be reckoned. I have always suspected that the former secretary of state could cope with many of the servitudes of our politics, the compromises and the conspiracies, all except the tedium.

Unless of course the thinning layer of gold dust on the New Labour enterprise is blown away in the coming storms and high seas. In which case we may not have heard the last of Mr Raphael Sinclair.

BARRIE

A week to remember. So I leave the FCO again, although this time my new best friend Cynthia asks me to stay on. I have the talk with Raphael. He desperately wants me to remain with him, but of course offers to let me go. He apologises about the pay cut. He's cagey about what he does next. Perhaps he doesn't know but I'm sure he has at least a partially formed plan.

Nigel's resignation from the Office was the bombshell. He'll work with us part-time and take up a post with a consultancy (of course a very ethical one) to help keep Marie-Claire in the style to which she has always been accustomed. But for Nigel, working for any boss after Raphael would be a comedown in every way, which is of course the reason I'm staying; that and the deep affection I have for him.

Marjorie, who could have got any job anywhere, will of course stay with him too. So it'll be a bit of a squeeze in the new block, even though the offices are larger than those in St Stephen's and Nigel will work mostly from his other rather palatial office in the public affairs company in Buckingham House Gate.

Then Raphael rings up to announce that Helen's leaving Battersea and that she's flat hunting for him (typical) in the Putney area (a bit of a trade-up but a healthy distance from the House).

The next day in our new office he drops one final nugget. When he had got back to Battersea the previous evening there was a hand-written note on the mat, saying,

"Congratulations. I didn't think you would do it but you did and I'm proud of you. It would be lovely to see you some time. Aidan XXX'.

He had added his mobile phone number. I noticed that the boss didn't hand me the paper for safekeeping but folded it carefully and put it inside his wallet. So the poisonous snake (who, to tell the truth, I hate even though I've never seen him) has wormed himself back in the frame just when Raphael's at his most vulnerable.

****

Raphael has put down a deposit on a quite large flat at the top of Putney Hill, next to the Green Man pub. There's a whole campus of these 'staircases' set out like a nineteenth-century Oxbridge college (but not a distinguished one.) I was given a private viewing and it's nice, looking out on to a large leafy courtyard, so not too much traffic noise, with mock bullion windows (which rule out double glazing), up two flights of stairs, and with two good size bedrooms, a nice sitting room; dining-room area, a modern bathroom, pokey kitchen and a small office - so, perfect. And of course Helen has taken on the furnishing of the place helped by her husband-to-be, portly Ted, who seems nice and about the person most different from Raphael you could wish to meet.

Raphael went off to some conference in Lille last weekend. He stayed a couple of nights longer than expected (though it seemed an unusual place for a Sinclair long weekend break). So when he finally came back today and insisted we go to a very quiet Indian place he'd found at the bottom of the hill down from his new flat (quiet, that is, until chucking out time) it was the inevitable, "I've met someone and this time, Barrie, believe it or not, he's not from the Mediterranean."

The 'someone' is a French academic called Nicolas, junior professor of comparative politics at Lille 2. He's also for once Raphael's own age, and according to the photo produced from wallet, a rather chunky bearded guy with bright eyes and a pleasant expression, not as glamorous as some in his back catalogue, but quite fanciable.

"It's not just a fling, this time. We were on the same panel on one of those 'What's left of the Left?' things, and we decided to go out for supper to some cheerful bistro. We then talked practically all night in my hotel room, with just the odd interruption. So I'm heading back to Paris this weekend where he's got his flat, not far from the Bastille."

Not as alarming as some of his previous dalliances, but it won't last.

****

His trips to Paris have become more frequent. They're becoming a double act at all the think tanks and research institute events that Nicolas can arrange. I think he's making the most of Raphael's unique status as a former UK Foreign Minister who actually speaks French. And now Raphael has just come back from their holiday together at a small hotel on the west coast, just south of La Rochelle. And he's so taken with the area that he's started looking for a small cottage in the same village as the hotel, St Palais-sur-Mer.

As his private life seems so sorted (for the moment) he's got some energy back and the last few days have been busy enough - articles written painstakingly by Nigel and me, but completely redrafted by him, and enough media stuff to stay in the picture. The line is generally supportive of the government, no personal attacks but some questioning about the direction of travel. And he's accepted no less than 17 'rubber chicken circuit' dos in constituencies up and down the land between now and November. This might just have something to do with him being a last-minute candidate for the NEC.

To bring in some money and to help pay for Nigel and give me a pretty good salary he's also doing commercial speaking (at around £15,000 a whack) but he's very choosy about who he speaks to, and has turned down all sorts of iffy directorships. But, courtesy of the Freedom of Information Act, he's still now one of the top five earners in the House.

****

Typical! He's got himself elected to the NEC at first go, just a few votes off the top slot despite not being backed by the Chancellor, the unions or the old hard left. And Helen got on via the women's section. Reports of the political demise of Raphael Sinclair would appear to be a little premature.

NED

>>>

From: ned.warren.1982@hotmail.com

To: martin.warren.78@hotmail.au

>>>

So we're all in clover. Angus and Rashida have got their PhDs from Florence in subjects which could have been in Sanskrit for all they mean to me; and now they're off on some post-doctoral programme to Harvard for a few years. Angus keeps getting articles published in top economics journals (my holiday reading of choice, but he sends them, and you sort of feel you have to try to read them).

Rupe is on ITV's new politics programme, started doing research but they quickly put him in front of the cameras. And of course he gets heaps of fan mail, not all of it from complete nutters. And he's moonlighting for Raphael Sinclair, doing a bit of stuff on cultural policy, free media etc. and keeps in close contact with his office.

And I, your devoted sibling, have landed a job at the main telecom union; not on the picket lines you understand, but policy stuff for the executive - a bit of a doddle really.

As for Aidan I thought he'd gone right off the rails, high as a kite from mid-afternoon and one-night stands, only twice nightly. He started to look like shit then it was hair trimmed, beard shaped, smart suit and off to Chatham House for an interview, which of course he walked and is now researching away on Far East issues. He's still livid that Sinclair never got back to him.

It was Rupe who had the explanation. It took Aidan and me at least thirty seconds of intense torture to get all the information out of him when he came round gagging to blab. At the Gare du Nord waiting for the Eurostar after covering the French elections he sees two men just standing that bit too close to each other, obviously bidding rather fonder than usual farewells; one of them a typical French intellectual, elbow pads on the faded sports jacket, cords, "all that was missing was a Gitane stuck to his lower lip and a copy of 'Le Monde Diplomatique' under his arm." The other was HM's former Secretary of State, clearly not best pleased to bump into enthusiastic young friend from Oxford, so it was hurried goodbyes and maximum embarrassment all round. By the way, I'm now sharing my little hovel in Chiswick with Aide and we take turns in forgetting to do the washing up. When mum came down two weeks ago she threw a fit but then spent four hours cleaning up for us.

Sorry to hear you're splitting up. How are the kids taking it?

If you want a very ample shoulder to cry on you can always fly over and sleep on the sofa here unless Health and Safety have shut us down first.

Love,

Ned

HELEN

It was impressive seeing Raphael at work on the NEC[10]; a manipulative genius. He did not intervene too much, was deferential to everyone and then just at the right moment swooped, made the proposal that no-one dared oppose and then congratulated someone else for having thought it all up. He worked hard to keep the staff on side, especially Bill Sampson, the national agent[11]. Bill was a cynical old bird: he always had Raphael and me in stitches with some of his mickey-taking but despite his lanky laid-back exterior his judgment was as sharp as mustard. And the great thing was that he was neither in the leader's faction, nor with his rival nor was he a tool of the big unions. Together with Maudie Hinton and Hattie Reynolds, who had both been elected the year after me, Hattie in the more competitive section reserved for constituency parties, we formed a pivotal group, and Bill fed us little snippets of useful information before the start of meetings.

When it came to choosing the new General Secretary, everybody assumed the choice would go outside either to the young City man who had been groomed by No 10[12], or to the union favourite[13] backed by his rival. So Raphael got himself appointed chair of the interview panel and roughed up the union candidate, who was genuinely pretty hopeless, so that when the choice boiled down to the New Labour clone from a finance company versus good old reliable Bill who had no enemies, the unions naturally blocked the PM's man and our friend romped home 20 to 7. This put Raphael's soul-mate in charge of the machine. That way he had early warning of seats coming up; so he could veto all-women shortlists if he had some male acolyte he wanted to push; or insist on them when - less frequently - his protégé was a woman. Pretty soon he was chair of the candidate selection sub-committee, again because of a stand-off between the factions; so he immediately started adding names of friends and allies to the 'A' list of priority parliamentary candidates. And all of this was under the radar, so oblivious were the protagonists in numbers 10 and 11 to anything other than the relentless prosecution of their very own civil war.

---

[10] National Executive Committee : the Labour Party's ruling body
[11] Responsible for ensuring the observation of the Labour Party's rules
[12] Malcolm Martin-Petrie
[13] Jack Matthews

Whenever he saw a vacant seat in prospect, he started to renew local acquaintanceships or offer to speak at a party meeting, spread the word a bit, and arrange a few introductions.

His relentless pushing for young and attractive new candidates, not all of them male, seemed to me to reveal a great deal about Raphael. He was genuinely in awe of youth, its vigour, idealism and sometimes insane ambition. He was quite simply infatuated with youth, and perhaps increasingly jealous of the young as he confronted the limitations of his own middle age, as well as feeling that they had freedoms denied to him or which he had denied himself.

And in the Commons, he seemed a fixture, not in the tearoom or one of the bars but in the chamber itself, feigning interest in even the most obscure debates, and sending little words of congratulations to humble new backbenchers for their meagre efforts. Even so, to many it seemed as if he was in semi-retirement. I actually had one colleague say to me, "Shame about Raphael. He seems to have given up on politics. A real loss. I suppose they'll get him a Mastership of a college or something pretty lucrative in industry." It only goes to show that the really masterclass politician is the one who does politics and you don't notice.

This did not mean that I always approved the ends to which he put his talents. Getting the party job for Bill was fine, of course. And the first people he pushed for vacant seats were worthy enough, but then he started one by one on his young acolytes scarcely out of university. They were all very saleable of course, good-looking, articulate, and highly intelligent but none of them had really done anything. And they had certainly not slogged it out at local party meetings or on the doorsteps in the pouring rain. Nor had they won their spurs fighting hopeless seats. No, this was the royal path for the privileged girls and boys, mostly boys, in his circle.

I did not take to Rashida Hussein[14], cold, weighing up each word to calculate the probable effect, but I could see that she was the right sort of candidate for a certain type of constituency. Angus Buchanan[15] was extraordinarily bright but so obviously knew it: he had an arrogance bordering on human cruelty. Rupert Dennison[16] seemed a typical media smoothie but talked so well and looked so handsome that it was inevitable he would be selected somewhere if he could just get

---

[14] Elected as MP for Bradford North-East, 200-
[15] Elected as MP for Mayberry South, 200-
[16] Elected as MP for Belper, 200-

shortlisted. Ned Warren[17] was the most likeable of the bunch but also seemingly the least ambitious; he looked and sounded what he was, a bright, amiable working-class lad who always seemed himself. But, sensibly, he had already told Raphael that he wanted to get more experience with the union first before trying for a seat.

Barrie Jones had told me in confidence that there was another in this group called Aidan Richards[18], who I had not at that time met and who according to Barrie was the most poisonous of the bunch, but who he said had really charmed Raphael. Barrie was clearly proud that he had put a spoke into that particular wheel, but gave me no details.

---

[17] Elected as MP for North-West Lincolnshire in a by-election, 200-
[18] Elected as MP for Mayberry, West, 200-

NED

Bloody hell! Rashida's only gone and got herself selected for a safe seat. She comes back from Harvard, goes straight to the selection conference, walks it and now she'll be elected for sure for this part of Bradford with the highest Pakistani population outside Lahore. The seat (majority 13,798 from memory) coming vacant was only because the sitting MP suddenly announced he was stepping down (Rupe claims it's due to an expenses fiddle about to break big).

I never thought she'd be the first to break into the big time but then she's always played it cool and she had Angus, who should have been the first, wrapped round her little finger.

What's the new bird like? Pics, please, so I can give my discerning judgment.

BARRIE

Writing books with Raphael gives me the highest of highs. He has the idea, and does a rough draft. I slog away at the research and do some heavy drafting. Then Nigel livens up my leaden prose, after which Raphael scraps half of it, and rewrites it all with clarity and verve. And he's generous with the acknowledgments, wanting to put us both on the back cover, though the publisher has drawn the line at that.

After the first book we did last autumn on the Middle East, which it's clear now is what they call a 'succès d'estime' (i.e. some good reviews in the qualities albeit tempered by unspoken disappointment that the criticism of his successors at the FCO was so muted and the shops hardly shifting any copies), the new one seems as if it's going to make more waves.

As I foresaw a few months earlier, it all started with young Dennison persuading him to do a polemic about dumbed-down media standards, the need for independent regulation, the dangers of media concentration to guarantee 'that elusive treasure, a free press'. Nigel was very dubious about the gratuitous attack on the press but Rupert prevailed, did some first-rate research I have to admit, and of course the final result is beautifully written. I have also to concede that Rupert almost matches Nigel's drafting skills. Anyway first indications are that's its selling moderately well because as Rupert points out, "there's nothing the media like talking about better than themselves".

****

I thought Paris was burning a little less brightly. The visits had become infrequent though they've still been on holiday together 2 or 3 times this year already. It all came out last night, with Raphael, fortified by four glasses of wine, admitting rather sheepishly,

"It's all got a bit monotonous. The Friday evening train to the Gare du Nord, a late supper in the same bistro near Nicolas' flat, the long lie-in on Saturday mornings, flâner around the bookshops before a light lunch, a walk in the Bois in the afternoon, and then dinner with some of his left-wing 'intellos' with ferocious discussions exclusively about French politics (a subject I now major in) - extraordinary how French academics are as insular as the British ones; another lie-in on Sunday, a late brunch and then the late afternoon train back.

"There are never rows, there's been no rupture, but I know he took someone else for a weekend at the hotel at St Palais. I have to say I did smirk a bit when I heard it rained all weekend."

So it looks like it's game over. Amazing to think I've never met Nicolas, and I don't think I'd have liked him and I guess he wouldn't even have noticed me. But Raphael could so easily have chosen worse. I wonder what's next.

NED

Something really is going on. We're only months from the election and my mates are all getting fitted up with safe seats. The first thing I knew about the plan for Angus was when he rang up from O'Hare airport and told me that Sinclair was pushing him for the seat adjoining his own in Mayberry (majority 7564 - not rock solid but looking good according to local by-election results: got to keep up, you know) because the sitting member has decided to step down (one of those wife ill, secretary pregnant stories) at the last moment. Of course it was swung for him by Raphael.

It now appears he may be trying to push Rupe for a seat in the East Midlands (Belper, somewhere I don't think Rupe had heard of until last week, but still an 8,722 majority).

And to think that I said to Raphael some time ago that I didn't want to try for anything until I'd made my way up the union ladder. I notice he's not come back to try and make me think again.

Aidan's moved back in after the latest tryst ended in tears (the other bloke's tears of course). He was a bit snooty about Angus and Rashida and has just gone off to North Korea for the third visit; not that even Aide would get up to any mischief there, would he?

Maggie dumped me last week after spending a night or rather half a night here.

Back to drawing board,

Ned

HELEN

Raphael was at this stage pushing too hard. After Angus Buchanan squeaked through with the Mayberry, South nomination, the machine went into overdrive for Rupert Dennison in the Belper constituency. Another safe seat, and another one for the boys. Of course Rupert with his charm, looks, self-confidence and just a hint of stardust saw off all the local challengers. Raphael always ensured that the competition on the NEC-approved shortlist was eminently beatable. So another twenty-something white male got the big break, with Raphael and Bill pulling the strings. It was an outrage but no-one seemed to notice because they were too worried about the latest polling figures which made it seem that all this manoeuvring might be a bit academic.

BARRIE

When he comes into the office yesterday he says nothing, just hands Marjorie a scrap of paper with a telephone number on it, tells her to get the call and then shoos us out of the office. The Frenchman back in the frame? But Marjorie tells me it was a UK mobile number. Not a word when he comes back but he leaves the office early, saying he had a meeting in Putney.

Today he comes in, a bit irritable and much hyped up. He's ages on the 'phone with Mayberry people and has at least two calls with Bill, both in their code, but with Raphael a little bit testy with him during the first conversation, almost assuaged after the second.

We have a sandwich for lunch, in the office, just the two of us. Finally he blurts it all out.

"At the weekend I had a visit from Felicity" (the MP from the other neighbouring seat), "the first since our spectacular falling out over the war. She tells me she's ill and she's decided to step down, and asks me to support one of her local union friends who would be even worse than her. I'm sympathetic, ply her with whiskey (probably not a good idea in her condition), mutter my warm feelings toward her stooge and then show her the door as quickly as could be decently arranged.

"I then had my first call with Bill, who after some hesitation agreed to go for the accelerator procedure because of the imminence of the election (that's when we give them the Henry Ford choice, "you can have any colour car you want provided it's black" or in this case provided "it's got black hair.")

My heart starts to sink. He went on, "And, in the end, we agreed to declassify it - so it's no longer women only."

"So who is to be the beneficiary of this little windfall? Or have you started to run out of good-looking young graduates from your old college?" I ask.

He flinches a little but ploughs on. "Well, I had thought of young Ned Warren, but he's happy enough with the union, and wants to sit this one out."

"And when did you have this conversation?" I ask, clutching at straws, seeing with mounting dread where we are headed. "After all he might have changed his mind, seeing all his mates getting fitted up, and he being the least obnoxious of the bunch."

He ignores this extra little insubordination and wades on, "He seemed quite settled in his view when we spoke. In any case we've got past that point now. I phoned up Aidan Richards and we had dinner at the little Indian place down the hill, you know, our usual." Remind me never to set foot in that place again!

He continues, "He was all sulky reproach at first, why had I not contacted him? Why had I not invited him to visit the Office with the others? And then when I finally got round to talking about the seat you'd have thought I was asking him for a favour. "I don't know, Rafs... " (I ask you!) "I'm enjoying ticking over at Chatham House, the North Korea book sold quite well (better than your first effort, I seem to remember) and, really, Mayberry, sitting around with you and Angus on wet weekends or listening to the latest gripe from Sid and Doris Bonkers about their hedges or their plumbing when I could be out having fun. It's very marginal so I'd flog my guts out for weeks and then lose. Or worse, win by the skin of my teeth, and then be jobless in five years' time."

"So we finished on a pretty sour note after I'd paid the bill, with him saying, "I'll think it over and let you know." So I started puffing up the hill, and then after a hundred yards stupidly turned round just as he did. He waved knowingly and then continued toward the river, probably planning a quick trick on the towpath.

"Well I was so furious I couldn't sleep. Then at one in the morning, the phone rings and it's "Really sorry to wind you up, Rafs. I forgive all those jiltings. And of course I want to do it but you'll have to hold my hand all the time. I love you to bits, so now get some sleep."

All pretence at annoyance now gone, he is in a state of exaltation. It is my turn to be angry.

"Raphael, you're making the mistake of your life. Let that little monster back in your life and he'll wreck everything. I know the type. And the whole Mayberry scene will blow up in your face."

He answers with cold deliberation;

"The election's being called tomorrow. This selection probably won't get a single mention. In any case I expect we'll lose the seat. And, Barrie, don't push it; I'm not going to accept lessons on how to live my life."

Silence: we both mutter 'sorry' and then we man the 'phones for a solid eight hours to set the whole squalid operation in motion. All because of that stupid encounter in Balliol quad years back. And all for that poisonous little wretch. But what really hurts most was that not once did he think to ask me whether I might be interested in standing; but then I'm forty, my hair's going grey and I've put on a bit of weight.

HELEN

When the heavily trailed election was finally called, there was even less excitement than last time. We expected to lose seats but to scrape a majority. The opposition was hopeless, our leadership patched up their internal quarrels, or hid them better from the public gaze. But it was Bill's overhaul of the party machine that kept the constituency parties going despite the falling membership figures. He raised the money and drafted all spare helpers into the marginal seats. And he set in place a team of young experts in what was then a novelty: social media. And in this area our effort was far superior to the Tory High Command, as blissfully ignorant of these new weapons of war as most of us on our side.

Raphael fought almost no campaign in his own seat, and all his party workers and those of his Scottish protégé were drafted in to help Aidan Richards in the most marginal constituency in the region. I went to help for a day. I had only met him once before and found him to be insolent and arrogant but with rather dissolute good looks. But in Mayberry he was transformed, as if he'd been stung by a hornet. Up at 6 every morning, doing 18 hour days on the stump; every school gate when the mums came to pick up their kids, every morning shift at the local glass factory, every early morning train from Mayberry Central, even the pigeon fanciers' weekly get-together, all subjected to his wayward glamour, hair now perfectly styled, the designer stubble, sharp suits, rarely a tie, with a brilliant white shirt open to the button which revealed just enough chest hair to turn on those susceptible to this kind of metrosexual appeal. He certainly seemed to have a rapport with the housewives and the shoppers at the local supermarket.

I was there for his debate in the parish church with the Tory candidate, a local businessman, and the clever-clever Liberal lawyer drafted in for the occasion; I feared that what he described tastelessly as his 'storm troopers', about 100 youngsters who followed him like groupies stalking a rock star, combined with his own aggressivity might lose him the debate but the charm button had been pressed: he was polite - even deferential - to his opponents and scored on all the policy points showing off his local knowledge shamelessly. He won the debate hands down.

We kept our parliamentary majority but a heavily slashed one. Both Raphael and I held our seats comfortably enough. His young acolytes did well, Rashida Hussein spectacularly so. After six recounts, Aidan

Richards held on by just 22 votes, with the lowest swing to the Tories in the region.

NED

I'll send you the swings and majorities separately but to cut a long story short, they all got in. Even Aidan. Thanks to me of course. I spent two whole weeks in sodding Mayberry shacked up in Aidan's tiny rented flat, which would be a pinch for just one, worked my balls off 14 hours a day, and then got plastered with his campaign team every night. I even managed to get off with one of his local councillors but when she woke up in the morning she had that 'dreadful mistake' expression emblazoned on her forehead and from then on she pretended not to know me. Aidan squeaked in by 22; only he and Raphael Sinclair - a fixture in the campaign because he had nothing to worry about in his own seat - seemed to believe he could win. So all my mates are now MPs. I could kick myself.

BARRIE

I've had a bad feeling about what's happened this week. Since the election we've been concentrating on the party executive stuff. He and Bill have been doing a lot to resuscitate the youth and student groups, which were almost on the point of shutting down, quite frankly. The party had lost a lot of support over the war, and now tuition fees is the big issue. But they've managed to find some quite bright young kids and in the words of that arrogant little prat Rupert Dennison, "Rafa's (sic) now grooming the next generation".

He's also doing a lot of stuff on Europe, which he says is being neglected by the party. The Labour ministers are in and out of Brussels as fast as they can, with no interest in building links with continental socialists. And of course his successor is one of those 'don't trust the food, don't drink the water' eurosceptics who hates spending a night in Brussels or Luxembourg. So it's Raphael who represents us on the executive of the European socialists and even sits on some working group drawing up yet another 'founding programme' for Europe's pathetic apology for a Left. A bit below his pay grade I'd have thought, sitting in boring meetings in characterless buildings with party apparatchiks from Lithuania and Malta. He must be the only real politician in the room.

He went to Brussels on Monday, came back the next day on a later Eurostar than we expected and didn't check up on us at the office. When I rang him last night in Putney, the line was constantly engaged. Today he came into the office looking pretty fagged out, but in sparkling mood. I recognised the signs.

So this evening I cancel my London Symphony ticket (much to Digby's annoyance, though being season ticket holders means we could negotiate a refund) and hotfooted it up Putney Hill, answering the summons. Here's the story in full technicolour (OK, so I didn't take notes but I know him so well I'd swear these are more or less the exact words).

"It was pissing with rain in Brussels, the train had been delayed, I didn't even have time to check in, I missed out on lunch completely, and I arrived at that tedious office block, soaking wet and straight to the meeting; the subcommittee chaired by that incomprehensible but garrulous little Hungarian. They accepted most of our amendments but the thing was dragging on because the Germans and the Dutch were being difficult on everything.

"The only little compensation was taking furtive looks at the young Portuguese who had drawn the short straw and was the notetaker. Pure eye candy. Not tall, but strong looking, with short jet black hair almost crew-cut, the obligatory stubble but neat, beautifully turned out in dark suit, white shirt and brilliant crimson tie. And then there's the eyes which show every emotion in a slightly exaggerated way, occasionally quizzical when listening to the latest inanity, with just a hint of mirth, but of course, deeply, profoundly soulful. On previous occasions I'd gone out of my way to thank him for sending papers on time, or drafting a good note, which I always do with staff but which I guess is not standard practice for many of the continental comrades.

"But I obviously couldn't stare at him all the time, and in any case I couldn't read any reaction in his face. I was by now almost catatonic with boredom so for once your call was welcome. I took my mobile down the corridor and into some rather untidy cupboard-sized office. Because you're such a chatter-box, by the time I'd gone back into the room, they'd shut up shop for the night. My young Portuguese friend had left a little note on top of my papers, "I'm sorry, Mr Sinclair, but the meeting finished suddenly. I do not know where you had gone. We start again at 9 tomorrow morning in this room. Please telephone me on the number at the end if you have any problem. Jose."

I hesitated but was sensible and tried to phone your chum, Cynthia, but she had a late Council meeting. And my friend Miranda" (my friend, actually) "was away on a business trip. So nothing for it but to get a taxi to my gloomy hotel just off the Schuman Roundabout, eat there and then have an early night. When I got outside it was still pouring down of course. You can't just hail taxis in Brussels and it was a good 10 minutes to the nearest cab rank. It was one of those moments when you just want to sit down on the wet but still dog-shit strewn pavement and scream profanities.

"Then suddenly out of the underground car park at quite a nick comes a small rather beat-up white Renault and it was my gorgeous Portuguese life saver. 'Can I give you a lift, Mr Sinclair?' I was tempted to say 'you already have done' but just jumped in the car. My hotel was in the opposite direction. The Brussels traffic was now grid-locked. He reversed the wrong way down a one-way street, using the pavement, but it served only to bring us juddering to another standstill. We waited and I finally plucked up courage, 'I suppose we could go for a quick drink, then I could get a taxi to my hotel when the traffic clears.' He does a curious manoeuvre and we're suddenly going in the other direction, downtown against the flow, past the Grande Place, deserted in the deluge, and then on to the Bourse area. We park illegally of course, then it's into this rather buzzy bar, where we have almost to shout, jabbering away about the political situation in Portugal and the UK, how he ended up in Brussels, my last book which he claimed to have read.

"Then Jose as I could now call him (but I remain Mr Sinclair to him) says 'Can I ask you something?' By this stage he could have asked me literally anything. 'Would you agree to have a meal with me? I know a good Italian restaurant nearby.' So, back to the car - going on foot even 100 yards being illegal in Belgium - another fancy manoeuvre and we double park outside the 'Luna Caprese' where he is clearly well known to the head waiter at any rate who plants kisses on both stubbly cheeks. Although I had no lunch, suddenly I'm not really hungry (or at least not for dinner). So it's a starter size plate of indifferent pasta, but followed by quite an effervescent zabaglione, lingering a bit over coffee, and, in my case, not one but two grappas to steady my nerves and stop me shaking, just wondering what happens next.

"Finally, the words I dreaded, 'I ought to drive you back to the hotel', followed by a pause, and then 'unless you'd like to come back to my flat for a last coffee. It's just round the corner.' I tried to count to five before saying what protocol demands in these cases, 'Well, just for a quick coffee, then. Thanks.'

"We drive into his underground car park under the small block where he has a flat. We take the lift to the fourth floor in silence. By the first floor he has taken my hand, by the second he has started kissing me, and by the time we've reached his floor, he has started to unbuckle my trouser belt. Before he has even closed and locked the door, clothes are being discarded. At his suggestion we shower together. Very much together in fact because the shower is so tiny that physical intimacy is the only option. Then to bed, but he's fastidious about precautions and obsessively clean: a shower after each bout. I took four showers before utter collapse. And then at about six in the morning it all starts again.

"When he goes down to the garage to fetch the car, I take a look around a flat I know I'm going to see so often. It's pretty tiny, like an old attic flat, with a small bathroom, loo, recently refurbished but not at great expense; an open-plan kitchen, again modernised but with just a small 3-ring cooker and no washing machine that I could see. The bed (one-and-a-half size, I guess) at one end of the living room with a nondescript dark green sofa and two armchairs, the desk and chair both from Ikea. Very tidy and clean except for the desk, cluttered with his computer, papers and the thousands of newspaper cuttings that mark out the true political obsessive.

"I shower, I think for the sixth time, he's prepared breakfast, a slice of toast and coffee (he'll have to learn about the tea thing) and then he drives me, now in a state of elation and exhaustion, to a meeting on trade policy which would have been unspeakably tedious had it not been for long 'gazing time' between the representative of the British Labour Party and the less than usually focused notetaker. Near the end of the meeting he comes over and just drops a little note on my desk, 'I telephone you tonight at home.'

"I got back to Putney shortly after 7, but there was no message. I began to pace the flat like some teenage girl who's been jilted after her first kiss at the school prom. Then at last after 9 he rings, 'Hello, Raphael. It is Jose. Where are you?' I reply, 'In my flat which is not really surprising as that's the number you've rung.'

"He continues, 'But where in your flat?' I reply, 'In my office'. He continues, 'I am on my bed. Why do you not go to your bedroom? I have taken off my clothes. Why do you not take off your clothes?'"

I'd had enough of this self-congratulatory indulgence by this point so said something like, "OK, Raphael, so you had telephone sex and without paying for it. No more details, please." He looks almost hurt and just continues with the narrative which involves at least two more calls before sleep was permitted. I am about to get the details of the early morning call, and the usual line about this being really serious this time, when I finally let rip, "For Christ's sake Raphael, this kid is half your age. He's just some politico wannabe who's latching on to Norma Desmond. Only it's not orange groves and film stars, it's bloody Brussels and dog shit everywhere. If this gets out you're finished and you take us all down with you."

He seems really hurt at my reaction, looking punctured for all of thirty seconds. I leave shortly afterwards, without the ritual hug, him doubtless about to pace the flat waiting for the next call from Brussels.

I am not in the least surprised that he has found some excuse to cancel some constituency engagements at the weekend. He slinked off to Waterloo for the Eurostar. When he comes back to the office, quite late on Monday morning, he looks as if he hasn't slept the whole weekend and is thriving on all this sleep deprivation.

HELEN

The first year after the election felt for everyone like treading water. We knew about all the tensions simmering at the top from Downing Street leaks and a string of books narrating the death throes of the regime. Raphael's young protégés made themselves as obnoxious as possible, clustered at the end of the third row below the gangway, making some ministers look like second-rate, poorly prepared fools, incapable of facing any serious scrutiny. Angus Buchanan routinely showed up just how hollow were all those claims by the Treasury team that the 'boom and bust' era had ended. Rupert Dennison could be lethally funny, quite the wittiest speaker in the party. But it was Aidan Richards who won gold in the obnoxiousness Olympics. He stretched the dress code to its limits but he managed to get away with the lightest of reprimands, while all the time writing withering articles in the press about how stuffy and cut-off from reality Westminster was.

His put downs of the more inept Foreign Office team were pitiless. But the loathing of his parliamentary colleagues became really intense when he suddenly started putting every penny of his expenses on his website: paper clips, biros and rubber bands included. Of course the picture that emerged was of a public official being unimpeachably transparent. The other gang members followed suit, starting the feeding frenzy which ended with several MPs being hounded out of Parliament and quite a few announcing early their impending retirements. Two at least finished behind bars. But what irritated his colleagues most was the media fawning of this paragon of virtue.

One or two profiles started to appear in the weekly magazines, mentioning in passing that he was openly gay, publishing more photographs than strictly necessary of the man voted 'sexiest politician of the year', some in quite clearly 'come hither poses', with his shirt unbuttoned to the waist, one with a crystalline white T-shirt over navy bermudas, revealing sturdy thighs and rather hairy legs.

But it was his reputation as the perfect constituency MP which they pushed, just adding to the resentment of his colleagues. He had initiated a 'Labour in the community week' every autumn, with the three Mayberry MPs asking their constituents to nominate a volunteer project for them, building a temporary hut for the scouts, doing up an old people's home, clearing some wasteland, and, despite opposition from the local housing committee, organising a 'paint-in', letting council house residents choose the colour for the outside walls of their homes. It was all a bit 'bob-a-job for politicos', and of course guaranteed local and indeed some national coverage for the three MPs and their little army of volunteers. Richards' rather smug, "We're putting something back into the community" provoked the ire of his more modest colleagues, but others felt obliged to follow suit grudgingly.

His compulsive localism landed him in deep controversy when he led the opposition to the building of a large incinerator plant near a school and in the middle of a residential area[19]. Despite the fact that the Labour group on the Council supported the project, he got Raphael and Buchanan involved, but reserved for himself the glamour of being arrested during a community sit-in on the main road to the works, which inevitably hit national news. When the project was cancelled, he attained local hero status.

---

[19] Four Ashes

NED

From now on, favourite, indeed only, bruvver, respect. OK the selection conference was fixed by the union, even if I was replacing one of the fallen during 'the great Allowances crash' who happened to be one of ours too. Raphael Sinclair didn't have to lift a finger but he did come five times during the by-election campaign (conscience playing up because he hadn't asked me again for the Mayberry seat). And, boy, didn't he bring some stardust with him; he looks better as he gets older, more groomed, Italian hand-made suits, fantastic ties matching perfectly, really smart Church shoes. Puts even me in the sartorial shade (joke!). Much speculation among the lads about the reasons for this, as you can imagine. Well, no more of this idle banter, I have the people's business to see to.

HELEN

When finally the leadership election came up, we had a couple of meetings with Hattie Reynolds and Maudie Hinton and one or two of the trade union group of MPs who Raphael had started courting. He was meeting his smart young friends separately, judging rightly that each little group would get up the others' noses. And he phoned Bill a lot.

The conclusion was that it was all sewn up for the long-time, loathed heir apparent. And that there was no point in standing for the deputy leadership either, "Why be the seventh dwarf?"

As Maudie Hinton shrewdly if colourfully put it, "if you won it, it's not worth a bucket of piss, and you'd be tying yourself in. Just be ready when things go wrong which they will. I know him."

Raphael told me later that he had had a meeting with the successor just days before he formally took over. It was all very affable, punctured with perfectly insincere mutual expressions of support, both ardently wanting to keep in touch, but no offer was made and none solicited because the Foreign Office had already been given to someone else (and the Americans would dislike it anyway) and the Treasury would have to go to one of the new leader's allies. Raphael was not interested in anything else anyway. The PM designate then said he would welcome Raphael continuing to build up the party: this left him unsure whether he was being told that his manoeuvrings in the constituency selections were being watched.

Just as Maudie Hinton had predicted, it all started to go wrong almost from day one. Policy cock-ups, lousy presentation and the lid coming off all the rivalries and factions. Within weeks the press speculation had started about passing the torch to someone from the younger generation (i.e. the one below Raphael's - generation in politics having a shorter duration than those in the real world); Raphael's name did not figure at all.

But despite the prospect of yet more years in the wilderness, Raphael seemed in great shape. He had lost a bit of weight, smartened himself up a lot, had obviously thrown away those old slightly frayed sports jackets which made him look like a don on sabbatical, the shoes now highly polished, and the suits perfectly pressed and for once fitting. Most assumed a woman had taken him in hand. Someone certainly had.

BARRIE

He came back yesterday after the break, looking like Cary Grant in his heyday. Hair swept back as usual, but neatly trimmed, nothing flopping over the ears or the collar, and just a few flecks of grey but looking as if this relaxation and prolonged exposure to glorious sunshine had disproved the irreversibility of the clock. He's lost a little weight, looks fit and rested. Of course I love Digby, but I do sometimes wonder what it might have been like if Raphael and I hadn't put the brakes on when we were both incompetently circling one another.

In any event, he wouldn't look like this if I'd been taking care of him. All of this is Jose's handiwork after the six weeks (yes, six weeks!) they'd been together at his cottage at the French Atlantic coast. I was made to wait until the end of play yesterday before getting the long version of the holiday:

"I knew he was insatiable in bed of course but the whole holiday was like boot camp: swims three times a day, whatever the weather, early morning stretching and something called 'Pilates', long coastal walks; no booze at lunch, no aperitifs, and just one bottle of wine for the two of us in the evening. Of course severe looks and the odd lecture whenever I light up.

"The rest of the day is like one long tutorial. First, English lessons, 'Why do you say it like that?' or 'What does "smirk" mean?' Then it was my world view, a potted history of Europe in 25 lessons. He even - wait for it - takes notes and then reads them out to me the next day and asks quite difficult questions about the replies I'd given but long forgotten so I have to wing it.

"He's rather a good cook, so it wasn't a case of trekking over to Marie-France's hostelry every day for the 'menu du jour' which was the routine with Nicolas who couldn't boil an egg. He'd even googled all sorts of experimental recipes with local produce.

"I took him to the golf course for what I'd thought would be a little knock-around where at least I could show off a bit; some of the members I've known for years gave us odd looks, ranging from mild disapproval to outright drooling. Inevitably, on the first day he was pretty hopeless, but he insisted we go back every day and by the end was trying to beat me."

Apparently, he's told the Portuguese not to be so competitive, which from someone who is not merely a bad loser but even a bad winner is a bit rich!

"He also dragged me off to Bordeaux four times to change my wardrobe, at pretty huge expense. 'You dress so English. Why do the English dress so bad?'"

But the telling of this tale told all. The little complaints and whinges couldn't mask that the holiday had, against the odds, worked. So I expect the weekends in Brussels to continue. The Portuguese is now a fixture we'll all have to cope with.

HELEN

You could tell that things had started badly and gone downhill from there by the fact that the Prime Minister even called in Raphael for a late-night chat in his House of Commons room, one October evening. Ostensibly it was to offer him a wide-ranging portfolio on presentation and organisation, with few resources and no authority to back it up. The offer was not seriously meant and not seriously considered. The real reason was to get Raphael to give his blessing to some of the Gang of Four[20] joining the government. The PM was paranoid about them, and the media loved giving space to their sniping. In particular he wanted Angus Buchanan 'to give ballast' to the economic team (which I think meant to shut him up and end the constant carping) and he was desperate to neutralise Rupert Dennison, whose mockery of the more third-rate ministers had now started to fill up the Commons whenever he got to his elegant little feet.

Of course all of them had qualities, except Aidan Richards, who was just a venomous attention-seeker and, in my view at least, a very bad influence on Raphael. But there was something almost sinister about the way they hunted as a pack, prepared for any meetings of our informal little group, and had clearly squared Raphael beforehand so that he accepted anything they came up with.

It is a matter of wonder to me, even at a distance from these events, the hold that these young and inexperienced colleagues had over him. Without him, they would have been nothing. He had brought them into politics, found them mostly safe parliamentary seats and was clearly in a different league. Was this just his infatuation with youthful vigour which had led to this subservience? Yet I noticed it was in their company that he came alive, shone and raised his game, whereas with others he would just tick over and drop in and out of conversation as the mood took him.

---

[20] i.e. Angus Buchanan, Rashida Hussein, Rupert Dennison and Aidan Richards

BARRIE

Raphael got back from his US speaking tour today, bursting with energy and enthusiasm. For a moment I fear he's yet again 'met someone' although the Jose thing is still very much on, apparently.

These tours are nice little earners and help keep Nigel on board. He calls the two of us into the office with the other dreaded words, "I've had an idea". He continues, "It came to me after I'd been talking to the dean of the Economics Faculty of one of the Ivy League colleges at a dinner in Cincinnati. He gave me a doomsday scenario for the financial markets, how America's a financial basket case, we arguably even worse and all of us on the road to perdition, which is now just round the corner.

"On the way back, I started thinking about something more comprehensive, a polemic, 'The Way We Live Now…Now.' And we have a go at everything: the irresponsibility of finance, the way governments are too feeble to stand up to corporate power, the increasing irrelevance of party politics, the dominance of quick returns capitalism, the fragility of the credit boom which is based on absurd property values, the decline in public services, the threat to jobs of US-led automation and digital services, the dumbing down, the abuse of corporate power, London as the tax fiddle capital of the world, rip-off Britain, our enfeebled constitution, our moribund politics. You know, a real philippic."

There's silence. He brings out a sheaf of papers from his slim black leather briefcase. "I just scrawled a few more detailed thoughts on the plane. Get Marjorie to type them up" (she's the only one who can read his handwriting). "Then call in Angus to draft the two parts on the economy and corporate power. Rupert can rehash the stuff on the media and dumbing down. I'd like to take a first draft with me to Brussels for the Christmas break" (so Portugal's still definitely on, then) "We should aim to have it out in March."

We gawp like goldfish at a standstill in a circular glass bowl.

NED

Of course no-one asks me to write anything for it, but Angus has had a big hand in it. And it shows, much more leftist than people would expect from Raphael, lots about us needing to make 'an uncompromising onslaught on the excesses of unaccountable corporate power', with good populist examples about banks and utilities and the supermarkets. And then Raphael himself put in the phrase about 'the tin in the heart of New Labour' which was of course what everyone's picked up. It's over the top about all the debt and a financial crisis; if he's right he's a prophet. If he's wrong he's just another moaning Minnie.

Aidan seems to spend all his spare time going to the boss' office, or dropping in on his flat up the road in Putney. This is a new development ever since he heard about the mysterious Portuguese love interest. Rupe wormed the truth out of Barrie Jones (Raphael's long-time assistant) when it became clear that something had happened. So now my flatmate is always having late Indian meals with the oracle of Mayberry, or even going to the cinema together. But he now always spends the night here which is a novelty.

My own love life has again become the crossing of the Sahara, after the unfortunate incident with the Party researcher, the wine spilt down her dress and me mopping up her breasts and getting slapped for my pains. Still as I am not even a D-list celeb, no press and no lawsuits.

HELEN

The book became the book. Despite what people thought, it was all written by Raphael, but a lot of the ideas - particularly the dafter ones - came from the gang, and early drafts had been done by Barrie and Nigel. It got some great reviews including in odd places: the Spectator, for example, loved the analysis though ignored the prescription[21]. It reached No 1 in the non-fiction chart after ten days and just stayed there for two months.

Of course he had some sublime luck. The first bank run and the collapse of the American sub-primes seemed to vindicate everything he had written. Suddenly he was 'the sage of Mayberry', never off the screens or the radio, the lone voice in the wilderness who had predicted chaos and collapse, but who had some ideas how to turn things round. The high command fumed but the constituency parties loved it.

But no-one - including myself - twigged that it was the first, perhaps unconscious, move in a leadership bid. All talk of challengers was about the younger cabinet ministers getting restless as things turned even sourer. Indeed I heard two colleagues (one in the corridor and one in the tea-room) saying that Raphael was on the verge of resigning his seat, to become vice-chancellor at Sussex, or to start a TV career here or in the States. He of course did nothing to counter these sillinesses from the headless-chicken wing of the party. He was his usual unflappable, charming self who just smiled enigmatically when anyone talked of the future.

---

[21] August 22nd 200-

EXTRACT FROM 'THE JC DUNNETT ANTHOLOGY (199- to 201-)'

This week I've broken two of my golden rules. I usually leave book reviews to my more erudite colleagues toiling away for the back half of the magazine but I cannot resist commenting on the latest book by Mr Raphael Sinclair, the former Foreign Secretary, which has proved to be the publishing success of the season, in part at least because it has been placed perhaps paradoxically in the non-fiction category.

And long ago I decided that interviewing politicians was a contrary way of seeking to understand politics. In the age of what a colleague has called 'the sultans of spin', no practitioner is going to give you an answer to a question which has not been rehearsed, tested on focus groups and put out for amendment to a dozen special advisers. But last week I found myself in the office of Mr Sinclair and the experience was not without interest.

The man has manners. After the shortest of waits chatting inconsequentially to his assistant, a Welshman who, if he is not careful, could give his nation a reputation for garrulity, and receiving a cup of rather superior coffee from his kindly secretary, he opens the door to his office, gives you a firm handshake, and guides you to a table where you sit opposite him to bathe in the warmth of what appears to be his effortless charm.

I study him. He is a good-looking man in his late forties, strong-boned and probably above his ideal weight, but I would say, although I am ill-placed to judge, that he takes some care of himself. And for a politician he is well turned out. I'd always imagined him to be a sports jacket type, with grey flannel trousers, a checked shirt and a tie to match albeit with a little approximation, while sporting what used to be called 'brothel creepers', those now out-of-fashion suede shoes. But no, he was, as they say, dressed to kill, a very smart dark navy suit, bespoke I'd guess, a light blue shirt and a deep purple tie, and black shoes, shined as if for a parade ground inspection. This is a man who cares for his appearance and may be on the receiving end of professional advice. Were it not for his size he could pass muster as an Italian corporate lawyer in a good way of business.

He has a strong voice he can project without strain, but he modulates it to create a sense of intimacy with his interlocutor. And all the time he fixes you with not a stare but a laser beam of concentrated interest. He *speaks sparingly, thinks before answering questions and shows he is following your reactions with utmost care.*

His replies when they come are sophisticated and littered with just enough historical and cultural references to make you aware that you are talking to a figure of some cultivation, but who refrains from ramming his erudition down your throat.

I try to take him on to the terrain of his latest book, which he dismisses lightly, with "Oh, you've actually read it. I thought it was a case of being a book to buy, talk about but not to read." I ask him about where he picked up the phrase of 'New Labour's heart of tin' which has entered our lexicon.

"Oh I got a lot of help for some sections of the book, the more complex policy stuff. But the judgment's mine, and that phrase is original. I wanted to sum up what is the deficiency of New Labour, and the way things have evolved, I feel that the beating heart of social democracy, our values, and our people are now almost an embarrassment to some at the helm of the party."

"But I thought you came in as a New Labour prototype when you were elected. Why have you turned against the, er, brand?"

"I don't recognise some of the things being done by government as New Labour. The tinkering with public education, allowing private companies to muscle in on the health service, and that's just two examples. And of course to ingratiate ourselves with corporate power we got carried away with a 'smart regulation' agenda (which was it now seems not always so smart) and the regulation became so light that future generations will be living with the crippling consequences. But for me the starting point was our fundamental disagreement over our external relations and what seemed to be a fawning attitude to Washington."

So far, so clear, and not a word out of place but when I started to question him about his acolytes, the young MPs who he helped to get into Parliament, there's a flicker of evasiveness in his gaze. "I think when you see their quality, and their burning convictions, you can easily imagine how a local conference of party members called to select a candidate might be impressed with their idealism and their eloquence. You can encourage youngsters to come into politics but it's the local parties which take the decisions."

Well, up to a point. Using his vantage point on the Party's executive and his network of contacts in the constituencies, it is now abundantly clear that he 'assisted' these local parties in making their 'sensible' choices about future representation.

Predictably I asked him about his future plans.

"People are divided about what publishing the book signifies? Is it a 'burning-of-boats' moment when you recognise you'll never be able to work with the different tribes of New Labour and start thinking of life outside politics? Or are you setting out a stall as the alternative if things go wrong, or rather, get worse for the leadership?"

He paused, and looked me straight in the eye, almost to unsettle me. "That's the trouble with practitioners of your trade, Mr Dunnett, even ones with great elegance of expression and clarity of thought. In the end everything comes down to leadership challenges or jockeying for position. You may find this hard to credit, but I just thought I'd say what I think, I'd warn the party of where we're heading and open up a debate which can't just be quashed. I can influence politics more directly by conducting that debate from where I'm sitting, as a backbench MP, serving his constituents and raising some questions. I'm not going anywhere."

And with that he was out of his chair, a little stiffly I thought, always a danger for a tall man in a sedentary profession. He managed to shake my hand warmly, bestow several warming smiles, utter his thanks and shunt me through the door in almost one fell swoop. A masterclass in bringing closure to a conversation with some elegance.

As I made my way out of the building it suddenly occurred to me. The much admired British theatrical profession had missed out on a great talent. I found what he said interesting, and believed not a word of it. I don't think I will interview another politician. In future I'll abide by my golden rules.

But if I were in the upper reaches of government, I'd keep a close eye on 'the sage of Mayberry' in the future.

BARRIE'S DIARY

He's spent Easter at the cottage in France, and when he came back yesterday I could see something was wrong. Sure enough, I get it out of him over three whiskies late at night in the Putney flat.

"It was pissing rain for seven days and Jose was bored and frustrated; no runs, no dips, no golf - I'm not prepared to get soaked for four hours, with the clubs so wet they slip in your hands and with the greens waterlogged. So it was a lot of mooching around the house, arguing about whether to go out for a meal, and him being difficult over my choice of TV programmes; and then I got just a little bit tired of the constant refrain about the innate superiority of continental socialists, and how much better the Lisbon government was at managing the economy than ours.

"But above all it was 'When will you let me come to Britain?', 'When can I meet your family, and your friends?', 'Are you ashamed of me?', 'Is there someone else?', 'You do not believe in commitmenting' (sic). When he announced that Belgium, Holland and Spain were introducing gay marriage and I showed zero enthusiasm that was the final straw; his dark eyes welled up and then he went on a sex strike for 24 hours so that we had even less with which to fill the time."

HELEN

Disaster struck at that year's May local elections. So great was the wipe out that coming third in safe Labour wards was a victory of sorts. Even in Mayberry the Tories swept the board. Many of my colleagues started to look at other career options.

NED

Angus in his worst head teacher mode had us round to their nice little garden flat in Ealing.

"He's got to go for it. Now. It's become such conventional wisdom that we've lost, it's self-fulfilling."

Rupert, for once not bubbly or smirking, just said quietly,

"We need to talk about Rafa. Angus, there's something you and Rashida don't know. Our spiritual guide in whom we invest all our hopes and more importantly our careers, is a serial shirt-lifter but deeply embedded in the closet. He's been having an affair with a very young Portuguese boy for about eighteen months; and before that it was a French academic, and before that God knows what…"

There was a pause which seemed to last for about two hours. Rashida went pale, like a vicar's wife who's just discovered that the curate has been emptying the collection box. She looked at the floor as if to detach herself from this intrusion of sordid reality. Angus, paler still, asked in a very quiet monotone, "And you didn't think to let me in on this little detail? We've been working our balls off to build up this guy, our very own Special Purpose Vehicle, and now just as we're about to raise the fucking flag you suddenly tell me he's gay. Well gee thanks guys! Guess that's put an end to that. We hunker down and wait to get smashed at the election."

Rupert rediscovered his piping Pollyanna tone, "Is it really such a killer? Just a few years ago an openly gay minister would have been unthinkable, now half the cabinet's 'that way inclined', according at any rate to Aidan who knows about these things. It would be a bit of a sensation, but it'll go down a storm with the LGBT mafia, the students, the yoof sections…."

Rashida interrupted coldly, "My people" (since when were they 'her people'? Is she playing the Muslim card? Whatever next, the bloody burkha?) "won't like it." But then she said something so chilling in that precise accentless English she has, "But I suppose that it's something we could exploit later."

I put in my twopenneth, "Mind you, the young Portuguese boy bit won't help; sounds like a beach pick-up at Albufeira."

"Well," said Rupert, "from what I hear that particular chapter is about to close." He gets all this from Barrie Jones, whom he flatters and bullies on alternate days of the week.

Throughout all this, Aidan remained silent. We drifted off a bit later with nothing settled.

HELEN

The June meeting of the NEC was just appalling. An irritable, distracted Raphael was in the chair. We had before us copies of a situation report distributed by Bill at the beginning of the meeting which we all had to hand back in afterwards. When we read it, all the backstairs whispering against the leadership seemed suddenly justified. The membership was simply collapsing. Some local parties were no longer meeting and had zero activities. Funds had dried up. Some unions were threatening to withdraw backing, 'not throwing good money after bad'. Morale was rock bottom. We were heading for a poor third in the general election. And the PM's ratings were even worse, with his economic competence far behind the Tory team, who for the first time ever were more trusted than Labour on the NHS.

As we broke up, pretty dispirited, I took the lift down alone with Bill. He said, "I'm seeing him tonight. He's got to go for it."

BARRIE

This was the week the tectonic plates finally shifted.

It looks like Jose is toast. I don't think he realises it yet, but I know the signs. The visits to Brussels have been cut right back. Calls, messages and now texts ever more frantic but not returned. Marjorie, who knows everything, does her perfect telephone act, "I am so sorry Mr Pinto. I am sure Mr Sinclair will get back to you as soon as possible. He is terribly busy at the moment. He has a lot of major meetings which he always prepares seriously" (if only). When Raphael did make a trip to Brussels last week, it was only at Saturday lunchtime, returning on Sunday morning for the good old standby, the default excuse for all political philanderers wearying of their flings, 'constituency business'.

When he came round on Sunday evening, fed up, and had shooed Digby into the kitchen, I asked, "Why don't you finish it cleanly for once?"

"It's very difficult when you've just walked through the door, savoured the energetic enthusiasm of the greeting you invariably get just to turn round and say 'Thanks and all that, but it's over'. And before you say I should keep my trousers on and blurt it all out before any steaminess, I'd simply point out that it's not so easy when you have in front of you this extraordinarily scrumptious person just in his boxer shorts but visibly keen to get down to business. But I guess that's not a problem you've often had to face too often."

This was so hateful that I thought about asking him to leave but I put it down to his general fractiousness.

As if this change in his personal life is not big enough, it looks as if he's about to take the biggest risk of his career. Apparently, on Monday night after the NEC, Raphael was collared by Bill Sampson. They go to Bill's new flat, the one he moved into after his wife died, and which he shares with his rather gormless son, Bo, who is road manager for a pop group I've never heard of. Bill prepares an omelette and salad, and then suddenly goes for him,

"When are you going to stop faffing around? You're behaving like a complete dilettante. I don't know whether you can save this party - indeed I rather doubt it - but what I do know is that we're dead if we don't get rid of him."

Raphael tells me he asked all the questions: other possible candidates from the cabinet to 'jump a generation' (Bill's reply was, "It won't happen because they're all gutless and they've all given up"); the risk of a more radical platform weighed against members leaving in droves because of the current insipidities; his private life, about which Bill already knew - at least the broad outline (" well, you'll have to clean it up a bit, cover your tracks, come out and that will give you some immunity in the party: no-one can attack you personally or they get labelled homophobic. Provided there's no drugs, underage sex or money changing hands, it'll be uncomfortable but you can ride it out. There isn't is there?") Raphael gives the appropriate reassurances: done the grand tour, no rent boys, all over age (just), no drugs and always precautions (a little white lie, this, since Jose has apparently relaxed conditions believing that he had now had some real commitment.)

By the time the plates are cleared away and a further half bottle of Tesco's finest blended whiskey has gone west, the conversation moves from ends to means.

So, yesterday, the day after this heart to heart, Marjorie, Nigel and I were called in to the office for an announcement of some solemnity despite starting off in an almost tongue-in-cheek style.

"You three have to be the first to know. You see before you a candidate for the leadership of our party. We are total outsiders, we have no organisation, no trade union support, no money, and no battalions. But we do have a bit of credibility, a record of being right, and a fresh approach. And we aren't tainted by being part of a failed government. But the greatest asset I have is you three, my great friends, on whom I depend and to whom I owe everything."

Of course he's hamming it up a bit, as usual, but he pulls it off, and inevitably all three of us are moved, with Nigel being the most obviously moist-eyed.

Then he starts dishing out orders. Marjorie and me to do a timetable; Nigel a media strategy and then, with him and me, a programme.

I think the tears were also for what was unsaid. Either everything we've worked for over ten years will bring about some real change, maybe even the top. Or it will be a spectacular shipwreck, the end of his career and for all of us the parting of the ways.

NED

Things are getting weird now. I'm sitting channel zapping while Aide's lounging in the corner reading something. Rupe drops in for a bit of gossip on his way to his place at Kew, which we've never been allowed to visit which fuels its own little bubble of speculation, but that's not the point.

Aidan suddenly says, "I think I'm going to make my move".

Rupe replies "Shrewd timing. We need something to tie him in."

Aidan replies, "It's not that. I've just decided it's what I want."

End of conversation. Rupe changes the subject to some story about the guys at No 10 at war with each other, and everything leaking. And I'm left there not knowing what the hell's going on, embarrassed to ask and wondering how I'm going to pay the rent if Aidan moves out. I know it's not very clean let alone smart but he could have said something.

HELEN

The weekend in France was actually my idea. At the end of June, Raphael just walked into my office at the end of 'the corridor of the damned' in Portcullis House (some childish idea of the Whips putting all the dispossessed together in one wing of the building). When he had finished making his obviously rehearsed big announcement, preparing doubtless for the launch, I simply said as prosaically as possible to bring him back to earth,

"You've got to get a team together. Your office is great, but even with your Bad Boys (the name everyone gives to the brats) this is not a team. You need some more women, some of the union MPs, a bit of organisational muscle."

He was unconvinced, "Surprise is everything. I'm nervous enough even about letting my kids into the secret. Any leak now and the whole cabinet, and the stooges in the PLP[22] leadership, will be all over the media, making public oaths of loyalty to the Dear Leader, rubbishing us, intimidating waverers and it's over before it's begun. Imagine if I assemble a larger group here or in my office, I might as well go down to the atrium and shout it through the security loudspeakers."

I wasn't giving up, "Then why don't you invite us over one weekend to your place in France? You've always said how off the beaten track it is. You could put some of them" (I hoped he heard me emphasising the 'them') "into Madame's hotel with all those fruits de mer you rave about. We'll have our privacy and we have less risk of leaks."

"Um, well I'll think about that", Raphael never liked other people having the good ideas. He liked even less my next conversational gambit.

"Raphael, your private life is going to be the big problem. This Portuguese boy, the papers will love it. Can you cope with this? Can he?"

He replied, "If by the Portuguese boy you mean my young friend who is ten years past the age of consent and quite able to fend for himself, all I'd say is 'don't worry.' He is part of my past but, I'm afraid, not my future."

I persevered, "He knows this?"

He paused then said, "Not yet".

---

[22] Parliamentary Labour Party

I concluded, "Well sort it out, Raphael, or it will destroy us all."

The good thing about my relations with Raphael was that I could speak to him with great frankness, the bad thing that he felt perfectly free to ignore my advice.

NED

Raphael called us over to his Putney flat; a first for me but clearly not for some of the others. A nice, airy place - no clutter but not much personality, just a place to kip I suppose. He was impatient to get cracking and came straight to the point, "I'm going to run for it and here's the plan." Many high-fives and expressions of enthusiasm, even if I think Angus and Rashida are still worried about the gay thing, although neither said anything.

So to plan the revolution, come August and we're all off to some village in the west of France where Raphael has his place, and where according to Rupe he organises his trysts. I suggest we all go in my car and stop off for a bit of serious wine-tasting in the Loire; no takers; Angus at his most pompous, "This is not a holiday. It's about changing Britain."

We were all sworn to secrecy, with Rupe insisting we change our email passwords every two days and our pin numbers every week.

Glad to hear you've met someone new and I look forward to meeting Sheila (is she really called Sheila or is this a wind-up?) during my first ministerial visit to Oz which should be in about three months!

PS The union's pushing me to stand for the national executive of the party. As Rupe said, "there's a big slob vote out there and now they have their man!"

BARRIE

The weather just gets worse. If it weren't for all the planning I'd have escaped the joys of London in July and headed south. But there's no let up.

Then on Monday disaster strikes. In the evening I drop some more docs round to Putney and it's pouring down permanently. Papers all over the living-room floor, when Raphael answers the phone. He goes into the study and shuts the door. I know what this is about, persuading his mum and dad to leave the family house and move into sheltered accommodation because they can no longer cope at home; the banal story of life's last phases being played out every year in tens of thousands of families up and down the country. His dad's got high blood pressure and can't really manage the stairs but won't hear of a stairlift. His mum's had several falls and is beginning to be very forgetful. I feel for Raphael because for once he's not in charge, and feels frustrated and guilty at the same time.

Suddenly there's a knock at the door so I answer it. Aidan Richards, in running shorts and sweat shirt, soaked and mud spattered, which really pleased me. But there was no pleasure in his face when he realises it's me.

Seeing that as usual when I'd been sitting on the floor I'd taken off my shoes and my shirt tails were hanging out, he asks, "What are you doing here?" (The usual Aidan Richards charm school greeting).

"Working, which is what I usually do here."

"Well", he says peremptorily, "I need a shower and somewhere to dry my gear."

"It's fortunate you happened to be in the neighbourhood."

"Don't get smart with me, Barrie, it doesn't suit you."

"It's down there, and you can probably borrow one of his dressing gowns till you've dried out before going home. He's on the 'phone to his folks."

"As it happens, Barrie, I do know my way around here. How long were you intending carrying on working now?"

"Oh, we only need another half-hour."

"Tell you what, Barrie, why don't you fuck off now? I'll tell him I sent you home early because I have something urgent to tell him and in private."

The murderous expression in those black, hard eyes, underlain with the permanent dark pouches, warns me off questioning this. Mustering as much dignity as I could, I tucked my shirt back in my trousers, put my shoes back on, placed my tie in my jacket pocket and left without us exchanging another word.

NED

I don't know what time it is with you but Aidan hasn't come back all night; not the first time but he left at seven for a jog and I get scared sometime he's going to pitch up dead after some encounter in a park or on the towpath.

BARRIE

Raphael arrived late in the office, barely greeted us and walked straight into his room looking tired and drawn. An hour later I got the summons to hear what I've been dreading for so long.

"As they say in the movies, 'It Happened One Night'", he started. "I'm sorry if he shoved you out. I didn't hear you go, and the front room was deserted, all the papers stacked, so I went to the bedroom, and there he was, lying naked on the bed, bedraggled, covered in mud, and his few clothes strewn on the floor still soaked through. But, as they also say in the movies, he appeared pleased to see me.

"All he said was, 'I need a shower, and I don't like showering alone.' I followed like a particularly obedient robot, undressed in the bathroom and the rest, as they also say, is history. But I realised that this was what I have been searching for the last ten years." There was a pause, he looked away from me and then started gabbling as if to stop himself from breaking down.

"When I reached for a cigarette after we'd had sex the second time, he took the fag out of my mouth and snapped it in two, and did the same slowly and deliberately with all the fags in the packet. 'That stops now,' he says." (Since when did he become a health freak?) "And he refused precautions outright, which given his track record worries me a bit, but he swears he has regular check-ups and there's nothing.

"When he gets dressed in the morning, having cool as a cucumber raided my drawers, taken a clean pair of my underpants, my best golfing bermudas but which are almost calf-length on him, and that dark green T-shirt I bought in Bordeaux last summer, he suddenly puts out his palm and says "I'll need a spare set of keys, and you'd better clear out some cupboard space. We'll bring my things over this afternoon." It took a moment before I realised what he was saying.

"I put up the feeblest resistance. 'Aidan, last night was wonderful and I think I fell in love with you that first moment in Balliol' but he interrupted me: 'If you want, Rafs, we can finish it now. No-one knows anything about it except Barrie, who obtuse though he is will at least have guessed this'. He made some pretty disparaging remarks about you. I don't know what you've done to offend him." I let this last outrage pass, as he continued, "He then added, 'But I'm not creeping in and out of this flat like some cat burglar.'

"In any case, he went on to say that unless I agreed there and then that he move in at once, it would all be over before it really began."

I set my facial expression to blank, awaiting the inevitable.

"So he's moving his things in tonight. We'll have to keep things quiet for a bit, but if I go for it, we'll have to go public."

My expression must have changed because he rushed on,

"I know this makes things a bit more difficult…"

I can't take it any longer, I start to shout or as near to shout as I do, "Difficult! Difficult! You've just blown it. It was bad enough with the Portuguese teenager, but you've got shot of him like a sex toy which no longer works" (sheepish look telling me that he hasn't yet told the kid) "but you go and take up with the world's least popular politician, a spoilt, infantile brat who is just using you for fun because you're suddenly going to get celebrity status; and then he'll start looking for new tricks. The party won't wear it. The public won't wear it. It's over. And quite frankly I don't think I want to be part of this anymore. It's like being a staffer in the Clinton White House, though at least there no-one knew about it before he was elected. It's so self-indulgent, so immature…."

I am now shaking with emotion.

He says kindly, which makes it worse, and quietly,

"I can't stop it Barrie; I just know it; it's Aidan I've always wanted. I know you hate these kids - what was it you called them yesterday, 'the Midwich cuckoos'? But they've turned my life around. I need you more than ever. I know I've made the mountain steeper but I still want to do it, and I still want you at my side. I cannot do it without you. And then we'll see what sort of party and what sort of country we have."

I walk out the door without saying a word. But I don't clear my desk. I go outside and walk along the Embankment under a slight drizzle, with the sky, the South Bank, the boats, the river and the bridges all bathed in a pale greyish brown light; remarkably quiet as if what was going on in my head crowded out all other noise.

After an hour, half of it spent sitting on a wet bench, with for company only a perplexed gull standing on the wall, looking at me balefully from time to time, I went back into the office, sat down with my hair still dripping, felt the sympathetic, warm but silent gaze of Marjorie, took off my jacket to dry, and started work on some more position papers for the campaign.

Perhaps Raphael does deserve some happiness, even if he's looking for it in the wrong places. Perhaps I'm just jealous. But we're embarking on something which could come crashing down in just a few weeks, and he just seems so reckless.

NED

I help Aide pack his stuff. He invites me to 'his' new flat for a few beers. I put on some CDs (all crap as you'd expect) then just as I've switched to a hard rock station in He walks, and one look tells me that I've outstayed a welcome which hadn't been proffered in the first place. I stand up, nearly fall over the coffee table, back out of the room, and say, "Well I'd better leave you two to get on with it," and then of course regret putting it that way.

I guess I won't see much of Aide until we get to France. Having him here has not always been LOL but I guess I'll miss him. At least I'll be staying in their cottage, not at some pricey hotel nearby.

******** END OF PART ONE ********

PART TWO - UNDER THE RADAR

NED

Dear Mart,

You're getting this by snail-mail. Too long, too much to tell by email, way too Hush! Hush!

Of course I wanted to get down there as soon as possible but my soppy agent had had some brainwave about spending four days non-stop at some regional youth club convention which was supposed to get me some good local publicity, it being a quiet news month; and I of course hadn't let on to her about my dirty weekend in France. Mind you, with nearly all my voters on the Costas or in Tunisia I had my doubts anyway about this convention being a game changer. So in the end it was a Ryanair weekend cheapie from Luton to La Rochelle, arriving Friday afternoon and leaving Sunday lunchtime.

I was to be the privileged one, sleeping in one of the spare rooms at the cottage. Just me, the two lovers and dreary old Helen Mitchison. "He felt he had to let her stay; and it was his revenge for me asking you before I got his permission. Still, you two can take it in turns doing the washing up," was Aidan's explanation.

Anyway, checking in further up the queue, and settling up for extra luggage (for a mere two days!) were my favourite slags, Maudie and Hattie, Labour's answer to Joan Rivers and Jennifer Saunders. I sneaked up behind them, gave their bums a little pinch, and got a mouthful of cheek straight back. All deadpan, some aspersions about my physique, had I had to pay for two seats? I got in my riposte about Ryanair now offering 'two slappers for the price of one' before we started to board. I of course get stuck in the back in between a young mum and dad because the dad refused my offer to let them sit together so he and his gizmo wouldn't be disturbed. They'd not read the handbooks about bringing up babies, force fed the child a lot of orange goop which he promptly brought up all over me, twice. Profuse apologies from little wife, quite pretty, and I started to forgive her a bit when she started sponging me clean almost down to my knees. Husband by this time dead to the world.

When we arrived, I get voted i/c luggage of 'the last two working-class women in the Labour Party', chuck it all on top of a trolley, Maudie at least having remembered to bring some euros. We walked through the small hall of the airport into pale sunshine, not yet hot, but promising. And there was Aide in altercation with a local security guard, pretending not to speak French, the other just wanting him to use the paying car park like everyone else and not being impressed with the 'Je suis un member of the House of Commons' line.

He (or Raphael) had hired a mini moke and looked in great shape, plain white t-shirt, dark navy Bermudas and grey deck shoes, he'd had his hair trimmed, the stubble shaped and was revealing enough body hair on chest, arms and legs to turn on Harriet, who kept pawing at any available limb when he started to drive. He was just like some star on a film set for the latest new holiday romance filler. I'm afraid all three passengers rather let the side down, though not for want of slap and baubles on Hat's part: my own below the knee flared tangerine shorts, green sandals (!) and the old Hawaiian shirt deserved at least A for effort. I had all the baggage on my knees so couldn't actually see much, which given the way Aidan drives down French D-roads was probably just as well. I noticed even the girls went quiet when we started cornering on two wheels.

When we finally arrived at the Hotel de la Baie at St Palais-sur-Mer, which of course didn't run to porters, I had to lug all the girls' luggage up very narrow stairs to their second-floor room, which admittedly really did have the 'stunning sea views', as advertised. When we came down again, Aidan was deep in (French) conversation with Madame about the evening's catering arrangements. She was sending over two waiters at the end of the afternoon to set up the buffet. We'd all be eating at her place the next night.

Madame is small, impeccably turned out in any weather, I'd say: her hair tied back in an old-fashioned bun, anywhere from 60 to 70, with a strong upper-class French voice, and the eyes of a murderess which were currently not even attempting to conceal her distaste for some friends of 'monsieur le ministre'. Of course Aidan was a different matter, it was already, 'Cher Aidan this', 'Cher Aidan that', and 'Chère Marie-France'. All over him like a rash, and him lapping it up. Despite her airs, Aidan delighted to relay tales of what a great chiseller she had been after she'd set up the hotel, following the early death of her husband in mysterious circumstances, "so mean she soaks the old used soap bars in hot water and squeezes them into shape to pass off as new".

"Now, Hattie, why don't you and Maudie waddle down to the beach? Then I'll expect you can explain to the barman how to serve your port and lemons and you can come along to our cottage at 6-ish. It's the fourth one, at the end, along the path up there."

Of course the 'our' cottage was the give-away.

Maudie asked, "Been having a good time, dearie?"

"Slaving night and day to give you two a weekend to remember", he replied without any pause, "and now I have my little helper everything will work like clockwork, I'm sure. Come on, Lurch, let's get going."

"Well, that's let the cat out of the bag" I said to Aide as we got back to the vehicle.

"Oh, they'll know soon enough, he's going to reveal all tonight."

"Wow, a double coming out," was all I could think to say.

We drove round the back lane for about three minutes and Aidan parked on the gravel outside the last house; we just walked through the door, completely unlocked. ("No need, Madame keeps her binoculars trained on the whole bay, woe betide any intruder.")

The kitchen was on the right side of a large living room, with an ill-assorted mixture of chairs, sofas and armchairs which diminished its size. Then we walked out into the garden, with a perfect view of an old-fashioned rocky bay, the coastal path running along the end of the cottage garden behind a foot-high wooden fence, on the other side of the path a small patch of rough turf and then a few rickety wooden steps making a channel through the rocks on to the beach of pale fine sand, interspersed with rocks haphazardly strewn every few yards, each cluster with its own ration of tiny pools, some with shrimps, baby crabs and a great profusion of limpets - some metaphor in there about the Labour Party, I think.

In the late afternoon sun, little families eking out the day, the sand-filled sandwiches all now consumed, their thermos beverages nearly all drunk, dads building sandcastles more absorbed in the task than the kids, over-compensating for the past eleven months of parental neglect, and the only sound that of the rare infantile shriek from one of those braving the water. This was exactly how it was, Mart, when you and I were dragged off to Hastings to stay at Auntie Beth's twenty years ago, only the beach here is nicer.

"I suppose you're not up for a quick swim?" says newly sporty Aidan.

"No", say I, "but I could murder a beer." He fetched a couple of beers (French pisswater stuff) from the fridge and we flopped down on two of the striped deckchairs at the path end of the garden. When I allowed my body to subside onto the canvas, I heard a faint ripping sound, so henceforth I stayed motionless apart from my right arm passing bottle to lips every few minutes.

"So how's married life?" I ventured.

"Well, I'm gradually getting him trained. When he was here with my Portuguese predecessor it was a bit of a physical marathon all day. I'm getting him to chill out, stop fretting, nagging me about the housework, or getting up at the crack of dawn; been a bit of an uphill struggle. To tell the truth it's almost a relief when he disappears with the couple next door for his 18 holes. That's where he is now, with Bill."

"So he's actually here?" I asked, a bit relieved.

"Yup, and we've get Bob Hatchway," (from the ATGM, the third-largest union), "and Paul Howkins," (trade union official now turned MP), "so the horny handed are on board. And then there's Louise Marchant, the only true New Labour throwback, but Angus and Rashida have taken her up…"

"So, what, 10 of us?" I ask.

"Well, plus staff, Fido of course," (he really hates Barrie) "and Nigel the quietest spokesman of all time… and then there's a bit of glam, Elaine Chayter."

"What, the bird who reads the news?"

"Evidently she had always been hitting on him at Oxford, he even hints they may have been an item, although I doubt she ever got to first base."

"God, bit confusing, you and your tribe. So… how are things, you know?" (How was that for brave?)

"If by that you mean 'how's the sex?' you disgusting fat perv, you'll have to pay fifty quid for a peep through the keyhole like everyone else." (I pretend to gag, but then why am I so interested?) "But as you ask, I've had to work quite hard to extend his repertoire but we're getting there. I think he's always been a bit 'wham, bang, thank you, mam' in this department. 'Mr Five Minutes, including the shower,' as they used to say about some French politician. But Ned, actually it's just we're so compatible. I like his company. We laugh a lot. When the passion fades, we'll always be best friends".

I found this planned obsolescence a bit disconcerting.

BARRIE

It's been great having two quiet days with Digby in the gite, just an hour from St Palais. Our room's a bit primitive, and Digby's paranoid about mosquitoes, but the food's great - we've taken the breakfast and dinner formula. He doesn't mind me being away for a couple of days. He'll read a lot and go for walks. And from my stories of the 'Gang of Four' the last thing he wanted to do was be shacked up with some of them in their hotel.

Of course he thinks we're all mad. "The Labour Party doesn't dump its Prime Ministers like that" was his refrain until I reminded him of very recent history. "Yeah but not for a queer who's having it off with another MP, half his age, while there's still all the past pick-ups hanging around". He's slightly overcoloured my reports and I do wonder if he really likes Raphael. Of course his main concern is about what all this will do to me, not so much losing my job because he has a naïve belief that I can walk into something else overnight, but how I'll react if Raphael gets smashed.

Of course, I'll be upset for him. He won't like leaving politics but he can always pick up directorships, he can write and he's probably the best conference speaker on the circuit. But what really concerns me is how he'll bear up when Aidan Richards dumps him, which he will, within weeks of the car crash we are now all intent on planning. I still hate Aidan, almost irrationally. It's not simple jealousy, at least I think not. It's just the arrogance, the cruelty, the overconfidence, the intellectual and sexual swagger. I looked him up on Facebook (not a 'Facebook friend' obviously, so only the front page) and there's this photo of him, dominating the page, striking a pose with a lascivious smirk, sprawling on a sofa, shirtless.

This is not the photograph of a politician or a party leader's spouse, it's vulgar soft porn. He's only just posted it, I guess, so I haven't seen anything in the press but when they do, it'll be everywhere, deliberately designed to coincide with Raphael's announcement, which just goes to prove what a narcissistic, self-obsessed gigolo he is, intent on playing Bosie to Raphael's Oscar. It will be Raphael who risks losing everything and ends up being miserable and alone. I want to speak to him to warn him but nowadays I can never get him on his own.

It's odd because in fact the last two weeks Aidan and I have been working together on the text of a programme for Raphael, and shielding it from the destructive maraudings of Rupert Dennison and, above all, from Angus Buchanan, who keeps dismissing it all as "reheated revisionist New Labour crap, insipid, vacuous and unreadable" but who rarely makes constructive comments because he's still sulking that Raphael didn't ask him to write it; a wise precaution otherwise we'd have the nationalisation of everything that moves and - for our family policy - the massacre of the First Born.

So Aidan and I sometimes find ourselves on the same side, but we communicate nearly always by email. Whenever I phone him, which I do as seldom as possible, he sounds distant, irritated verging on hostile.

All in all I'm pitching up at St Palais with a heavy heart, hoping others have already arrived because I really couldn't take spending quality time with the happy couple.

HELEN

I came by train from Bordeaux to Saintes, Ted having dropped me off ridiculously early, amid goodbye pecks saying how worried he was about all the grief I was letting myself into. At the station I had bumped into Louise Marchant[23]. Our seats were far apart but we arranged to share a taxi at the other end.

Louise Marchant had been a rising star of the New Labour firmament. A pretty, neat woman, with warm friendly eyes, always impeccably dressed. She had on a pale salmon cotton dress, and flip-flops, sufficient for Arcachon, where she and her husband had been staying and currently enjoying a real heatwave, less obviously so for the breezier Charentes Maritime. Her career had juddered to a halt when she had been unceremoniously and unfairly sacked, taking the bullet for yet another cock-up at the Borders' Agency. She had become the latest Home Office human sacrifice; it never seemed to occur to the No 10 machine that there might be an alternative to the scenario of some of the press only having to call for someone's head three days running for their wish to be granted. Still, these collaterally damaged ex-ministers could turn out to be useful recruiting targets for the cause.

The reservations we had about Louise were political not personal. She was so New Labour it hurt. Before she had become a minister she had even penned a piece calling for compulsory health insurance to replace state funding of the NHS. But her dislike for the new PM, the blatant misogyny of his team, the grisly prospects for the party, brought her closer to the Sinclair circle. And she had struck up a girlie friendship with Rashida Hussein, despite their rather different politics, and was almost a fixture at the Ealing flat Rashida shared with Angus Buchanan, who seemed prepared to turn a blind eye to her revisionist tendencies. And Rashida was just looking for allies to further her own cause: she needed some women collaborators as she was going to be a hard sell with all that Muslim baggage.

I managed to shift my seat to sit with Louise for the last 15 minutes of the journey. She told me she had been nervous about the weekend and had sought cast-iron guarantees about the confidentiality of the operation. She admired Raphael and had a very high opinion of Angus, although some of his views she thought were "pretty extreme". For Rupert she had developed a great fondness, "He's so…hot. He just teases me all the time," she giggled in a fluffy little way which was

---

[23] MP for West Hampstead, 199-

slightly irritating. Aidan Richards on the other hand she loathed. "He hasn't a good word for anybody. He's so self-obsessed, so good at putting people down...I don't understand how Rashida and Angus put up with him. Must be some university thing, you know, all that 'ferocity of friendship' ".

As we took our small cases off the racks, she whispered "Of course this isn't going to work. But it might embolden Derek to have a crack at it." So that much was clear, she was supporting Raphael as a stalking horse, hoping like many others that Derek Jamieson, the young, rather smug but smart Foreign Secretary would step in and take the prize once the PM was wounded. Derek had solid government experience, was very bright, but so distant with colleagues that he almost warded off any possible faction forming which might support him. He always seemed to hesitate when occasions presented themselves, probably concluding quite perceptively that the next general election would be the one to sit out. He was certainly young enough to do so.

So it was clear where Louise's loyalties lay but I decided not to pass this on. We had little enough support among the MPs for us to start making some of even our tepid supporters walk the plank.

Talking of the little devil, ahead of us in the taxi queue was none other than Rupert Dennison, looking his usual dapper self. I would have let him take his taxi alone but Louise hollered and he beckoned us to jump the now long line. And I have to say he kept us amused for the full forty minutes' journey, bubbling with his joyous energy, making sarcastic but acidulously witty remarks about colleagues, distant acquaintances or even his supposedly close friends, quite indiscriminately. He was genuinely funny about his very old-fashioned hotel at the front in Biarritz, imitating doddery waiters spilling the drinks, creaking floorboards, the lift which created a frisson of excitement as it stopped and restarted between floors, the loud and unpredictable plumbing, and the lottery of the hot water taps. And after all this, it turned out to be Hotel Imperatrice Eugenie, only the swankiest hotel in South-West France, where he was staying "with friends". These Sinclairites had private lives which made the Bloomsbury Set seem straight out of the pages of *Cranford*.

They dropped me off at the cottage and headed over to the hotel, more grist for Rupert's anecdotes in all likelihood. I arrived a little sweaty and flustered to find that Maudie, Hattie, Ned Warren and Aidan Richards had beaten me to it. Ned and Aidan were also staying with us at the cottage, not my ideal choice for fellow country house weekend guests and a bit of a surprise. It was Aidan who opened the door and just said briskly, "Ah, Helen, your bedroom is second on the left up the stairs. Glad you've made it. We'll need someone to do the dishes." Before I could think of a riposte to put him in his place he hightailed it back to the garden for doubtless more congenial company. It sounded to me as if Hattie, Maudie and Ned were not on their first drinks.

Raphael had been taking a shower upstairs and emerged from his room wearing only that old pale blue dressing-gown I remember so well from Putney. He gave me a warm hug and seemed really pleased to see me. "This is a big day for me. I really wanted you here." I could not help looking past him through his open bedroom door. The unmade bed had pretty obviously been slept in by two. I was filled with a kind of morbid terror.

NED

I was doing my life and soul bit. Social, spiritual and alcohol lubrification. Aidan didn't help one little bit, and his mood darkened when Helen arrived, flustered and anxious. He kept going back indoors to text and read updates from his laptop.

At last Paul Howkins and Bob Hatchway arrived from their cheap hotel in Saintes. Their taxi driver had pretended to get lost five times. "Fucking French" was Bob's pithy summary of their adventure. Of the two, Paul was in some ways the bigger catch - secretary of the trade union group of MPs. Not unlike some others in that neck of the woods, he looks like he's a pretty heavy boozer; he's certainly a chain smoker. So I pushed him out in the garden, with a cheery 'smoker's corner' since the house is smoke-free (the only social behaviour 'reform' ever to be associated with Aidan), and gave him a beer. It was great to have this rough, acne-covered Geordie with the tell-tale reddened eyes and smoky voice, a great antidote to all those New Labour smoothies. He's not hard left, but got pissed off with the New Labour crowd and is willing to give Raphael a go, and take the stick for it.

Bob Hatchway, bearded, beer-gutted but with a soft panda smile, is also taking risks just being here: number two in his union, and on the National Exec., his union has always been solid for the PM.

Having done my 'hostess with the mostest' bit, keeping the boys in beer and Hat and Maudie with stronger stuff, I opened the door to let in Bill Sampson and his son. Bill was on cracking form about the golf game and describing Rafa, kept using terms like 'Mulligans', 'St Antonio's' and 'winter rules' which just went over our heads, unlike the shots of our esteemed future leader, which barely took flight. The boy, Bo, who must be about 25, stood in the background, looking as if he'd rather be somewhere else. Quite tall, with a mop of curly brown hair which looks as if it gets a basin cut every six months, a bit plump (yes, Mart, I've lost 4 lbs this summer so I can talk), tongue-tied, with a gormless almost semi-permanent half-grin on his face. Aide, who'd met him a couple of times earlier in the week, had said typically "No sign of human life on that particular planet" but as I get talking to him, I suddenly realise he's not as daft as he looks. He certainly knows the pop business (he's a road manager for several groups) and I could just detect a bit of hero-worship for Rafa, for whom he'd been caddying most afternoons and who is always great at treating the socially ill at ease with graceful attention. Great political and social skills we suave top drawer politicians deploy!

Then in come Rupe and Louise Marchant. Rupe almost literally exploded from the path into the garden like a swirling dervish, immediately laughing, talking his head off, a bit minimum service for Bob and Paul, and skirting round Bo, who inevitably had managed to place himself bang in the middle of the garden as the small groups formed at its periphery. Hat and Maudie got a bit of goosing, then Aide was pushed into a corner for a quick gossip. When he sees me it's the usual, "Ned, darling, if I'd known it was fancy dress, I'd have brought my harmonica." But he does lift the mood.

Nigel Bolton arrived, leaving the lovely French wife at her folks' Medoc Chateau, glad to get away from his heavy duty in-laws, I'd think. Barrie on the other hand slipped in looking tense and nervous, and immediately latched on to Bob and Paul in the quiet corner. Compared with Rupe's grand entrance, Angus and Rashida seemed quite meek. The only serious upstaging was by La Chayter, who arrived in a limo complete with chauffeur only wanting a peaked cap: the car can only barely have squeaked through the D roads. She's so glam, we were all almost speechless, except of course for Rupe, who gave her a little peck and escorted her round the clusters to make the introductions. Rafa and Aide, who had joined him upstairs for what seemed like a long time, finally descended, doing the greetings, giving Elaine a long hug, as she whispered quite distinctly, "Lovely snug place darling but who are all these dreadful little people?"

Rafa said, "I think we are 'au complet' as they say in these parts."

BARRIE

When Raphael finally comes downstairs, preceded just a little too obviously by an almost triumphantly smirking Aidan Richards, I thought how wonderful the boss looks, tanned but not sunburned, wearing a pair of pale cream slacks, with a dark blue shirt over the trousers, and dark blue deck shoes. But because I know him best, and because I know what he has to say, I can feel the tension and hear it in his voice.

But the words are warm and welcoming, making sure everyone had their drinks, "Everyone, fill your glasses up, then come inside, and after we've had a bit of a talk about things, we can attack Madame's buffet, which we can polish off outside if it's not too chilly."

Everyone was seated except me (typically, obliged to loll on the floor), Aidan who sat on the bottom stairs, and Bo who was propped half-hidden behind the sofa, which had to bear the weight of Hat and Bob, with an uncomfortable-looking pert Louise squeezed on the end. Oh, and Raphael himself, who roamed the room throughout the proceedings. He asked Bill to start us off.

He gave us the full doom and gloom works, the polls, the feedback from the constituencies, morale at rock bottom, the collapse in membership, the winding up of dozens of branches and the near-bankruptcy of the party.

"If things don't change, we'll come third, get between 22 and 23% of the popular vote and hold on to just under 200 seats, so a net loss of 150. I say to those of you who are our elected masters, any of you with majorities of less than ten thousand have a good look at the vacancy notices in your corner shop next time you're passing. And to our younger comrades, he stared at Rupert and Ned in particular, if you survive the cull, which is by no means certain, you can look forward to between 10 and 15 years in opposition, if the party survives at all, which from where I stand is far from guaranteed. And how have we got here? The wars blew away the trust, the great rivalry of the two Titans did us massive harm, the policies were wrong and we have the most unpopular Prime Minister since polling began. Easy."

Suddenly even Hattie looked completely sober.

HELEN

I had never seen Raphael so nervous. He had to clear his throat several times and kept taking gulps of water which Bo, Bill Sampson's son, would then fill up as if on cue.

Instead of the usual perfectly rounded sentences flowing seamlessly one into the other, it was a series of almost disjointed phrases, his voice with a kind of strangulated quality, as if he were about to confess a terrible crime; and devoid of the kind of authoritative tone he usually employed when he was urging any particular course of action.

"If you want to. I'll go for it. Someone's got to. You heard what Bill said. And perhaps it'd flush out someone from the cabinet to throw his hat in the ring. But it's not about me or someone else. The policies are simply wrong. We need a programme. We must talk about that too. The obstacles are huge. And I'm so much not the ideal candidate. I've got no union base. And in the parliamentary party we'll have the whips gunning for us; and the payroll vote won't back us. A lot of people think I've moved on anyway. And I have in a way. I'm not certain I want the job even if I could get it. I've found other interests, doing things I want, with the people I want, I care about.

"And then here's the thing. I've begun a relationship. And it's with a man. And he's younger than me. Quite a bit. And he's a colleague. Aidan, here," (He walked over to the stairs where Aidan Richards, totally expressionless, sat on the bottom rungs as Raphael placed his hand almost paternally on his shoulder. Aidan put his hand up to touch his), "Aidan and I are together. He's changed my life. I love him more than anyone or anything in the world."

NED

There was this dreadful silence. It was probably just thirty seconds but it seemed to drag on into infinity. Hat was the first to break the ice, "Waste of two fit blokes if you ask me; I dunno why I bothered to get dressed up," which provoked a kind of collective sigh of relief.

Angus weighed in with, "It doesn't make things easier but attitudes are changing", as if it was prepared - which it must have been. Bill said, "You'll have to be open about it from the start, which you won't like because you're a private person. But I don't see how anyone in the party could say anything. It will give you a kind of immunity; if any of our people attack you they get labelled homophobic. The wider public and the tabloids, well, that's a totally different kettle of fish."

Rupe, upbeat as always, "It's precisely what you need. It's an attention grabber. The LGBT brigade will love it and they've got great organisation. Students, the kids will go for it big." A little over the top, I thought.

Rashida, also put up to it, I think, said quietly, "We'll have to be careful how we present this to my community. But if we handle this sensitively, they'll go along with it. But you have to have effective surrogates for the campaign, and start working out the messages we'll need to deal with the fall-out." Bob and Paul looked a bit blank, but said nothing.

Finally Angus concludes with an almost harsh, "Look, let's settle this now. Who's in?"

There was a smattering of yesses and "I'm ins", and then a little cheer. Rafa looking relieved and finding his normal voice back, said simply, "Thanks. Now I could do with a drink, and then let's eat. Tomorrow we discuss the campaign. Angus and Bill to lead off. And in the afternoon, it's the policy wonks who have their go - we'll even have a bit of paper."

HELEN

I had seen it coming but was as horrified as anyone there, probably more so. My problem was not having a gay candidate but the choice of partner. Aidan Richards was in my view about the most unsuitable possible: cynical, self-regarding, manipulative, with what would almost certainly be a string of past lovers ready to crawl out of the woodwork. He was loathed by nearly every Labour MP for his narcissistic self-promotion. He was cruel: I had seen the way he treated poor lovesick Barrie - calling him Fido quite openly. He seemed to me to be quite incapable of love. Raphael had always been hopeless with his personal relationships but this was a disaster.

But the die was cast. I joined in the largely artificial celebrations, knowing how we all felt manipulated by the careful choreography after the announcement, which closed down any serious discussion. So we refilled our glasses and piled up our plates with some wonderful seafood prepared by the local hotel. The evening was mild, the sun was fading beneath a very low level of cloud just above the horizon, and there was already the outline of a full moon which soon would glisten on the calm sea and provide a welcome distraction as we filed out into the garden, sitting on deckchairs or the low wall separating us from the neighbouring garden.

I sat on the wall with Paul Howkins[24], who was chain-smoking and whose plate was almost empty. We were joined by Bob Hatchway[25], Hattie and Maudie, "the other grown-ups", as Paul called them. Every ten minutes Maudie, who loomed over us, would scrounge a cigarette from Paul. Bob sat on the grass. Hattie did her beached whale impression lying on the wall. At the end of the garden there were whoops of laughter from Rupert and Aidan at Ned's clumsy juggling of plate, cutlery and drink, followed by a string of doubtless sarcastic witticisms from Rupert. Rashida, a couple of feet back, quietly observed the group of which she was meant to be part.

Bill and Angus were in earnest conversation about the campaign. When Barrie joined them he inevitably started taking notes. Raphael had a few words with Elaine, still in deep shock I guessed at the announcement. He introduced her to Nigel Bolton[26] and they climbed down the wooden steps to the beach, precariously holding drinks and plates, to talk about

---

[24] MP for Tyneside, East, 199-
[25] Deputy General Secretary, ATGM
[26] Spokesperson for Raphael Sinclair since 200-

'comms' and 'messaging'. This left Raphael surprisingly in fairly deep conversation with Bill's son, Bo, but he had always had some kind of empathy for the party wall-flower, one of his endearing characteristics. Or was it yet another way of creating the indelible impression and recruiting another follower 'until the ends of the earth'?

As we started picking up plates with just the debris of the prawns and crab claws, Elaine came over and speaking just to me said, "Well, quite a turn up. Why couldn't Raphael have chosen someone just a little less sexy? Some forty-year-old telly tubby who did the washing up. The trouble is when people see them together everybody will be imagining unmentionable thoughts, and some won't feel comfortable about it. But, hats off, he certainly had both of us fooled."

BARRIE

Well it's nearly all crashed before we've even got off the ground. I guess only Ned and Rupert knew; maybe Angus and Rashida. Bill, who must have known he was gay, looked as if he'd had the stuffing knocked out of him when it became clear who was the object of 'the candidate's' affections. Raphael is nearly fifty, good-looking and single so it's not rocket science to guess that he might, just, swing the other way. But announcing it like this, and with the lover there lolling on the staircase like an insolent brat, almost daring people to say something – that was what was so intolerable! The one I really felt sorry for was Helen, who's chased him for years, and then accepts to be his submissive 'beard' even after she finds out he's gay. Now she's got to share the cottage for two days with the leader, the lover from hell and the Court Jester. Only someone as emotionally stunted as Raphael could land everyone, including his best friends, in this situation. But, more and more I think, for Raphael friends are simply those most easily sacrificed.

But you've got to hand it to the political class. Lightning strikes, the corpses are everywhere but within minutes conversation resumes, situations are managed, plans made and new stratagems devised. By midnight when last orders are called (or shouted, by Angus, of course) little breakout sessions have been formed, brimming with campaign plans, every amateur communications strategist bursting to share his or her expert insights, programme pointers, the ideas flowing as copiously as Madame's Muscadet.

When those of us staying at the hotel finally wound our way a little unsteadily along the path, lit by a full moon, a kind of silly, almost hysterical, merriment has taken over. Then there's a shriek, and we catch up with the advance party of our group, Angus and Louise, who point at the ground, and there in petrified motionlessness sat the largest toad anyone of us has ever seen. We watch it for a good two minutes before it hops in almost stately fashion to the turf on the beach side of the path. "Well the PM made it after all," is Rupert's quip. We'd all had enough to drink to find this hysterically funny.

Next morning Madame gives us a rollicking about the commotion we'd caused as we entered the hotel, at well past midnight.

Anyway, I've been summoned for eight in the morning for a 'working breakfast' by Angus who's intent on dragging Bill and his boy early from their campsite. Raphael's chat to Bo this evening outlasted the normal call of duty, trying to make the socially timid a little less out of things. It turns out that Bo is not merely keen to help in the campaign but has huge social networks which he felt can be tapped for drumming up help and raising some cash. He's the nearest in our group to a techie and he's volunteered to do the website, the social media and the twitter account as well as launching the new internet presence of the candidate. So Bo has been passed on to Angus and it's a bright, early start tomorrow, so I'd better turn in. Missing Digby, dog tired, with a faint headache already (so no idea what I'll feel like in the morning) and generally pretty melancholic.

NED

When the others finally left, Rafa was in expansive mood. He asked me to put on some of his crappy CDs on their fairly antique player; so it was - would you believe it, Mart? – Helen, me and Rafa dancing to 'Johnny and Mary', and Martha and the Vandellas, and singing along. Even Aide seemed less condescending than usual. When Rafa put on 'The Sun Ain't Gonna Shine Anymore' with him and me singing in harmony with Scott Walker, I felt so happy I could have burst.

HELEN

I got up early the next day and found Raphael downstairs making a pot of tea. After we had drunk a cup, he suggested we walk down to the sea's edge for some fresh air to clear our heads. "When we're back we'll get the boys to make us some breakfast", a pretty unlikely scenario, I thought.

We walked down the garden and crossed the path onto some rather unsafe wooden steps down to the beach. The tide was far out, almost out of sight in the early morning mist; for company we had just two old men pouring salt down small holes in the damp sand, trying to fool the razor fish that the tide had come in early. Nearer the rocks a couple of dogwalkers were out early.

I didn't want to spoil his moment with a row, so I just said softly, "So I guess it's serious this time?"

"Yes. I have to keep pinching myself it's for real. I can't help the timing; I've fallen hopelessly in love."

"Well", I continued with a little more emphasis, "well I hope he's worthy of you."

He stopped, and turned to me, and put his hands on my shoulders, "There are two Aidans, Helen. There's the abrasive one, full of front. And then there's the insecure kid who puts on an act but who craves affection, which he gets from me in spades. And he's also a bit my project."

"Well", I forced myself, "I wish you both every happiness. I really do."

"Thanks Helen," he gave me a warm bear hug, "Best mate".

Half-way back to the cottage we could just make out sitting on Madame's terrace an intense-looking quartet, finishing their copy: Angus was easily recognisable, the fair hair, straight-backed in his chair, the leader in any circle; Bo Sampson holding up a notepad (I had been cross the night before when Rupert Dennison had made one of his cheap childish remarks while Bo and Raphael had been chatting, "Look it speaks"); Bill, and Barrie taking notes and talking simultaneously.

NED

Next morning at what must have been 5 a.m. at the latest, I suddenly needed to sneeze. And there was a weight on my bed. It was Aidan, sitting in the briefest of briefs and torturing me with a feather duster.

"Wake up, sunshine. Time for you to get started in the kitchen. The boss and droopy drawers have gone for an early morning constitutional so you can use the bathroom, provided you leave it in the state you'd wish to find it … on second thoughts, forget that."

I was finding this new bootcamp approach to weekend living a bit hard to take. Anyway I scratch myself and stagger down the corridor to the bathroom for a pee. Disaster: as I come out I find Helen and Rafa have returned from their stroll on the beach and I'm starkers. I cover myself with my hands and bolt back into my room. Helen looks at me witheringly, "Oh, for Christ's sake!" then she glanced through the bedroom door to see Aidan stretched out on my bed with a lascivious look on his face. She turns round to Rafa and says, "Honestly, Raphael, if you can't keep these two kids in order, how can you expect to run a government?" Rafa seemed to be trying to conceal his amusement and started issuing orders to us like a demented house master.

BARRIE

Today, Saturday, was meant to be the main day, and so it has been. It didn't start very well. I had just served myself at the hotel buffet when Angus hauls me outside with, "Oh there you are. Come and join us. We're doing the campaign plan on the terrace." He corralled Bill and his boy to a table overlooking the beach, from where you could clearly see Raphael's cottage. It was pretty cold in the early morning mist and I'd left my jumper upstairs, intending to take it when we left to head over to the cottage. I was only really there as a glorified notetaker. Angus seems to think the idea that I might have something of interest to say about the organisation of the campaign quite outlandish.

But it's Bo who was the discovery. He rattled off ideas about the campaign office, volunteers, 'flash mobs' to turn up wherever Raphael appears, just summoned by text messages. On the website he's already quite advanced with a concept, all very interactive, but controlled, supporters posting 'selfies' (a new one on me); building a massive email list; advertising on Google to get our posts upgraded, placing clips on YouTube and promoting them, details on how to design a smart Facebook profile and feed the unquenchable appetite of Twitter - all the paraphernalia of the early twenty-first century political campaign; a world almost as alien to me as it is to the candidate.

Angus announced that he'd commandeer Ned and Bo for Monday to bring in 'the best and the brightest' of the Socialist Youth and the Labour Students to form the nucleus of a campaign team.

"If a lot of Labour kids are in on it, they'll brag about it, and our cover will be gone," I ventured.

Angus answered, slightly annoyed at me for interrupting his flow, "Well without some volunteers getting trained up we'll have no resources to run the campaign."

Bill concluded, "Damned if we do, damned if we don't. We need to come smartly off the starting blocks, otherwise we won't have the numbers in time for Conference."

And then Bo added intelligently, "You only need to call in three or four at this stage, let them organise their own flash mob for the launch, and get people available for something vague for a few days afterwards. And kids if they're motivated can probably keep their mouths shut better than politicians," I was impressed.

"Yes", said Angus, "tell them it's for a new blitz on the BNP or the English Defence League."

An hour later we all assemble at the cottage, except for Bo who had been sent off to the village by Angus on some errand. They'd cleaned the place up, which must have been Helen's work, since neither Ned nor Aidan looked in any fit state to lift a finger; and as for Raphael, housework is something (like so much else!) others do for him, which, of course, doesn't stop him being quite fastidious in the demands of order and cleanliness he makes on them. That's why Raphael and Aidan will never last, but I digress.

Raphael started us all off by telling us that Angus should run the campaign. No-one dared demur. So, by now chairing the meeting and after some spine-chilling stuff about leaks and hacking and blagging (some newspapers get access to NHS records and the like), Angus handed over to Bill to remind us all of what the rule book says about dumping the leader of the party. "It's a bit primitive and is crying out for reform but people are scared to touch it lest the whole thing shatters. If we're in office you need 20% of the elected MPs (that's a total of 75 MPs, Maudie) to nominate a candidate for leader, knowing full well that their signatures will be public, which is a pretty daunting prospect if your constituency officers or trade unions are strong supporters of the PM. Ridiculously there's no time limit to gather signatures but the NEC would have to call time after a month. In other words, if Raphael announces in late August, or at the latest early September, he's got max. three to four weeks to pull in the signatures or he's dead in the water."

And this is only the first sploshing litres of cold water on any enthusiasm in the room. Louise piped up with the obvious question, "And if we get the names, what next?"

The Authority replied, "It's the NEC which sets the timetable and the rules of engagement - the debates, for example. But the shortest absolutely incompressible time to distribute ballot papers, CVs, statements, the separate trade union balloting, with a real push would be two months."

"But that takes us into December. It'll tear the party apart." Angus frowned at this flicker of insubordination from Louise, his protégée, but it was Rupert who interrupted with, "….which is why we'd be daft to try it unless we weren't convinced that without it, we're toast."

Far from being put off, Louise continued, with a question which was perhaps unwise given the suspicions about her political allegiance, "Bill, have you allowed time for other declarations? If we get the signatures, wouldn't we have to allow some weeks for others to join the race?"

Bill squashed this quite neatly, "It could be a short period because all this will be happening in the build-up to party conference, which every MP is supposed to attend - well, that's the theory - so they'd all be on tap to sign anybody's papers. And they'd only need 37 because once a contest is going to happen, the threshold drops. Bit unfair on the trailblazer but that's our daft rules for you."

At this point Bo arrived bearing 10 medium-sized magnetic blackboards. As he placed them in different corners of the room, Angus explained to an astonished assembly.

"Comrades, pretentious geeks from the communication world call this game 'stakeholder mapping'. Bo's going to prepare 250 little flags, each with the name of one of our backbench colleagues. Then we put the little magnets on one of the 10 boards. Over there's board 1, 'certain to sign' which I hope means all of us here; then there's 'quite likely to sign', then 'possibly likely to sign'; down to board 5, 'don't knows' right down to board 10 - 'can't sign my name' or 'wouldn't sign for Raphael Sinclair even after 24 hours of water torture'. Bo and Barrie will write up the names, then talk to each of you about those you know personally in the PLP. By the end of play we should get a picture of our target signers."

Quite clever really. There was even some humour in his words but none in the way he speaks them. Of course everybody assumed this was Angus' idea, but the suggestion had come from Bo over breakfast.

While all this business carries on, Helen asked, "Raphael have you given thought to how you declare?"

"Not certain. I'll need to talk to the party. We'll probably do the launch there in Mayberry."

Bo then added almost robotically while multitasking - writing names on the flags on the kitchen table, "Gotta make it a big event, kids, flags, music - good pics."

Rupert warmed to the theme, "He's right. Could you and Angus bus in some kids for the night?"

"Yeah," said Angus, "I've already texted three of our youth section people I can rely on. We'll see them on Monday, and Ned, you're coming." This seemed to wake up Ned, who was as usual sprawled out on the floor, as if dozing after a hard night.

Rupert continued, "It's gotta be a rock star moment, not like when those Tory head bangers challenged John Major, with six borderline nutters sitting round a table."

Nigel spoke for the first time, tentatively. He's always conscious of the fact that people don't really think he's one of us - just the high-flying young diplomat with the rich French wife, having a dilettante career break with his erstwhile boss.

"Don't forget, Raphael, you're on Desert Island Discs the last Sunday in August."

Both Aidan and Angus looked witheringly at Nigel, as if he'd missed the point of the conversation with some frivolous aside. But Rupert's the sharpest of the lot, "Great launch pad. The double coming out. Soft landing as you leave the safety of the closet… ."

"You can't declare on the radio, you've got to do it to a party audience," thus spoke the traditionalist Paul, horrified at the breach of etiquette now being canvassed. He gets some support from Hattie, Maudie and Bob, until finally Raphael cut through everything using the voice which brooks no dissent, or even further discussion.

"Here's how we do it. On the Saturday night I meet my local party officers. I'll have to say a word about my new personal circumstances, (nodding in the direction of Aidan, seated as always at the bottom of the stairs, looking bemused by all this, and occasionally texting, probably the odd - both senses of the word - (hopefully ex) lover) "and go into the 'can't carry on like this' routine, and get their endorsement, which we'll already have fixed in advance with the chair and secretary. Then Sunday morning, I do the show, come out between tracks and hint that I'm thinking of throwing my hat into the ring 'to save the party I love'. Then at the end of the afternoon, we do the launch at a big party event in Mayberry with as many kids as can be mustered for the occasion."

Elaine interjected, "I know the producer, she and I were at school together," (at least she didn't actually say Benenden) "I'll have a quiet word with her to make sure it's handled right. It's a huge scoop for them."

Now Angus started bullying Nigel and me into doing things for him. I couldn't handle the PLP lists with Hattie and take notes of the policy discussion at the same time. When I whinged politely he shouted at me. Raphael cut through all this with, "Angus, remember Barrie and Nigel are my old friends. Without them I wouldn't have got through this dark period. With me they aren't staff. They are friends as important to me and to us as anyone else in the room". All this was said quietly and to some effect.

As if on cue, Ned rouses himself, and said sleepily, arms folded over his tummy, "There's just one thing which worries me, Rafa, can you tell us what you've chosen for your eight discs because if it's anything like what you made us listen to last night, we're dead before we've begun?" The perfect comment to lighten the mood; once again, memo to self, don't ever underestimate Ned Warren.

NED

By lunch (if you can call it that, mostly rabbit food with a few shrimps, and a choice of three kinds of bottled water!) we'd made some progress; a bit of an idea how to proceed, and how to manage the campaign. The first 'most likely 35 to 40 MPs' had been assigned to Maudie, Hattie and Paul for initial but vague soundings-out - their patter being, "Just happened to be in the area, going up the line for a conference, how about you giving me a cuppa for the road?" Then talk about the situation, the "road to perdition" (a Rafa phrase) but absolutely no talk of Sinclair at this stage; then the public launch with some big rallies to set the place alight and to place small bombs under the backsides of a few more MPs; Bo – what a find, this kid! - will set up an office in some not very conspicuous part of South London. We start to bring in kids to man the phones, keep the website topical and lively and put bums on seats at rallies.

Then Helen and Louise will start putting out some feelers to their friends in cabinet, again no talk of Rafa, just sounding out, starting the chat. Rashida and I will do warm-ups at rallies (!); Aidan writes the final programme. Bill to feed us as much of the party's internal mailing list as he dares. Bob and Rashida to handle the money. The very hot Elaine (who gives me a withering look every time I wink at her which is often and her coolness just turns me on more and more) will front press conferences but Nigel will do the general media briefings and think up good lines for quotes. Barrie to carry on as minder and confidant for the leader, and Angus will do everything else. As he made clear, despite a well-deserved dressing down for being rude to staff. So we've got our marching orders.

HELEN

After lunch divisions started showing. The document on economic policy was torn to shreds by Angus Buchanan as 'insipid', 'puerile' and 'to the right of the Tories', which prompted Ned Warren to lighten the mood by saying, "apart from that, you liked it?"

In general Angus kept pushing for leftist and radical policies which some of us felt were too anti-business, inimical to the aspiring classes and abandoning completely the centre ground. When Hattie Reynolds and even Paul Howkins tried to point this out, we all got ferocious tongue-lashings. In the end, Angus just ground us down, so we ended up with full nationalisation of the banks, a wealth tax, a transactions tax, public control of 'strategic utilities', financing job creation schemes through a state bank which in the longer run would be the only one to be guaranteed by the state, and what he called 'an Emergency Economic Powers Act' which would enable the government to take control of any firm to save jobs.

On corporate responsibility, better deals for consumers and small-scale suppliers he was sounder; and we all liked the cap on bonuses, the return of the lower income tax band, as well as a cut in VAT to 15%.

Louise Marchant was the only one to hold out against the Buchanan blasts, she could match his economic arguments with her City background, and she came out bravely for pension and welfare reforms, the old New Labour themes, now pretty much out of fashion. In the end she had to fight off Maudie Hinton and Paul as well.

After a good hour of ferocious argument, we agreed a programme of 'progressive responsibility' for public expenditure with the pain spread out over five years, and then we had a separate row on tackling tax evasion, which Angus seemed to think was the magic wand.

I ventured, "It's like waste in public spending, we're all against tax evasion but we've never managed to do anything about it."

"Because you never even tried," he shot back. I thanked him for personalising this. "It's simple, HMRC[27] makes an estimate of tax owed by large corporations and the superrich and then levies it. They can appeal, but first they pay. And the nondoms[28] pay too. If you're British

---

[27] Her Majesty's Revenue and Customs
[28] UK residents agreed by HMRC to be regarded as non-domiciled, thus benefitting from significant tax advantages

and want to live in Belize, South America or Jersey, fine. But you pay. The Americans do it, for Christ's sake, and so should we." Game, set and match to Angus on that one!

When Louise asked about capital flight, he came back with all his rocklike confidence in himself, "then we close the markets and ban capital movements for as long as it takes." Her reply that this would breach EU law was dismissed with "by the time that lot get round to doing anything, we'll have moved on." This from someone who professed to being an avid pro-European!

All this was breath-taking stuff and clearly worried most of us, until Bob Hatchway said with his usual drawl, "After all, this is just to get us heard, to put us on the map, for the leadership. We're all old enough to know we're going to have to water this down if we ever look as if we're going to win." This piece of worldly cynicism helped smooth things. I thought Rashida was going to come back on this but she held her tongue, and Angus, as if she'd programmed him by remote control, did likewise.

By mid-afternoon we had agreed to abolish the House of Lords as a first step, with setting up a constitutional convention as a five-year exercise and a referendum at the end of it. The Church of England would go too, but the monarchy was spared, as abolishing it would wreck the chances of getting the Constitution through. Public party funding was in, voting reform kicked off into the longer grass of the Convention.

Rupert Dennison then blasted his way through the media debate, insisting on rules against media concentration and a tough new regulatory framework. Nigel Bolton tried to tackle him on a few details but Rupert was always unstoppable in these discussions: unlike Angus, he usually got his way with a winning smile and was all the more effective for that.

Hattie and some of the others insisted on some specific pledges on health, old-age care and housing. The graduate tax would replace tuition fees. On transport we accepted greater public control of the railway companies and networks. Louise managed to sneak in a new commitment on the 'greening' of all new house and commercial building projects. Rupert then made a pitch for prison reform and cutting back on the more security-obsessed policies pursued by successive Home Secretaries. But there was no appetite to change current immigration policies, with Maudie and Paul leading the charge against any liberalisation here.

It was nearly 7 p.m. by the time we finally got on to foreign policy and then there was a real explosion. Aidan's paper was in the main acceptable; the parts on the Middle East finely balanced. But in introducing it he made some pretty incendiary remarks about the wars. "We've really got to go big on this: the deceit about WMD[29], the legal issue, the quagmires, the regional disaster. It's your clearest red water between you and the government. Say you'll pull the troops out of both theatres[30] before Christmas, and you'll set the campaign alight. And a full public judicial inquiry into both wars. Set it up immediately, people on oath, all transmitted live. And we scrap Trident and go non-nuclear."

Paul and Bob both shared trade union concerns about scrapping Trident and Hattie had regiments on her patch serving at the fronts. She said, "Hang on, Aidan. I can't say to my widows, or my parents or my orphans, 'look your dad, or your son or your hubby's died for nothing, and we're just upping sticks like the Americans in Vietnam."

He shot back, "So you'd prefer us to be saying 'don't worry because there'll be more body bags coming back soon'? This is how we motivate the whole of the Left in the contest. Duck it, fudge it and we'll never get off the ground."

With impeccable timing, Madame then rang up to enquire when we would be coming over for dinner. But the row on how hard we went after those who supported the war dragged on a bit. There were other loose ends to be tied up. No-one had got exactly what they wanted.

It was only when at last he spoke that we all realised Raphael had said not a word all afternoon. This was classic Sinclair, impassive, seemingly paying attention to every word, unmoved by the vehemence of the arguments, confident that the final word would be his. He'd been watching a playground fight, and now the master in charge blew the whistle.

"Madame is getting fretful about dinner, so we'll have to adjourn very soon. I've listened to everything that's been said. Our favourite young scribe (Aidan) has noted down all the points. I'll think it over and then put my own pen to paper. I have the feel for what should be in my programme. You've all made your views clear. We must set a radical

---

[29] Weapons of mass destruction which were the justification for military intervention but which were never found
[30] i.e. Iraq and Afghanistan

tone, a rupture with the present government but not so far outfield that people would feel uncomfortable.

"Now, Barrie, you and Hattie have been having a bit of harmless fun all afternoon. Explain all these little flags you've been putting up on the blackboards."

"Well, it's not great." Barrie paced up to blackboard 1, "25 we're pretty sure of getting. Another 15 here" (blackboard 2) "we're fairly optimistic of getting." He walked over to the other end and blackboard 10, "80 here we won't get, and the remaining 255 (straddled over the intervening seven boards) will be hard work. We'll need 40 signed up very early after the launch in order to create any momentum. Hattie and I have drawn up a list of MPs for Maudie, Paul and herself to start contacting when we get back, just the general sounding out at this stage."

Raphael's eyebrows lifted a little, and he set his lips firm, saying, "So 75 is a pretty tall order." Before we broke up, Rupert insisted on handing round a 'dos and don'ts' list to give more cyber security. He printed it off Aidan's laptop. For someone who is so nonchalant about security for the general public, he's single-minded when it comes to campaign confidentiality.

NED

We were all pretty knackered by the end of the day. But the thought of drinks and nosh kept us going along the path. I tried a few chat-up lines on Elaine who suddenly stopped dead, put her hands on my shoulders, "Don't waste your breath, sweetie. In my league. Not." Once in the upstairs room reserved for us, I knocked back three glasses of the house white in short order to console myself and saw with pleasure some huge plates of Madame's best fruits de mer dominating the centre of the big table.

She joined us to see if we were alright, clearly a bit taken aback at the way modern era parliamentarians from the land of Churchill dressed and behaved. When the sole was served, she returned, saw that Bo had clearly no idea how to fillet it on the plate, and tapped his shoulder to get him to give her his seat. Once she sat down the white flesh almost flew off the bone with four deft strokes of the knife. Bo, who's a good bloke, I think, went bright pink but we all cheered her artistry.

BARRIE

He is just so much the master at these occasions, gracious, affable, the well-chosen words to put everyone at ease, "Good point you made just now, Maudie,", "Excellent idea, Bo." He joined in the scabrous comments on the MPs on our lists, of which the best was Hattie's "he tried to grope me in the lift once", answered without pause by Ned, "No, he didn't Hat, it was just a small lift." Later Rupert asks the serious question, raised originally by Bo, "What shall we call ourselves." It was Ned who answered, "How about 'the Insurgency?'"

HELEN

At the end Raphael just stood up, said a few words of thanks, asked us to put the differences we'd aired so strongly that afternoon to one side for the greater good. He invited us to "start this great adventure. Remember what's at stake is not me, or our futures. It's whether our party survives, and what sort of future lies ahead for Britain. I have deep affection for you all but I suggest we get some rest. To those of you I won't see in the morning, have a safe journey; and my deep, deep thanks." We all stood, cheered, some of us - Hattie, Paul (surprisingly), me (of course) and Ned (inevitably) just a tiny bit choked. The next morning I left the cottage early for a couple of days with Ted before the return to the fray. Nearly everyone else was already on their way back.

NED

We'd arranged to have brunch at a café in the village, just Hat, Maudie, Aide, me and the boss before the two 'girls' and I took the early afternoon flight back. As we were leaving the house, Raphael said, "You lot carry on. I've just got to ring my folks."

It was colder and mistier than I'd thought so after about a hundred yards I said to the others, "I'll catch you up. I'm just gonna grab my anorak." As I got back to the cottage I could hear his voice saying "Mais je t'aime". I was as quiet as I could be but even I understood it was French he was speaking, and although I can't really speak any more French than what's strictly required to order some eats in a motorway pit stop, I could tell that he was consoling someone who sounded pretty close to him.

After a minute or two he concluded with, "Of course I love you too. See you soon," or something like that. I'd tried not to be noticed but as my anorak was still upstairs I couldn't make myself invisible. There was an awkward silence. I just had to say something and out it came, "Do you usually speak to your parents in French?"

He suddenly seemed older, diminished by being found out. He just said, "Ned, why don't you sit down? It's the classic complicated situation. Someone loves you, and you can't break it off on the telephone. You've got to be with him in person. And I just haven't had the time."

I just stayed standing and said, "Do it, Raf, please find the time. Or this could turn into a disaster. Besides, Aide's my best mate. I'll have to tell him if you don't break it off."

BARRIE

Would you believe it? He gets back on Monday evening and phones me late at night. Even for someone as emotionally stunted as Raphael this beat all the records, "Barrie, I'm never going to have time to go to Portugal to tell Jose, and by the time he's back in Brussels we'll be even busier. Could you do it for me? Go down to Setubal for a weekend, it's not particularly nice, but you could even take old Diggers down to the Algarve afterwards. It's not far. And it's all on me of course. Just look him up, arrange to meet him - he's a really sweet kid - break it to him gently, the needs of the campaign, all that. No need to mention Aidan at this stage... Oh well, if you won't, you won't." He rang off, obviously hurt at discovering that there are limits to what even I will do for him.

NED

Went to Angus's flat in Ealing early Monday morning, first day back, still recovering from 'le week-end'. Rashida's off somewhere but Bo was already installed. I made a mess of the coffee-making - the old trick of the electric kettle placed on the gas stove- so you suddenly get this odd smell of burning rubber; then I spilt half the tray as I stumbled over a low-lying table cunningly placed below the radar on my flight path. I get looks from Angus, who was hyped up explaining the big plan to just the three kids who can be trusted.

There's MariLisa Ngowo, a pretty chick doing a doctorate in philology. She's Nigerian and head of the Labour students. Then there's JoBoy Miles, a bright kid, paler than most of us after a day at Margate, but part-Caribbean and the pin-up of Labour Youth, all street patois and noisy but in a way that shows that he's bright enough. And finally Angus has brought along Gwilym Rhys, smart young trade unionist, on the NEC and chair of Welsh Labour. Angus goes through the routine, how we're all fed up with the trimming and the feuding and the triangulation. How we're going to lose big. How Rafa's been proved right on the war, on student fees, on the credit crunch. By the end of the spiel they're on board. JoBoy will get us a flash mob for the launch in Mayberry, and just keep them on board battle buses for the other meetings. He says "sixty, easy, man. Just tell them there's an anti EDL demo in Mayberry - do it all by text." MariLisa reckons she can sign up 6 or 7 of her mates to do the office, run the machines, feed Twitter and the website. She and Bo have this caricature of a techie conversation, all about downloads of clips from YouTube, Google adverts, Facebook sharing, clouds, Instagrams, yammers and Mings. Even Angus begins to lose interest at this point. And Gwilym thinks he can get some young union volunteers to act as a little Red Guard operation for the candidate, following him, filling halls, building the atmosphere. They talk about music for the venues but I caution, "Be careful, Rafa has strong views about music and they're not mine or yours. Bo, you'll have to check him out on this."

It's all wing and prayer stuff. The numbers ain't great but it's all we've got at the moment.

In the afternoon, we go down to Streatham, a dingy, insalubrious, disused office just off the high street. And yes, even I thought it stank. Was that a rat I saw running for cover as we opened the door? Bo had found it on Internet, really cheap, and rented it off his own bat. As he's won Angus' confidence he is given some autonomy. He says he can install phones and everything in 3 days, and we pass ourselves off as an internet start-up if people ask, which, in this part of the world, they probably won't.

In the evening we head back to Angus's to talk money with Rashida. The boss has laid down the law - no contributions more than a thousand quid and no corporates. Bo and MariLisa design some on-line donations, with a choice of £10, £50, £100, £500, and £1000 - "you'll see" says Bo, "most will give a hundred." But the donations can't be sought until the launch. Until then it's advances just to set the office up, hire equipment, buses and the launch itself. Rashida says everyone who went to France should chip in a thousand, to which Angus adds a bit sourly, "and that includes staff. They're earning more than the members. And Nigel's wife is a vineyard heiress." When Rashida pointed out that Marie-Claude couldn't contribute as a non-national this did not go down well. Angus, in his absolute element - bullying, bossing for Britain (can't say England) - the ultimate political obsessive.

BARRIE

Raphael's in a curious mood. Shuts himself off for hours, plays old favourites on his CD player using his enormous old-fashioned earphones which make him look like a WW2 pilot; plays around with bits of text which bear no relation to any of the notes Aidan or I have drafted for the personal programme or what will now be a personal letter to some 40,000 people whose names have been slipped to us by Bill (councillors, party chairs and committee members, union staff, reps, local branch officers). Marjorie's had to add in names from other sources every day and to try to avoid duplications. From the bits I've seen, Angus' more radical tone has not been softened and he's "going big on the war" to quote his partner. He's also practising lines and structures for stump speeches.

On Wednesday, in breezes Elaine, blows me a luvvie kiss and closets herself with Raphael. He tells me later that she's spoken to her producer friend at the Beeb. They'll trail the programme as 'Desert Island Discs just occasionally makes the news. Sunday will be one of these times.' The presenter is now primed that she's got a double coming out; "After all", her producer friend had said "this one's always reluctant to be too intrusive and it'd be a shame if we got to the closing credits with Sinclair having to start shouting, 'I'm gay and I'm standing for PM'." Security will be guaranteed by pre-recording only on the Saturday, and out-of-area. Nigel, who sat in with Raphael and Elaine, has offered to prime the World at One presenter mid-morning so that he could reorganise his programme. Rupert has wangled himself a place on the sofa of one of the main breakfast shows doing the review of the Sunday papers.

What do I think about Rupert? Well, he's wonderful to look at, and I'm flattered by his compliments and his flirtatious sweetness, but I know he's just using me to gain access and to pass on messages. But it beats Angus treating me as if I'm some old codger or a college scout; or Aidan Richards who considers me as the enemy (though I guess that's spot on).

Yesterday I asked Raphael if he had had the conversation and he said that he'd try to find a half-day for a quick return trip to Brussels, but with no overnight stop. So he obviously doesn't trust himself.

HELEN

By the end of the first week after France we had made precious little progress. We had agreed that those of us contacting colleagues would meet up at some half-way point, the nearest for all as the crow flies, somewhere in the Derbyshire countryside. Paul Howkins had chosen some crummy little village pub which was quiet and looked to be on the skids. We recounted our adventures and at least Hattie Reynolds and Maudie Hinton told the story of their slim pickings with some crude wit to lighten the evening. Some of our fellow MPs had simply given up and were already sending out CVs or returning to teaching or in a few cases the Bar. They just didn't have any fight left in them and were totally demoralised. Fear was also a factor in those constituency parties dominated by trade unions close to the PM. Of Barrie's initial list of the 'most hopefuls' we had only got 15 who had said they would sign up for a challenge. Hattie had one bright spot: two women not classified as anything more than outside chances were so fed up with the misogynistic style of the leadership that they would back almost anybody to take him on. Paul added on two more from the trade union group worried about the austerity measures just announced.

So two weeks before the launch we had got just 20 likely signatures plus our own, barely a third of the way to our target.

In their discussions, the alternative most mentioned was the Foreign Secretary, Derek Jamieson. He wasn't particularly liked but people felt he was competent and performed adequately on television. They liked Brian Dawkins, the Home Secretary, who was brilliant with people but seemed lightweight. Only two mentioned Raphael, in both cases only then to dismiss him, one saying what a shame it was that he was obviously quitting politics; "joining the list of 'The Best Prime Minister We Never Had', which is now longer than the list of those who have held the post".

NED

I've gone underground with Rupe and Bo. We slink into Mayberry and visit a couple of venues. The local Methodist Hall is hopeless, gloomy, poor acoustics (Bo's expert judgment) and seats 600 which we'd never fill. Forbidding, no atmosphere.

The Richard Crossman Memorial Lecture Theatre at Mayberry Uni (yes, I didn't know they had a Uni either) is better. Bo simply says, "I could do things with that stage but I'll need a couple of days to get it knocked into shape". Which means paying over the odds for room hire. Having talked to the security people he's bribed them not to make any fuss about numbers if we overshoot. And he's also slipped someone fifty quid to cancel an event the previous evening which would have interrupted the massive reconstruction he's planning. The kid's a genius.

HELEN

Half way through the phoney war there was the first of the articles inspired by Nigel Bolton in the Guardian, talking about the mounting despair in the party and the frailty of the leadership – "one heave and it would topple over...The party now faces the stark choice, make the change or risk coming third and losing 150 seats in one fell swoop." There was a little speculation about those who might limit the damage but no mention of Raphael. The author of the piece was close to the Foreign Secretary so this was brilliant planting of material.

Meanwhile, Louise Mitchison and I had started our casual drop-in sessions on ministers we knew, just testing the water. No-one relished a challenge, except for two (out of the four) women cabinet ministers who were fed up with being treated as window dressing by the macho mafia in Downing Street. No names were mentioned but one could already sense the beginnings of a febrility which was starting to take hold.

By the end of the second week the trawl by Hattie, Maudie and Paul was making almost no progress. The number who might commit had risen to 26 or 27, plus the nine of us from St Palais. We were not even half-way there. And the main problem was hope - or the lack of it; "Why add to the misery if we're going to be smashed anyway?" was one reaction. One of the Welsh God squadders even said (to Maudie of all people), "If the good Lord himself moved his celestial residence to No 10, we'd still be flung from our seats."

BARRIE

I've seen the first draft of his letter. Beautifully written of course, modest and personal. I love the start, "This is the letter I thought I'd never have to write. I've always sought unity. I've not allowed personal ambition to overwhelm me but I cannot just stand by and see our party, its principles and our shared hopes smash into the rocks. We need above all a new direction."

He showed it to Angus, who hates all the "schmaltzy perso stuff" (which is the best bit) and made some eighty proposed changes. But he held back a bit because he knows Aidan has had a hand in all of the drafting, and can't push his luck too far.

Rashida treats me now with a little more respect or at least she does when she's tapping me for a £1000 advance. We're all having to put money up front. And this could be only the first instalment if Bo's rallies, which will cost a bomb, don't raise some serious money. I don't know how I'm going to tell Digby, who thinks we're saving money to buy that pretty little cottage deep in the Dorset countryside.

HELEN

With a week to go there was a helpful piece in the Sunday papers repeating all the dire predictions for the future, depicting the leadership as rudderless and paranoid and reporting the growing pressure for someone 'to step up to the plate'.

But on the Tuesday, an article appeared from the Foreign Secretary in the Times under the heading of 'Why I support the Prime Minister', which talked of the 'supreme folly' of a leadership challenge from 'some discontented backbencher' just as the first fruits of necessary but unpopular policies were being seen, and how wickedly irresponsible it would be to allow ourselves the distraction of a leadership challenge at a time of economic peril when we were fortunate enough to be led by the right Prime Minister to steer us through the crisis and who enjoyed the full support of his colleagues. He then acknowledged that the government had to sharpen its presentation and hinted at deeper disquiet about shortcomings in the No 10 machine. But, he continued, "instead of forming little cabals of young supporters", experienced politicians should take the lead in defending the government. "The party will round on anyone who threatens our unity and lets in the Tories."

It was, of course, Jamieson's own leadership pitch for after the election and a pre-emptive strike against any ex-minister on the back benches planning a challenge. We started phoning each other, each convinced that this was a leak, with that reference to 'the young cabal'. Ned Warren and Aidan Richards felt sure that Louise Marchant was the culprit, the latter saying with his usual elegance how she was "always sucking up to Jamieson, like some over-the-hill groupie." Angus Buchanan on the other hand told Raphael that Rashida had Louise's solemn word that Louise was still very much on side, had leaked nothing and had had no contact with Jamieson since the weekend in France. Raphael ordained that there was to be no witch-hunt, no recriminations and above all no reaction. But I suspected then that he believed Louise to be the source of the leak.

The next day's Telegraph had a helpful piece about Jamieson's article being the sign of a deal struck with Downing Street that a public declaration of loyalty would assure him a clear run after an election which even No 10 now assumed all but lost. This was clearly designed to discredit both the leader and his putative successor. It had been dreamed up by Rupert Dennison and then passed on to Nigel Bolton who, with Raphael's blessing, not only got it placed in the most read broadsheet but then proceeded to give it further traction with slightly different spin for a number of other outlets.

Hattie Reynolds rang me up late Wednesday night, which in itself was unusual. She was agitated after a call from the Chief Whip[31]. In his nasally tones and flat East Anglian accent, he had just said, "I hear nasty reports, Harriet, about some of you and the other ladies going round the countryside whipping up discontent and disaffection. Let me put it to you straight, Harriet my girl, either you stop or I'll start ringing around your union branches and start speaking to your CLP officers. Understood?" and slammed the phone down.

It was all seeping out. And I did begin to wonder just what the purpose of all this was. Had we just trapped ourselves? We were just three days away from the launch. We had just 31 promises, plus ourselves, and of those who were on board only 20 could be expected to sign early.

---

[31] Rt Hon Philip Webb, MP for East Harwich

EXTRACT FROM 'THE JC DUNNETT ANTHOLOGY (199- to 201-)'

Generalisations become accepted wisdom because they are invariably proved correct. In the political world, the Tories are regarded as predisposed towards disloyalty with not a shred of remorse when they come to dispatch leaders hitherto treated with the most ostentatious and obsequious displays of public reverence. Labour is the natural habitat for squabblers, complainers and malcontents. But they stick to leaders with disgruntled and morose devotion even when the signposts to the precipice are six feet high and the commander-in-chief continues hurtling towards the cliff edge.

I just wonder whether this might not be about to change. I've heard the whispers about signatures being collected, the tell-tale declarations of fealty from putative contenders, and stories of telephone lines being installed in dingy premises south of the river. This tittle-tattle resurfaces normally about every two to three years even in balmier times.

What has drawn my attention this time is the number of articles being penned by some of my colleagues in the more serious broadsheets, spreading gloom and despondency - in terms remarkably similar - about the impending fate of 'this great movement of ours'. These opinion pieces have been 'placed' in a fashion which is rather professionally coordinated and with conclusions that have benefited from a guiding hand close to one of our cleverer politicians.

I now believe a challenge to the Prime Minister to be a distinct possibility. The gauntlet could well be thrown down in a few weeks and whoever steps out of the shadows may well be the first of several, including some senior cabinet ministers, so convinced have some become that the oblivion now facing them threatens any chance of their beloved party returning to government in the next generation.

A sitting Labour Prime Minister has many levers at his disposal. But an open challenge would be a novelty with quite unpredictable results.

NED

I love going down to Streatham each morning. There's a real buzz, and some extremely hot items who are all nice to me and make me coffee and don't nag if I make a mess because the place is a total mess anyway (pizza cartons, coke bottles, plastic takeaway containers half-empty and half-closed, and paper strewn all over the place). And the loo's pretty iffy although that's me just being fastidious (there's always a first time, Mart).

But there's energy and the thrill of it being sorta secret. We keep getting new volunteers, they've built up a mailing list of nearly 90,000 and the website's nearly ready. I saw the dummy last night - brilliant.

There's never fewer than 15 in the office, and all here till pretty late each night. Angus paces up and down giving orders. Bo sits on the dirty floor in a corner, his laptop appropriately on his lap, running through all the logistics for Sunday. We'll need 2 buses for Mayberry. On Friday he's moving camp to Mayberry, staying in Aide's old flat, supervising the rebuilding of a Lecture Theatre. The college authorities will have a fit.

I'm still worried about the choice of tracks for Desert Island Discs. My offer to supervise the selection having been turned down, it'll be all Beach Boys, Motown, such a turn-off. Still it's preferable to spin (ha! ha!) doctors choosing for him records he'd never heard of which is what usually happens. Even Aide's been kept out of it.

BARRIE

I've seen the final version of 'The Letter'. Aidan has spotted two grammatical errors, one split infinitive and one misspell, so he's pleased with himself, which is his usual state of mind. Raphael seems more relaxed than ever, even managing a round of golf with old business chums on Thursday when he could have used the time more profitably making a quick trip to Brussels for 'the conversation'. I don't know this Portuguese kid, and 'vendetta's' an Italian concept but I fear the worst. He'll find out soon enough like everybody else. Tomorrow - Saturday - Raphael will pre-record his broadcast...

****

I just hung on at the house, much to Aidan's annoyance, to get the post-broadcast report. We got nothing out of him, "I think it went not too badly. She's such a nice girl. Stunning too. Great if we could get her on board."

NED

We've all decamped to Mayberry for the weekend. Rafa took Angus and Aidan to the officers' meeting in an office just off the Labour Club - according to Aide "your typical Labour Party dump - all odours of stale beer and fags, with the obligatory stained carpets and ripped styrofoam arm chairs". Anyway the meeting is all pre-cooked with Tom Carter the local party chair (bearded trade unionist with a beer gut that makes me seem positively dapper) and the secretary Rodney Wills who's also the boss's agent, described by Aide as "your average sad Labour Party misfit" which is unfair 'cos he's a brill organiser. Anyway, according even to Aide - no sweat, all in line, raring to go but sworn to secrecy until tomorrow midday when the balloon goes well and truly up. Rafa did say that one or two of the slower souls didn't quite seem to grab the significance of two of their local MPs shacking up together, and both of them men, but no-one dared express any qualms under Tyrant Tom's chairmanship.

Before that I'd whiled away the time preparing supper with Helen, Rashida, Elaine, Nige, Rupe and Barrie - well, to be more to the point I'd volunteered as food-taster in chief ('just in case there's a traitor in the midst going to poison our hero'). I got banned from the quite small kitchen but not before I'd yanked a 6-pack from the fridge. All the others except Maudie and Hattie - who are remaining undercover until later to make something of a flounce out of government to give us a bit of momentum - will arrive here tomorrow morning so we can all listen to the favourite programme of the English middle-aged middle class - "the classic comfort food - essential nutrition of the intellectually stunted and culturally primitive" as Rupe so encouragingly called it. Actually I quite like the programme which I guess just proves his point.

Before their meeting we'd all gone off to the Lecture Hall to see the marvels worked by Bo. Think a mixture of a US nominating convention, the set of 'Strictly' and the sight of Cleopatra's arrival in Rome and you begin to get the idea. Everything's done by lighting, there's a huge video screen behind the rostrum to the left, and the set's pale grey but bedecked with flags - Red, Union Jack, Europe; the stage now slopes so that the speaker seems to walk up a hill to the left side and then up to the rostrum which juts out into the middle of the crowd (sort of 'climb every mountain' inspirational). Acoustics and sound brilliant - heightened so that when he puts on a track it's almost like having on really sensitive earphones, a kind of audio 3D.

There's twenty people all hard at it, hammering and fiddling with wires. Just a few seats have been reserved, while the hall now has a capacity of 450 but which will look like many more if we manage to half-fill, which evidently we will, easily.

Again secrecy for the music choice, which worries me like hell because I'm supposed to do a 3-minute warm-up and I don't want to come on to the strains of 'the Sugar Plum Fairy'. Actually I'm nervous as hell and won't sleep a wink unless mightily sedated with significant quantities of knock-out beverages.

As we leave, Rupe asks Bo, "How much is all this costing, for Christ's sake?" to which came the reassuring answer, "dunno, but the boss says, 'go for broke'."

HELEN

Aidan Richards refused to allow any of us to stay at what he now referred to as "our house" so after we had been shooed away we went on after midnight to a late-night pub, 'the Indian Halls', in the old centre of Mayberry, in one of the few streets which had escaped the bombing in 1941. Of course Hattie Reynolds and Maudie Hinton were still undercover and Rupert Dennison had gone back to London for his breakfast programme the next day.

We looked back at where we had come from and the distance still to go. Barrie, in particular, was very agitated, seriously overworked, emotionally strained and hating having Aidan Richards around. Paul's hands were shaking from fatigue. Almost every ten minutes he would disappear for one of his sixty a day. Angus was white, tense and silent. Rashida hardly ever said anything in any case, and was probably rehearsing her warm-up remarks for the rally. Bo joined us late, having solved some complex rewiring problems. Only Ned kept up our spirits with a stream of silly anecdotes, reminding us, "hoy, this isn't a wake". Rashida asked him what he intended saying at the rally, "Oh, like the boss, I'll wing it, but once I'm out there you try and stop me! It'll be worthy of Fidel", which was a little bit what we had feared.

BARRIE

The big day. First I watch Rupert on the sofa doing his suave accomplished stuff and looking like a young Brad Pitt only more clued-up. He picked on two articles in the Sundays (both planted by Nigel), 'Labour's Race to the Bottom', and 'Who will Rid Labour of This Liability?' He made no mention of Raphael but managed to drop in, "I think the clamour from activists, trades unions and supporters is now deafening. We're going to have to make a change and the PLP is waking up to it." He was asked 4 times to name a possible challenger, and refused with the formula, "It's up to whoever has the courage to stand to announce for herself or himself, but I believe the call from the party is being heard." This was the main news at the end of the programme, and someone pointed out that Rupert was "known to be close to the former Foreign Secretary Raphael Sinclair but who has refused to comment".

TRANSCRIPT FROM 'DESERT ISLAND DISCS',

30th August

"My castaway today has been described as the most intelligent man in British politics. Foreign Secretary at 40, he resigned on a great matter of principle. Since then his writings and speeches have given authority to all his criticisms of New Labour, which he memorably described as having a 'heart of tin'. He, almost alone, forecast the economic and financial crisis. He is of course Raphael Sinclair, the Labour Member of Parliament for Mayberry Central.

"So, Raphael Sinclair, how serious is the crisis facing the Labour government?"

"We're in a triple bind: the wrong policies to take us out of the crisis - champagne years for the super-rich, austerity for the rest of us; foreign wars which are sacrificing the lives of our young women and men in conflicts which arms could never resolve; and a sclerotic politics with leadership which is out of touch. Reviled."

"Wow. That's quite a charge sheet. So it's the Prime Minister we should blame."

"No. Changing the leadership without changing the policies makes no sense. It's the direction the ship is travelling - basically straight towards the rocks - that's the real problem. The names and faces of the crew and how good they are at communicating – or, in this case, not - that's all secondary."

"What's your first record?"

"My father loves Ella Fitzgerald. Her records were on all the time at home. I love so many but my favourite is 'Every Time We Say Goodbye'.

****

"Was your childhood a happy one?"

"Yes, wonderfully so. My parents gave me a stable loving home. I was good at school, well, not at sport, but I made wonderful friends there I've kept. Dad and mum were both teachers but it wasn't some hot-house atmosphere. It was all a bit of a soft landing. Teachers didn't earn much in those days but we had no financial anxieties. And I didn't really worry about getting a job, unlike kids today."

"Your second disc?"

"Usually new versions of great old songs don't add much to the original, but the teaming up of Roy Orbison and K.D.Lang to do 'Crying' turned a standard into something with huge emotional power."

****

"University must also have been a good time. You certainly got all the glittering prizes."

"Well, not the academic ones: too much time doing politics leaving not enough time for the library. But also the people like my colleague Helen Mitchison, and one of your colleagues Elaine Chayter, remain among my dearest friends. I wish I'd worked a bit harder, spent a little less time in pubs, a little less politicking in the Union but I had a great time there.

"Record number 3 is another cover; mum loves Dionne Warwick's 'Walk on By' but this jazzier, more soulful version by Aretha Franklin just adds a new dimension to it. And it's pretty heart-breaking."

****

"You have this flying start in life and then you start working for a trade union. Why this choice?"

"Well, it wasn't just any union. It was the teachers' unions. I just felt that with the dedication demanded of your state school teachers, and the daily challenge they face, it seemed to me they deserved better conditions and a bit more respect. One of the things New Labour has done which I never disparage has been to improve the conditions of the profession, and all that extra money spent on schools. But I'm uneasy about the new Academies because they could in the wrong hands undermine the principle of 'universal' education. And tuition fees is a blunder which is bound to put off kids from poorer backgrounds."

"To lighten the mood, disc four is Betty Everett's 'Getting Mighty Crowded.' I dance appallingly but to this I dance."

****

"From the unions to Parliament, and then a meteoric rise. Foreign Secretary at 40. How did you feel about that?"

"The most mixed of feelings. I was very close to Rory, shocked by him dying so young, and uneasy about stepping into his shoes. And then soon after we were on the assembly line to war."

"Which you opposed. And over which you resigned. Did you think of challenging for the leadership then? Some people thought you could have brought down the government."

"Oh, the answer's simple. You don't start a civil war in your own party when your troops have just been sent into a ground war abroad. Remember we moved very quickly from seeking that second UN resolution to bombing Baghdad. So the only thing I could do was resign. And in the circumstances I could do no more than take a very personal stand."

"The fifth track is Don Henley's 'The Last Worthless Evening". I liked the Eagles when I was a kid but when he went solo he became one of the great singer-songwriters of all time. I could have chosen half a dozen of his tracks."

****

"So, you're in the wilderness, and you become the foremost critic of New Labour. In your last book you said it had a 'heart of tin.' So you'd like to go back to Old Labour?"

"It has a bad press, and there's been some heavy historical revision but it wasn't that bad. Old Labour or real Labour created the NHS, the modern welfare state, equal rights for women, liberated an Empire and fought apartheid. There's a long list which we should respect. But you don't go back. There's a new agenda to tackle: corporate abuse, young people without jobs, archaic institutions, media power, and I could go on..."

"But only to our next record..."

"...which is by Nat King Cole. His voice is so distinctive, all those cigarettes, but his songs are the transcript for all our romantic feelings sixty years on. A tough selection to make but this very slow version of 'The Very Thought of You' is just sublime."

****

"Raphael Sinclair, judging by your discs you're a very sentimental person. Love sounds important to you. Yet you've never married. Your private life remains private. What's the story here?"

"I've had wonderful women friends. I love working with women. But my relationships are with men. Over the years I've had several very deep relationships and this year I've started living with a partner for the first time."

"Can we ask about him? Have you two known each other long?"

"Yes. Quite a few years. He's become a colleague in the Commons, but despite the complications we decided two months ago that our love was too important for us to be apart. So what do you do when you're in a stable relationship? You move in with each other, spend as much time together as possible, be a couple."

"So he's a colleague?"

"Yes, Aidan Richards from the neighbouring seat in Mayberry. And we've both decided we wish to be together, forever."

"This is going to be a big shock for many people. How have your friends and family taken it?"

"If they're friends, they'll be happy for us."

"Your last but one record?"

"I saw Nina Simone perform in Lille. She was half an hour late, insulted the audience but then played and sang wonderfully. I've chosen a real tearjerker, 'The Other Woman'- listen to the piano with all that classical training, the melody and the sheer desolation of the words."

****

"People say, Raphael Sinclair, what does he do next? Something's got to give because we can't see you going back into government under the *present PM. Do you go off and write books, lecture? People have mentioned you as a possible Master for your old college. Or do you try to change things in your party? Will you, Raphael Sinclair, challenge for the Labour leadership?"*

"I've long stopped day-dreaming about becoming Prime Minister as most young MPs do. It's a pretty thankless job. But when you think you see so clearly what's wrong and a leadership falling so short of the moment, the time has come to step forward. I think the PM should go, and tonight in Mayberry to my local supporters, I'll announce my own intentions."

"But surely the odds against an outsider ousting a sitting Prime Minister are just too overwhelming?"

"Well, I think it's the party which needs to make that choice."

"And won't your revelation about your personal life just make things that much more difficult. Is Britain ready for a gay Prime Minister?"

"We'll see if Britain is indeed ready for its first openly gay leader but I have confidence that we have become a more open society which tolerates diversity."

"The last disc?"

"I heard this from a tape of a young Portuguese friend of mine. It's by a Spanish singer called Antonio Vega who died recently, and it's called 'Para bien para mal' and I just find it beautiful if very, very sad."

****

"The usual questions we ask of our guests seem almost out of place after all you've said to us this morning. I guess you wouldn't cope that well on the Island?"

"Oh, I'd be in deep depression after about half an hour and dead from malnutrition in three days."

"We're giving you the Bible and Shakespeare, what other book would you take?"

"Middlemarch, the greatest novel in the English language, which describes early Victorian society in all its complexity and is still massively relevant."

"Your luxury?"

"A photo album with pictures of those closest to me."

"And if the big wave comes, sweeping all but one of your discs out to sea, which one would you save?"

"Difficult but it has to be 'The very thought of you' because the very thought of that very special person moves me beyond words."

"Raphael Sinclair, thank you very much".

NED

We all sat there in the front room listening to every word, hardly daring to breathe, all twelve of us (and me trying to stop my tummy rumbling - no cooked breakfast and nerves about tonight). Of course I'd have liked to comment on his selection, but chickened out. In fact they weren't as crap as I'd thought.

I kept watching Rafa - impassive, like a Roman commander surveying a battle; and Aide, total concentration, blinked twice with the declaration of love at the end, with his Adam's apple bobbing up and down as if swallowing a lot; and then a fleeting cloud passing over his face when the 'young Portuguese friend's' record was played. (Bet Rafa hasn't told the kid and this is a message as some kind of 'we'll always be friends' consolation prize which will just make matters worse when the boy hears it.)

When it was finished and that familiar old signature tune started up, Aidan just said, "OK" in a flat voice. Rashida said, "More than OK. You got the messages across brilliantly", thereby skating over the 'coming out' bit. "I'd give the music 7 out of 10," I concluded magisterially, "middle-of-the-road, but quality middle-of-the-road".

HELEN

The midday bulletins following on immediately from the programme led with the announcement, and the inevitable, "If he's successful, Mr Sinclair would become Britain's first openly gay Prime Minister." In five minutes the first of a swarm of journalists and photographers arrived at the front gate of the house; and all our mobiles started ringing at once.

It was such fine late summer weather that some of us took our calls in the garden. Poor Mrs Sinclair would have been devastated had she seen the signs of neglect in just the two months since she and her husband had moved into sheltered housing. Weeds strangling what must once have been a beautiful border of gaillardia and delphiniums and lupins; the grass clearly still mown from time to time, but no-one doing the edges.

Barrie telephoned the local police to send around some officers to stop the journalists from trespassing on the front garden or sneaking round the back.

The main lunchtime news bulletin devoted some twenty minutes to the story. There was instant reaction from the chair of the Parliamentary Labour Party, "I'd say this to Raphael Sinclair, who's an old colleague: don't do this, Raphael, don't rock the boat. Our people don't want the distraction of disunity,"- a line promptly peddled by two cabinet ministers close to the Prime Minister. The potential cabinet rivals were more circumspect, and others kept their heads down.

We had decided to field Rupert Dennison, who was almost sickeningly brilliant: "People will be less interested in his private life; they'll care more about what he'll do for them"; "you're obsessing about sex; the BBC should get over it; the public have." And then he had another theme, about giving him a chance and then, finally just a hint of menace, "Labour MPs will have to make their own decisions. But before rushing into this they'd be well advised to listen to their local parties and their constituents who are fed up with the drift and crying out for change."

BARRIE

I spent most of the afternoon fielding calls and with Marjorie's help fitting in the avalanche of press requests which Nigel and Elaine keep throwing at us. We worked on a grid which Bo has mapped out and which includes thirty big meetings in three weeks, with face-time for MPs, local media stops and short visits; worse than a general election schedule but only the beginning.

The website will be up at 7 a.m. tomorrow, and that's when the letter goes out. For Rashida the top priority is the donations campaign. She took me to one side and said that Bo's campaign could cost us up to a hundred thousand a day; in a week we'd be bankrupt. I've already chipped in £5000, in five dollops. Digby doesn't know of course and will be beside himself. Others like Elaine and Helen and Nigel have stumped up even more. I still can't make out Rashida, so cool, never offside politically, yet with just enough warmth in her smile to make you think there's maybe something more than pure calculation there.

Aidan and Raphael spent the afternoon indoors just for some down time. Have I misjudged Aidan? Perhaps he really cares for Raphael. Or is this just the trick of a lifetime?

Of course when the news crosses the channel, there'll be a crisis, all thanks to our pusillanimous, cheating, egocentric, emotionally disfigured but brilliant leader.

NED

I get to accompany Rafa to meet the kids who've come early for the show. They've been corralled into a hall just 200 yards from the lecture theatre. JoBoy has done more than deliver - there's three coach-loads here plus a local 'flash mob' summoned by text and who would be going straight to the venue. So it'll be standing room only!

The kids are pretty fired up, and then Rafa gives them the works, how it's not about a candidate but an uprising for change. "If we leave it to MPs, there'll be no leadership election, no new PM, no change of policy. There'll just be crushing defeat at the election and you lot facing a Tory Britain until you're all middle-aged.

"But you can set the party alight. You can create the force for change that even the most jaded and cynical MP will have to listen to. To pull this off, we'll have everyone against us: the government, the party machine, trade union general secretaries, the press, the City, big business, the bureaucrats, the bankers. You name it...

"All we've got now is a candidate, a set of beliefs and a handful of young MPs and you.

"Here's what I ask: give us three weeks of your life and all your energy and your force. Just take us through to party conference in three weeks' time. If we get that far we'll have forced this thing wide open and given the party a choice. If we don't, at least we'll have made the case. At least we'll have tried. At least we'll have done our duty.

"We've got no money, no organisation, so I need you to travel with me to every corner of the land to fight for change in Britain. We can't pay you; we'll find you somewhere to sleep - not grand hotels, mind - and we'll feed you but it'll be tired sandwiches and carefully rationed beers.

"But you'll be part of an insurgency. And you'll never forget the days ahead. And I'll never forget you."

And with that and before the cheers had subsided he had slipped out of the room leaving MariLisa, JoBoy, Gwilym and me to do the business, assign tasks and ferry them to the meeting.

BARRIE

When we get to the hall I am speechless. The whole set complete with the walkway to the rostrum and the flags billowing on film at the back (Bo having decided that real flags were inanimate and therefore had to be junked). On the rostrum, a huge legend, 'The Sinclair Insurgency; A Mission of Hope'. The place is jammed packed, with people three deep standing at the back walls or sitting on the floor. I'd guess 600+, maybe more. Rupert is already spinning a thousand. There's a bit of a scuffle with press blocking the view and one cameraman's sound boom hitting a woman councillor in the face. But it looked great.

NED

Would you believe it? I had just arrived at the hall, and Angus lords it up to me and says, 'You're stood down, Ned, sorry. But we're running late and if we have 2 warm-ups we'll miss the 6 p.m. bulletins. Sorry. So it's just Rashida."

What can you say? Of course it's Rashida. She got him to dump me so that she can shine alone.

But she looked pretty sensational: all cream twinset and one line of small pearls. And confident, no notes, just her 'second generation Pakistani' routine and owing everything to Labour. Praise for Raphael, and then "it's a great honour for me to open this campaign to take Raphael Sinclair to the leadership of Labour and to No 10."

Then the wall of sound as he walks on to Betty Everett, getting her second outing of the day, but this time at least it's well-adapted to the situation. I'm squeezed against the side wall, between Aide and Rupe, my best friends ever, and we're all kind of proud. He walks to the rostrum, the cheers deafening, and he looks great. Rupe whispers behind my back, "Looking pretty fit..." Aide replies, "Well I had to put him through his paces."

HELEN

He could have come out and read the Mayberry telephone directory and the crowd would still have gone crazy. Indeed it was by some distance not his greatest speech. It had all the arguments, and some good punch lines about the banks, big business, rising inequalities. But Angus had fed him too many figures and he misspoke twice which was a sure sign of the pressure he was otherwise hiding so well.

But it was the war, "the illegal, reckless rush to war," and the aftermath and the casualties and the sheer ignorance of geography and history which almost took the roof off.

"Our national reputation and the proud peace traditions of our party have been sacrificed on the altar of America's imperial destiny and the base and remorseless interest of black gold."

When it got to policy it was sketchy still, and he seemed for a time to lose pace, but then built again into a riff borrowed from an American politician years back, about "Come home, Britain, from foreign wars...Labour come home from sordid backroom deals with bankers...Labour come home from selling off our cherished public services to private interests..." and so on. This worked after a fashion, and then he went into his peroration about the Insurgency and the Long March and concluded simply - a typical Sinclair bathos moment, quieter but with real authority,

"Yes, tonight, my friends, I stand before you as a candidate for the leadership of the Labour Party and for Prime Minister."

This was the prelude to a standing stomping demonstration of ten minutes and he left the hall through the crowd, with the old Martha and the Vandellas song, 'Dancing in the Streets', as accompaniment.

BBC News at Ten, after a twelve-minute report on the launch and the day's events, the newsreader announced, "And now over to our political editor in Mayberry."

"So tonight Raphael Sinclair begins the impossible quest for power. The hurdles are formidable. To try to remove a sitting Labour Prime Minister at the height of an economic crisis is quite frankly quixotic. Labour is traditionally the party which is most loyal to its leaders, even those who are not perceived to be performing well. And getting 75 MPs to publicly declare for a contest - the minimum threshold just to trigger a vote - is against all the odds.

But three things will be worrying No 10 tonight. The Prime Minister has still not had the endorsement from half of his cabinet colleagues, including the three most senior. There'll be a lot of arm-twisting going on and the cabinet will rally round, but that it's taking so long will unnerve the PM.

His staff will be worried by the sheer enthusiasm and vitality of the crowd in Mayberry tonight. This was no re-run of the stage-managed rally in Sheffield all those years ago which back-fired on Labour's election campaign. This was raw and raucous and of a kind I've not seen at any political rally in the last thirty years.

But what will be most dispiriting for the Prime Minister will be that the youngest and most gifted of the Labour intake at the last election and Labour Youth are lining up behind Mr Sinclair and giving an inkling that his campaign against all the odds is likely to be the most fascinating show in town as we enter the conference season."

BARRIE

Back home at 2 in the morning; don't wake up Digby. Log on, all the clips chosen by Bo are already on You Tube with many more hits than expected. And I've just had a text from my old friend Miranda in Brussels to say that's it's all over the continental media. Even the Portuguese ones, I guess.

********   END OF PART TWO   ********

PART THREE - STEALING A PARTY

"Fasten your seat belts, it's going to be a bumpy night"

Margo Channing, from 'All About *Eve*'

EXTRACT FROM 'THE JC DUNNETT ANTHOLOGY (199- to 201-)'

If I was for a moment tempted to indulge in a little self-congratulation for my most recent piece on a possible challenge to the Prime Minister I hold back for my failure to connect the spurts of activism of Mr Sinclair and his young acolytes with the organisation of a coup. The member for Mayberry has been playing a long game. His resignation on what he chooses to present as a matter of principle preceded a prolonged period of quietism, the careful manipulation of the party machine to propulse a number of young admirers into parliament and to build up a war machine at a time when the official structures of the party are deeply atrophied, all the while creating a wide expanse of crimson water between him and the New Labour clans. His challenge has the semblance of a programmatic basis to widen the appeal beyond the simple and obvious statement of fact that we currently have in the age of television and 'social' media a Prime Minister who lacks even the most basic communication skills.

Much attention has been paid to the hurdles erected by Labour's rule-book to shield a sitting Prime Minister from a formal challenge to his leadership. And the Parliamentary Labour Party has always shown a pusillanimous disinclination to dislodge leaders, even when their continuation in office has been so detrimental to the interests of the party.

The tactics of the undertaking seem to me to offer a way around the regulatory obstacles. Those MPs who quaver at the wrath of Number 10 and the pressure of their regional party hierarchs have to be made more afraid of a citizens' revolt among local activists. The Labour party is a shriven shadow of its former self. The influx of marauding teenagers carefully deployed and in awe of this latter day Cincinnatus and his young gladiators will seek to take over the party bottom-up. If this brittle shell starts to crumble, you will begin to hear the menacing sound of a clamour for choice, "the party must be given the right to decide".

And they will not lack encouragement from certain quarters in the press who will welcome a rowdy tumultuous distraction from the tedium of the party conference season, now so stilted and stage managed that only the most sophisticated Kremlinologists have found something worth reporting.

I think I might break the habit of a lifetime and buy a ticket for Brighton, which come late September might offer a bracing few days to blow away some of those old political cobwebs.

BARRIE

Actually I'm happy not to be staying at the house in Mayberry. I can't take anymore the rows that Raphael would have to have to win over Aidan and mitigate the latter's sustained hostility, or the deliberately noisy love-making aggravated by Aidan's little trick of leaving the bedroom door slightly ajar just to make me uncomfortable or jealous. Which of course it does, a bit. And when I do stay there I get duties like taking coffee to the royal suite in bed, where Aidan is lolling nude texting (to ex-lovers, I imagine) or reading the papers I have gone out to look for 2 hours earlier. God I hate him!

On Monday morning I ring Bo in Streatham really early - the office already busy by the din of things. The website had gone online and the letter with the appeal had gone out to 78,000 addresses at 7 a.m. on the dot. These addresses are gold, email still being the best direct means of getting supporters motivated: personal but quick. By lunchtime 12,000 had signed up for the Sinclair Insurgency and the first donations, courtesy of some new internet payment system, had started rolling in. Bill had insisted that to each 'insurgent' we automatically send a party enrolment form.

Raphael went out early to the Mayberry BBC studio for the main Radio 4 interview at 8.10 a.m. He was not at his best - struggling to take the interview in the direction he wanted, on the defensive with repeated questions about the struggle to get the signatures and about how it felt to be "the first openly gay man to seek the top job in British politics". He answered all this calmly, politely and then something finally snapped, and there was a little explosion, "We've now talked for 15 minutes about my private life and about the complicated internal procedures in Labour's rules, and not one question about policies which could end the crisis and bring jobs back to Britain. Is the BBC now so dumbed down that you've lost all interest in things which matter to people?"

The interviewer replied tartly, "Oh, I'm sure we'll be having other interviews on your policy proposals."

To which he replied quickly before they can cut him off, "But not with you, I assure you."

As a parting shot it almost worked, concluding an otherwise lacklustre performance.

We then do a teleconference, with Raphael in Mayberry and Angus, Rupert and me in the Commons office. Angus full of gloom, as usual.

"So far, you're just a speech. You've not got a programme, just a series of punchlines and sound bites: just like New Labour at its worst. No sense of urgency. No detail. You've got to stop improvising.

"And your schedule's mindless. Why Leicester and Coventry? You're not campaigning to run some Midlands regional authority. And what precisely are you going to talk about today?"

Raphael replies silkily, "Well, good morning, Angus. How are you today? I hope you had a good night's sleep.

"The thing I really appreciate about you, Angus, is the way you make your point with such finesse, such old-fashioned charm.

"As a matter of fact I thought I might give education a whirl at Leicester University; you know, tuition fees, the free public system. And then this evening, with a more mixed audience, a bit on fair trade, minimum ILO standards and human rights in trade negotiations."

"It's not good enough, Raphael", came back the voice down the line with the almost imperceptible Scottish accent, practically shouting, "you've got to go hard on the economy; go for the banks; the world of finance and hit them with the Emergency Powers stuff. Create a sense of urgency."

Raphael now sounds bored with all these reprimands and asks for Streatham to be connected, and we managed after a bit of fiddling to get hold of Ned.

NED

The morning after the rally, I did my first ever 3-way 'telecon'. Not as good as a threesome, but almost! Rafa just wanted to be comforted about the kids working flat out, replies to the letter, hits on the website, dosh coming in and figures for the YouTube clips - very good but more for the choreography of the meeting than the extracts from the speeches. How was the tweeting going? And who's editing the tweets?

I got rather fed up with this restless time-wasting and decided to try out something.

"Rafa, I've had an idea," (predictable cheap comments from Rupe), "why not start a virtuous circle operation?"

"Explain, Ned, for the other three's benefit" (Rupe, Angus and Barrie, I think), "they just might not have immediately grasped the full import of your inspiration."

"Well, some people who don't support you might just sign for contradictory reasons."

I was getting nervous now because I sensed they were all listening and I wasn't really sure of my ground, but I struggled on.

"If they think this thing is not going down the drain straightaway, some other possible candidates might give their supporters a nod and a wink to sign anyway, along the lines of, "Well, Sinclair can't win, but it throws everything open, so if he gets the numbers our guy can come into the race, while old Rafs gets all the blame for the disunity. You know, the Heseltine thing, 'he who wields the dagger...'"

"Go on", says Rafa, no smart put-downs now from anyone.

"On the other side, if you were a No 10 sidekick you'd be thinking, if we're gonna get a challenge, best be Sinclair 'cos he's too left and, um, a bit colourful and he's not got any union backing. If there was a contest they might think they could take you out but won't be so sure about someone from the cabinet; so organise a few signatures, get him to the starting line so the other rivals in the government end up missing the bus. You know, you become everyone's favourite stalking horse. Do you get me?"

A pause and just as I was thinking we'd been cut off, it's Rafa, "Ned, so you're not just a pretty face after all. Angus, get on to Hattie and Maudie and Helen, and see if they can run with it. And then get Nigel to place some stuff on, 'The real interest of the PM…', or 'The real interest of Jamieson or any of the others', so that suddenly signing for Sinclair is not an act of disloyalty. It's holding the party together! The Warren paradox!"

I walk round the office beaming with pride and then find a few more excuses to hang around. Some of these girls are real lookers, particularly Melanie, who's doing the donations stuff. A plump softness I really go for. She brings me over a coffee in the last unused polystyrene cup, but then I've got to get to Coventry because I'm not allowing them to pull me off the bill again.

HELEN

The first couple of days after the Mayberry launch of the campaign were unsettling. There was wall-to-wall coverage in the media but it was extremely hostile; there was a big font on the front page of one of the tabloids - Sinclair's policies: Defence - Surrender; Foreign Policy - run from Paris; Economy - tax, nationalise and tax again; Media - state control and censorship. And photos of Aidan Richards taken from his own Facebook pages which were border-line pornographic, although it has to be admitted that large numbers of women and indeed men would probably have found them sexually enticing.

But Bo Sampson's technical operation, run out of Streatham, went well, with good early returns. I wasn't there for the first rallies but the media interest and JoBoy Miles'[32] flash mobs resulted in large turn-outs: 500 at a hall on the Leicester campus, 600 at the civic centre in Coventry, about the same numbers for an open-air event at an Asda car park in Birmingham (with the added bonus that the local manager tried to get the police to move the crowd on); and 750 - filled to the rafters - in the local theatre in Wolverhampton.

Raphael of course was totally allergic to messaging, always spoke apparently off the cuff, and with predictably mixed results. In Leicester his attack on tuition fees went down a storm. But in Wolverhampton his pieces on trade evidently went over most people's heads until he started including a whiff of protectionism, with great lines about slave labour, child workers and "executing trade unionists" in some of our "most favoured trading partners". This was an unashamed pitch for the union vote.

He chose the Asda car park to make his tirade against supermarkets rooking their customers, exploiting their suppliers and their staff, destroying our town centres and flogging cheap booze to young people. The shoppers seemed to like it even if they were laden with shopping bags filled with goods bought from these same commercial pariahs.

Angus Buchanan was relieved when the economic themes appeared in the Wolverhampton speech, with some ritual bank-bashing, but also a tough line on corporate abuse and tax evasion. Because he knew off by heart the figures from Angus and Barrie his confidence bowled over his listeners. Nigel Bolton's genius in feeding nuggets to the media ensured that at least some of the message got through the firewall of editorial

---

[32] A leading member of Labour Youth

hostility. And with the PM in New York for the General Assembly of the UN, there was no coordinated response from the leadership to the radical messages from his new rival.

I shared the platform with Angus at the first Insurgency press conference after the launch. Nigel and Elaine had gathered a good crowd - not just the usual lobby people - and some twenty TV cameras; and Angus presented our figures in the most favourable light: 22,000 had "joined" the Insurgency since the launch; 15,000 had donated nearly £800,000 all in small contributions, with more than 10,000 joining the party, what he described neatly as "the collateral bonus". He announced we now had 28 signatures for the candidate ("so we're nearly halfway there on day 3, week 1") but of course the figures included all of us, the remnants of the old Campaign Group[33], some of the dispossessed and a few women bitter at being passed over; and there was no mention of the drunk who had been cornered all evening by Hattie armed with a bottle of whiskey and a biro. I think the press bought into Angus's bravura because they wanted to, they really needed this fight to give some life to the long conference season.

At lunchtime, the main radio news programme relayed all this and then had the PM's main ally in the cabinet to comment. After the ritual lines about "distractions" and "disunity", he went further, "And, you know, I'm not sure the country's ready for a gay PM. It may all go down well with the London media but what I'm hearing from hardworking families in my constituency is that people are uneasy about someone who isn't sharing the challenges of family life in Britain today. Raphael Sinclair's lifestyle is very different from theirs. I'm no homophobe of course but having a gay leader won't help us win an election."

---

[33] A group representing the traditional left-wing of the Labour Party

NED

In Streatham when we heard it we whooped. "He's fallen into the trap!" shouted one of the girls. Within minutes the switchboard was jammed and the site went down. By 4 p.m. we'd got 5,000 more supporters and loads more money. But when Angus came in it was a stern, "I don't want anyone saying anything until we've reacted on 'PM'." The Lord hath spoken.

BARRIE

We heard it when we were en route to Wales for two events staged by Gwilym and his people, a few miles apart but with a surge in interest building in the afternoon. Just me and Raphael in the car, and Eddie behind the wheel. Eddie, the grizzled driver from all Raphael's elections, an old union driver ("with a mistress in every car park" according to Rupert), who knows everything and says nothing.

Raphael seemed totally unconcerned. When Angus rang in for the go-ahead for the responses, he just says, "if you think fit", "OK" or "you think so?", as if commenting on some supermarket special offers.

Rupert had been put up for the interviews and, as always, he's superb. We heard him just as we pulled into the Students' Hall at Aberystwyth; "I never thought I'd hear a Labour minister stoop so low… we had a great record on equality and diversity until now and he's destroyed it at a stroke…they must be really rattled…of course we know he wouldn't have made this pre-planned outrageous personal attack without the express approval of the Prime Minister…the Sinclair Insurgency now calls on the Prime Minister to disown him and then sack him. Failure to do so would not just position him on the side of bigots; it would be a failure of leadership."

The next 24 hours were dominated by coverage of the vacillations in the PM's camp about how to react, divisions in the High Command, reprimands to their colleague from two openly gay ministers, five 'out' backbench MPs signing up, and a boost for all our campaign indicators. Raphael's own themes for the day, youth unemployment and industrial regeneration, made little impact and even fell rather flat in the second meeting at Cardiff City Hall, packed, masses of media, and ever more youth volunteers.

At last at 9 p.m., right at the end of his speech, he gave his own reaction and the hall fell silent, "I hear that the Prime Minister's closest colleague has been considerate enough to give us the benefit of his wisdom about my private life. He is of course acting under licence. The organ grinder will in time doubtless gift us with his own views. All I would say, and I will comment no further on these trivialities, is that I'm asking you just to vote for me, nothing else."

The understating of what seemed like pent-up outrage but which may also have been artificial had the whole auditorium rising to its feet in a demonstration of support. Back in the car he just says, "I thought that went OK, didn't you?"

NED

I just love it at the Streatham office. Streams of volunteers with a high fanciability quotient, the mess and the squalor; it's like being back in my own sty only with lots of women. Bo's a fucking genius, just gives orders for the day and people get on with it.

But nothing lasts forever. Angus has sent Maudie here (she's still undercover) to get the place cleaned up and generally put a bit of stick about. I think Angus believes I'm a serial groper and need close supervision from the one woman in the world who is under no threat.

She and I do 'positive vetting' with interviews for every volunteer, to weed out undercover journos and spies from the various New Labour clans, Tories, loons and just the terminally sad. So there's not many left after all that but still it's a good old crowd.

Any case, a worrying turn of events this morning. We'd just sent off a mob for a set of rallies in the North-East (Durham, Newcastle and then into Yorkshire - real enemy territory) and there were just eight girls in the office and me (my sort of ratio) - they're all doing tweets, uploading take-outs for YouTube, updating the site, that sort of stuff - except one, Julie from Willesden who I'd persuaded to give me a quick neck massage, when the police arrived. And not your average plods coming to complain about the noise, the overflowing bins (all those take-away pizzas), drugs (?), sex on the back patio with an intern (I wish) or yet another complaint from some supermarket supervisor wanker about us holding a rally in his car park. No, these two were senior, one in uniform with a peaked cap and medals to show for it. In they walked, showed their ID, and the one called 'Chief Constable Gibbons' asked, "Could I ask who's in charge, sir?" They managed to conceal their astonishment when I told them who I was and what my day job is. "Are you the campaign manager?" he asked and I thought, "oh gawd what have we done?" but replied "the campaign manager is Mr Buchanan, but he's off on the campaign trail, and I'm holding the fort." The other guy ("you call that plain clothes? I call that old clothes" - Groucho, late forties), Inspector Weller, who's from MI6, guides me into the back room, much to the amusement of the girls, shuts the door and says, "We're getting a record number of death threats and hate messages about Mr Sinclair, we think some are from just the usual nutters, but we believe some may be from more recognisable terrorist groups, including Islamist radicals but also some extreme Christian groups and some close to the English Defence League". "And the political office from No 10?" I asked, but they chose to ignore that.

Anyway they are now insisting on much tougher security, more bods around the candidate, more protection at rallies and walkabouts, and, wait for it, "close protection" at the house in Mayberry and the flat in Putney. And I don't just mean a couple of guys having fags in the police car or standing under the lamplight, but a bloke indoors with the candidate, full-time. Aide will hate it.

I call up Angus and then Bo, who refuses any changes to the format for rallies or to give early sight of the 'grid', which he changes all the time anyway. And there'll be no stopping the 'up close and personal stuff', the walkabouts, the short stops in shopping malls, all that. I then phone Aide and ask, "How'd you like a third person in this marriage?" I explained about the live-in bodyguard and got the answer I expected, "No way…unless he's seriously hot".

HELEN

Looking back on that first week, the first breakthrough was the unforced error from the PM's side. Raising the gay issue was inevitable; it wasn't necessarily homophobic to ask whether the country would tolerate a gay PM. But what backfired totally was who was asking the question and why; the malice intended, the source and its inspiration were sufficient to make it a tipping point.

But by the end of the week, our greatest fear was loss of momentum. Yes, we had hundreds of volunteers, more every day, but they were nearly all from Russell Group universities, having a bit of fun before term started. And, yes, some cash was now coming in but not enough to pay for Bo Sampson's extravaganzas. And, yes, there were huge rallies but numbers were swollen by JoBoy Miles' storm troopers, the media hordes and the curious.

Raphael's own speeches seemed to be running out of rhetorical steam. Although Barrie and some of the others tried to feed him new lines, he kept going back to the comfort zone of his own punchlines and the old messages honed through years of practice.

And the real business - the collection of signatures - was painfully slow-going. By the end of the week, even after the 'gay issue' had run its course we were stuck at 35, with no idea where the higher numbers were going to come from.

Rupert Dennison, who has his dark side despite his winsome appeal, was the one who hit on something to raise the stakes. Just before a short press point on Friday, he corralled Angus and me in a corner and said, "We start placing commissars in key constituencies where we judge we might get extra signatures. They just go around the local party members saying, "people must have a choice", "let the membership decide". A little local intimidation from the grassroots, and some of the colleagues will start to crumble. And it gives them a let-out, 'I still support the Prime Minister but I believe Mr Sinclair has the right to his day in court.' So Angus went to the press and, skating over how slow was our advance, aired a new line, "It would be a democratic travesty if MPs conspired to deny party members a choice. Local party members should be balloted on whether they want the right to choose; and if their MPs don't get into line with the wishes of their constituents they should be deselected."

It was almost admirable the way that Angus refused to do anything by half measures. For the more spineless in the PLP, just months before re-selection procedures would be gearing up, alarm bells started to ring. By the end of the day 50 of the best of the kids were dispatched to the seats where with a bit of tender duress we could hope for a signature. To help them on their way, they had written instructions from Angus with lots of dos and don'ts, and lists of addresses and telephone numbers for each seat provided by Bo's father.

NED

I'm the nearest Bob has to a soulmate in High Command, apart from Paul who was still trekking around seats in the north to get a few more signatures. So it was me he rang on Friday night to tell me, "They've pulled Rafa". Roughly translated this means that the TUC general council, meeting on Friday night in Llandudno to put the finishing touches to the agenda for their conference, has decided by 18 votes to 15 to cancel the traditional 'fraternal greetings to conference from the chair of the Labour Party", who happens to be Rafa, and who was intending to make this the big pitch for the union vote and for support from the trade union group of MPs.

This sacred ritual, part of the liturgy for nearly a hundred years, sign of the unbreakable and immutable links between the two wings of Our Great Movement etc., etc. has quite simply been scrapped. Bob said that three cabinet ministers and some of the Downing Street satraps had been hitting the phones for days.

I brought the news to Angus, on one of his rare visits to Streatham, planning every detail of the trip to Scotland, "whose hand to shake, who to kiss (not blokes), what to eat, what to drink" as if Sinclair was on a visit to the Chrysanthemum Empire, and needed protocol tips. After all, he's called Sinclair so there's probably some Scottish blood there somewhere, poor bloke.

Anyway we then had a telecon thing with Rupe, Bob and the boss. Rupe was at his most psychopathic, "It's great, really. The line is first the MPs don't want you to have a choice; and now the Union barons want to stop you hearing him." He and Angus were all for street demos outside the hall and kids storming the doors, until Bob interrupted with a formidably quiet, "Don't be so fucking juvenile. These are professionals we're talking about. And they're not going to cave in to a few shouty Oxbridge kids. Come on! We work to overturn it from the inside."

"Tell us about the procedure, Bob"; at last Rafa said something.

"Well at the start of business on Monday morning any delegate can move 'reference back' for the agenda. Paul and I can make some calls. Hattie and Maudie will do the women's network in the union delegations. Delegates don't want to be in this dogfight, but they're pissed off with the government which has been stringing them along for 10 years, and they're nervous about anything symbolic which seems to cut the link. So on this you'll have the conservative vote, which, at the

TUC, is not something to be sneezed at." I've never heard Bob use such a long sentence.

Rupe came back with something about "a bit of street theatre", but Rafa cut him off with, "We'll do as Bob says".

But when Bob had rung off, Rafa said quietly to us, "But I think I'll go there, come what may, and I don't want to travel alone." He's a duplicitous bastard, but he's my duplicitous bastard.

BARRIE

He's exhausted, even if his tan is being topped up by this Indian summer during his outdoor stops. Hardly a drop of rain ever since France.

I can see his heart isn't always in this thing. All his speeches are still off the cuff, but he now occasionally misspeaks (unheard of), the syntax is often just odd, not even a semblance of structure, and the content is repetitive. Or is it just that I'm judging by different standards? The audiences seem to lap it up, he's still for them the great orator. One or two of Bo's more discerning flash mobbers who've been to most of his meetings will say, "he wasn't on form tonight", "I still don't get his economic policy", "and he's a bit too negative". Last night, at the big rally in Newcastle (the last stop before Scotland), he did some new stuff on the Constitution, the Lords, the Church, but it was not right for this audience, who wanted more on jobs, schools and hospitals.

In the really cheap and not very clean hotel on the outskirts of Carlisle (the only economy in this lavish campaign is on the candidate's accommodation) I finally had a few minutes alone with him in his room before the nightly call to Aidan (checking in or checking up?), who is confined to barracks this weekend, working on regional unions and a handful of local MPs. This seems to me a risky deployment given that Aidan, despite his new status as 'First Lover', remains a hate figure in the PLP.

I ask him what the matter is. He passes me his mobile, "well, check out my texts, in the past two days". In the last 24 hours, there are 3 messages from Aidan, perfunctory stuff, a couple of barks from Angus and 37 on a thread from an 'unknown' with a Belgian number; some in English, some in French, and two in Portuguese - all variations on the same theme, "Call me"; "call me or elese" (sic); "I hate you"; "you never loved me"; "I'm getting an HIV test tomorrow"; then as the day wears on the tone becomes more threatening, "I'm coming to you"; "I will have my own press conference"; and then, and these are the politer ones, "I kill that bastard"; "I kill that bastard and then I kill myself" (and me thinking, if only: the perfect scenario, Richards dead and the Portuguese falls on his sword).

"I keep thinking, he'll get over it. He'll find someone else easily enough. But it's getting worse. I don't know what to do. I've rung him a few times, but either he shouts Portuguese obscenities, or cries, or slams the phone down. I'm really scared what he might do to himself." (Sinclair shorthand for what he might do to him).

I resist the temptation to express my hope that he pass from talk to murderous action, coming over to apply some extreme prejudice on Aidan, but for once I'm stumped for words.

NED

On the phone all weekend to every friend and every TUC delegate I'd ever met or had a beer with in any bar or any pub in the last ten years. Paul and Bob have circulated us all with 'to be contacted' lists. Because the Supreme Being is now home in Scotland escorting Raphael, where it's all going well apparently but not meriting any press coverage in more civilised territories to the south, and being at a bit of a loose end, I phoned Aide.

"Hi, I'm here with my new best mate, Bud, we've been for our run, had our showers and now we're having a couple of beers before I get tucked up in bed", was his description of his evening with 'Bud', the new live-in 'body' for the chief. But if the great white hope was in Scotland, why was his lifeguard in the cosy little Mayberry house? "Oh he's just getting used to the lie of the land, debugging us, securing windows, locks etc. But if you see your friend, Inspector Doings, tell him if he's got more lads like Bud in his stable, bring 'em on." How's he hitting it off with Rafa? "Oh", he says, "they've not met yet. He's the big surprise when the conqueror returns on Monday night."

HELEN

The Monday of the second week of Raphael's campaign was another important moment. At 9.30 a.m. on the dot, "the shrivelled old crone" (Rupert Dennison's description) from the shop-workers' union who I'd had to endure for three years on the NEC and who was a lobotomised supporter of the PM began to bang the gavel and call the conference to order. She moved the agenda be adopted. There was some shouting and Bob, nimbler on his feet than one might have imagined from his girth, almost sprinted to the rostrum. He moved the 'reference back' of the agenda[34], saying that whatever the reasons, stopping the chair of the party from addressing conference was like cutting the historic link, that Raphael had the right to be heard, and that delegates were grown up enough to make up their own minds. There was a storm of applause from delegates and from a suspiciously young crowd who packed the galleries. After a bit of procedural wrangling and some unhelpful remarks from my friend in the chair, the reference back was carried by a show of hands, and Raphael was back on the bill in the traditional slot for Wednesday afternoon.

---

[34] A procedure at the Trades Union Congress whereby conference delegates instruct the Executive to reconsider its proposals

BARRIE

We got the news as we were travelling south to a big end-of-afternoon open-air rally in front of the large cinema museum in Bradford. Bob telephoned in and interrupts Raphael's excessively gushing thanks with a sharp, "I want to go through your speech with you. I want to hear the specific commitments you're going to make, and to help me, pass me to Barrie so I can tell him what you need to say. We don't want another performance, we want some commitments. And something else: I don't want to see any more of your throwbacks from Brideshead in our galleries. When I saw them there this morning I nearly let the agenda go through on the nod. We agreed no outside pressure. This isn't the Labour Party here, we don't play your silly little party games. Don't fuck with us, Raphael."

Before he mounts the steps in front of the J.B. Priestley statue, all bronze, coat-flapping, with pipe firmly set against the wind, Bill rang in to say we've reached 38, 'half-way there, with two of the three getting jittery about the deselection threat. And a union groupie we'd lost yesterday is now back on board."

After the rally, which really went well, eight hundred, mostly Pakistani, with Rashida doing the warm-up, Raphael took a call from Aidan, and said nothing for a few minutes afterwards, after which he mused, "It appears our efficient security services have provided us with a live-in bodyguard for the duration; or as Aidan says, 'a ready-made ménage à trois'. Aidan describes him as 'perfectly presentable'."

My heart slumped a few rungs lower.

HELEN

At Monday's rally in Leeds, buoyed up by the news from Llandudno[35], Raphael seemed at last to have got his act together. His economic message was broadened out to "there's no contradiction between financial responsibility and economic growth". And he started on what sounded like the beginning of a plan. And then for the first time in the campaign he used Angus's "five-point plan to bring the money home" and made the centrepiece of the speech the tax evasion issue, including some quite credibly complicated stuff on corporate tax, with brilliant examples of eye-watering fraud and a 'blacklist' of tax havens, and the companies that used them, including the mention of a few company directors who had had New Labour honours bestowed on them. And he rounded off with some good populist stuff about tax evasion dwarfing social security fraud, "both indefensible but there's a question of degree". The largely Labour audience packed into Leeds town hall lapped it all up.

I had hoped for a chat when we went back to a crummy low-cost hotel on the outskirts of the city, but he pleaded 'a slew of messages' and 'prep' for the TUC speech on Wednesday. Bob had sent him a stack of notes which were completely incomprehensible. "He's an impressive guy, but essentially illiterate" was his judgment. And he seemed distracted in the car as he fiddled clumsily with his new smart phone.

---

[35] That allies of Raphael had successfully overturned an attempt – instigated by the Prime Minister's team – to prevent him from addressing the TUC Conference in Llandudno in his capacity as chair of the Labour Party

NED

Crept up to 40 names on Tuesday and I'd finally got a date with Lizzie from the Streatham office, an embonpoint capable of stopping the traffic, not the best complexion I've ever seen and those glasses don't do her justice, but I've never been one to obsess on looks, and all I ask is the same indulgence. But then at the last minute the Laird summoned me to Boston (Lincolnshire, not New England, worse luck!) to do the warm-up for the boss. Great crowd, and Rafa in good form, although complaining of backache from all those hours stuck in the back of Eddie's old Fiesta. He covered health (doctors' hours, creeping privatisation) and schools (stop the tax concessions for public schools, and more resources for kids from deprived areas).

But as the Labour people start to love him as the new People's hero, the press is really out for him now, with headlines about 'Labour heading redwards', but it's a kind of game. They play up his left-wing pitch to frighten voters to the Tories and because they really want him to win because we'd be a lot more colourful and newsworthy than this lot. And within the party the red label doesn't do Rafa any harm after all these years of careful, disciplined positioning in the safe centre. Our people want to live a little. Nigel's managed to get a good piece in the Independent and the Times along the lines of 'Now it's getting serious'.

I saw this Bud for the first time tonight. Shortish, stocky, very fit I'd imagine, with this blondish crew-cut and really kind blue eyes. And very respectful too, kept calling me Mr Warren and 'sir' before I told him to chuck it. Aide says Rafa's quite taken with him.

BARRIE

Yesterday time seemed to hang heavy. We arrived in Llandudno early in the morning, having stopped at a motel outside Crewe with nylon sheets on our beds. Between quite sharp showers, Raphael insists on going for a walk "to stretch a bit, and get some air", now trailed by his head bodyguard, called Bud. Seems a nice kid, a bit shy, very discreet, and pretty muscly I'd judge from the way his white shirt hugged his top. He's always alert, which is just as well, but there's a reflective look in his beautiful blue eyes. About 26 or 27 I'd say. Not my type but I could imagine that some would find him hot as hell.

But not I think the candidate, who was just focused on the speech, which is a bit make-or-break. Bob joins us for breakfast (limp white toast, one rasher of cold greasy bacon, an egg fried for the first time last week and refried daily since, and a brown lukewarm liquid resembling neither coffee nor tea - and I thought being in Europe was meant to change all that), having skipped the morning session for last-minute prep. We go through my draft, which has become Raphael's jottings, and get some blistering criticisms from Bob. "Give them some of the commitments they want, but don't overdo it or they won't believe you. No razzamatazz, and keep any of your camp followers (no pun intended) quiet in the galleries."

The drive to Llandudno was quite short and we had time for snacks in Bob's hotel room (much nicer than the ones we stay in but nothing's too good for the workers' representatives!) so that Raphael can do quick meet-and-greets with some of the union bosses, each getting 15 minutes on their own. It was mostly Raphael listening, taking notes, and being respectfully cagey about making too many promises apart from being always "ready for dialogue". He did have a good line about being the candidate for "the unity of the whole movement" but mostly just kept probing their arguments.

We entered the hall by a back entrance (orders of the hostile chair, "to avoid any fuss"). As he walked to the stage at 2 p.m. the Sister was calling the delegates to order, but without any enthusiasm, she'd have been happy enough if they had continued chatting throughout his speech. Raphael was doing humble, his suit not too smart, the tie nondescript (all the Portuguese effect now absent), a pale blue shirt, nothing too flash, no concessions to trendiness.

He started well, welcoming the decision to reaffirm the link with Labour which he valued so strongly and which these fraternal greetings typified.

Then it was straight to the point, "As you know I'm running my campaign but today I come before you as representative of the whole Labour Party. So those of you expecting me to criticise the government of the leader of the party will be disappointed." (A new riff on 'I've come to bury Caesar not to praise him').

He continued with the litany of all the things that Labour and the Unions had done together and which should be celebrated ("Put a wedge between us and we suffer; unite and we can change Britain. Together we built the NHS, state education, safety at work, decent pensions, workplace rights and the minimum wage" – this got the first applause).

"And together we can create growth, full employment, modern public services and responsible banking and make the living wage the new national minimum."

You could tell they were beginning to like what they were hearing.

Then he spells out five quite specific ideas on industrial policy, employment, incentives for youth employment and training, an investment bank, "fully guaranteed by government" and "trade based on reciprocity, ILO standards and respect for human rights". He'd now got their full attention.

Until that point it had been solid, delivered with authority, but lacking the usual Sinclair pyrotechnics. The hatchet-faced bag in the chair was looking ostentatiously at her watch, itching to bang the gavel. It just needed a little something extra. At last it came, as he turned to her, with the full Sinclair glare,

"Madam Chair, allow me to say a few words about us, the Labour people. Of course everyone - party, government, the unions - has their own roles to play. But this must always be with respect. Let's be frank. At times Labour in power has treated the unions like an embarrassing old aunt in the corner, sipping tea and nodding off. At times we've seemed almost careless about our common mission as if the relationship is past its time."

By now they were almost willing him on, as his voice started its steady surefooted rise up the oratorical mountain.

"Our advisers tell us if you want power you must distance yourselves from the unions. We must deregulate. We must chip away at workplace rights. We should let the private sector into our public services, one step at a time, but now swarming all over them like locusts. We must stop talking about equality. The words 'social justice' must be banished from our lexicon".

The pause, and then full throttle, "I say something else. I say it's time the Labour Movement got off its knees. I say it's time we stopped apologising for who are, for what we believe, for what we stand."

By now most of the delegates were doing just that, they were standing, and the cheering was beginning to compete with the peroration. The galleries of course were going berserk.

Almost superfluously, he shouted above the tumult, "I say it's time to stand up for our Labour values, our Labour principles, for equality, for social justice, for the betterment of our people and the indissoluble community of our beliefs."

An ovation like I've never heard or seen before. Bob whispered to me, "That's the greatest speech I ever 'eard." Some of the old lags were in tears. The stomping, the shouting and the clapping see us out of the hall, unaccompanied by the graceless old hag in the chair, who alone stayed put and banged her gavel as if her life depended on it.

NED

We watched it on the web stream in Streatham, Bo and about 20 of us. It was all low key to begin with, Rafa seeming matter of fact, almost offhand, and then he begins to soar, and soar, and soar. By the end we're all standing, cheering and hugging (particularly me and three of the girls, although only one seemed not in a hurry to end the proximity). And within 15 minutes of it being over Bo and two of the girls had uploaded the best clips on to YouTube, the website and Facebook. The bits with "It's time to get off our knees" got the most hits of the week, nearly a million in two days.

And then came a massive spike in the number of his followers, 140,000 plus and with it, at last, some serious money.

EXTRACT FROM BBC1'S 6 p.m. NEWS EDITION,

first item

Mr Raphael Sinclair, candidate for the Labour leadership, won a standing ovation today with an uncompromising defence of Labour's links with the trades unions…. (Extracts from the speech)

And now over to our political editor in Llandudno.

"This may have been the turning point; the day when 'the children's crusade,' as Downing Street insiders have dubbed it, came of age and a serious challenge to the Prime Minister.

"Trade Union conferences are usually pretty staid affairs. Today this one was different. Old TUC hands I talked to can't remember an occasion like it. The climax with the phrase, "It's time this movement got off its knees" could be the game-changing moment in a campaign which has now set alight both the industrial and the political wings of the Labour Movement."

HELEN

I chaired the meeting in Watford for Raphael the day after his triumph at the TUC. The crowds vastly exceeded the numbers expected, the atmosphere was lively to the point of being almost raucous, and as we walked to the door of the hall from Eddie's[36] car he was literally mobbed, with some people just grabbing at his hair and his jacket. His new minder, a nice young man called Bud[37], polite and level-headed, seemed very sensible, not heavy-handed, only intervening when someone tried to relieve Raphael of his rather smart watch.

In the car afterwards, I asked Raphael about Llandudno. He said, "I knew I could do it. Just coming into the hall, I said to myself, 'Now you really perform.' Bob did a great job to prepare me but in the end I tore up his rulebook and just trusted my own judgment."

He was almost preening, so I brought him down to earth with a little reminder that he had always been scornful about 'the special link' between us and the unions.

"Of course it isn't healthy but you've got to sort out party financing before you can break the link for good."

Even I was taken aback with this breath-taking cynicism. But it was great to see him on form, except that his back was obviously giving him some pain.

---

[36] Eddie Smith, a retired trade union official who used to drive Raphael in election campaigns and who had volunteered for the Insurgency

[37] The police had insisted on giving Raphael protection as a result of the number of death threats being received. Bud Mitchell was head of the team.

BARRIE

We made an early start from the flat in Putney. When I call to pick up the candidate, Aidan is wheedling the bodyguard to make some more tea and toast, which I would have thought was not in the job description but about which this nice kid makes no complaints, indeed he seems to relish his housekeeping duties.

Later when we were alone, I asked Raphael if it was embarrassing to be making love with Aidan when the minder was in the next room; an intrusive question but the sort of thing which I know that Raphael loves answering.

"Well I tell Aidan to keep the noise down a bit, which of course just encourages him to up the decibels."

As we arrive at the first of four stops in South London high streets, before the big rally, we get another episode of 'The Inspector Calls'. "How was it working out with the new bodyguard?" More concerns about the shambolic, rowdy walkabouts, the absence of any controls on who attends the rallies. Raphael was curt but polite and said firmly that he would accept no further constraints on his activities. They handed him a beige folder which they said was for his eyes only. He then ostentatiously handed it to me, defying them to query it, which of course they didn't.

While he was doing Lewisham market, lost in a scrum, I sat in the back of the car and read it. Pretty lurid stuff; each threat registered, and then a second column, clues as to provenance. Pages and pages of the stuff. What struck me was the sheer diversity of the potential sources: anti-gay; islamist militants; extreme right, all threatening but seemingly small groups acting alone; although one spin-off with links to the old National Front might have some neocon finance from nutty Californian sources.

They are proposing some extra security around the house in Mayberry and outside the flat in Putney; in the grounds of the OAP home where his parents now live; and doubling up security at every rally and appearance. The final requests were that secrecy about venues for walkabouts be increased and that the Streatham operation be tightened up.

We talked it over before we get to Southwark High Street, the second stop, and he gave the go-ahead to most of this. "When Maudie resigns, get her to take over the shop at Streatham, and take Ned out of the operation. Get him on the road. Whatever his qualities, running a tight disciplined ship sure ain't one of them. And I hear he's becoming a bit of a groper.

"Oh, and you might tell Nigel to leak a bit about the death threats; you know, "first they wanted to silence him - now they're changing tack." Even Nigel baulks at this for a while, but one or two stories do start to appear, or are they from Rupert's operation?

NED

My first press conference, but kept on a tight leash by Angus. I got to read out some of the numbers: registered supporters, new party members, cash flowing in, campaign team, twitter followers (huge since Rupe took it over, which he does, just adding what he feels like - I don't think Rafa even knows what Twitter is) and Facebook friends. All this was good but all the hacks wanted to know was the number of MPs who'd signed.

Angus just said, "We're expecting fifty by the weekend", which was a bit of a let-down, particularly after Bob and Paul had signed up three of the general secretaries albeit of the second tier unions. I thought we might at least have got a few of their sponsored MPs.

Afterwards he said to me he's deliberately playing down the numbers. "I'm not lying," he said defensively, "it's just we're calculating it differently. It's signatures actually received by Bill that count now. We seem to lose a tiny bit of momentum today to pick up more tomorrow."

With the journalists, Rupe goes completely overboard about the PLP, "They're still trying to deny the party a choice although their constituency parties are all signing up for Raphael Sinclair."

When I got home on Friday night, I had a message (not an everyday occurrence for 'Ned no-mates'). "Would Mr Warren please ring back the Secretary of State on this number?" It was some hoity-toity bird from the office of His Lordship, you know the one they brought back and I always call Lord Snake. So I ring, and it's,

'Hello, Edward, it's so good of you to ring back. We're really impressed with the campaign you're fighting. You've been noted, you know. Why, the Prime Minister himself said to me just the other day how impressed he was with your, er, performances. He'd like you to join the government when all this is over. Why don't we meet up for a cup of tea early next week so we can have a quiet little word about your future? The PM's not cross about your campaign, thinks the party needed shaking up a bit, but we know that sometime soon, the whistle goes and school-break is over. So it's time to think about getting back on board. My office will be back in touch on Monday.

"Goodbye, Edward, and have a lovely weekend."

I committed all this to memory, then rang up Aide, and then Rupe; did great impressions. LOL.

By the way they're pulling me out of Streatham. From Sunday it's Maudie who'll bring her own brand of the Reign of Terror to the office. Angus and Rafa think she should put some stick about. It's not, absolutely not, because of any 'inappropriate behaviour' on my part despite Aide's suggestion. So from Monday it's the Ned Warren roadshow, should be good for my own campaign to get on the NEC.

HELEN

It was Angus Buchanan who decided when we should start pulling out 'our' ministers. He went for the Saturday, a week before Conference, to make the splash in the Sundays, to buck us up a bit for the last few days, and to present the picture of the PM's camp as crumbling at the edges.

It was also Angus who decided that Saturday was the time to give Aidan Richards his first 'outing' at a press conference, hoping that the news about the defections and the extra signatures would deflect excessive prurient attention away from the personification of the sex life of the candidate. So the three of us took to the stage but of course all the hundreds of cameras were trained on Aidan, who had inevitably prepared himself meticulously for the occasion: the hair a bit shorter, swept back neatly, the stubble trimmed to the right length, the crystalline white shirt and a thin tangerine tie, and a smart tight-fitting Paul Smith black suit. And he smiled, not snarled; and when he smiled and his eyes softened, even moistened a little, I suddenly realised what Raphael saw in him.

The camera loves him. He did not need to say anything and indeed on this occasion was silent until the very end.

Angus then announced the seven ministers who had defected and who came in as their names were announced, in a 'come on down' routine; they were all absolute unknowns[38] except for Hattie Reynolds and Maudie Hinton, who had at least appeared on 'Question Time' and some other shows on and off and who were called on last.

Everybody could do the sums. We had reached around 56 or 57, with a week to go. I made the point that we had deliberately not approached cabinet ministers because we did not want the government falling apart. But the Times man asked the question which was to dog us all week.

"Given what cabinet ministers have all said, it doesn't look as though you're going to get the support of a single cabinet minister. So if Sinclair wins, how does he form a government?"

---

[38] The five others, all Ministers of State, were Sylvia Jones, MP for Workington; Matthew Hardacre, MP for West Norwood; Chris Harris, MP for Mansfield East; Jean Williams, MP for Aberdare and East Merthyr; and Ahmed Fazari, PM for Colchester Outer.

Angus snapped back, "It wouldn't be the first time that a Prime Minister brings into government those who weren't his most ardent supporters."

The journalist, a smooth young man with rather attractively greying hair in contrast to his boyish face, continued, "But how big a clean-out will he make?"

I said, "He wants the most competent people possible. And a broad church. He relishes debate but he'll expect people to rally round his programme."

He did not give up, "But that means he can forget the whole present cabinet, who disagree with him on practically everything. So there'll be quite a few novices at the table, won't there? In an economic crisis."

Angus was emphatic in his attempt to close this line down, "In this party, we're all democrats. We will all unite to deliver what the party membership has decided."

It was almost a relief when the tabloids moved on to the comparatively safer terrain, questioning Aidan about his sex life with the candidate. "How long had he known Raphael?" "What was all this media attention doing to their relationship?" "If Sinclair becomes PM, would he be a consort, and accompany him on official visits?"

I admit that Aidan answered all the questions with a kind of resigned charm, like a Hollywood celebrity answering the umpteenth question about a new squeeze.

BARRIE

The Sunday papers are all over the place. "Government Wobbles as the Insurgency Forges Ahead"; "PM's Support Collapsing"; and in the Observer, "Now Jamieson is the Frontrunner", accompanied by a long interview with the Foreign Secretary in which he manages to convey the tepidest support for the PM alongside hints of a personal programme if his boss falters.

The same paper has a big profile of Angus, "The Campaign Mastermind", from "world-class economist to running the Insurgency". In the colour supplement there's five pages on "Sinclair's Insurgents" with lots of photos, particularly of the 'Glamour Group', Rashida, Angus, Louise, Rupert and 'the leader's partner', all looking pretty fabulous. There's a great photo of Ned, his shirt flapping over his trousers like a fourth-former, in full spate at a rally; Harriet in a bar looking as though she'd been there for some time; and Maudie ('the office manageress') apparently about to bite someone's head off, literally.

The back-room team barely gets mentioned. Elaine and Nigel at least get photos ('The TV star' and 'The diplomat'). Marjorie ('the gatekeeper'), Bo ('the road manager') and I ('bag carrier, eminence grise, close confidant) all figure in a diagram with Raphael at the centre, but without photos.

I'm a bit miffed, but as Digby points out, "This way at least you won't get stalked, or start receiving obscene suggestions."

All the papers relish the 'Labour at War' stuff, "The Last days for the PM", "Labour's New Tax Threat", "Labour abandons the centre ground", "Return of Red Labour", and that's just a small selection.

At last Digby and I turn to the Mail on Sunday and the attack I've been fearing throughout. Of course they go big on Aidan, the Facebook page, some ten anonymous quotes from previous pick-ups, all under the banner heading, "Britain's Next First Partner?", sub-headed, "Labour chiefs warned about the Aidan Richards problem". Bad, but not catastrophic. I phone Nigel at about 10 to ask why it's not worse, "Oh, I think it's obvious. They all think he's going to get the leadership which is what they really want because what we offer them is good copy - daily thrills and spills - and then they'll try to smash us at the election."

But he points out something I'd missed, a smaller piece in the Express about "Team Sinclair worried about Sex Revelations", referring to past lovers, the French academic, the Italian, the Greek, and a Brazilian. But they'd got none to make a comment. And no mention of the Portuguese, which strikes me as odd.

As we head off for a Sunday tour of the Medway towns, with five rallies in five hours, I ask him if he's still getting the texts.

"No, not a peep for several days now. He must have got over it" - a piece of shattering Sinclair wishful thinking (but how typical!).

NED

I do the warm-ups in all the Medway rallies and, if I may say so, with all due modesty, they love me. They practically have to yank me off stage I'm enjoying it so much. Rafa's really at ease now, almost playing with the crowds, but still word perfect on the economy stuff, having mugged up on the economies of each town we visit, knowing which local industries to promote and which had suffered from the banks. And then each time, the big theme stuff at the end: today - banks, tax evasion, inequalities (great vivid stuff on health inequalities), the end of macho politics, the need for older and younger women in politics, and his showstopper, the war.

Now we're in our stride we don't really need the flash mobs any more, not that that stops them from coming. I missed the big Bristol rally last night but Bo says there were ten thousand, with big screens outside the venues. At each of our Medway stops there are overspills.

Mind you we need better crowd control. Someone bit my hand at the entrance at Gravesend. And people have started to want to have a bit of Rafa. His watch went at Rochester, one cufflink in Gillingham, two shirt buttons in Dartford, and in Chatham, his whole jacket sleeve. I hope that suit didn't cost much. So he did the speech in his shirt sleeves, and with a tear in one of those. Great pics of course and he loves all the jostling and excitement. The journos have never seen anything like it outside football matches and pop concerts.

But it's tough for the security guys, and Bud was looking seriously worried at the Chatham stop. And it's not all exuberant supporters: there's quite a bit of jostling at the back of the rallies and some EDL louts shouting, "No Pooftahs here" or some racist stuff. But it's small beer so far.

Bo's gone off his head. He presents the final week's programme to the boss first, and then to Rafa (cos that's how it is these days), and then pretends to both of them separately that the other has approved it. Cunning little bastard, always with that slightly vacant innocent smile. Anyway it's big rallies for the last five nights; ending up with the monster, the Wembley Arena (capacity a mere 12,000) and then a big party on Brighton beach at the weekend, the day before Conference begins on Sunday afternoon.

Love it, love it, love it. But dreading what all this costs.

HELEN

We rode the crest of the wave at the beginning of the third week. Bigger and bigger crowds; some of the MPs were even forced to recant by angry local parties who made them sign Raphael's nomination in public: the 'Commissars' dispatched to the regions by Team Sinclair had done their job.

But already the media had started to move on. Because they now all assumed Raphael would get the signatures they had started to write the script for the different hypotheses. First, there would be a three-month slugfest with both men fighting each other to a standstill, and both in competitive bidding with the supporters of the former Prime Minister. Scenario 2 was precisely the entry of Derek Jamieson, the Foreign Secretary, into the race - the prince over the water, the successor anointed by the previous regime. Of course this was the possibility we most feared because it offered a real generation leap. And in him the party would have got someone who communicated better without ditching all the New Labour legacy. In any hustings, Raphael could see off the PM. Derek would be a tougher proposition. Rupert Dennison believed in scenario three, what he called "the quick kill", but, at this stage, he did not spell it out because we would all have dismissed it as fantasy.

BARRIE

We've reached 70 this morning, with three days to go before Brighton. All the indicators look great, and the money's pouring in. I told Digby we might not have to sell up after all! Just as we were about to leave the house in Mayberry for the start of the East Anglia leg (Norwich, Ipswich, Cambridge, and two more market towns) Raphael held me back and said, "You're not coming out to play today. I want you to do a bit of work for me. Start thinking about the week of Conference and the first weeks after."

"Well, Angus and Bo have got all that in hand, I think. You know, the hustings, the itinerary...," I said.

"But", he cut me short, "supposing, just supposing it is scenario 3. We get it by default next week." There was a pause, and he continued, "I know it's the least likely but technically it's possible. Suddenly, maybe even a week from today, we're in Downing Street. Then what the fuck do we do? Oh, and then just one last thing. A question, purely hypothetical, mind you. What's the minimum time between dissolution and elections? Is it three full weeks? Three weeks plus one day? Or really four weeks?"

I felt a bit shivery when he left the room.

NED

The sound of wheels falling off. Aide rings up. Rupe says a paper's located the Portuguese kid and he's ready to talk; and they're gonna pay for him to come over to Brighton, to piss on our parade.

I spoke before my brain kicked in, "But didn't Rafa tell him?"

"What do you mean?"

"But...", I was so flustered because I'd never told him about overhearing Rafa's call the day we left the cottage in France.

"You mean he never broke it off? He never told him? The kid learns about it on Portuguese TV?" Aide's voice mounting an octave as it all dawns on him what he's discovering.

I just whistle, and say, "Fucking Hell'.

"The scumbag (a reference to our revered candidate) is on his way back here (the Putney flat) now. Hold on to your hats..." evil relish emphasising each syllable.

BARRIE

It just defies belief. We got back to Putney at midnight, two more rallies under his belt, one in Hackney, one in the Hammersmith Palace, both packed - Harriet does great warm-ups, and Rashida's just so professional. He was all buoyed up, the standard stump speech, but a little extra each time. At the first rally, and for the first time, he spelt out the wealth tax proposal. At the second, a ten-point plan, on growth, apprenticeships, research, easing planning restrictions on green investment, pretty standard wonkish stuff, but in his mouth almost poetic. Fresh, radical.

And then, unexpectedly, a new punch line, "I need your help" (three times, with growing volume each time). "Come with me to Portsmouth and Southampton tomorrow. Come with me to Wembley on Friday night for the biggest political rally in a hundred years. Then come with me to Brighton, to the big beach party, Saturday night, and stay through Sunday when we change Labour and Britain forever."

In the car he was on a high, looking forward to a nightcap, while all I wanted was the tiny small bed in the spare room, and I really was just a little dreading being greeted by Aidan, who makes me feel about as welcome as a large verruca.

When we arrived, there was more security than ever, and this time police with flashing lights. Bud's sidekick, Kev, all pink and big ears and gauche, stepped forward and whispered to Bud, who came out to meet us and said, "I'm afraid we've had a bit of a situation here, sir. A woman turned up with a young foreign gentleman demanding to speak to you. He looked at his notes, and continued, "She said, he'll want to speak to me when he hears what I have to say. And there's this video camera filming us. And the young foreign gentleman seems very upset. Anyway I ring Mr Aidan who comes down, speaks to the woman, and then turns to the foreigner, says something to him in French, and then he takes the other gentleman upstairs, and tells us to "fling this fucking old hag off our lawn, or do her for trespass." She tries to slap him, so we lead her away. It gets a bit out of hand, and the cameraman intervenes, and his camera gets smashed while we stop him from seeking to enter the building." He allowed himself just a flickering grin at this somewhat varnished tale of security thuggery.

"Any case they get escorted away, cautioned, and we've cordoned off the place."

Even Raphael's pooterish buoyancy was deflated by this. He suddenly aged, as if all the accumulated fatigue of the past few weeks had caught up with him. And I could see that his back was playing up, as if the pain was triggered by the tension of the moment. We walked up the two flights, Bud walking ahead of us. As we entered the flat I saw a very smart crimson hold-all in the hallway I didn't recognise.

We walked into the living room, the nice ostrich feather pattern curtains from Liberty's which I helped choose with Helen, all drawn; only a couple of lamps on. In the left corner, as it were, Aidan, white with suppressed fury. In the right, this beautiful but small boy, with very short dark hair, stubble, wearing a light beige jumper, black trousers, and very smart black leather shoes. He has the most beautiful expressive black eyes but they were now reddened with tears still falling intermittently, long dark eyelashes, and - the giveaway - very full, sensuous lips.

"Hello, Jose, how are you?" asks Raphael with a kind of 1930s drawing-room comedy heartiness.

"Let me introduce you. You've met Aidan, I think. And this is Barrie Jones who runs my office, and Bud who makes sure that no-one takes a pot-shot at me. It's great to see you."

This was too much for both young men. Jose started blubbing noisily, and Aidan let rip.

"I really don't believe you, Rafs. You never tell this poor bastard, and now you walk in like some throwback from a Noel Coward play. In a moment you'll get him (pointing at me, he hardly ever uses my name) to 'make us a lovely cuppa'."

By now Jose was weeping and emitting keening noises like a recently bereaved widow at a Levantine funeral.

I decided to take Bud out to the kitchen, indeed to make some tea but also to give the threesome a few minutes on their own. After he had filled the kettle, obviously now quite used to doing the household chores, he said, quite acutely, "I think Aidan (no longer 'Mr Aidan' I note) made the right decision to get him up here and get rid of the journalist. Best if I sleep in the car tonight, I think."

"Or I could go back to my place. My partner hasn't seen me for days."

"No," he said, surprisingly firmly, "better if you stay here to calm things down a bit."

When we went back to the living room, the tableau had hardly shifted, although Raphael told me later, "You missed a few moments of high melodrama, what with Jose's recriminations, "you are not a Christian", which is true enough, but nor's he. And then we had the threats; "If I have HIV I take you to court"; "I am selling my story"; "I will follow you everywhere. I come to your meetings and I stand up and shout, 'He cheats on me and he'll cheat on you'". The best bit was when he said of Aidan, "He's kind. Not like you. You're cruel. You use people and then throw them away.'"

Maybe it was just the fatigue but by the time we'd had a second cup Jose had subsided and I tried a new gambit and ask him, "How's the campaign being seen in Brussels?" He seemed to snap out of it and for five minutes gave us a perfectly lucid account of the interest we'd generated, how the continental media had written us off at first but how we'd now become the big story, and then how all his friends wanted us to win. "But not me. I hope you lose. You are a bad man."

Raphael finally spoke, and I felt too embarrassed to be present but couldn't think of an excuse to leave the room. He got up off the sofa which we'd been sharing, goes to the hard-backed seat where Jose-Miguel was sitting, went down on his knees in front of him, put both hands on the boy's calves, looked him in the eye and said, "Look, Jose, I love you very much. You changed my life for good," he started to stroke the boy's face as the tears welled up again, "But I knew Aidan a long time before we met. He was my first real love. And I'm sorry. I've behaved really badly. I want you to forgive me. I still love you deeply. I want you and me to stay this close to each other and forever. I'd like you to be here for me during the campaign… ."

This low theatre went on for another five minutes, with reminiscences about playing golf together and Madame's fish soup at the hotel thrown in. Pretty abject but it seemed to calm down the boy, now reduced to just a deep sulk. I didn't dare look at Aidan while his partner continued to make such a spectacle of himself, quite impervious to any sense of dignity and self-respect.

Then suddenly Raphael got to his feet and said in a tone as if, "problem done and dusted", "Sleeping arrangements. Jose, could you bed down in here, because Barrie's already occupying the spare room? Bud, our bodyguard's been sleeping on the sofa during the campaign and says it's quite comfy. I'll go and get some bed-linen. We'll talk more in the morning and, Jose, I mean it. I'd love you to be at my side for the rest of the campaign."

At this point, Aidan shot out of his chair and said, "Excuse me a moment while I go and throw up."

But in the end the three of us made up the living room sofa bed and I got everyone a glass of water for the bedsides, and we all went to our rooms.

In the middle of the night, there was clearly an incident and I heard voices and doors opening and shutting. Rafael told me about it while he and I were having toast made of course by Bud, Aidan having left the house early with an ominous farewell shot, "We talk later, a serious talk and alone". The boy didn't appear at the table.

"Aidan of course refused any talk or anything else last night. Then at 3 in the morning, suddenly Jose's in our room, saying, 'I'm cold, the bed's hard and I'm lonely,' Aidan just turns over, and for one awful moment I'm on the verge of making space for him and saying, 'OK but just to sleep,' but for once in my life I do the sensible thing, get out of bed, find him an extra blanket, take his hand to lead him back to the sofa, hold him for a few minutes, kiss him just briefly, then return to bed."

All of this in front of Bud who carries on doing the washing up! I despair about Raphael! His immaturity and narcissism is going to bring us all down, it's just all so egocentric.

I then got another anecdote about the morning's ablutions. "I'd just taken my shower and was brushing my teeth while Aidan's in the shower. Just as he steps out and I'm drying Aidan's back, in walks Jose, without knocking, and just walks into the shower as if we're not there."

I went to the office early to get the news digest from Nigel, and of course The Express led with its aborted scoop, "Message to Love Rat Sinclair; I'm coming after you". There was a shot of the melee outside the front door of the Putney block, but the journalist had piled mistake on mistake. She had banked no quotes before she accompanied Jose to the flat, didn't get good quality shots because the main camera got smashed, and was completely wrong-footed by Aidan inviting the boy in.

So the paper gave more attention to the police roughing her up than to the story she was meant to cover.

Rupert and Nigel spent all morning trying to damp down interest in the story but it was Angus who held the key to killing it.

BBC TV NEWSFLASH 12.30 p.m.

Raphael Sinclair is now an official candidate for the leadership of the Labour Party. His campaign manager, Mr Angus Buchanan, has just made the following announcement outside the Sinclair headquarters in Streatham, "At just before midday this morning, Mr Sinclair got the 76th signature from a Labour MP on his nomination papers. He is now the official candidate to give new leadership to Labour and to Britain."

Our political editor is in Downing Street.

"Well, he's done it against all the odds. Labour's rules requiring the signature of 75 MPs to trigger a contest when the party's in power make challenging a sitting PM almost impossible. But in reaching the magic figure the challenger gets real momentum.

Now that we know there will be a race, the question becomes, who else will join in? Attention is focusing on the Foreign Secretary, Derek Jamieson, who has many admirers in government but whose loyalty to the former Prime Minister may be held against him. Or there's the more emollient figure of Mr Brian Dawkins, the Home Secretary, described to me as "the man with no enemies" or the Deputy Leader, Marsha Worthington, champion of women's issues.

But the man sitting in an office in the building behind me has been likened to former US President, Richard Nixon, who was famously "not a quitter". One of those closest to him said to me just ten minutes ago, "Look, Raphael Sinclair's trumped all the other potential candidates. His people will trash any johnnie-come-lately runners. But we all know he can't win. The PM has solid backing in the cabinet, most of the union leadership and most MPs. To Mr Sinclair the hoopla, the roar of the crowd, the smell of the greasepaint. To us, the victory."

"Well, maybe. But the Sinclair bandwagon continues to roll. Tonight it's two more huge rallies in North and East London. And then tomorrow, the big gamble - can a British politician fill the Wembley Arena and make it the biggest political meeting in a hundred years? And then the wagons roll to Brighton for more events and stunts to prove his appeal to a younger generation generally so turned off politics.

"So as of midday today at any rate, Mr Sinclair is the one to beat."

NED

Spent two hours trying to calm Aide down and stop him from doing something stupid. It's all "revenge"; "I'll make him suffer"; "...and if I just walk out, he'll be dead in the water. So much for 'Rafa4PM'"; (Bo's campaign button we have to wear all the time) "toast". "You should have seen him on his knees in front of the kid, it was such ham, 'Forgive me. I want to be friends. I never want to hurt you', like a Donald Sirk script only more melodramatic with lousy acting. As the abasement sank lower, I almost felt sorry for him. Almost.

"And as for you, you little fat fucker, why didn't you tell me he hadn't broken it off? I'd have gone to Brussels myself."

I made a pathetic attempt to defend myself, "But he promised me."

"And you believed him? And then the kid comes into our bedroom obviously in search of consolation. Actually, he's a really sweet kid, completely out of his depth. He's got these fantastically dark wide innocent eyes, and looks as though he's permanently about to burst into tears. And a really hot little body..."

He stops suddenly, smirks a moment, and I think, "Oh dear."

HELEN

The last stretch before Conference got off to a rough start with the story of 'the ex' pitching up in all the papers. I was cross with myself for not checking up whether Raphael had had the elementary decency to end it all cleanly with this Portuguese boy. So typical of men; anything to avoid a confrontation. If it had not been for Angus's announcement that we had hit our target, we would have been knocked sideways.

On his way to the first of the big rallies on Thursday he picked me up and we went together to Streatham where he thanked all the kids, some fifty packed into the two offices, and gave them the usual spiel about "not the end, the beginning of the end, not even really the end of the beginning, but, let's admit, a great start." He signed autographs, chatted a bit, kissed a lot and bathed in their collective adoration. He was relaxed and seemed rested; one would never have believed that, according to Barrie, he had had practically no sleep because of the Portuguese lad turning up and, to my amazement, spending the night in the Putney flat.

In the car he had a long conversation with Bill Sampson on the telephone. I eavesdropped as best I could, and Raphael nestled the phone between our ears. The NEC was to meet on Saturday morning in Brighton to set the timetable and conditions for the contest. Raphael kept bombarding him with questions of which the most crucial was what the conditions were for others to enter the race.

When Bill said they would need 37, Raphael asked, "How come we had to get 75, and they've only got to find 37?"

"There's a logic, you need a higher figure to trigger a race which might not happen, but once you're going to have a contest you go back to the same situation you'd have if there was a vacancy. You just need to prove you have at least some significant PLP support."

"Well, Derek will easily get 37."

"If he stands," Bill said. To which Raphael replied that he was sure he would.

"Unless you set your young dogs on him to frighten him off."

There was a pause before Raphael asked the next question.

"What's the minimum amount of time between triggering the contest and the deadline for tabling candidatures?"

"Well, I don't think you can decently set it before Tuesday at midday. And that's very short but of course all the MPs are likely to be in Brighton for once, since you've managed to turn the conference into an affair of some interest."

"Well let's say Tuesday at 6 p.m.", concluded Raphael.

Bill continued, "And I don't think you can chair the Saturday NEC meeting."

"I'd thought about that. I'm not going to resign as chair because I still want to open the Conference. If I don't go on Saturday, do we still have a majority?"

Bill replied, "Just. I make it 14 to 11, but there's always waverers."

I whispered to Raphael, "Who's chairing if you're not there. Don't tell us Marsha, please."

"Thank Christ, no," said Bill, who detested her. "No, it's Paul, as vice-chair."

"That's a relief. But you'll have to put him through his paces, Bill, and tell him there's no quick fag breaks. He sits there throughout."

Eddie had to drive us round the venue, the Michael Sobel sports centre in Islington, twice while Raphael kept up the interrogation about dates and hustings, when the ballot papers would go out, deadlines for posting them, the count and finally, "So what you're saying is that the earliest possible date for the result, cutting every imaginable corner, the incompressible minimum is November 30?"

"And that's with a lot of corners cut."

"But that's two months. It'll pull us all apart."

"Well, we knew the risks when we went for it." At least Bill did not shirk his share of the responsibility for the impending civil war.

There was another pause, but still Raphael would not hang up as we did another lap. But it was Bill who broke the silence, "By the way, the votes are piling up for the NEC elections" (the annual contest for the Party's executive).

"When do we announce?"

"Sunday afternoon, just before you bring down the gavel to call us to order."

"I guess it's quite a test for us?" mused Raphael.

"Oh if you manage to get any of your tykes on to the NEC at first go, that'll worry them."

I now insisted they hang up. We were by now thirty minutes late and the press flotilla was deeply confused. One cameraman had already fallen off his motorbike. And I was beginning to feel dizzy. But just as he put the phone down, he picked it up again, and tapped in Rupert's number. But with this call I was not allowed to listen in to Rupert's replies:

"Rupert, slight change of plan. New message for tonight and tomorrow. We go big on Jamieson, all guns blazing. Try to frighten him off. See what he's made of. The heat of the kitchen and all that. And get some staffers to stop loafing about in Streatham and trawl through his record, and you send me some lines for Barking later.

Rupert then obviously asked something about the Portuguese lad because the reply came back, "Well I very much hope he's on his way back to Brussels by now, a little tear-stained and perhaps a bit wiser."

The reply clearly was not what he had wanted to hear. I think Rupert had told him that his house guest was going nowhere for a while.

NED

Aide told me at midday that he'd agreed that Jose could stay over for the weekend; but in Brighton he'll have to share the house Rupe and I have rented, just behind the sea-front at the Hove end, and around the corner from the old Palladian building where he and the boss have taken a flat. It's about 20 minutes' walk from there to the Imperial and its bar, and then another 4 minutes to the Conference Centre. Seems quite a hike to me, but Raphael has refused staying in the Imperial suite to which as chair he's entitled. He wants a bit of fresh air and some space. I thought the whole point of Party Conferences was you take up residence in the bar and start getting them in, until you're ready for the curry house, before you then fight your way back to the hotel bar until the early hours. But we're being Spartan this week. Marjorie books us these places miles away, and valuable drinking time will be lost. So Hove it is.

And I'm not sure how Rupe will take to the Portuguese waterworks, in constant flow, blaming the perfidious Brits, according at any rate to Aide, who now sees it all as a huge joke. Then he says he's actually "really sweet" when you get to know him, how he's beginning to feel sorry for him, and how my job is to cheer him up. This is obviously the new compassionate Richards which lasted about thirty seconds, when I got the warning uttered with the usual menace, "He's your responsibility. Don't let him out of your sight for a moment. Now Bud and I and my new Portuguese friend are going for a run on the Common, and afterwards we'll refresh ourselves with a shower." Jesus.

BARRIE

When Aidan rang me in the early evening he was unusually polite and uncharacteristically cheerful. "Word from our masters is that it's 'Get Jamieson' time. Could you possibly dig out some quotes from him? Anything on the torture allegations? Support for the wars? That sort of thing." And before he rang off, it was, "Thanks Barrie. That's great. See you later". This uncharacteristic warmth is actually rather unsettling.

HELEN

On the Thursday night in Barking Town Hall, before a capacity crowd, with the new aura of "official candidate", Raphael was in blistering form. With the wind in his sails and with total confidence he set about doing a total demolition job on "young Lochinvar", as he has anointed the Foreign Secretary.

"Labour's looking for a new direction, a new programme and a new commitment, not a makeover for the TV cameras. People won't understand it if we saddle ourselves with the most ardent supporter of these ruinous illegal wars. People won't understand it if we elect a lapdog to do America's bidding. People won't understand it if we choose a leader who's going to be spending the next few years answering questions about complicity with torture, the security services running amok, government-sanctioned kickbacks to sweeten arms deals with nepotistic totalitarian dictatorships, or our appeasement of Washington's limitless appetite for snooping on the whole of Britain, on me of course, but on you as well.

"Derek Jamieson has his qualities. He has been the loyal servant carrying out a failed policy. He's sincere. He's the only person left in Britain who supports the wars.

"Whatever the political question we as a party face, the answer is not Derek Jamieson".

He had said quite enough to blow Jamieson out of the water but the tirade didn't stop there. And the press lapped up the blood now spilling on the carpet.

"And to any cabinet minister who suddenly has an attack of courage after sitting on the side-lines, I have a message for you."

"We will hold you responsible for the actions of this government. Your record will be laid bare. There'll be no hiding place. You cannot distance yourself from the government which has failed. You took the shilling."

All of this in a tone of magisterial rage and scorn, like the Prophet bringing down the Temple. The hall was ecstatic, I was unmoved and said as much in the car on the way back.

"If we win, you've got to work with these people. What you've just said basically to the whole cabinet is 'You're all shite, and you've been crap ministers'. Well, you won't be able to form a government without at least some of them, and now they'll all be bearing a grudge, big time."

"Look, Helen, if we win I want a government which looks very different. We can't just pretend we've had a rupture with the past and then recycle the whole team. Who do we really want from this old guard anyway? They don't have the faintest idea what a principle is, let alone any notion of resigning for the sake of one. They're mostly just limpets on the rock. Take away their special advisers, their civil servants, their nice offices, their cars, their status and they'll fall apart. If we win, they'll be on their knees begging for jobs.

"Anyway, I want a small cabinet, parity and some new faces."

And then it dawned on me, with growing dread, just to whom those new faces might belong.

BARRIE

I got back late to Putney to confront a scene of cosy domesticity, with Aidan giving orders to Jose about the ham salad which was to be prepared for Raphael's late supper. The Portuguese now trots after Aidan like a pony going through carefully plotted paces, and treats every word from him with total reverence. Aidan was the least sullen I'd ever seen, so I assumed that the two young men had spent the better part of the day together.

When Raphael came back, Aidan was provocatively indifferent and Jose put back in place his hang-dog look, almost dropping the salad bowl on the table like a Soviet-era waitress in some state hostelry in eastern Siberia. He plonked the wine into people's glasses and said nothing. I could see Raphael's post-rally high evaporating rapidly. But he managed to thank Aidan and me for the quotes we'd sent and which judging from the 10 p.m. news he'd put to good effect.

He then asked a little too pointedly, "So, Jose, how long before you head back to the capital of the Belgian Empire?"

Before Jose could reply or burst into tears, Aidan intervened, "You said last night you wanted him to come to Brighton with us, so he is. And he's staying with Rupe and Ned round the corner."

His Sulkiness then said, "I want to stay with you, Aidan, and him," pointing at Raphael but not looking into his face.

"Sadly, not possible this time, we've only booked a one-room flat."

"I don't mind," says Jose, not archly but as an assertion of his position.

"The press will just love it when they discover it's a small bedsit, and with only one bed," said I, proud of my bravery, but not totally confident as the sexual temperature began to rise.

After an uncomfortable pause, Aidan finally said, "Barrie's right of course. But we'll see lots of you, and you'll come to all the private parties. Ned will show you around. You like Ned."

It was like talking to a child. Raphael, lost in some personal reverie, finished his salad (which was, I have to say, very good), refilled his glass and went to bed.

Jose said, "I'm not tired. Can we go to a club?"

I put my foot down and said, "No, we cannot," with firmness, but realising of course that I'd not been included in the invitation.

"Aidan?" he whined.

Aidan replied in a tone of feigned or perhaps genuine regret, "Sorry, but tomorrow's a big day. Perhaps in Brighton."

I'll put a stop to this if it kills me.

NED

My big day. I star at the press conference but Angus hogs all the key announcements, the 90 signatures, the 300,000 supporters and the 150,000 new party members we've signed up - making us bigger than at any time in the last 40 years - and the £9,465,843 and 18 pence we've raised (love the detail, so Angus). We've now got one thousand working full time in the field and for free.

Then he and Rashida do the anti-Jamieson stuff. He's all blunderbuss, while she uses some stiletto quotes which are of course more lethal. I get to do the practical announcements for Wembley; press areas, accreditation, filming, how much it all costs (I'd committed the lies to memory), the band Bo has arranged and the running order (Rashida, me and then the boss). Elaine then deals with the usual questions about cabinet members' attitudes, the party election timetable and the NEC results. She's just so much the pro - word perfect once she's well briefed. The fact that she hasn't a political idea in her head is of no matter. The hacks respect her and she adds some class and glamour; it's a great turn-around. She was the middle-aged woman discarded by the Beeb and now she returns in triumph. I worship the ground...

****

Then we start packing up for Streatham, to be bussed up there for 6. Maudie's directing operations but we're not shutting the shop. Bo and Angus have decided that we keep the HQ on for the party election - but next week of course we'll have a small set of offices for conference, also at the Hove end, to run the floor management. Bo has ordained that we start the campaign officially on the Wednesday, the day after the PM's speech, to stymie any bounce he might get from it. Maudie bullies and hectors all the kids, but she's a fair dragon and they start to love her.

****

Hat, Louise and I go by tube to Wembley. Far quicker than any other way. Louise tells me she feels she's been underused in the campaign and senses a coolness between her and Raphael ever since France. I tiptoe gracefully (as per usual) around the possible Jamieson candidature but she snaps back, "I threw my lot in with Sinclair. He's torn us apart quite frankly but now only he can put us all back together again. Derek can't win. And I think he knows it. But I've not - repeat not - talked to him. At all." Harriet, probably acting out of some sisterly solidarity, rapidly changed the subject.

When we finally got to the arena and sneaked in a special high-security side entrance for "the platform party", there appeared to be thousands milling outside even though there was still ninety minutes before "doors open". I've been here before as have you, Mart, remember when we saw Springsteen, and later on Madonna? But inside, when I peeked through the door leading off from the dressing rooms where the platform party would assemble, all breath went out of my body. The size, the scale, the huge double stage that had been set up, with Bo's pet group, the Brass Monkeys, who would do the warm-up and then the other side with four tiers of seats where Angus would place some of us and lots of the kids. Then there's the rostrum, 50 feet out from the stage, and set low so that the speaker would only be a couple of feet higher than the nearest in the audience, who would indeed be near, touching-distance. And then the six giant screens so no-one misses anything, and the whole place festooned with flags.

The rostrum backdrop was simple, all black with just "The Sinclair Insurgency" picked out in white. On every one of the 12,000 seats one of three flags (European, Union Jack, Red), and the "Rafa4PM" buttons.

Hat, Louise and I were just dumbstruck, but also deafened as the wail and screeching of the testing of equipment almost drove us backwards. Louise, who's a bit of a professional moaner, was fretting, "It'll never be ready in time. I hope to goodness it's full." But Hattie was brimming with optimism, "It'll be full alright. I just hope the collection boxes are all in place because this is costing a fortune."

Bo was everywhere, with his plump expressionless face, his pale skin, the mop-head cut, the black turtle-neck, black trousers and trainers. Does he have any other clothes, because he doesn't stink or anything but he's always wearing the same things? Or has he got a wardrobe just full of black trousers and shirts? Never mind, he's the real star of our campaign.

Just after 6.15 p.m. they opened the doors and people started flooding in. And our lot started to arrive backstage. I chatted with a couple of guys from the band and tried to sound cool. Louise pointed out that my shirt tails were hanging out, but Maudie in an approximation of a smile said, "Chuck it, it's his trademark."

Rupe arrived, tense, hyper. Angus, grim and pale. Paul, smoking down the sink in one of the dressing rooms, praying no alarms would go off. Bob, his chubby fingers fiddling with his mobile, relating latest news, all about us of course; Barrie, fidgety, going through some draft notes for Rafa which he knows he'll never use; Nigel, impassive but grinning and glued to his smart phone. And Elaine, glammed up and I'd do anything to plonk a kiss on her. And JoBoy, MariLisa, some of the kids and one or two of Rafa's old Mayberry crowd. Getting mighty crowded, back stage, all of us there.

The last to arrive is Aide, with Jose in tow. He's quite solicitous about the boy, who is wide-eyed, allowing himself to enjoy things a bit, and clearly besotted with "kind" Aide. I'm not that way inclined but Jose is all short bushy hair, neat little frame, and eyes that seem to "run the whole gamut of emotions from A to B in about 30 seconds" (Dorothy Parker, I think). Aide points to where he'll sit, between Rupe and Helen, tells him again to speak to no-one and to leave with me straight afterwards as we're off to Brighton tonight.

Some of these gay guys love living on the edge, what on earth persuaded Rafa to bring him here and then to Brighton? Or is this Aide's doing? A kind of tortuous revenge.

I keep peeping through the curtains. As far as you can make out with the full wattage of the lights bearing down on you, it looked full. As the Brass Monkeys wound up their second set - they're good, they know how to heat the place up and we come out in the shadows from the lights trained on them to take our seats as unobtrusively as possible. When the set's finished, the lights go out for ten seconds then come back slowly on our part of the stage, the signal for Rashida to come forward, to deafening cheers.

Because she's so pale-skinned and wearing a white jacket, white skirt and a black turtle-neck, with just one string of silvery beads which flash, it's almost like a black-and-white film. All you can really see is her small, elegant frame and her shadow, all the rest coned in light, surrounded by an invisible multitude. This is the Hollywood Bowl.

She's amazing, nerveless, so self-assured while I'm a bag of nerves, wishing to Christ I'd gone for a last pee, with butterflies flapping about furiously in my stomach, almost sick.

"Ladies and gentlemen" (I swear she adds just a tinge of Pakistani to her accent) "my parents came from Karachi forty years ago. They worked hard, all the hours of the day, to save money so that my home gave me and my sisters the security to study and to help us through college. They always taught us that one party in Britain believed in equality and giving life-chances to people like us. And that's the Labour Party. I believe, and tonight I see I'm not alone, that Raphael Sinclair is the man to take Labour forward, to uphold its great traditions of fairness and freedom, and to make Britain stronger. Thank you."

All delivered in a deadpan voice, just slightly upping the volume when she mentions Rafa, but it works. It's unoriginal, uninspired, but it does the trick. As she came down from the rostrum, we pass, kiss and I'm suddenly there, feeling a bit woozy, alone and knees knocking, and this wall of sound.

I start, "When Rafa told me he wanted to take on the world and fight the leadership, I thought he'd gone a bit crazy. But I followed him because I believe in him. And I now think we can win. But we ain't won yet. We need to take the battle to Brighton tomorrow, and then when the campaign opens to keep at it, and bring our message to the country. Let our party on Brighton beach be the signal to every delegate, every member, every activist, every Labour voter. We're here to win this thing, and then let Rafa change this country forever. Ladies and gentlemen, I give you Raphael Sinclair."

That's all. I'd stuck to the script. I'd stuck to the time. I loved them. They loved me. The applause almost smashed my eardrums. I walked my way back to our lot, got kissed, tickled, head-patted, and almost fell onto the chair. Then a moment's quiet, the lights lowered, and a beam picks up Rafa coming down one of the aisles from the back, relaxed, smiling but not too widely, shaking outstretched hands, indifferent to all the camera flashes from the press and all the audience with their mobiles, and all to the wonderful Betty's 'Getting Mighty Crowded' (yeah, I know, I wasn't a fan before). He walks past the platform party, stops to shake hands with Bo, Angus, me, and to kiss Rashida, Hattie and Maudie, and then a hug for just a few seconds with Aide. (I try to avoid looking at our young Portuguese friend during this).

Then he walks out to the rostrum, and it's clear this is no Sheffield rally (you remember Mart when one of our leaders blew it at the big pre-election rally just by getting carried away with all the enthusiasm). No, lesson learned and it's all presidential. For twenty minutes he mounted a frontal assault on financial power, quick profits, exploitation of workers, consumers and then a great bit on what we're about as a party and the need to rediscover our principles in this different world, "Not managers, campaigners; not administrators, idealists; not desiccated pragmatists but socialists - democratic, open-minded, tolerant, listening, responsible - and socialist. That's what we're about.

"This isn't about winning office. It's about what you do with the power once you get it. You change things for good. You strive for social justice. You fight for equality. You combat cruelty and tyranny abroad, indifference, vulgarity and hardship at home. True patriots want to see Britain as the world standard for fairness, tolerance and human decency. It's our way. It's the British way.

"They may tell you that winning an election on a socialist platform is impossible. I say winning on any other basis is a worthless bauble. If I win I promise you nothing less than the irreversible shift of power and wealth from the few to the many. As someone once said, I can do no other."

Then it was into his "Help me" refrain and it was all over. We surrounded him, hugged him, kissed him and hugged each other as the waves of cheering just carried on and on. I kissed Elaine smack on the mouth which earned me a quick squeeze of my left nipple, but good-natured though. Then he walks back the way he came in, to the sound of Ella and 'Swonderful', with the crowds trying to snatch bits of him, to touch him, to kiss him. We make our way out the side entrance, pick up Rupe's car and with the kid head off in the night to Brighton.

The greatest day in my life, Bruvver.

BBC NEWS 10 pm

Mr Sinclair's gamble pays off. More than 12,000 crowd into the Wembley Arena for the largest political rally in a hundred years, as more than 100 Labour MPs sign his ballot papers...

Now over to our political editor in Wembley. "The crowds are still dispersing but for a couple of hours here tonight we saw a different politics come to Britain. Mr Sinclair found the mood and language not just to set the crowds alight - quite frankly, they were already pretty excited - he got them to commit to carry the battle to Brighton tomorrow, and then beyond. And in this appealing to British traditions he's starting to find a tone which could reach a wider audience. Those Conservative strategists who consider Mr Sinclair unelectable and who have therefore been hoping for his victory may be starting to have second thoughts about what they wish for."

BARRIE

I went back to my Digby after the rally. He'd cooked a rather wonderful vegetable lasagne although I think he might not have pre-cooked the carrots enough because they were a bit chewy (but I say nothing of course!). We watched the late bulletins and Sky News and of course our great night - and it was a great night - just dominated everything. And the Portuguese nightmare seems to have receded a bit, even if the Portuguese hasn't.

The next morning I went with Raphael to meet up with Paul in his House of Commons office, which was great because early on a Saturday morning the whole place was deserted. Paul was dreadfully nervous, kept his window open so that he could smoke without the detectors going off, and was grateful to be put through his paces again. Then we drove over to Putney to pick up Raphael's things for the week (three suits, about twenty shirts all crammed into two suitcases). He now has three dress advisers on hand, Elaine for TV, Aidan for everything else and Jose, who was the first to take a hand in Raphael's appearance.

We each lugged down a suitcase to the waiting car, where Eddie took over. I could see that just carrying the one bag had been agony for Raphael, much wincing and a bit of a gasp as he lifted the case into the boot.

In the car I asked him how things were on the domestic front. "A bit calmer, I'm still getting a lot of torture, mostly mental from Aidan, but at least some semblance of normality has been restored. Jose went down to Brighton last night with his two minders, under strict instructions to keep him away from journalists, photographers and gay clubs. Aidan went down first thing, and Bud's there already casing the joint."

All this was said cheerfully, but then the mood changed and he got deadly serious.

"I'm not tempting providence, Barrie, but we have to cover all eventualities. I think Angus and Bill have done all the planning for the contest. But just suppose, for one moment, we reach the deadline for candidates and we're the only ones standing. Suppose the Prime Minister bottles it?"

"Oh he won't," I dismissed the idea, "you've said it yourself: prising him out of Downing Street is an SAS job."

Another pause; "Well I still think that. But I'm not absolutely sure. He's a manic depressive of course, but so far we've seen nothing manic. Indeed no activity at all. He's hardly on TV at all this weekend, except for the breakfast show tomorrow. He's petrified of being humiliated. And if his fear trumps his doggedness, he might just walk. I don't know..."

Another quite long pause, and he continues, "Barrie, give some thought to the sudden death scenario. What happens? When? What sort of team do we put together? Who gets which jobs? We'll need a first week grid."

I liked the 'we' of course and want to feel part of it, at his side, but I also felt dread. So I said my piece.

"Raphael, may I say something? I don't know how much more I can take of all this intensity. The 24/7 stuff, the emotional bits, rushing from home, to the office, to Mayberry, Putney. And I know Digby's getting fed up. And if you win and we carry on, I just don't feel I can stand up to it."

There is a long pause. I'd spoken facing front, trying to concentrate on the words. But with his hand he softly turned my face to his, and looked me straight in the eye and just says, so quietly it was hard to hear above the traffic, "I realise the strain I've put you under. And my being silly has made things worse. And I apologise if Digby's cross with me" (which I hadn't actually said, but which was close to the mark) "but I can't do this without you... ." Such a manipulative bastard!

He carried on holding my chin with his hand, stroking it slightly, his dark eyes holding mine. I wanted to cry but managed to say, "I don't say I just up stumps, but if you had intended offering me some chief of staff role, I just think it would be better to be some background policy wonk. You know I don't like the public stuff anyway."

"Well, there'd be the cabinet secretary to run the service anyway. I was thinking about bringing back 'Cruella De Vil' (our name for Cynthia, who's now Dame Cynthia, Montcalm)" he continued, a bit more upbeat (and he'd let go of my chin!)

I just said, "Christ, the service will hate it."

"Yup, well that's a bonus. She was the best ambassador we never had. These bloody mandarins, they're so macho. Let her at them, I say." He was now enjoying the thought.

"Seriously though, Raphael, you'll need a proper head of staff who's just loyal to you. And if I may I've even got a suggestion."

"So you have thought it through, my clever little puppy." He tickled me, quite oblivious to the fact that Kevin and Eddie were witnessing all this. I tried to make him serious so continued,

"You know my friend Miranda Fawcett, you've met her several times in Brussels. Well, I think she'd like to come back. She knows how to manage staff. And she'd be a terrific foil for Cruella. What do you think? She'll be in Brighton today and tomorrow. I could get hold of her and you could see her. And of course she's devoted to us."

"To you, you mean, clever clogs?" and he started tickling me again until I removed his hands quite forcibly from my ribs. His general friskiness was beginning to disturb me.

Fortunately his mobile went off and a series of conversations brought an end to 'our' moment of playfulness.

To Angus, he just snapped, (which is what he's decided is the only thing that works with his pushy campaign manager) "...and get a grip on those kids. I don't want the place run over like the Sack of Rome. Respectful, quiet, no intimidation, no flag waving in the hall, and at the beginning just a few buttons. We should go for the slow build."

To Marjorie, "Can you free up time on Sunday morning? I'll need to see a few people; and no press stuff."

As we neared Brighton, he finally rang Aidan, and had to shout because I can hear deafening music coming from the receiver.

Aidan shouted something like, "Keep it down, you lot, it's sugar daddy."

He was evidently with Ned and the boy. Rupert, doing "something useful" was not there.

"Well, perhaps you two could think of doing something useful as well," he suggested.

Aidan replied to the effect that they were doing something useful, keeping "your ex" happy and occupied, which was pretty much a full-time operation. He asked how long we would take.

Raphael replied, "We should be there in fifteen minutes, so sober up, take a shower, because then we'll have to walk the promenade to the Centre."

As a parting shot Aidan asked if he'd seen the early edition of the Standard. I downloaded its front page on to my laptop. There's a photo of Bud, Jose-Miguel and Aidan in shorts and T-shirts going for an early morning run, under the legend, "Training for the top?", with the caption, 'Sinclair's boys getting fit for conference'. I feel for Bud who will be deeply embarrassed by this unsubtle innuendo. Jose won't get it. And Aidan will revel in the exhibitionism of it all.

When Raphael looked at the screen, his face was a mask: he didn't say anything.

HELEN

These trade union types certainly knew how to manage a meeting. Paul Howkins, well primed by Raphael, Angus and Bill, steamrollered everything through. The nominations deadline was set for Tuesday at 5.30 p.m. There were some protests from the two members of the committee who were obviously supporting Derek Jamieson but they got a dusty answer from Bob, "If Jamieson can't get 37 signatures by then when the whole PLP's milling around, or supposed to be, he'll never get them."

On the Conference Arrangements Committee, the PM's people had mounted a challenge to stop Raphael from opening the conference with the "Chairman's address". Paul simply said, "In that case, we scrap the leader's speech on Tuesday. If you stop Sinclair, then we stop your guy."

Some on the committee complained about the intimidation of MPs by young activists or "hooligans" making them support Sinclair. Again, Paul just put them in their place, "at least we've got some youngsters on our side." And so it was all wrapped up in 45 minutes, effective but not very pretty.

I caught a train from Victoria in mid-afternoon, jam-packed with delegates, journalists and hangers-on. I had lost my anonymity and kept being filmed or photographed or just accosted. So it was quite difficult to take the call from Raphael asking my impressions of the NEC meeting and telling me to start working on cabinet ministers. "Not Jamieson. If he wants a word, he calls. But the others can have a call or see me tomorrow morning. And tell Marsha to come by my suite at the hotel about an hour before Conference begins."

"Why so precise?"

"I'm going to ambush her."

NED

We wandered over to Rafa's flat round the corner in Hove parade at about 4 p.m. Jose had had a shower at our place and then paraded around stark naked, as if nothing could be more normal. I think he thinks I'm "one of them" just because there are no girls in evidence.

But oh so BORING. "In Portugal we do this." "In Portugal we do that". "This is how the Socialist party of Portugal works". And now the new thing is, "How do you say this in English?" "How do you pronounce this?", "What does that mean?" After an hour of this, I finally snapped and said, "You won't need so much English when you go home." This gets a "fuck you off" (so he's getting to grips with the vernacular). Then Aide says, "That was pretty heartless" (yup, Aidan Richards, of all people!).

When Rafa arrives at the flat he looks tired and nervous, so takes a bath, and seems even more inscrutably withdrawn than usual. Then Rupe was summoned to come back and mind Jose until the Beach event while we walked along the promenade, just me, the boss, Aide and Bud. We were soon joined by a handful of exuberant delegates, then a dozen or so, and by the time we'd crossed the boundary into Brighton and were making our progress on the Promenade, word must have reached the press because we were just surrounded by hundreds of cameras, crews, hacks, supporters and the curious. When we finally reached the Imperial, we're the armed forces of a small nation state. Of course I love it all, and so does Rafa but he doesn't show it. Just the time out he takes for a quick word with some on-lookers, or passing delegates, or the odd MP shows how he's relishing his moment.

We arrive at the hotel entrance where we waste time while the manager fawns all over Rafa, and because Aide has left his badges behind thinking that his charm would swing it, and that it was better than having any plastic on the lapel of his latest Hugo Boss acquisition, a sharp blue velvety jacket, over the regulation shocking white shirt. Confusion reigns until your heroic little brother takes charge and starts to throw his not entirely inconsiderable weight around so that the barriers are finally lifted at this absurd Checkpoint Charlie they've established in Brighton's premier hotel. All this because the First Boyfriend has been too vain to wear a badge.

Then the manager gets a bit miffed when he learns that Rafa has no bags to be brought up because he's not actually staying at the hotel but will be using the Imperial Suite as a campaign office. But was it really necessary to use that tone "Goodness, I'm not staying here" as though the room was substandard or hadn't been properly cleaned?

When we finally get inside the suite, it was bedlam. Far too many hangers-on. "Hi everybody" says Raphael with his snarling charm, "Now Maudie, sort this lot out." Within five minutes, everyone's favourite prison wardress had booted all of them out, except Rafa, Aide, Angus, Barrie, Nigel, Elaine and Marjorie. Bo was off somewhere and soon we saw precisely where: he was directing operations on the beach, along with what looks like some 700 assistants. For the hotel suite Maudie would act as bouncer, liaison with the outside world, doorkeeper and totally untamed Rottweiler.

The bedroom itself was reserved for "the Royal Couple" (Maudie's phrase, not mine), or for Rafa to receive passing figures from the Labour pantheon. Marjorie had blocked off time in the run-up to the party and then the next day until the commencement of proceedings at the Greatest Show on Earth, the 107th Annual Conference of the Labour Party. Rafa took Marjorie's list and struck off 3 names ("timewaster…I wouldn't give him houseroom and he knows it…") but then added a name which we couldn't see however hard we craned our necks. Then typically it was, "You know what I fancy, a nice pot of tea and some of their cinnamon toast and tea cakes?" Don't 'cha love it?

BARRIE

Hattie, Helen, Paul, Bob and Louise were our designated floor managers (or "street-walkers", as Rupert puts it). He, Nigel and Elaine, on the other hand, worked the press enclosure, the first-floor studios and the press room. I just hand on scraps of information for them to feed the vultures and deal with one or two of the more delicate errands I've been set, unbeknownst to anyone else, I think - which chuffs me no end. I phone the two ladies, one weekending in her place in the country, at Burford; the other spending part of her Saturday afternoon taking the last Eurostar to St Pancras to check in late tonight.

Both are pretty surprised to get a call from me and to be told to be on hand for a follow-up in the next 48 hours. Before 5 p.m. they were unsuspecting, now after 5 p.m. they're very suspecting.

Raphael took tea alone in the bedroom, while the others texted, or in the case of Ned and Aidan just watched what was happening on the beach and made off jokes about passers-by gawping at the ever more elaborate preparations on stage. Occasionally Rafa passes me or Marjorie a little note with instructions; one, to me, just said, "Check out contact details for Lorna Delaney, and tear this up." I know him so well, but just occasionally even I can still get surprised. What on earth could he want to talk to her about?

Lorna Horrocks, now Baroness Horrocks of Risborough and currently vice-chancellor at Loughborough, former MP, former Europe Minister and, little detail, a Tory! They know each other quite well, have shared conference platforms on disarmament negotiations, Europe and the Middle East. They'd spent some time together when he took over her portfolio when we won in 1997. But why Lorna Delaney? Some foreign policy adviser role?

Really we were just filling in time. I sat in the corner making deliberately illegible jottings about possible cabinet holders. I sent him in a list with 22 jobs. It came out half an hour later whittled down to 12. I tried not to gasp. I sent it back in with 15 and it came back with 13 plus a minister for Europe, in attendance. Then he told me to follow him back into the bedroom, and I could see Aidan's irritation.

Raphael was lying on the bed in shirt, trousers and without his shoes. He asked, "Did you find out the answer to that question about minimum periods for having elections?"

I replied, "I spoke to three people, the head of the Commons Library, a friend of mine who's a constitutional lawyer, and an expert at UCL. They're unanimous, the absolute minimum for an election, say, on the 29th would be to have the dissolution on the 7th - the Wednesday. Not the Tuesday."

"That's 100% sure?"

"1000%"

I paused before posing the obvious and pointless question, "You're not really thinking…"

"Not really, I just like to know these things. You alone know I asked you the question. You tell no-one not even anyone - and I mean anyone - out there", pointing to the sitting room.

I bask in this confidence.

NED

He started receiving calls that afternoon from union general secretaries and from one senior minister. Rupe has now deposited Jose on us and gone off to do "something less boring like counting the pebbles on the beach" (clearly tired of the intellectual challenge of a lengthy conversation with our Portuguese friend). When I finally get him up to the suite, Aide comes over and says, "I'm bored out of my skull here", and "Rafs only speaks to Barrie who won't let on what's happening, even when I give him Chinese burns. Let's go down to the beach and start getting in the mood for a party." So the advance party goes downstairs. When we weave through the scrum we look out at the beach, the sea and the frantic activity all round us. And what does our little ray of southern European sunshine do? Well, he moans of course. "It's not a proper beach. There's no sand. And it's cold." (Which it isn't except by Oz standards: it started off damp and grey but it's now really sunny, with just a light breeze).

HELEN

I contacted seven or eight cabinet members; how things had changed. A few weeks before and I would have been greeted with a little smile, an almost pitying, "How are things, Helen?" or "Let's have a catch-up soon." Now I was treated like the plenipotentiary of a major power, with "Is there any chance of you putting in a good word?"; "I'd really like a chat with Raphael, but I know he's so busy"; "I so agree with what he's been saying about Trident, but of course we're not allowed to open our mouths in cabinet", and "I'd do anything to be part of his team."

The only two I spoke to who were really standoffish were the Chancellor, "He's turning this into a complete circus. He's run a great campaign, I grant you, but there's no way he could run a government. And who with? That bunch of teenagers?" and the Home Secretary, Brian Dawkins, as friendly as ever but very clear, "Bloody hell, Helen, they're running amok. I had a really rough time with my local committee last week. But I made it clear - I believe in old school Labour politics. You elect a leader, you back him, end of story. Raphael should have stood last time. The PM's only been there just over a year, and had really tough stuff to deal with. He's been to hell and back to save the economy. He's earned his chance to take us into the election."

Time and again, the big negative was "Team Sinclair". People were afraid of Angus Buchanan, didn't like being treated as dimwits by Rupert Dennison, had no respect for Ned Warren, and seriously loathed Aidan Richards.

Brian was most interesting in the way he brought our conversation to an end. "Put it this way, if the PM does stand, I back him. If he doesn't and Derek stands, I'd back Derek, and campaign for him. But I'm not convinced he will."

NED

After 6-ish people started drifting to the beach as the sun started to slip below the outline of the Old West Pier ("Why don't you repair that place? You should see Oporto now…" from my least favourite Iberian). The bands were still warming up and people started to pour on to the beach. By the third act, and the inevitable Brass Monkeys (has Bo got a percentage?), the two layers of promenade, the surrounding streets and half a mile of beach were full to the brim. Aidan had slipped back to the hotel, leaving a small group of us near the stage, Rashida, Hat, Paul and Tom, the beardie from Rafa's seat), as well as Jose showing off his moves to a small throng of female and male admirers. Bo fights his way over to us, "Word from Angus, they're running a bit late, so Rash and Ned do the warm-up." I realise I've only got my old anorak and jeans but stardom beckons.

BARRIE

Of course we left it to the last possible moment, the Brass Monkeys had done their three regulation encores, and we were now having a Sinclairite medley from the 60s (Martha, Dionne, Diana, and Mary Wells). At last the boss, Aidan, Angus, Helen and I walked out of the hotel into the throng. Raphael, ignoring all the instructions from security, blandishments from Bud and common sense, just throws himself into the crowd, "my very own bain de foule" he shouts at Aidan. The spotlights are on him as he took ten minutes to reach the stage, where Ned was in full, unstoppable flow, firing on all cylinders, recycling old Ned jokes, shirt all over the place, laughing at himself and making the crowd laugh with him. Is this the new politics?

So to the strains of 'The State of Independence', Raphael's hauled up on to the stage, takes off his jacket, and walks to the mikes, the politician as rock star. The changed politics in front of our very eyes.

"I'm told by my friends in the police that we have 80,000 people here tonight. You came here for the music. You came here for spectacle. But you also came to take part in a little revolution. You came to change Britain."

HELEN

Of course the speech was light stuff. It lasted just over 5 minutes, but he struck a chord, and seemed almost choked with emotion when he finished with his professions of love for the party, for the people and for his country. Finally, he just added, "I hear the call to serve. Tonight I answer it. Give me the chance to change Britain." No policy, no substance but the Sinclair style, the emotional catch, the master at the top of his game.

And there was one last trick. When he finished, all the lights went out and there was just one firework, a silvery gold shooting star which shot up into the black starry sky before exploding into a massive storm of gold and silver rain which lit up the whole beach. Bo Sampson told me afterwards that this single firework had cost £20,000; he had ordered it direct from China and until that morning had believed it had been lost in transit.

The lights came back up and the music started up again, but Raphael and Aidan wended their way through the crowds (I was relieved to see not hand-in-hand, but so obviously a couple, bound together by hoops of complicity).

As the crowds surged round them, it was obvious that the police had lost control. People were snatching at them, their clothes, Aidan's hair was thoroughly roughed up (which he must have hated). Raphael lost buttons from his jacket and his shirt, and his wallet ("Nothing in it, just a few quid and some photos" I was told afterwards, intrigued by the obvious questions about the photos), and someone struck something sharp into his head, drawing a little blood, not serious but a warning that passion once roused could tip so easily into violence.

NED

What a night! Even my little bundle of Southern misery says "wow" at the firework. I get to speak to about a hundred thousand people and they all love me. I go to the hotel bar and don't need to take out my wallet. Raphael and Aidan slip through the lobby and out the back to go back through the side streets, on foot, alone except for Bud, with the sound of the party, which continues until well past midnight, as backdrop. Rupe's surrounded by hacks; the women have gone off to work the phones, lobby ministers and see regional delegations or union bosses. Bo's still on the beach, supervising the dismantling of the set and the clearing away of tons of rubbish, cartons, bottles so as to head off criticism about "Sinclair litter louts" adding to that about "Sinclair louts". Barrie's off fretting about timetables. And I'm here holding court in the Imperial bar, getting mightily smashed, and with my tedious compañero who I do not let out of my sight.

BARRIE

Early on this Sunday morning I traipsed over to the boss's flat, to be greeted with civility by Aidan who even offers me coffee, instead of spitting out instructions as to how he likes his. He then went off for his daily run with Bud, on to the promenade in the opposite direction from Brighton. I'm beginning to wonder about the lover and the bodyguard! But Raphael seemed almost relieved when we were left alone.

He told me everything was alright after "an early night, much kissing and making up. I think I'm all forgiven". He then started on about the "quick death" scenario, which to me is a bit tempting providence. He'd already done some lists, keeping nearly all the junior ministers in their posts, except for obvious enemies; he was cagey about cabinet, "Helen of course. And at least Hattie and Maudie have some ministerial air miles. And I need 50/50."

"Does that mean Rashida?"

"In the right job, why not?" he asked but I knew then his mind was made up. "She's super-bright and a bit of a scene-stealer on the road."

"But she won't take it if you leave out Angus."

"Well, no," this after a dutiful pause.

"Rupert's very bright."

"Isn't he just? And Ned's a total star. The party loves him. You just wait for the NEC results."

There was a pause before he finally added with great awkwardness, "The difficulty will be with Aidan."

I knee-jerked my reply, "No, Raphael, no." I was surprised at my own vehemence.

"Well he won't like being outside if all his mates are in."

"No, Raphael."

There was a difficult silence before he changed the subject, just as I could actually taste the bile rising.

"Did you manage to track down the secret women in my life?"

"Yes, I saw Miranda on the promenade this morning. She'll meet us just outside the restaurant we're going to tonight after the opening session. She'll pitch up in the pub next door so we can haul her out whenever you want."

Nigel arrived with the press digest. Nothing but Sinclair of course. The Telegraph had a great montage of Raphael's face and the firework exploding. And the Guardian centrefold had just the firework, but page after page of the young crowd, "hearing Sinclair's message of hope and change." There was a funny piece by their sketch writer comparing the speaking styles of Rashida, Ned and Raphael. Nigel then went back to the 'office' in the hotel while I rather pointlessly made a few notes for the speech.

Aidan and Bud returned, taking turns in the shower but spending perhaps just a little more time together in the bathroom at handover point than was strictly necessary, or is this just my febrile imagination? When Bud emerged, wearing just a towel, I realised quite how attractive he must be if you like perfectly formed muscular tough young men with blond cropped hair and blue eyes. But really he's not my type.

Raphael's mind was elsewhere, "Can you get me Angus?" he asked. I passed him my mobile (since he hardly ever uses his own, as if he still considers it a vulgar contraption not to be shown in public.)

"Angus, I've been thinking," (warning signs start flashing) "you know we said today we play it low key," (actually this had been Raphael's idea) "...not too many buttons, quiet galleries, our people restrained. I think that's tosh. We should go full throttle today. The big bang. Let them take the roof off. Anyone not wearing a button's a cissy. If that's intimidation, let's intimidate. Time to blow the whistle. End of school break. The message to the PM today must be "it's over"; and for any challenger, "don't even think of it". We want to create the sensation that we've had the campaign, now let's get on with the revolution."

I don't know what Angus said but he got a curt, "Just let's do it."

HELEN

Raphael and Aidan Richards arrived at the Imperial Suite just before lunch, and Marjorie Delaney, who had been such a loyal support to her boss for so many years, had ordered a seemingly endless supply of quality sandwiches, petit fours, tea and coffee. Hotel staff and security had managed to clear our corridor of most of the journalists and other snoopers. After chatting with us for a while, Raphael took sandwiches into the bedroom and told Marjorie to start the calls. He spoke to five members of the cabinet but did not tell any of us, not even Barrie, what was said.

After an hour or so Angus Buchanan just barged into the bedroom to relay a message from the cabinet minister closest to the PM: "He says they're impressed by the campaign. The PM would like to work with you. And this time it's the Treasury. If it all works out after the election he'd stand down and you'd have a clear run. He also promised me a big job. I just said I'd tell you but that any conversation had to be between the two principals. The guy just says, "Yes the PM would be delighted to get a call from Raphael", to which I replied, "…and I'm sure Raphael will be pleased to take a call from the PM."

Of course no such conversation would ever take place. Raphael judged that time was up. And the PM was too proud to beg.

BARRIE

The highlight of the afternoon was the visit from our esteemed deputy leader, Marsha Worthington. And this time I was allowed in to pour the tea.

It was pure drawing room comedy from the word go.

"Have some of these fancy cakes, Marsha, they really take you back."

"You've had a wonderful campaign, Raphael". Pause.

She continued, "I really admire the momentum you've created." Another pause, Raphael just smiling sympathetically but impassively.

She persevered, "You've been saying a lot of things about policy some of us have always agreed on… ." (Still no reaction)

"I expect you to win. I don't think he'll want to be humiliated." Raphael's silence continued.

"Some of us have been wondering if we could help out in the new government… and whether you'd given any thought to jobs in your team… (her neck had now turned bright pink) and of course if you still want me as your deputy I'd be very happy to carry on serving."

There was another exquisite pause so she ploughed on, "For myself I think quite frankly I deserve a proper department."

And then the icing on this particular fancy cake, "Like the FCO, for example."

I fear for a moment Raphael will choke on his slice of Black Forest Gateau, and when he spoke at last, there was a kind of strangulation in his tone which I recognise as his way of suppressing giggles. Marsha just seemed relieved to have elicited any reaction whatsoever.

"Marsha, I really appreciate this. And I sincerely look forward to working closely with you. I think your talents have not always been recognised in the way they deserve. A deputy leader of the party should have a proper job in government. Of course it would be inappropriate to think about specific departments at this stage. But I'd want you close at hand, so sending you on all those tedious trips abroad might not be the best use of your talents.

"Now we've got to go downstairs shortly, and I expect you'll want to change" (a really nasty little one this as she'd obviously put on her best dress and would now feel obliged to put on something else). "Please tell your colleagues that when this is all over, come what may, we've got to close ranks. I'm hugely looking forward to working with you."

The climax of this little piece of the theatre of cruelty was the way he said, "Now step out through this door, it's more discreet," gave her a little kiss, while opening the door to twenty bulbs flashing and the British media witnessing at first hand the apostasy of Marsha Worthington. They smiled at the cameras, hers a simpering, embarrassed clenched-teeth job, and his a huge triumphant grin.

NED

When he finally emerges into the salon (not as much of a saloon as I'd like) to join Angus, Aide, Helen, Hat and Paul, I pass him the phone with Bill on the line. And daring now in my new position as BMOC I put the conversation on parrot.

"Are any of you tossers interested in the NEC results or have you still got the vapours after your tryst with our divine deputy?" asks the sardonic party bureaucrat.

"I'm mildly interested," says Rafa, feigning a yawn.

I take out my notebook for the scores. For the trade union section I make it 6 for us, 5 for them (the PM's lot) and 1 somewhere in the middle.

For treasurer, Bob ousts an old union hand by a staggering 3 to 1 majority. In the women's section, it's a clean sweep, Maudie top, Helen at number 2 and Louise just scraping on. Then for the constituency members' individual votes, where there's seven places, my heart stops.

Bill drones on, "Well to my surprise, Aidan scrapes in at number 7, just 20 votes ahead of the runner-up. At number 6 (now he's sounding like that old DJ Alan Freeman on 'Pick of the Pops' who mum used to love) the gorgeous Rashida; in at number 5, for the first time, our Paul; then a startling success for another newcomer, Rupert, straight to fourth place. The lovely voluptuous Harriet manages her switch from the women's section in style and races to the third spot. Our old geriatric emblem of the past" (a hard-left throwback now kept afloat by good old fashioned Labour sentimentality) "cedes the top spot for the first time in ten years, to be replaced by…our very own Mr Ned Warren, top, and by a margin of 50,000."

They all cheered: Raphael embraces me and I collapse in the only vacant armchair. Only Aidan seems able to control his elation.

Is his mediocre result because he's put too many people's backs up? Or do people still not feel at ease about his affair with Rafa?

Without another word, Raphael slips back into the bedroom to change the shirt and tie and to prepare for the walk from the hotel to the conference centre, a mere 100 yards but it could take a while with all the press mob and the fans.

HELEN

After the preview of the results we crossed the road to the special platform-party NEC side-entrance. We were all pretty thrilled except for Aidan Richards who seemed out of sorts. He should have counted himself lucky to get elected to the NEC at all. He was very good at the constituency work, of course, but it seemed to me that he was just too arrogant, cliquey and divisive. Rupert Dennison had many of the same faults but concealed them beneath his infectious enthusiasm. And of course it was obvious why Angus Buchanan had not stood, given his innate ability of making the maximum number of enemies in the shortest time possible. It is always a failing in a politician not to suffer fools gladly; Angus refused to put up with them at all and tended to make even quite clever people feel deeply stupid.

But it was lovely seeing Ned, so unpretentious but so happy. He held my hand until we took our seats in the hall, mostly to steady himself. As we sat, a hundred cameras flashed as the new star was recognised.

The security was so painfully slow that it took ages to get everyone in the hall, to the extent that Elaine and Nigel feared we might miss the early evening bulletins.

The hall had been shaped to resemble one of Bo's rallies. A simple backdrop, lit in a greyish purple, with the three flags, and a rostrum projected way out into the audience, almost halfway up the gangway and only a foot higher than the floor, to create an intimacy even in a vast overflowing auditorium. Bill had given his son carte blanche for the design, and for once it was the party, and not the Insurgency, paying the bills.

Half an hour behind schedule, the lights dimmed and Paul, Marsha Worthington[39] and Bill walk on to the stage to repeated cheering. Paul stood up simply to say, "To open the 107th Annual Conference of the Labour Party I call upon Raphael Sinclair, the outgoing chair of the Party to make the opening address."

The hall exploded.

---

[39] MP for Brixton, and Deputy Leader of the Labour Party since 200-.

BARRIE

Not vintage Sinclair but it didn't have to be. The cleverness of it was that it was not too blatant: the need for mutual respect and tolerance in the days ahead; the long litany of Labour's historic achievements; the great personal commitment of all our leaders past and present; the need from time to time to assess whether what we are doing is right, whether it advances "the abiding principles which caused brave men and women to take the parliamentary road to socialism".

He then started on a series of points prefaced by the two words "They said" without ever explaining who "they" were.

"They said that an internal debate would rip us apart. But here we are, now half a million strong, more party members than at any time in the last fifty years.

"They said you can't get people enthused about politics anymore. Not enthused? More enthused than this and it's time to call an ambulance. In the past three weeks we've brought a new generation into politics. We've set the party alight. Now we light another fire to bring politics closer to people, to meet their needs and concerns, to advance our principles: peace, equality, redistribution, the public accountability of private power and social justice for all.

"To these enduring objectives I commit the rest of my political life, and all the resolve of the whole Labour Movement."

Not merely policy-lite but weightless, almost meaningless, but the demonstration that followed lasted nearly ten minutes, with hundreds standing on their chairs, waving banners and cheering.

As he left the rostrum with the ovation unabated, Bill had to read out the NEC results. They had already leaked of course but there was a bit more delirium when Ned's result was read out, creating a minor riot.

Pity the poor old mayor of Brighton (a rather washed-out looking Green lady) as she gave the traditional, official town welcome to the hall, as people stampeded for the bars, the press interviews, the stands and all the usual conference distractions.

HELEN

Most of us drifted back to the 'royal suite' in the Imperial, all on cloud nine, except Aidan. Then when even Ned Warren had joined us, having unusually refused countless offers of a celebratory drink, Raphael behaved stupidly. He just said,

"Well done to all of you, the new masters of our party. You see, Aidan, how well Ned did. Nice guys don't always come last. And petulance and general brattishness, even from someone studiously showing enough chest hair to move hearts of stone, don't always cut it."

It was just a silly immature remark but Aidan walked out and slammed the door. At times, Raphael could be incredibly emotionally obtuse and insensitive, as I knew full well.

NED

I felt bad about the way Raphael had humiliated Aidan in front of us all. I rang him on his mobile; he was just walking up the promenade with Bud. I said, "Don't forget the restaurant at 8, and don't boycott it. He didn't mean it. He's just overtired, and takes it out on the one he loves." You didn't know about my side-line as an agony aunt, did you, Mart?

He replied, "It's just one more thing to add to the account in my revenge ledger. But I'll be at the restaurant."

BARRIE

Raphael really socks it to Aidan and I'm so thrilled I could hug myself. At last the little bastard has to take some of what he dishes out all the time. But when he slammed the door I sense new danger.

Raphael called me into the bedroom alone, winked, our old complicity renewed in full, and then said, "Now, we'll need to start some planning. I'll be working at the flat all day tomorrow and Tuesday until after the PM's speech then it'll be out of the traps before he's even sat down.

"I'll need to see Angus, Rupert and Bo on campaign stuff first thing tomorrow."

This all seemed a bit phoney and I ventured, "You really think there'll be a campaign after this?"

"Well today was a show of strength to whip up such an atmosphere that anything can happen. But we must also plan what we do if it's all over on Tuesday. We'll do some lists tomorrow. By the way, is the Queen still at Balmoral? Better she comes back soon. Do we know anyone at the Palace to raise discreetly the hypothetical question?"

"Don't forget we're meeting Miranda at around 10.30 during the dinner", I added.

"For me it won't be during, but after. I'm so knackered I'll be going back to the flat early. Let others carouse."

NED

The dinner was upstairs in a private room in a popular fish restaurant at the beginning of the Lanes. Lots of mayhem when we arrive, when Rafa comes in some of the other diners downstairs (all delegates) just stand and clap.

I was to sit between Hattie and Maudie, "below the salt" (Rupe of course) but when I'm not looking, Jose (who invited him?) takes Hat's place. To my surprise Aidan sits himself next to his erstwhile rival, all matey, and starts pouring wine down him as if they've announced the start of prohibition in thirty minutes. So Hat is promoted to the top end of the table, next to the boss, with Helen on the other side, then Rupe next to Helen and Angus at the corner between Hat and Maudie.

After quite a few rounds of the bottle, and just as the starter is served, Rafa gets up and simply says, "I owe you everything. You know what I feel for you all. I want to thank just three people, Angus for engineering what could be the political upset of our lifetimes, Bo for making the impossible actually happen and …Aidan, the love of my life. We cheer a bit, but Aidan's face is impassive, and then he carries on pouring drinks for Jose which he proceeds to mix.

After the main course, Rafa gets up, puts on his jacket and says he's "all in" and he's still got one or two people to see. As he passes our end of the table he bends down and whispers in Aide's ear, "I need you with me, now", conciliatory but commanding. At first I think Aide is going to refuse but after a moment he also leaves, saying nothing. I carry on joshing with Maudie and listening to Rupe's impressions, particularly of the boss, which are hysterical. I rather ignore Jose and I'm not going to let him spoil my evening of triumph with his special blend of melancholy, homesickness and sexual pining.

By the time dessert appears, his head almost falls into the ice-cream. And when coffee is served I notice he's gone - to the loo I imagine. When we get up to leave Rashida pays the bill, "This one's on the Insurgency. It's the first and last time entertainment expenses have been paid by the campaign", she adds firmly. I search for the Portuguese in the loo, nowhere to be seen, then in the street. I catch up with Rupe and say, "We've got a situation. Kid's gone AWOL; he's drunk as a skunk and I'll cop it."

Rupe replies sweetly, "Don't worry sweetheart, he'll have followed Aidan and Raphael back up the promenade to the unfashionable end;

and then he'll invite himself into what I seem to remember is their one-bedroom flat."

BARRIE

We met up with Miranda just outside the appointed pub. She does rather stand out I realise! She's seriously tall, taller even than Raphael, and with shortish yellow hair and rather startlingly bright clothes. Tonight she had on a crimson leather jacket and a black top and skirt, and, astonishingly, high heels. She's a warm soul and oozes Yorkshire plain mateyness. She hugged me, shook hands with Aidan, who she remembered from a Brussels Information trip he'd made shortly after being elected, and then walked off for a quiet word with Raphael. When they return, they both smile and I could see that the match has been arranged. She and I went off for a quick drink, while Aidan, who didn't even say goodbye, led the way back to Hove with Sinclair, followed by Bud.

****

This morning - very much the morning after the night before - I got to the flat at 8 a.m. Bud gave me coffee, two pieces of toast spread with some butter substitute, and an apple. Aidan was pleasant enough but I sensed the atmosphere and was a bit relieved when (just as yesterday) he and the 'body' went off for their run on the promenade away from town.

No sooner were they out of sight than I asked Raphael, who was clearly intent on having a dress-down, no appointments day by the look of things, "So was it kiss and make-up time last night?"

"It was a bit of a rough ride, actually. On the prom it was just the 2 of us, well, with Bud of course. I kept on being stopped by delegates or MPs or well-wishers and each time Aidan just carried on walking so I practically winded myself keeping up.

"When I asked him to slow down a bit he turned round and said, 'You've got a choice, we can have our row here and now in front of the next cluster of fans and hangers-on or we can have it in the flat, but row there will be and sooner rather than later.'

"Once in the door, he just stands there, looks me in the eye with a kind of really hateful defiance, and says, 'Is this policy of humiliating me in public now a fixture or just a passing fad? First it was the little matter of your affair with Jose not being quite over and you just forgetting to tell me. So he 'knows nothing' (imitation of the boy) and I get not even a moment's prior warning.

'Then today I manage to get on the NEC at my first attempt; not brilliant, but not bad considering you've given me no role whatsoever in the campaign. Then you shovel a heap of crap on my head and make me look like some poor loser in front of my mates.

'And what you did to the kid is unforgivable.'

"I of course couldn't let that go. 'Well, that's a turn-up, the new altruistic Aidan, the one who really cares about my cast-off. A few days ago he was a boring little jerk, now he's someone to be protected and cared for.'"

'I've got to know him better, that's all.'

'How much better?'

'Quite a bit if you must know. He's a really sweet guy, vulnerable, not at all stupid but just out of his depth. He needed a bit of help.'

"So like an idiot, I say, 'I'll bet he did. So when did you start sleeping with him?'

'I knew you'd throw some jealousy fit if I stuck up for him. As it happens he did try it on and, yes, I was tempted. I didn't sleep with him and whatever happened was just one tiny incident of no consequence.'

"I just shouted, 'what happened?'

"He replied, 'It was just one little moment in the bathroom in Putney, when you'd left me there alone with him. So nothing.'

"I was so angry and upset I felt as if I was choking. I just went to bed without saying anything. After a while he came into the bedroom, undressed and got into bed. We lay there for a while, not saying anything.

'It really was nothing, you know. I did it to punish you, that's why. He's got over it and it meant nothing to me. I still love you, though I don't know why.'

"A few minutes later he climbed on top of me. I resist at first, but then I cave in and we have a great night. When he got up this morning, he took some papers out of his jacket pocket and said, 'as you're technically unemployed all day, you can fill this out.' It's the form for a civil partnership. He adds, 'It's not urgent. November will do.' God I love him."

I said nothing. But as if on cue, Aidan and Bud were back from their run. Raphael and I carried on working.

NED

Jose-Miguel still hadn't pitched up by the time we got back to the flat and I was worried because he'd been so maudlin and totally wasted. Next morning there was a knock on the door at 9-ish, and although I was still bleary-eyed and sporting only a bath towel which didn't quite meet round the waist, I let Bud in.

"Sorry to disturb you but there's been a bit of bother with your young Portuguese friend."

My heart sank but I managed a defensive, "He's not my friend."

"Apparently", Bud continued, absolutely straight-faced, "the police found him wearing just his briefs, with hoops around his arms and legs, stuck to the ground, on the grass in front of the Pavilion. He's rambling a bit, keeps asking for the boss or you or Aide (!). I couldn't get Aide on his mobile and I don't want to trouble the boss, so could you nip down to the station?"

Frankly I'd rather be in Salt Lake City than here now. This is a fucking catastrophe. Anyway I ring Rupe and we meet up at the station. He was in the interview room wearing some ill-fitting clothes and covered in a blanket, looking like death and shivering. I put my arm around him and true to form he starts to cry.

"I go to this club. All men, older men, some in leather. They give me drinks. I thought they are kind. They took me to places to sleep downstairs. They try to take my clothes. I fight back, but is three or four. I do not know what happen. It was no good. Some people take me on the grass, they put iron rings round my legs and arms. I am there a very long time before someone comes. I lose voice. I feel ill. I want to die."

Rupe speaks to the duty staff to keep him there a bit longer while we arrange for someone to take him back to Brussels. I tell Aidan and he comes straight to the station, kicks everyone out while he has a word with Jose alone. Rupe and I then talk for some time to Bud to make sure we keep this as quiet as possible as long as possible. By the end of the day he's on his way out of the country, with one of the girls from the Streatham office who's kind and mothering.

HELEN

Even at their best, policy debates at party conference are never interesting. At this one, the attention was everywhere but on the hall. The bars and cafes round the stands were hives of rumour and speculation. At noon on Monday came the announcement that the Queen had returned from Balmoral in the morning to receive the Prime Minister. For three hours all media attention was on the Palace and Downing Street. At 2.30 p.m. he left No 10 alone. A few minutes later the black Jaguar drove through the gates at the Palace. Just after 3 p.m. came the official announcement, "The Prime Minister has tendered his resignation to the Queen. He will leave office as soon as his successor as leader of the Labour Party is elected."

At 3.30 p.m. he made a statement on the Downing Street steps, mostly to thank his family and staff and wishing the best for his country. It was short and dignified and silenced the bars and corridors at the Conference. But any feelings of solidarity and remorse were short-lived, as thousands of the politically obsessed started to hyperventilate about successors, strategies and odds. The main question was now whether Derek Jamieson or one of the other cabinet heavyweights would at last throw their hats into the ring.

NED

I said to Rupe, "If he'd known about our little local difficulty he might not have gone. Rupe replied, "We did well to sit on it this long. I give it to the end of the afternoon before it's out."

I asked, "Has anyone told the boss?" to which he replied, "That's Aidan's job. He got us into this shit with his 'encora un poco mas vino, hombre'. It's so typical of his self-indulgent capriciousness which will ruin it all."

BARRIE

Rupert informed me about all this saga in mid-morning but said that Aidan should be the one to tell Raphael, as it's all his "fucking fault". Well, up to a point. The real blame (as so often) lies with Raphael himself. But I couldn't sit on this so I told him. He was aghast, "This could kill us. It's the whole gay lifestyle thing. How did Ned let him out of his sight? I suppose expecting him to be sober and disciplined is like putting Aidan in charge of a campaign for sexual abstinence." I refrained from snitching on Aidan getting the boy drunk.

He had repeat calls with Angus, Rupert, Elaine and Nigel.

By 5 p.m. the story was out, and it was worse than that, there were the photos. Some cretin had taken shots of the boy obviously drunk, stripped down to his pants, laid out on the grass with hoops around his limbs. He looked so pathetic, so defenceless in the photos. I just felt for him.

Fortunately, even the British media couldn't quite put this as top item the day of the PM's unexpected resignation. But the BBC did carry it as second story, "And there's embarrassment for the frontrunner to succeed the Prime Minister, Mr Raphael Sinclair. One of his friends, a Portuguese national working in Brussels, Mr Jose Durrao Pinto was found undressed and tied to the ground on the lawn in front of Brighton's Royal Pavilion at 6 in the morning. Mr Durrao Pinto has since left the country."

In the course of the evening the full story seeped out - how he had spent the night in Brighton's roughest gay area, but how he was totally drunk when he arrived was not mentioned or explained.

By mid-evening, the press had retrained its focus on this, so much more interesting than the stale old story of the nation's political leader falling on his sword. It was now, "how Sinclair's ex-lover passed his last hours in the UK". All the commentators were talking of the "gay issue", safely submerged in all the political correctness of the campaign but now back on the agenda big-time. So the tabloids were full of "the sex questions Sinclair has to face". Whichever way you looked at it, we had handed the press all the weapons required to kill us and they were now landing the first blows. The speculation now was all about "potential candidates in the cabinet beginning to think the race isn't over after all".

HELEN

Elaine Chayter and I had had our ups and downs over the years but I was forced to admit that when Angus convened the press conference almost as an act of desperation, she played a blinder. She sat alone with Rupert and came out fighting.

"So young man on his own gets drunk in Brighton, loses his trousers and is victim of a cheap stunt. Well, hold the front page.

"He did nothing illegal. He was out of his head with booze. People take advantage of him, and the police pick him up in the morning. He's not a politician. He's just a silly young visitor who can't hold his drink."

But of course the story did not end there. One of the tabloids dug up the photo of Aidan, Jose and the bodyguard doing their run, with the caption, "Sinclair's current lover, his past lover and another man…in happier times." Others followed suit, "the future of our country in these hoops?", "The Club where Sinclair's lover met his fate".

One unnamed cabinet minister was quoted as saying, "It's like a gay Dallas comes to the Labour Party. In a few weeks we'll be sighing for the monotonous sobriety of our regretted PM".

And in the course of the evening the rumours started that Brian Dawkins, the Home Secretary[40], was about to emerge as the man to unite the warring wings of the party. Brian was a competent but not outstanding minister. He had worked his way up from modest beginnings, people liked him and he spoke language people could understand. He was a more formidable threat than Derek Jamieson, who had his admirers but aroused no affection and was just too right-wing for the prevailing party mood.

The immediate reaction of Angus and Rupert was to mount a spoiling operation against Brian, "not really leadership material", "not quite up to it", "undistinguished record", "economically illiterate" and "backed the wars". All this was done without any authorisation from Raphael, who seemed almost to have disappeared. I just shouted at them to put a brake on this, "It's just going to make him more likely to stand". And as the evening progressed and alcohol loosened tongues and dulled senses, one adviser of the former PM actually said, on the record, "Well what do you expect? It's the way these guys live. Drink, drugs, seedy

---

[40] MP for Bristol, Avonmouth, 199-

bars and public sex with anyone who's available. I dread to think what will come out if Sinclair wins." Of course he was immediately reprimanded, but not before he had done his duty.

BARRIE

Tonight we were as downbeat as we were up in the heavens 24 hours ago. So typical, Raphael withdraws into himself, stays indoors and doodles with his lists, which now seem pretty irrelevant.

I was in the flat with Aidan, curiously subdued, and Raphael watching the evening news when there was an interruption for a live interview on the steps of one of the other hotels; it's Brian Dawkins who simply says, "I'm not going to stand. I've got some support but it's a helluva job, and I'd rather help others get us through this crisis. If Derek Jamieson stands, I'll back him. But that's his decision. And if at the end of tomorrow Raphael Sinclair is our leader, then I'll back him. We have just got to come together".

When he was asked about the "gay bar story", he said, "We're only responsible for what we do. We can't be held responsible for the mistakes of our friends. I think this young man's been through hell and we should leave him in peace".

You can almost hear the sound of his ratings soaring.

Afterwards, I tell Raphael what a relief this is. But he replied, "Well, yes and no. He's powerful backing for Jamieson." He then went into the bedroom and shut the door to make some calls. Later, we heard on Newsnight all the subterranean briefings against Jamieson, rehashed from last week, about complicity in the war and the accusations about torture. Is Raphael behind all this? He certainly knows and does nothing to stop it.

NED

Things got pretty nasty here last night. Some of the old guard get a bit physical with some of our kids and at least two fights break out in different bars. Anyone wearing a Rafa button is likely to be told he's a faggot or worse. So much for the Labour Party "coming together to heal the wounds".

HELEN

The clouds had cleared by Tuesday and the bright morning sunshine which greeted the delegates tramping to Conference seemed to mark the closing of a chapter or least a slight leavening of the atmosphere. The press was awful but Jose was now old news. And contrary to our fears there were no new revelations, merely the confirmation that the boy had been out on his own while the candidate and his partner had been having an early night in their rented flat in Hove. But the media story of the morning was all about Derek Jamieson. Would he stand? Or wouldn't he? With everybody counting the hours to the 5.30 p.m. deadline.

BARRIE

Aidan was even more sheepish this morning than he'd been yesterday. No coffee or toast on offer in the flat, no run with Bud. So what Rupert has hinted is true: out of sheer spite he got Jose drunk to disgrace himself and damage Raphael. Stupid, attention-seeking little wrecker.

Shortly after I arrived he went out to meet up with Angus and Rupert, "just to talk things over". My guess is they're plotting who gets which job, but for themselves. And with Raphael they know that what they want, they get. He's just so bloody emotionally dependent on them. It really is just an infatuation with youth and a fear of disappointing "his boys".

Raphael was restless all morning, trying to speak to Jose, on his mobile, his landlines, by text. Finally at midday he succeeded. He relayed the conversation after, with his usual quite skilful impressions, "He's in a desperate state. Hiding with friends at a house just outside Brussels and he's got a sick note for work for three weeks (apparently easily arranged over there). He doesn't think he can go back to his job and says he'll have to go back to Portugal; but hates that because it's been all over the Portuguese press, and his parents are mortified.

"He kept on saying, 'I am so sorry', 'Can you forgive me?', 'I didn't want to hurt you,' 'Please say you forgive me,' 'I love you', you know the way he stresses all the vowels, really sweet. I just commiserate and say, 'I love you, Jose', 'Let's leave it for now but I'll come and see you when next I'm in Brussels'.

Oh dear!

HELEN

That Tuesday lunchtime few dared leave the Conference centre because it always took hours to get back in, even for those of us who were members of the NEC. I just chatted with delegates over a couple of quite disgusting sandwiches and polystyrene cups of tasteless coffee. In fact, one would have found out more by watching the television in an hotel than could be picked up in the hall and the foyer, but there was this atmosphere, the feeling that something momentous was about to happen and that people felt genuinely uncertain about how it would work out.

Suddenly a smartly dressed young man in a dark suit came up to me and whispered discreetly, "Mrs Mitchison, the Foreign Secretary would be grateful if you could spare him a few minutes". I got up as unobtrusively as possible and followed him thinking that he was so polite, so different from the young men who surrounded Raphael. We went to one of the small offices reserved for senior cabinet ministers, with a security guard on the door. The young man left us alone after I had turned down an offer of yet another beaker of coffee.

We were silent for a few seconds; Derek looked pale, drawn and thinner than I remembered, and on edge in his voice and in his tone.

"Hi, Helen, well another fine mess and all that."

I let him continue.

"You know Raphael better than anyone. Is it going to be a revelation a day? How much worse can it get? It's so undignified. Come back Monica Lewinsky, all is forgiven."

"Derek, this has all been got up by the press. He and this young man were together for a time. They broke up, and the boy takes it badly, and gets paralytic. It's unfortunate, yes, embarrassing, but it's a nine-day wonder."

"You know, Helen, until this I was struggling to get signatures, now they're flooding in. We've just gone past the minimum, nearly the whole cabinet's signed up."

This was interesting because 37 is less than an avalanche, and a cabinet signature was less of an advantage than it might once have been.

"So", I asked, "you'll go for it?"

"Do you know, Raphael hasn't even spoken to me once? All I get is piles of excrement poured on my head by his young hooligans every time there's any question of my standing. I'm surprised they haven't said I should be arraigned in front of the International Court."

"Raphael hasn't spoken to you, but have you tried to speak to him?" I countered. "I think you should. He's still up in his flat in Hove. Here's the number. I'm not going to be the go-between for you two guys."

BARRIE

Just after 2 p.m. the 'phone rings, "Derek Jamieson here. Could I speak to Raphael?" Cold, no "please" of course. If you're a SPAD you get used to it. I passed the phone, Raphael waving me to stay, but of course I could only hear the replies.

"Well, you'll have to take your own decision, Derek. If you stand, at least we'll have a real contest....No I won't take that about my people...We've had a lot of things thrown at us. Really personal stuff. So of course some of my young friends lash out a bit...

"I really haven't decided who I'd want doing what, and it looks as though I'm going to get two months to think about it...If it were that quick, then of course I'd want some people to stay in post...

"Derek, I can assure you that I have absolutely no animus against you. I'd want you in a senior position...

"No, I can't offer you any specific post until I'd have seen the whole picture...No I can't promise you that you'd stay at the Office...Well, we can't go much further then… ."

I thought it was all over, when Raphael suddenly said, as if it's an afterthought, "Just one thing, Derek, there's this Brussels job, the Foreign Policy supremo. I can't make any commitment of course but I just wanted to know, independently of all the rest, if there'd be any interest on your side."

There was obviously a pause, and it wasn't just that I couldn't hear any reply because I could then hear him starting to speak after about thirty seconds. Then Raphael wound up, "Thanks anyway for ringing, Derek. We'll probably be in touch after you've made your decision."

He sat there silent for a few minutes, then said, "Tell Bud I want to go for a walk, clear my head for half an hour. You go back to the conference, keep me posted. I'll only answer the phone from you or Marjorie" (a limitation duly noted). He went downstairs still in his trainers, heading off, just him and Bud, walking away from the centre of Brighton.

NED

At 4 p.m. the word's out, Jamieson's going to declare, and he's got the signatures, half the cabinet have come on board. We crowd round the set in the NEC suite, only our lot allowed in the room, Ned rules.

Ten minutes later Jamieson walks out beyond the conference pens to speak to the fifty journalists and the outstretched mikes. He looks good, sleek, but white as a sheet, nervous. An aide hands him a note, and his own mike. Bit of a scrum but he's not enjoying it. He waits a moment then says, "I'm grateful to many colleagues asking me to stand for the leadership of our party. I did not wish for this vacancy. I did not wish for an election.

"I have spoken this afternoon with Raphael Sinclair. I accept his word that he wishes to work with me and other cabinet ministers for victory for Labour at the next election and for sensible policies to help the country overcome the severe problems it faces. I have decided in the interests of party unity not to let my name go forward - "

The rest was lost in whoops and cheers, shouts of "Bottled it! Bottled it!", we started jumping and hugging. Even Aidan smiled and laughed, the happiest I've seen him for days. Only Angus growled, "We're not going to let that fucker cling on in office if that's what he's after. That I promise you."

BARRIE

Raphael had deliberately not taken his mobile for the walk. But Bud had his. He tells me later how Raphael didn't really want to speak to Angus when he insisted on being passed to him. He gives no reaction to the news, but responds sharply to the suggestion that he had done a deal with Jamieson. But the walk is foreshortened so that when we spoke a few minutes later he was back in the flat, he says he'll have to go the Palace that evening, then "take possession of 10, Downing Street", and come back here in the night. "We'll then work on the cabinet, announce it tomorrow morning and I'll speak to Conference at 11-ish.

"Oh, and you can tell the Palace I'm bringing my partner, who'll be presented to the Queen".

"They'll never wear that", I say.

"Then tell the Keeper of the Bedchamber, or whatever else the fucker calls himself, that either she receives both of us or I just move straight into Downing Street."

"Wow", I said, (and how considerate of my predicament in having to negotiate this - for Aidan, of all people!).

I then asked, "And when are you coming here for the announcement?"

"I think it might be best just to stay out here. I feel a bit shaken up by all the stuff with Jose. Send a car for the heliport when we get a time from the Palace and we'll meet up there. If I do a victory lap at conference it just wastes time."

I almost shouted at him, "You can't be serious. They want to see you."

"Well, they'll have to wait. I'll go and change and shower now." He rings off, graceless, distracted, almost cold.

I just could not believe it. I rushed over to tell Ned, who was crestfallen when he heard, Aidan standing by seemed almost not to care. But I notice he's already smartened himself, somehow changed his tie since the morning (but when and where?).

Ned grabbed my phone, redialled, and almost whined, "Raf, you've gotta come. No-one'll believe it if you don't. It's rotten. Please come. We deserve the moment."

I can just hear Raphael, "Oh well, if you insist, Ned." Ned shouts out "result", looking at the mobile, now switched off.

HELEN

As if in contrast to the morning with its brilliant sunshine accompanying our gloom and anxiety, the rise in our spirits came as the weather broke. A gale had sprung up from nowhere, even deep in the Conference centre we could hear rolling thunder, and heavy rain pounding the roof. As the clock ticked away during the afternoon, Raphael phoned to tell me to track down Bill Sampson, which wasn't difficult as I was chatting with him and Paul Howkins in the NEC room. Bill took the phone and walked with it to a quiet corner, or as quiet as any room could be when Rupert Dennison and Ned Warren were in it.

When he came back, Bill asked, "Why do simple, when you can be complicated? Helen, love, can you find Brian Dawkins? I need a word before the announcement. He's not answering his phone, and I need to stay here just in case we get a last-minute surprise". I looked into the hall, which was now about half full, and it certainly was not for any interest in the debate on the turgid NEC document, 'Transport 2020', nor to listen to "a screeching sister" (Rupert's description), a delegate from Surrey, getting overexcited about car pools. I saw one of Brian's trade union friends and a couple of minutes later we had tracked him down near the stairs in the corner of the foyer. We walked together back to the NEC room, him his usual cheery self, and me thinking that I was sometimes more useful than Raphael's young acolytes because I knew the party and the way it works backwards.

NED

As 5.30 approached I was shaking with excitement. And He rang me (me!) to get the gang together in the leader's suite after the announcement. And he told me to find Aide, tart him up a bit - "tidy up the stubble, sober tie, get the shoes cleaned" - because at about 7-ish they'd be going to the Palace by helicopter. The Queen had agreed to receive him as 'First Partner'. "I'll be on my way in 10 minutes, and I'll come in from the back of the hall and sit with my delegates, so you tell Tom and Rodney to keep a place between them. When I go up to the platform, you get the whole gang to follow, including Tom and Rodney and some of the kids."

I rushed off in all directions simultaneously, not a pretty sight!

BARRIE

He was on his way at 5.15. I just had time to phone Bill with the choreography for his entrance. Marsha took her place on the platform, which now has seats only for her, Bill and Paul and one other. Someone handed her as discreetly as possible a bouquet of dark red roses, clearly not for her, as she laid them carefully on the floor, by her seat.

I had fixed everything with the Palace. Her Private Secretary, with a deeply fruity voice, was huffy about it all, made things complicated but in the end submitted because I could tell they're a bit shaken by all this. I sorted that Raphael would speak to Cynthia at 6-ish. I'd primed her a bit and I think she was pretty intrigued by it all. And I'd put the Baroness on stand-by, who was (understandably) confused at getting a call; I don't really know what it's for but I guess he's going for the Government of All The Talents bit, and she'll end up in some job advising him on foreign or security questions. Miranda was on the train back from Brussels, having hardly had time to get back to the office before turning round. We arranged for her to join the gathering crowd in Downing Street, where the TV crews were busily filming packed boxes being taken away by removals men. All the main stations were by this point covering Brighton and Downing Street live non-stop.

Ned was running around like a blue-arsed fly, tipping people off that they should join Raphael as he walked to the platform after the announcement - even Nigel and me plus quite a few kids. I spoke to Angus - pale, distracted, joyless as ever! - lined up for "the first conversation". For myself, I felt as if I'd swallowed a dozen amphetamines and my head was about to explode.

Just before 5.30 there was a commotion at the back of the hall, now totally jam-packed. Raphael had slipped into the hall alone, and unnoticed for about 15 seconds, before a thousand camera lights picked him out, just as he took his place in the front row of the second block on the left, between Rodney (puce with embarrassment but glowing with pride) and Tom (looking his usual surly self but giving Raphael a comradely hug).

Just after 5.30 Bill came on to the platform, followed by Paul and to my surprise, because he's not even on the NEC, Brian Dawkins. What's up?

Paul, who had taken over the chairing again, thanked the last speaker in the debate, a junior Transport Minister, and asked for a show of hands on the document, which made people laugh because they had no idea what was being debated, let alone what the document might contain. But old fashioned Labour proceduralism prevailed and the body of party policy had been enriched with proposals which the government could then studiously ignore.

It looked to me as if all safety precautions had been thrown out the window. The hall and galleries were now so packed that it was almost suffocating. I think a thousand friends from the press must have been there as well.

Much gavel banging from Paul. At last the smoky Geordie tones announced, "I call upon the General Secretary, Bill Sampson, to make an announcement." Bill stayed at his place, using a smaller mike on the desk in front of him.

"At the close of nominations for the party leadership, I have received from 185 members of Parliament (whistles, gasps) nominations for Mr Raphael Sinclair (cue for the first practice round of wild cheering and the concentration of all attention on the impassive senatorial face of the Man of Destiny, sitting in the middle of Row 1, Block 7, on the left. Rodney and Tom are in most of the shots beaming around the planet.)

"At the deadline for nominations, this was the only name received."

Paul, quickly, before yet another explosion, "The chair recognises the Home Secretary, Brian Dawkins". Difficult not to recognise someone if they're sitting next to you, so much for all this heavily scripted spontaneity.

"Comrades, friends, let's make this unanimous. I ask Conference to acclaim Raphael Sinclair as our new leader and Prime Minister."

At last the flood gates open. Conference stands, cheers, stomps, and the cameras hunt for malcontents and turn their attention to 'the pen' where the ministers are corralled, and where they now, with varying degrees of reluctance, join the ovation, even the Foreign Secretary putting his hands together slowly and limply as if marking time to a particularly tawdry ballad from the 1950s. Two diehard friends of the former PM can stand it no longer and walk out, but Conference Arrangements had placed them at the rear anyway. The Chancellor sits motionless after a couple of perfunctory claps. Above in the gallery, hysteria has broken out.

After ten minutes of this, Paul starts banging the gavel for all he's worth.

"I take it that's a yes, then. I declare Raphael Sinclair leader of the Labour Party and invite him to take his place on the platform.

The procession lasts a further ten minutes, he is of course milking the adulation, intimidating any residual opposition in the party, and sending a message to the outside world - this is different.

HELEN

By the time Raphael had made it to the platform and as the audience had shouted itself hoarse, Ned had placed us standing behind the five chairs, all of us beaming like some huge production team going up on the stage for the Oscar for this year's Best Film.

He stood at the centre of the stage, not at the projecting platform but just in front of the desk with the five chairs, ensuring that all of us are in the shots. We were a rather diverse bunch, the "beautiful people" of course, the kids, and some a lot older figures gnarled from decades of life in the party. Ned Warren, Hattie Reynolds and I were a little tearful, naturally. Even Angus seemed moved. Bo was there, his face blank with that slightly idiotic half grin; Maudie Hinton with a smile she allowed out only on special occasions; Paul Howkins and Bob Hatchway, the true professionals; Nigel, texting of course; Elaine dressed up like the Queen of Sheba, relishing the triumph of our old mutual friend, the man we'd probably both have wished to be accompanying to the Palace (I could well imagine the make-over she would have given Downing Street and Chequers); Rashida seeming to relax a little, although she was never less than studied in all her poses and in every outfit; Louise Marchant looking eager but apprehensive; and in the first row, to one side of me, Rupert Dennison (the glint of exultation); Angus Buchanan (impassive but with just the hint of satisfaction at the job done); Aidan, impenetrable, his beautiful dark eyes, the eyelashes any woman would die for, the unblemished skin apart from the residual bags under his eyes, the little beard perfectly shaped, the hair shorter and sleek, the charcoal grey suit, the blinding white shirt and the plain turquoise tie, the personification of a kind of dissolute glamour, whose life was about to change forever. Was it love that you could read into those eyes? If not, he had trapped himself forever.

And then on the other side of me little Barrie Jones, holding my hand as if to steady himself, and with him at least there was no doubt, true love for the man he knew so well and who despite that continued to idolise.

When at last he addressed us, Raphael kept it short and simple.

"Friends, I thank you from the bottom of my heart. This is the deepest honour to which any progressive politician can aspire, to lead the Labour Party. The party I love.

"I will have an opportunity tomorrow to talk to you about my programme for bringing change to Britain and to introduce my team.

"Allow me tonight the luxury of some more personal thoughts: for my parents who brought me up with so much love and who instilled in me the values of a just society; for my friends from my days at college who are friends for life, Helen and Elaine, now my spokesperson; for my staff for so many years, Marjorie, Barrie and Nigel, who kept me going through the wilderness and whom I love beyond measure; for all my friends in Mayberry who've sustained me in good times and bad - Tom, my local chair who tries and fails to keep me in order, Rodney, who does all the work; my fantastic campaign team...(he reeled off several names) - and then Angus, my campaign manager and the most talented young leader in Britain; Rupert, the great force of nature I want on my side, not anyone else's; Ned. Every party should have its Ned...but probably only one. And the most important to me, Aidan, my life partner who I love with all my heart."

This emotional hurricane had kept the audience on its feet, the cheering now a constant background flow.

"Tonight while you celebrate, Aidan and I travel to the Palace" (a reference which generated an extra spurt of cheering and sounded the death-knell of any last-minute attempt by the Palace to downgrade Aidan's status). "I then form my government. Tomorrow I speak to you again as your Prime Minister and explain how we change Britain together.

"Thank you. I'm moved beyond words. I hold you all in the greatest respect and the deepest affection."

NED

I couldn't see through my tears. I had to sit down when he finished.

BBC1 JUST AFTER 6.30 p.m.

"So Raphael Sinclair takes over the Labour Party. What began just a few weeks ago as a tiny group of malcontents grouped around a middle-aged middle-class politician who'd been out of frontline politics for almost a decade has transformed itself into a mighty machine which has swept all before it.

"As Mr Sinclair prepares to take the helicopter laid on by a civil service adjusting to the change and which will land him and his partner, Mr Aidan Richards, on to the helipad at Buckingham Palace, it will be dawning on him that taking over a demoralised political party, ousting a sitting Prime Minister, seeing off all rivals, rallying the troops, enthusing thousands of young people and organising a mass political campaign which has been the most spectacular in recent history: that was the easy bit.

Now he must govern."

******** END OF PART THREE ********

PART FOUR - OCTOBER SURPRISES

BARRIE

Ever since Jamieson's announcement, I'd been taken up with fixing the Palace protocol while Marjorie established the links with the Downing Street staff, started to assign offices and prepared contact details for those who will need them. A helicopter booked by Downing Street is scheduled to take off from a supermarket car park in the north of Brighton and arrive in the Palace grounds. My hope has been that we'd be able to leave Brighton soon after 6 which proves wildly optimistic. Although we aren't involved in any of the festivities, they create a kind of general tumult in the building and along the promenade. Raphael shows no sign of adulation-fatigue: he loves being mobbed and insists on having quick huddles in a tiny office off the NEC room; first with Angus which lasts 15 full minutes until his young campaign manager emerges white as a sheet; Marsha and Brian were in for less than 5 minutes each. It all took longer with Derek Jamieson, who looks grim-faced and sullen as he then goes off to fight his way through the milling crowds of Sinclairites who hold him in special contempt. There are lots of shouts of "Bottled it!" as he walks on, which can have done nothing to improve his disposition.

I was not in on these meetings and just hovered outside the cubby-hole until Bo of all people pulled my sleeve to take me to one side to say, "Just tell him it's not Louise but Hattie who leaked. I checked the tapes." He then disappeared in the throng leaving me to grapple with all the ramifications of what he'd said: the question of the culprit and - more upsetting - the method of detection used.

When the convoy finally leaves for the make-shift heliport an hour late, I am relegated to the second car with Marjorie and Elaine; the boss was in the first with Aidan (or "the first toy boy" as Rupert now calls him quite brazenly) and Bud. As we wait at the car park for clearance Raphael scrounges a cigarette from one of the drivers, which Aidan promptly snatches from him and dissolves in his hand. When he does these things I can see it's not out of any concern for Raphael's health, it's just a demonstration of his power.

There was no possibility of debriefing in the helicopter, which is far too noisy. When we arrive at the Palace gardens Elaine, Marjorie and I are whisked off to Downing Street to hang around outside the door for an hour - a good job that it had stopped raining - while waiting for the new PM's arrival. (I can hardly believe I'm writing this after all the highs and the lows of the last few weeks!) At least I was able to rescue Miranda and get her past the gates.

HELEN

Our first evening in power was quite extraordinary. The delegates created a kind of VE day atmosphere in and out of the hall but several of us elected to watch events on the three TV sets in the NEC room. Much later than scheduled as we saw the helicopter take off, Rupert says in a stage whisper, "I'm not religious but I'm allowing myself a little prayer for their safety: otherwise it's Marsha."

We saw the helicopter arrive in darkness and the Jaguar ferry just Raphael and Aidan to the porch, where they were greeted by the Queen's Secretary, a very tall man with the bearing of an ex-Guardsman, silvery hair and good-looking in a distinguished sort of way. Raphael seemed unhurried and nonchalant despite having kept the Queen waiting for more than an hour. Aidan turned to the cameras and for a few seconds waved at non-existent crowds, but hogging all the media attention until Raphael said something so that they could mount the steps side by side. All sorts of disquieting points were being made about the equality between them and the power each might have over the other.

Then there was nothing for almost an hour until the release by the Palace of two photos, one of Raphael with the Queen, and a second one with Raphael presenting Aidan, which was I have to admit a little bit of history and raised a big cheer in the NEC room now overflowing and taken over by the sans-culottes, helping themselves very liberally to the drinks cabinet.

The channels all switched to Downing Street: a few minutes later Raphael and Aidan got out of the cars at the gates and walked up through a huge crowd of supporters. The cordons had disappeared and they were both mobbed (there had been instructions from Rupert Dennison, "good pics; less stilted and artificial than in 1997" - he never leaving anything to chance). It indeed chimed with the idea of a popular uprising. I caught glimpses of Marjorie Delaney, Elaine Chayter and Barrie, who was accompanied by an enormously tall blond woman of about my age who someone whispered was an old friend of Barrie's.[41]

When Raphael moved forward to the mike, the last act in the ritual of the transfer of power in Britain, our heaving, sweaty, boozy room fell silent.

---

[41] This was Miranda Fawcett, who was to become Raphael's Chief of Staff

He just said, "Tonight the Queen has asked me to form a government. I accept the commission and pledge to carry out my programme for transforming Britain. We start tonight. I will appoint an administration for change. Then I go to Brighton to hold my first meeting with cabinet colleagues and to address Conference tomorrow morning. Radical, irreversible renewal is coming to Britain."

He promptly turned round and, just for a second, brushed Aidan's hand as they walked through the door. Rupert, who despite his loyalty to the new regime could never resist a sly comment, whispered, "If Rafa's back wasn't so dodgy I swear he'd have carried Aidan over the threshold."

NED

I get the lowdown via texts from Aidan. Angus, Rupe, Rashida and I have a tense meeting here just outside the bog on this floor, which I'd been sent to inspect to make sure no-one was in the cubicles to overhear. I then have to lean against the door to prevent any intruders coming across the four of us hovering in the gents.

Angus tells us that Rafa has asked him to be Chancellor (or rather Minister of Finance and Economics, a new fancy title, the Treasury just abolished and the old Business department thrown in for good measure). So you'd think he'd be over the moon but he was beefing that contrary to all his promises Rafa's going to keep Derek in the cabinet, at the Justice Department, doing all the constitutional stuff until the next election. Angus protests but Rafa stands firm and says "Take it or leave it. And after the election he's toast. But now he's useful to calm things down, and he keeps the Right on board."

Now personally that all sounds pretty reasonable but you'll know from my earlier bulletins what an absolutist Angus is. And he still hasn't accepted. And he's egged on by Rashida, who keeps parroting, "this sounds like the first decision and the first sell-out". Rupe just says, "Don't be such a cretin, Angus. Chancellor at thirty. What more do you want?" Pretty clear really. Angus thinks we'll all get something, except maybe Aide who'll have to wait until people get used to the loyal consort bit walking several steps behind his sovereign liege and lover. Bit unfair really, what with Aide having the most marginal seat.

Back in the NEC room, or Ned's place as it's now called (!), I have to fight for a drink, the hoi polloi having ransacked the bar. Talk about lowering the tone. Hat and Maudie both seem half-cut. I get a text from Aide about the Palace, "R goes in 1st and I get stuck with oily toff who says how we'll all enjoy Balmoral next year and puts plump pink hand on my knee & leers." When at last they release the photo of Rafa, Aide and Queenie, no-one dares say "Three Queens", but there's a huge cheer and there are more later when they occupy Downing Street.

Aide texts from inside, "Upstairs with Bud to check it all out. Pokey. Smaller than Putney but cleaner than Chiswick".

Ten minutes later, "Bud's raided the mess kitchen in the basement now preparing salad. Won't please R who's starving. I'm off to change".

Another 10 minutes, "Now clean & beautiful. Bud now in shower & is really part of family. Marjorie says we return at midnight. Get everyone to drinks at yr place".

Last text of the evening, "R says he wants to speak to us all individually tonite. Some odd people pitching up here".

BARRIE

It all starts a bit brutally. Raphael calls in the Cabinet Secretary alone. He comes out shaken because he's just been sacked, replaced by Cynthia Montcalm who returns to confound her enemies in the Deep State.

Marjorie's worked out the phones and is starting on the 'must call' list. First up the US President, who seems pretty hazy about who he's talking to, what happened to the other guy ("Is he on the mend? Great guy. Shame he fell ill."). All this relayed to me afterwards by Raphael. Then the French President ("flattered me for speaking such good French"), the German Chancellor ("cool, precise, joyless") and the Commission President ("a bit patronising in an oleaginous way").

Cynthia's already showing the whites of her eyes. Friendly to Marjorie and to me, through gritted teeth she simply said to Miranda, "I suppose we'll just have to try and rub along together".

Then there are more calls to cabinet ministers being told they were getting their cards. Finally towards 9.30 in the evening he calls in Miranda, Marjorie and me to be told his list of the "stayers" for the cabinet. Marsha becomes formally Deputy PM and gets a new Regional Affairs Department (so the ancient Scottish, Welsh and Northern Ireland Departments are to be scrapped, just like that). I blanch, but say nothing because I know when he's made up his mind. Brian has agreed to stay at the Home Office (relief all round); old Bradley Mortimer's back at Defence, "years of experience and he's anti-Trident and will face down the armchair generals". Arthur Rillington stays on at Health ("he's got good ideas, he's brave, he speaks his mind, New Labourish but not so as you'd notice, the regional accent helps").

And then the first real whammy, Derek is to get Justice and run the Constitutional Convention. ("He's such an ungrateful turd. Lots of handwringing and whinging and downright gracelessness, and I had to throw in a few sweetener hints about the Brussels job.") But the real knockout, "I've decided to give young Angus his head, let him have a Finance and Economics Ministry, we scrap the Treasury and the old Business and Trade Departments; let him try out all his ideas. It'll either be our very own economic miracle and he'll be our wunderkind, or it'll all end in tears. But we can't do the half-measures, it's got to be our "rupture". It's our big test. We'll have to go for it. When I told him I thought he'd pass out."

"Talking of which, what does one have to do to get a sandwich round here? I'm starving. Has Lorna arrived? Well send her in so I can give her the shock of her life too. Then I'll nip up to the flat and see what Bud has been able to rustle up. Then it's Brighton here we come. I'll speak to the others one by one. Marjorie, you can ferry them over from the partying. We'll give Elaine the list so she can announce it at 8 a.m. live, and we'll get them together at 10.30. I'll speak to Conference at midday. Now where's Lorna?"

We walk out, and I almost feel faint. I can't believe it. He's handing the British economy to this kid: this bright, precocious, petulant kid. He may be "the best economist of his generation" if you believe his own self-promotion, but he'll be eaten alive. He's so left-wing it'll make the Great Leap Forward seem pure Chicago School.

And Marsha as Deputy PM? She'll be even more Lady Muck than she is now. And has he given a moment's thought to what it means to amalgamate all these Offices? Or how it will look?

And keeping Derek? Our people will see this as a betrayal - the first of many. The archpriest of New Labour. The warmonger. Complicit with torture. All the sniping from the sidelines. Of course it's only tactics until the election but it's hard to swallow.

HELEN

We had drifted back to the house rented by Rupert Dennison and Ned Warren at the Hove end which of course I had to tidy up. Rupert's little bedroom was clean enough, but the rest was a tip; and I did not have the stomach to go into Ned Warren's bedroom. Some of the others had brought considerable quantities of alcohol but most of us were too tired and drawn to start drinking large whiskies. At just after midnight, Raphael arrived looking fresh and relaxed. He worked the room in about fifteen minutes flat, and then he walked back to his flat to see us one by one.

He called me in first, which was kind. It was not really a surprise when he offered me education with the universities thrown in. It was what the press had expected. It was what I really wanted. I tried to pump him for more information, but all I got was a warm embrace as I was sent on my way.

NED

I try to sober up, drink four black coffees in a row, get stomach ache and then the runs. Finally at one in the morning I get called in to see the headmaster expecting a good caning.

"Ned", he says as if pleasantly surprised to see me walk into his little flat in Hove in the middle of the night. He's the picture of benevolent calm, all relaxed, with a light blue shirt unbuttoned at the top, dark grey flannels and slippers.

"I want you to be our business manager."

I look blank, gorm all gone.

"Leader of the House, you know, plan our work, all that. But I'm combining it with the Chief Whip's job, you know, keep the party in order. Big man, big job." His eyes twinkle with amusement.

I suddenly feel very sick and too scared to speak, lest all the booze and food starts seeping out of every orifice. I just nod, stand up, hug him, walk downstairs, onto the street, enter the house, where the doors are open and the music's playing loudly, and rush past everyone straight to the loo.

BARRIE

It's 2.30 in the morning when we all get summoned back in for the completed list.

"Lorna's agreed. Tickled pink," Raphael chortles triumphantly. "Just see them gasp. A Tory baroness as Foreign Secretary in a radical Labour government. That'll get them all choking on their cornflakes. This is world-class triangulation. And the thing is, on Europe, defence and the Americans she's as radical as I am." Hugely pleased with himself. (His sudden elevation has clearly made no change there then!).

We go through the list and it gets worse and worse. I'm happy for Helen at Education. She'll be good at it, progressive but rooted, knows it off by heart. Paul gets Transport. Fine. I had told Raphael about my chat with Bo (the thought that his events organiser had been bugging his campaign team didn't seem to faze him in the slightest) so Louise is reprieved and becomes Budgets Minister in Angus's empire and saves her place in the cabinet. Harriet, the leaker, still manages to keep the Pensions and Welfare portfolio (the only explanation given later by Raphael was "serves her right"). "The airhead leaks so she's rewarded with having to find welfare cuts. Don't fancy her chances for the NEC next year." This is straight out of the Harold Wilson text book, "How tactics trumps everything in politics". Rashida gets Housing and Local Government which is fair enough and pretty important for the economic strategy. Then he brings back that old warhorse, Margo Horsfall, for about the eighteenth time. She's been resurrected from some Old Labour graveyard just to honour the parity pledge.

Then it's Ned, "He's so good with the Party. He'll do the Commons leadership, and we'll combine that with the Chief Whip job. It'll be such fun having him next door in Downing Street." (I'm sure this is Aidan's idea). And Rupert gets Media and Culture, as we'd been expecting.

"Got all that?", he asks.

I ask, "And Aidan?", guessing and dreading the answer.

"I can't really bring him into the cabinet. But No 2 at the FO, the Europe job, deputising for Lorna in the Commons, and attending cabinet. It's not too bad a package. Did all that myself once." All this is said as if he feels I might be concerned that Aidan is getting a raw deal, which really isn't my worry.

"Now, Marjorie, could you wake up Elaine at around 7 with the list so that she can do the announcement for 8. I ought to go and put my head down for a few hours. Could you pop next door, Barrie, to get them to turn down the racket or we'll have the police round?"

So that's it. Clever and reckless in equal measure. A really small cabinet (the public will like that). Numerical parity (the voters couldn't care less but it's a pledge kept). Bring in a few New Labour people for a bit of reassurance but some really big jobs for the new generation. Add in an old Labour throwback, plus Marsha (so deeply unattractive older women are well represented - slap my own wrist for outrageously non-PC remark!), and then rock everybody's socks off with a Tory baroness at the Foreign Office, which gives you the excuse to bring in your lover as No 2 because "goodness, Lorna's in the Lords, so I'll guess I'll have to have Aidan at cabinet meetings after all. Aw shucks!"

You've got to admire the artistry forged from all this low cunning. I couldn't stomach going back to the party now going full pelt at the Ned and Rupert flat. I just couldn't face Rupert in all his superbity; Ned slobbering all over me; Angus planning the revolution; or the sight of the Consort savouring his clever little triumph. So I've just walked back to our place in steady drizzle to commit all this to paper.

BBC 8 a.m.

"Raphael Sinclair has formed his government. It's the smallest peacetime administration in a hundred years. And it has as many women members as men. Over now to our political editor…

"He could just have brought in some new blood to the lower ranks. He could have limited the number of changes just to steady the ship. Like Mrs Thatcher in her first government, he could have kept the team of his predecessor, bided his time and struck later.

"Raphael Sinclair has done none of these things. He's cleared out most of the New Labour regime. There are a few survivors in middle-ranking posts. But mostly it's a clean sweep.

"The young radical economist, Angus Buchanan, takes over the whole direction of the economic and financial policy of the government. The old Treasury, the dominant power centre of British policy, just disappears. The new job combines the Exchequer, that's what the state spends and what you contribute, macro-economic policy and the old Trade and Business jobs. Apart from the Prime Minister, the levers of power are in the hands of a thirty-year-old with a stellar economic reputation in some circles but no previous government experience.

"All Mr Sinclair's most prominent young supporters are handsomely rewarded, including the popular Mr Ned Warren, who combines the job of Leader of the House with that of Chief Whip, and with the title of "Minister for relations with Parliament".

"Women get equal billing and the most startling appointment of all, Baroness Lorna Horrocks, a Thatcher-era Tory MP, as Foreign Secretary, will raise eyebrows here in Brighton. But as the PM's spokesperson, Elaine Chayter, in her first official press conference said, "She's sound on Europe, disarmament and the Middle East. What's not to like?".

"And Mr Sinclair hasn't overlooked his young partner, Mr Aidan Richards, who becomes Europe Minister, deputises for Baroness Horrocks in the Commons and attends cabinet.

"There are all the traditional balances, north and south, Old and New Labour, all at the table. And the electorate may take kindly to the scrapping of all of those departments. Only time will tell what this most radical restructuring of government in a hundred years means for the policies it will pursue."

NED

<-<-<-<-<-<-<-<-<-<-<-<-<-<-<

#@nedwar82

<-<-<-<-<-<-<-<-<-<-<-<-<-<-<

Only got this job cos they wanted me in 12 Downing St to raise the tone of the neighbourhood

HELEN

For day after day Raphael had dominated the news. But the announcement of the new cabinet caused its own sensation. The New Labour crowd felt dispossessed. Some of our hardliners were angry Derek Jamieson had survived. And there was much muttering about putting a Tory peeress[42] in as Foreign Secretary, although this subsided when people saw that she had consistently criticised Labour foreign policy from the left not from the right. Some people liked the small cabinet approach, although quite a few PLP hopefuls could do their sums and saw the narrowing of horizons. The parity was appreciated, and at least twice I heard delegates saying, "and he hasn't felt the need to appoint glamorous young women", which did make me wince.

But the sensation was the rocket launches of the careers of Raphael's girls and boys (well, mostly boys, actually). There were a few snide comments from some old homophobes about "the hot totty faction" (by which I supposed they meant Angus Buchanan, Rupert Dennison and Aidan Richards, but hardly Ned).

So after this furore it was something of a surprise to see how supremely relaxed Raphael was when we all met up in the Lord Mayor's parlour for the first meeting of the Sinclair cabinet. It all started late because Raphael had insisted on walking from his Hove flat in pale sunshine accompanied only by Aidan, the bodyguards and about a thousand journalists and on-lookers.

The Mayor's Office was almost too big for us. I was placed next to Marsha, who it had been decided should now sit opposite the Prime Minister. Angus was on Marsha's right, and we faced Brian, on Raphael's left, and the pert birdlike features of Dame Cynthia Montcalm[43], the new cabinet secretary - an appointment almost as astonishing as that of Lorna Horrocks. I could not quite quash the politically incorrect thought that Raphael's obsession with titled Tory women of a certain age, like his enthusiasm for the music of Donna Summer[44], might just be a "gay thing".

---

[42] Baroness Lorna Horrocks, Conservative MP for Yorkshire North-West, 1979-1997
[43] A career civil servant who had been Raphael's Principal Private Secretary at the Foreign and Commonwealth Office
[44] An American disco singer whose song 'State of Independence' had become the Insurgency's unofficial anthem

Sitting behind the PM on flimsy collapsible chairs were poor Barrie Jones and Miranda Fawcett, his new chief of staff, a hugely tall girl, very bright and with a strong Yorkshire accent, and a long time Labour supporter. She obviously got on well with Barrie, although she was almost twice his size.

Ned Warren seemed to think that the plate of biscuits in the middle of the table at his end was all his until Maudie quite audibly smacked his hand and said, "Mitts off, fatso". He then managed to spill tea all over the papers of Arthur Rillington[45], the reconfirmed Health Secretary, who looked extremely cross. Brian Dawkins took some of the sting out of the incident by saying something like, "I see young Warren's already making quite a splash". As the camera crews did their final rounds of the table I studied four faces in particular. Aidan spruced up, hair brushed back but fairly short and beautifully tailored, his face with its superior knowing expression, but a kind of defiance in his eyes, tempered by just a flicker of tenderness when he caught Raphael's gaze. Rupert, supremely confident, with a brilliant navy blue shirt, light jacket and narrow white tie. It had to be said that at least two of Raphael's acolytes really know how to dress. Then Angus, staring ahead, not speaking either to Marsha on his left or to Bradley Mortimer[46] on his right; all fierce volcanic concentration, adamantine, with an almost intimidating authority.

And then finally I looked back to Raphael, laughing at some little anecdote with Cynthia and Brian on his flanks, as if posing for one of those 'sharing a joke' photos in the Tatler you pick up in doctors' waiting rooms in middle-class areas. So totally at ease in his new position but glancing just once at the far end opposite from Aidan, where sat the brooding presence of Derek Jamieson, contemplating just how much he had become the outsider.

Raphael beckoned Barrie to crouch by his side and whispered something, whereupon Barrie and Miranda shooed out the cameramen, and thus began the first cabinet meeting of the Sinclair era. It was all rather perfunctory: a 2-minute homily about confidentiality and quotes from the 'Instructions to Ministers', and a short glare at Ned who appeared to be tweeting, and the need to respect the views of others. Angus Buchanan then gave a report on the economic situation, the attack of the jitters in the markets which had greeted his appointment,

---

[45] MP for North Bedfordshire 199- : Secretary of State for Health since 200-.
[46] MP for Manchester South-East, 199- : Secretary of State for Defence since 200-.

and the likelihood of an early loss of the UK's triple A rating[47]. He then switched to the question of the minimum wage but Raphael cut him off, "I'll probably have to say something later to conference if we ever get there".

Then Baroness Lorna Horrocks was given the floor about the weekend's EU meetings which she did with great aplomb; totally unabashed at being surrounded by 'the enemy', completely on top of her subject, the great old pro, and funny too, with her concluding aside, "and if I make a mess of things I'll have this young man" (pointing at Aidan) "to hold my hand and prevent the UK from disgracing itself. God help us!" To my surprise instead of snarling, Aidan gave a warm beatific smile.

Raphael kept looking at his watch (which had an unusually large face, with huge numbers so that he did not need to squint when he looked at it, or put on his glasses which he hated doing in public, or indeed just reveal that he was counting the seconds before he could move on). Finally he said, "Look, colleagues, we're already running late. I want a few words in political cabinet. So Cynthia, if you could leave us now." Cynthia, forewarned, had already scooped up her papers when Lorna's stentorian tones interrupted with "If it's political, I'd better leave too". But Raphael said, "No, Lorna, you stay. You're a full member of this cabinet". This was said firmly to stop some of the more tribal of us like Paul Howkins or Maudie Hinton from querying the continued presence of the Tory.

When the room settled down Raphael just said in a matter of fact way, "When the euphoria subsides, we're going to get a lot of stuff in the Tory press about how we should have an election because we've changed PM twice and we lack legitimacy. So I think we should at least give the question a little attention". There was a bit of muttering in the ranks which he quelled by raising his voice just a notch.

"I know there's no constitutional obligation whatsoever but I'd like your views."

These came fast and furious, nearly all arguing strongly against an early election. Marsha, "the party's not ready"; Brian, "we need to settle the ship"; Paul, "we ain't got the money to fight an election"; and Derek, unpleasantly, "It will look like cut and run but you'll doubtless do as you please". Angus sounded rather detached, which surprised me, "From an economic point of view, things are bad now and I don't see any likely

---

[47] The rating of the country's credit worthiness by the leading credit agencies.

short-term improvement". Ned's was the best comment, "Blimey, only just worked out where I should be sitting".

Only Rupert was clearly in favour, "We've got momentum. There are a lot of people out there" (pointing in the general direction of the promenade), "who are just spoiling for a fight".

Throughout all this Raphael remained poker-faced, taking note of every remark as if he was Cynthia's junior, deputed to take the minutes. At the end he just said, "Thanks everyone. That was pretty clear. Now I think we'd best be off back to the hall. We're already running late".

NED

<-<-<-<-<-<-<-<-<-<-<-<-<-<-<

#@nedwar82

<-<-<-<-<-<-<-<-<-<-<-<-<-<-<

First cab. Hogged the biscuits. Spilled tea over my new ex-friend Arthur's papers.

BARRIE

Another piece of sublime artistry. He goes through all this rigmarole knowing it's just a sham. He, Bill and Angus decided days ago (or why had he got me checking out the dates so carefully?). So we let everybody talk on while he doodles. When they leave, Miranda and I sit with him, knowing not to interrupt. Then more doodles and on a couple of cards, 4 or 5 headlines just in case he blanks. In other words, the first speech as Prime Minister is to be made up as it goes along. Winging it as usual. Why did we ever think he'd change?

When we go out the front door of the town hall there are just hundreds of press, trampling all over the late autumn flowers which had thrived in their beds in the generally balmy Indian summer. Then we force ourselves along when one of the reporters shouts out the question, "Why won't you call an election?" He just laughs. The security, even reinforced since yesterday, is almost losing control. Bud looks tense. Bill rings me up, "Where the fuck are you? Do you realise how late you are? I thought you were meant to be his minder. You couldn't mind a rotten tomato." To which I just reply, "Charming".

We make it to the side door of the Centre just as the cabinet is trooping on stage to wild cheers, Lorna flanked by Brian and Bradley Mortimer as if for personal protection, but the crowds have started to feel some enthusiasm for her. We watch all this from the wings. The volume is ratcheted up for Donna Summer's 'State of Independence' (one of Bo's favourites). The hall is now in paroxysms as Raphael takes his place between Paul and Marsha. Once again the legal capacity limits have been completely ignored and it's just five or six thousand shouting themselves hoarse.

Paul stands and just says, "I can hardly believe the words I'm going to say. Ladies and gentlemen, the Prime Minister, Raphael Sinclair". Cue for ten more minutes' joyous tumult.

NED

<-<-<-<-<-<-<-<-<-<-<-<-<-<-<

#@nedwar82

<-<-<-<-<-<-<-<-<-<-<-<-<-<-<

How can he possibly build on this?

HELEN

He tried of course to effect the change from rebel warrior to statesman but the crowd were baying for 'his greatest hits' so he scoured his memory for the phrases delegates wanted to hear. He was improvising but fully prepared. Then he started on a list of policy announcements and decisions.

BARRIE

He tells everyone about decisions the government has taken that morning (ones which of course he hadn't even mentioned in cabinet!). So the minimum wage is immediately upped by 15%, with the living wage in 4 years' time. A VAT cut to 15% across the board. A new tax holiday for any SME creating jobs. Trident renewal stopped in its tracks. The defence bill cut by 25% in 2 years. He says he'll go to Helmand tomorrow with Bradley (who unfortunately mouths "Fuck" on camera) to announce that all British troops from both theatres will be back by Christmas but accompanied by training of local public administrations and a lot of support for education of young girls in both countries.

"And this is just the beginning. This is what happens when you back me. You voted for change. Now you get it."

After another 20 minutes of governing-as-you-go-along there was a sudden pause, a long pause. He suddenly seemed deeply uncertain.

NED

<-<-<-<-<-<-<-<-<-<-<-<-<-<-<-<

#@nedwar82

<-<-<-<-<-<-<-<-<-<-<-<-<-<-<

Christ he's blanked.

BARRIE

Just seconds before it got embarrassing he continued, "Of course our opponents will say you've no right to make these changes because you have no mandate. This is the Tories and their new constitutional doctrine. In a country which thanks to them doesn't even have a constitution. I want to deal with this argument head on. They say you must have an election when you change Prime Minister. They didn't say that when they dumped Mrs Thatcher.

"So let me be clear. We go to the country when we choose."

Another long pause. Tension mounting in the hall.

"I've thought about this long and hard. The reason we don't have to go to the country is twofold. We've not got a presidential system. We vote for a party to carry out its programme. It's not who leads the government that matters. It's the programme which counts."

Another long pause.

"But there's the rub. The trouble is we're not a business-as-usual government. I'm not the continuity Prime Minister. We are a government which is new, brimming with new ambitions, new policies. We are transformative. To bring about this break with the past, this rupture, to take the path of transforming everything, we don't need an election for constitutional reasons. We need it for moral reasons." (Then slowly he starts to build.)

"We need an election because it's the right thing to do. To change Britain I need the engagement of the British people to accompany us in making the change. Last night I obtained the Queen's authorisation to dissolve Parliament. This morning I consulted cabinet. Today Parliament is dissolved. The general election will be on October 18th.

"We fight. We fight the fight of our lives. We fight as if our future depends on it. We fight to transform Britain. We fight to win."

He lulled them, he jolted them and then he electrified them. The faces of his cabinet colleagues tell the story: perplexed, then aghast, then on their feet, then cheering their heads off like the rest of the crowd.

BBC NEWSFLASH

Raphael Sinclair shocks his party. On day one in office he has called an election for October 18th- the minimum period possible. Saying that he needed a mandate for transformation and citing "moral reasons", he brought the Labour Party Conference to a rousing climax and shocked commentators and Opposition politicians alike. Over to our political editor in Brighton:

"This morning after all the surprise appointments in his cabinet we thought Raphael Sinclair had brought the last rabbits out of his hat. But at noon today Sinclair the conjurer produced the biggest surprise of all: the snappiest of snap elections. He reckoned that the Conservatives and sections of the press were going to call for new elections and would harry him as long as he refused. Now they must renew their acquaintance with that old phrase, "Beware of what you wish for". Mr Sinclair knows it's a tall order. Labour still flatlines in the polls below 28%. There's still a lot of blood on the carpet after the defenestration of his predecessor. To many his programme sounds frankly alarming. But he has energised his party and electrified our politics. We're in for a bumpy three weeks."

NED

<-<-<-<-<-<-<-<-<-<-<-<-<-<-<

#@nedwar82

<-<-<-<-<-<-<-<-<-<-<-<-<-<-<

Driven (!) back to London pm, post a few celebrations in the bars. With little Arthur in car. Still cross. No 12 gloomy so I'll call on my mates down the street later.

HELEN

I was angry with myself. Of course Raphael had been planning this all along. I later learned from Barrie that only Bill and Angus had been involved in taking the decision. Bill of course had used the time sensibly: buying up advertising space, hoardings and blocks of time at printers, and booking venues. The appeals for donations and volunteers were up on the party's website the moment Raphael had sat down. These men can sometimes keep a secret. The rest of us were pretty shell-shocked. I thought I knew Raphael so well but his gambling sometimes blindsided me.

When I visited my new Department at the end of the afternoon I had the distinct impression that it was a case of "Let's not waste too much time on her. She won't be here for long". So I decided to lay down the law. Raphael had given me a free hand with the rest of the ministerial team, so I kept two and brought in a couple of women friends from the backbenchers. We had our first departmental meeting at 8 in the evening and agreed the main lines of policy: we would halt the academies programme, starting work on the switch from tuition fees to a dedicated graduate tax and finding some extra resources for inner city schools.

BARRIE

In the car back Raphael was his usual flippant self, joking rather archly with Bud whom he seems to have adopted, giving me the odd tickle (which I once would have pined for but which I now find unbecoming, and for me demeaning). He phoned around, got Marjorie to fix up some appointments back at the office. Over the phone he then hired Dame Elizabeth Jones-Wright (known to everybody as EJW evidently), another FCO battle-axe, as his diplomatic adviser (probably just to rile Cynthia) and a young diplomat from UKREP, Helena Chandler, to be his EU adviser - a bit superfluous really. When he speaks to Helena he says playfully, "I shall want you to keep a close eye on this new Europe Minister and make sure he doesn't get up to any mischief". If only he was joking.

He then talks to Bradley at length about their trip to Helmand and gets fed lots of briefings from Cynthia, EJW and from the great Lorna herself. He loathes the idea of the trip but feels he has to make it. We're hardly in the door of No 10 before Miranda presents him with a 'To do' list as long as your arm. Elaine almost drags her off him to prepare him for the 6 p.m. broadcast on all channels on the election announcement. I scamper to my little cubby-hole and start jotting down stuff for the manifesto.

He's established himself at the middle of the long table in the cabinet room (the first PM to do this for decades) because he finds the parlour "cramped" and likes space for his papers, which, contrary to some of his predecessors, he will actually read. Miranda, Nigel and I get half an hour with him (and a cup of tea and some biscuits, which he wolfs down - from our plates as well, there being a little bit of Ned in all of us) before we are joined by some officials. Miranda and EJW take him through the programme for Helmand. He almost baulks at the lunch in the squaddies' mess ("so artificial"). For the speech to the troops, Nigel runs through the messages, "Pride in your work, contribution made, now looking for political solutions, the savings we make in bringing you home must be used to make lives better for you and your families". He queries this, and asks for lots of figures about what savings really would be made and what could actually be done about soldiers' families' accommodation.

In all, the travelling will take up 20 of the next 24 hours and he'll be completely exhausted. All this just for a few photo opps. But he'd be crucified if he didn't do it.

NED

>>

From: ned.warren.1982@hotmail.com

To: martin.warren.78@hotmail.au

>>

The broadcast was good enough. Straight to camera. Felt as if it was off-the-cuff which it never is with Rafa. But he doesn't use the teleprompter. "Why I had to call the election"; "if we're going to make the change, I need your support". A bit later he rings me and tells me to start work on the candidates' list. Didn't immediately twig at first, but he spells it out as if speaking to a very backward child. A snap election two years early means lots of parliamentary candidatures undecided. In this case the rules say it's the NEC which can impose candidates ('force majeure', look it up). I subsequently discover there's at least 150 seats going begging, with quite a few of the old guard of MPs retiring, some in disgust.

He just says to me, "You draw up a list and we go through it when I get back. It's our chance to shape the parliamentary party for good. I want lots of women" (don't we all? Well, I guess not all), "ethnics, our kids. But above all, our people".

I pluck up a bit of courage. "Shouldn't we shift some of our people to any safe seats going? Like, er, Aidan for example?"

"Nope. It'll look like the old chicken run. And I want him where I can keep an eye on him."

I really hadn't intended telling Aidan all this but when just after midnight I went round to inspect their living quarters at No 10 (poky as hell, mine's dowdy but swank) and after a few snorts of the hospitality whiskey, Rafa being safely out of the picture, I finally blurted it out. Aidan, who'd been drinking a lot less than me, said nothing but just stared in the distance. Next door I think they went to bed early.

EXTRACT FROM 'THE JC DUNNETT ANTHOLOGY (199- to 201-)'

A column for a fortnightly magazine allows the writer a little perspective on recent events rather than the servitude of a frenzied scramble for scoops and the tyranny of deadlines. But I confess to some frustrations over the last four weeks since the fevered launch of Mr Sinclair's quest for power. Hardly has one had the time to remove the cover from one's faithful old Remington but some new sensation has sent the Labour roller coaster on another splash into rough waters or soaring towards the heavens.

I recognised early that the key to success for the insurgents in sustaining any national momentum lay in feeding the press's considerable appetite for mischief while under the radar screen meting out some good old-fashioned intimidation to force MPs to support the leadership challenge. What I had not reckoned on was the brazenness with which the coercion would be applied: young commissars from our top universities dispatched to the regions to ferment revolt in a manner worthy of the Red Guards, egged on by the quite frankly chilling aggressivity of some of the Caudillo's immediate circle. We have yet to become fully acquainted with Mr Angus Buchanan, part raging Glaswegian bull, part Robespierrian chilly calculation, but I would counsel against entering into argument with him. Another Labour left-winger was once described memorably by the then Prime Minister as "an Old Testament prophet without a beard" and Mr Buchanan's religion is of the merciless, vengeful sort. With his equally radical partner, "the Lady Macbeth from Karachi" as she was once irreverently described, one would find it hard to believe that managing all aspects of the British economy will be anything more than a staging post on the road to fulfilment of their shared ambitions.

And in Mr Rupert Dennison the Prime Minister has found the perfect Goebbels for the Insurgency, with no dissimulation too huge to be deployed when it comes to defending the cause and with a talent for Orwellian paradox that would not have disgraced the old Master and which makes the linguistic doublespeak of New Labour seem like plain old English. His infectious chirpiness and fine fair features are there almost to mock us, so strongly do they contrast with the sinister manipulation and dark arts of which he is the prime instigator.

We know less of Mr Ned Warren, the insurgency's Court jester. The public persona is well established, the bluff, cheerful, Estuary boy, who looks as if he's auditioning for the role of a teenage Billy Bunter, just about to raid the tuck shop. But those small, twinkling eyes and the studied sloppiness tell their own story. One insider at the Court of

Raphael Sinclair tells me that he has the sharpest political brain and a willingness to wield the stick which will come in handy now that his rather plump paws have got their grip on the machine. He will dispose of any opponents of the new ascendancy with a hearty good-natured laugh.

But it is the fourth member of this murderous quartet who alarms most. The phenomenon of an older man attracted to the point of infatuation to a good-looking younger male is a cliché that stretches back to prehistoric times through antiquity, the Roman Empire and on to Oscar Wilde and to many relationships in both social life and the workplace between men of different age groups. But to many the snarling aggressivity and extreme views of Mr Aidan Richards make his physical proximity and emotional closeness to our new Prime Minister a matter of concern. One would guess that what Mr Richards wants, Mr Richards gets. In the event of a Labour victory, which despite the stubbornly persistent Tory lead can still not be ruled out, one can only guess that Mr Richards will want a lot.

The new cabinet roll-call is a fascinating balancing act which is clearly destined for a short shelf-life. Mr Derek Jamieson and others will have to justify to their maker how they can sup at the same table with those who quite openly call them war criminals and serial liars, for that was and is the core narrative of this Insurgency. Into this mix of revolutionary jackals and capitalist road-runners is thrown the portly form of a former Tory minister to head up what used to be called British diplomacy. This was a Sinclair master-stroke, a degree of reassurance in enlarging the 'big tent', a wonderful distraction from too close an inspection of the qualifications of the younger set who have been propelled to the top table, and a cover for giving his paramour a place at the cabinet table, given the objective need for the baroness to have a surrogate in the House of Commons.

The fact of having an openly homosexual Prime Minister has so far been greeted with almost tearful expressions of joy by the British progressive establishment. Headlines around the world are rebranding Britain as a paradise of liberal tolerance and diversity. Whether this will lead to a durable change in public attitudes towards those with minority sexual preferences may depend on how often are repeated incidents such as the spread-eagling under croquet hoops on the lawns in front of the Royal Pavilions of the near-naked form of one of the Prime Minister's youthful ex-lovers. One suspects that Mr Aidan Richards, to name but one, may have a carnal back-catalogue which could titillate tabloid readers for years to come.

For the moment all is audacity and swagger. Mr Sinclair took the most reckless gamble in summoning us to the urns for October 18th. This was a master-stroke, aware that the market gloom would be momentarily lifted by the possibility that the new regime might last only a few weeks, keeping the new Jacobin ministers from wreaking excessive harm by sending them out in battle buses rather than allowing them to issue fatwas from Whitehall, keeping the thousands of insurgents mobilised, playing to the British sense of fair play which ordains that the new crew be given its chance, and lulling us into the comforting thought that Mr Sinclair's highly developed sense of honour pushed him into taking this noble risk.

The real reason for the snap election is to be found elsewhere: that middle England may begin to tire of the permanent revolution, and that the longer the campaign, the more likely that press scrutiny, suspended in this general atmosphere of mass hyperventilation, may begin to examine more closely the programme of this latter-day Committee of Public Safety and the personalities of its leading members.

Mr Sinclair has fired the starting gun for a race against the clock.

HELEN

We had a decidedly difficult start, not helped by Raphael's absence the first full day in office. He was visiting the troops in Southern Afghanistan and just about managed to avoid conveying the message that their comrades had fallen in vain and that the two wars had been a waste of life, time and money. When he came back the fatigue of the campaign, the conference and the trip to the front had completely exhausted him, and he disappeared from view for 36 hours.

I learned from Maudie Hinton, who had become by this point quite an ally, about the candidates' list which had been cooked up the day before by Ned and Bill. About 200 new people had been assigned to seats, some of them really safe, and all loyal to the new dispensation. There would inevitably be outrage in some of the CLPs not being consulted at all during the exercise, and there were one or two sloppy mistakes like naming a new candidate where the sitting member was not standing down, and listing one girl twice. This outrageous packing of the Parliamentary Labour Party went through Friday's meeting of the NEC on the nod, and gave us some bad headlines on Saturday.

I did notice that Aidan Richards had not been shuffled to a safe seat, which might have explained his behaviour later that weekend which was sullen even by his high standards.

But it was on the manifesto that things went seriously sour.

Raphael, still comatose after his exertions, had hardly a hand in the first draft, which was written by Angus, Rupert, Rashida, Aidan and Barrie. It had some good points. It was short. It was well written, thanks mostly to Rupert and Barrie. But their effort was entirely repellent to large chunks of middle England and many of our own members: an utter repudiation of the last ten years followed by promises of more state control, intervention, tax hikes, some sops to special interests and little about things most people cared about.

Everything was on display: the Emergency Economic Powers Act, nationalisation of the railways, state control of the utilities, the maximum wage, abolition of the Lords, disestablishment of the Church, breaking up the banks with only those putting their money in a new State Investment Bank having their deposits guaranteed, scrapping Trident, deep cuts in defence spending, no third runway at Heathrow or high-speed trains, scaling back the Olympics, a new top income tax rate of 75%, VAT cuts, fast-track planning for green projects, foundation hospitals to go, academies to be phased out and the living wage introduced within four years' time.

To be fair, Raphael had said all this in the campaign. But seeing the catalogue in five crisp pages brought one up short.

All the tensions between us blew up at Chequers. Raphael had invited all the St Palais gang for a meeting there on the first Saturday of the campaign. It was for all of us, excluding Raphael, our first trip to the PM's country residence: he did say he had had to entertain some foreign dignitaries there when he was last in office. We arrived for coffee at about 10, took our cups from the drawing room into the rather grandiose Long Room, where a large square table had been set out, and were given this text to read. Within twenty minutes we'd read through it. I had thought Raphael seemed pent up, and now I understood why. As Barrie later told me, he'd finally gone through the document just before breakfast and gone ballistic, almost shouting at Barrie about "the Longest Suicide Note in History - the abridged version".

When we had finished our study of the masterpiece the 'realos' (Hattie, Paul, Maudie and I) started to argue that the draft was just too extreme. Angus replied tartly that the text was merely "a compendium of what Raphael had said during the campaign, as you would know if you'd paid attention". He then added with menace, "Or are some of you just hankering after a return of the previous regime, but this time with a smile?".

Rupert then pushed his line about attacking corporate power and abuse, and some twaddle about "the primacy of politics".

When Raphael tried to calm things down by saying, "well, things get said in campaigns", Aidan interrupted him with a sour, "We all know you well enough by now to realise you don't believe half the things you say," which was such a shocking assault but with sufficient recognisable truth in it for the conversation to judder to a halt. Raphael continued gamely with a point about priorities and signals, but he had clearly been stunned by his partner's public display of ferocity.

In the discussion Hattie Reynolds and Paul Howkins made useful points about including two or three things which could attract lower middle and working class voters: a cut in energy prices, or better childcare. Angus dismissed this as "topics not a programme", and Rupert added, "any moment now and you'll be saying we should have a pledge card", but Maudie snapped back, "well at least with the pledge card we actually won an election".

So it continued until Ned tried to bridge positions by saying, "Why don't we start with saying what we're about, and then say, and these are our first steps?"

Aidan looked as though he was about to bite Ned in the leg, but Raphael intervened magisterially and closed our conversation in the way that only he can. "People have aired their views and made some helpful suggestions. I'll ask Barrie to do a bit of redrafting and circulate it late tomorrow just before cabinet. Now why don't we have some lunch?"

"Just one moment," this was Angus at his most stentorian. "You've chosen your cabinet, Raphael, and I can see the logic in having some of the old regime there. But Derek Jamieson? He oughtn't to be in the Labour Party, let alone the cabinet. I want your solemn promise to us here and now that if we win this thing, you'll sack him."

Raphael was now irritated and simply said slowly like a teacher repeating some instruction for the umpteenth time, "It was useful having him on board to steady the ship. He is reassurance for some outside the party, and some in."

Aidan piped up, with demonic glee in his expression, "I'll go along with that. So if we win, we won't need that reassurance anymore. So, just tell us that on the night of October 18th you'll sack him."

Harriet, looking nervous, almost tearful, talked about "you always having to personalise things. Let's just leave it to Raphael's judgment".

"It's not his judgment I worry about, it's his word."

There was almost a gasp at this but Bill shut everyone up with, "then even if he does make the commitment you want to hear, you won't believe it anyway. Silly boy". Several of us laughed at the put-down and we went in for a very late lunch, which was mercifully light, a perfectly acceptable poached salmon with salad, followed by gooseberry syllabub, and a couple of glasses of rosé. We had more or less survived our first 'cabinet row', and over lunch amused ourselves with tales from our new ministries and the reactions of the mandarins. Rupert in particular made us laugh hugely.

Only Aidan and Barrie were staying on, so just before 4 p.m. we went to our cars and missed out on what could have been a perfectly pleasant autumn walk in the grounds, with the sycamores and oaks turning colour nicely.

NED

Lunch was OK except that they'd obviously forgotten the main course but everyone's too polite to point it out. No one invited me to stay so I missed out on what was probably my only chance of a night at Chequers. I think Aide had tried, but Rafa wasn't hearing of it. They were due for a good old row anyway.

BARRIE

I tried to work on the computer in my room, but amazingly it's a poor signal. I rushed tea, then later just bolted down a bit of dinner, before scurrying back up the stairs to finish a first draft. It was a meal of a different kind, a real dog's breakfast: radical intentions, pragmatic measures and a few populist proposals (really just what Ned had been saying).

To be truthful I was not sorry I couldn't linger in the drawing room after supper. You could have cut the atmosphere with a knife. Aidan spoke not a word at dinner but I could hear the shouting and the rowing down the passage while I tried to wrap up the text in my bedroom.

At 11, Raphael came into my bedroom, bare feet, just wearing a polo neck top and pyjama shorts, looking dejected and tired.

"He's just impossible. Incredible. He gives me a Chinese burn - look you can see the marks (true, there were little weals on his lower left arm). It really hurt. Then he bites me. And after that he comes on to me. We've just had some truly awful loveless sex. Now he's kicked me out, and locked the door. Can I sleep here?"

I raised my eyebrows. As usual he tried to justify himself, "The other bedrooms aren't made up, and this is a good-sized bed. Look, I'll put the bolster down the middle."

I say, "Not a good idea, Raphael. You know how complicated that would be. I'll finish the text and then get someone to drive me back into town". I was showing him some of the text on the screen, when Aidan pushes open the door with his foot - it hadn't been shut, thank goodness. He's got just a towel round his waist. He asks Raphael plaintively, "When are you coming to bed? We've got a heavy day tomorrow."

He sits on the bed and I can see that his eyes were red. "You see, Barrie, sorry to disappoint you but I'm not throwing him over just yet. He's a bastard, but he's my bastard. He'll sell us all down the river. Me first. 200 seats to give away and he turns down a safe one for me. So I'll have to spend three weeks locked away in the dreariest town in the western world, with moronic supporters and hangers-on, and snooping journalists salivating at the idea of me losing my seat. And all this while everybody else is whooping it up on 'Team Sinclair; the Road Show'. I think, Raphael, you'd actually like me to lose the seat so I'll have more time to be the loyal little spouse, staring up at you in adoration during your phoney speeches, like Norma Fucking Major!"

To which Raphael replies gently, "More like Mamie Eisenhower, I'd have thought," which made all three of us laugh.

The two of them go back to bed, and during the night I am awoken several times by those unmistakeable sounds as their relationship careers on its rock-strewn path.

Everyone has rows, Digby and I have rows (mostly about Raphael and his impossible demands and whether I still love him), but I thought no-one could ever have a row with Raphael. Which just goes to show the poisonous effect Aidan and his little mates are having on him. And to make matters worse I couldn't sleep properly because, to tell the truth, part of me wishes he had stayed in my room.

HELEN

All members of cabinet had received by hand copies of the manifesto in the early hours of Monday, to give everyone a couple of hours to read the thing before the meeting. It was obvious that Raphael and Barrie had worked hard on toning the document down but for most people there this would not have been apparent as they had not been privy to the first draft.

We waited for Raphael to come through from the parlour, followed by just Barrie and his towering sidekick, Miranda Fawcett, all greens and purples that day, Cynthia being absent as this was political cabinet. Lorna immediately offered to leave and her offer was as instantly refused by Raphael. This was probably pre-arranged because he knew she was a true ally and because her presence stood at least a faint chance of keeping Aidan under control, Lorna Horrocks being the only person in the room to whom he showed any deference. A friend on the FCO team told me that she just kept throwing work at him, all day and all night, to prevent him getting distracted, and that she was finding him rather constructive on European and Middle East questions.

Raphael made a brief introduction, saying the manifesto must represent change lest we ended up being positioned as incumbents. But on specific issues, the text was open for amendment. Derek, almost white with fury, although in fact he never seemed to get any sunlight, but subdued in tone, intervened immediately and laid into the draft which he called, "immature, economically illiterate, statist and repellent. It discredits everything we've done in the past 11 years". Ned, probably trying to defuse things, came in with "but apart from that, did you like it?" which I have to say made some of us laugh out loud, despite ourselves. But Derek Jamieson and Arthur Rillington didn't share in the general mirth.

Raphael responded in a tone of sweet reason, cutting off Angus and others with, "Then let's go through it, and see where we can find the common ground on any changes you think would improve the text".

Then Aidan spoke, although as minister in attendance he didn't have the right to intervene unless his ministerial brief was under discussion and only then on special invitation of the Prime Minister.

"Oh, for fuck's sake, Rafs, there's no point. If he gets his way, we'll take out all the good points and be left with just some New Labour crap."

Raphael gave a good impression of being unperturbed, but replied with courteous firmness. "Thank you for those helpful comments, Minister of

State, but you will benefit from respecting the rule that ministers in attendance are just that. They attend, and only intervene on their subject and when invited so to do." Aidan looked at him with a ferocious glower but Derek was again the first to speak.

"No, Prime Minister, I welcome that last statement. What your friends want is to get me out. There is no way we can amend this text into something I could agree with. It's better for all if I leave now."

Raphael flashed a look at Angus, Rupert and Aidan as if to say, "Don't dare say anything", and then spoke, "Derek, I am prepared to compromise, which is what counts round here. I'm suspending the meeting for an hour. I'll see Derek and Arthur in my parlour. The rest of you could go through the less controversial sections on foreign policy, Europe and development. Marsha, if you wouldn't mind chairing this".

He said this with such authority, leaving Derek and, after a pause, Arthur no alternative but to follow. As he left, he tapped Barrie on the knee to join the conclave.

NED

Text to Mart

ooooooooooooooooooooooooooooooooooooooo

>Stand by for trouble. Heads about to roll<

BARRIE

Just about the worst meeting of my life. Raphael alternately wheedling, cajoling, threatening ("You think your local party will still nominate you if you rock the boat like this", countered by Derek, who stood his ground, saying, "If this is our manifesto, then we'll all be looking for new jobs".) Throughout, Derek was haughty, disrespectful and with real hatred in his eyes. But having Arthur there was a master-stroke. He's a Barrie Jones-league wonk, can't read a sentence without wanting to make at least five amendments. And deep down he clearly did not want to walk, which Raphael had realised, so he kept making suggestions "for improvement" which Raphael sometimes accepted, saying little things like, "that's very judicious, Arthur. Yes, that goes in". And bit by bit Derek saw that his only close ally was gradually being prised free of him.

So the railways aren't to be nationalised but "brought under effective public control"; the Emergency Economic Powers Act will be an enabling measure for the first twelve months, and not be renewed; we would set targets for deficit reduction after all and all departments would be called on to contribute. Gay marriage could stay in although Arthur really opposed it (shame really, because when he takes his glasses off he's quite fanciable in some lights – at least if you like small, chubby guys!!). Drug liberalisation is, however, out.

Throughout all this Derek stayed silent. So after more than an hour's policy discussion in which I'd been allowed to participate, Raphael said, "I think Barrie has noted all the changes we've agreed. Shall we rejoin our colleagues?".

We then troop back in, Raphael first, with me trotting behind, trying to complete my notes, followed by Arthur, serious, and then, after thirty seconds, Derek. And I can see the disappointment on the faces of Angus and Rupert that he is still on board.

Raphael says, "I think we've made some real improvements to the text. I'm going to ask Barrie Jones to read out slowly all the changes we've agreed; then I'll ask Miranda to do the same for your sections because I want us all to have a sense of ownership for all our policy".

I was pretty nervous, but got through it with just one or two stumbles. Angus and Aidan looked murderous. Derek stares at his hands. But I got nice smiles of encouragement from Brian, Helen and Ned.

In the two hours' debate after the presentations Raphael behaved extraordinarily. He keeps calling Brian, Arthur and Bradley for their amendments, and almost completely ignored Angus and Rupert. But as exhaustion started to set in it was Rupert - who's the cleverest of the lot - who saves the day. In his fluting chirpy tones he just says, "You know what people say, - if no-one's happy with it, then it's probably OK. And that's where we are".

"Well said, Rupert", says Raphael as if they've prepared this in advance, which is always possible. "I know you and some of my other young friends are disappointed with the outcome. It's less radical than you'd have liked. But I ask you to meet us half way. Can I take it that our election manifesto is adopted?"

Angus was about to ask for the floor, but was interrupted by Derek who says, "I'd like a few hours to consider this. I can't sign up to something I've not even seen in writing. And I insist that all the briefing against me stops now".

Raphael was tensing up, I could tell from the nerve at the back of his neck. And he was uncomfortable, his back playing him up. He said very slowly, "I'll come down like a ton of bricks on any minister briefing against colleagues. But, Derek, I can't allow an extension. When we leave this room we need to be able to say that we've got a manifesto. It's been a really good discussion. You and Arthur have made excellent contributions". (Not true; Derek hadn't proposed a single constructive change.) "And everybody's had to pour flagons of water into their bottles of wine. So let's consider it done."

With this he stands up and walks out of the room. Cabinet over. And as Rupert said, no-one's happy. As we leave I get compliments from several members including Arthur. But the episode was really just a masterclass in politics from the great artist himself.

NED

Text to Mart

ooooooooooooooooooooooooooooooooooooooo

>Derek bottled it again. Habemus manifesto. It'll do<

HELEN

It had been an exhausting and tense meeting. At one stage I had thought we were going to lose two members of the old guard, maybe three. But thanks to Raphael's extraordinary dexterity we got through it, and this despite the childish hooliganism of Aidan Richards and Angus Buchanan. Barrie Jones was a terrifically skilful draftsman and I have to admit that both Arthur Rillington and Bradley Mortimer made sensible compromise proposals, respectful of our victory, but avoiding any explicit condemnations of the last government. And just the good-natured and sometimes really funny interjections from Brian on their side and Ned Warren on ours helped to defuse the charged atmosphere.

I began to realise then that Ned was on his way to becoming a really adroit politician, and that the bumbling incompetence was all for show. And then there's Rupert Dennison, so clever at playing both ends against the middle, winding up the discussions with brilliant little flourishes. He never seemed to end up on the losing side. And he has that extraordinary voice, rising and swooping, full of energy and optimism. At one point Lorna whispered to me, "our Prince Rupert[48] of debate" (a reference I had to google afterwards).

And then there was the Prime Minister, impassive, speaking seldom, allowing the debate to flow, and then when the discussion had wound up at a point where he felt comfortable he announced the conclusion with an authority which brooked no dissent.

Afterwards we went back to our departments, all drained by the eight-hour cabinet marathon. I worked on my boxes until one in the morning, clearing the decks for the campaign.

---

[48] Prince Rupert, nephew of King Charles 1 and a flamboyant Cavalier general during the English Civil War.

NED

After cabinet we were under instructions to split up and then reassemble an hour later in number eleven under cover of darkness. Rashida's laid on sandwiches (as if this was a pleasant change from the campaign trail) and two different kinds of tea, one of which makes you want to pee all the time. There's a bout of recrimination, mostly directed at Rupert and me, for having joined in the cosy consensual stuff. The most vituperative was actually Rashida, who likes playing the ideological high priestess. But today for once her mask of calm reticence slipped, and she really let us have it.

"If you had just stood your ground, we'd have a stronger platform and we'd have got rid of the old gang."

Rupert tried condescending, "I get Raphael's tactics: we concede a bit, keep up a facade of unity and then after the election's won, the knives come out. There are times, my sweet Rashida, when a little compromising can bring you closer to your goal."

She went for him, Miss Goody Two-Shoes now transformed into a she-devil, "You really believe that he'll sack them after the election. For someone who thinks he's so clever, Rupert, you can be extremely stupid. He wants them there to counterbalance the socialists. If they go, he'll know he's next. We always knew he wasn't one of us, but simply the least unacceptable. He's worked it out. He needs Derek, and that crowd, so he can arbitrate and duck and weave. After the election, he'll use them to neutralise us. And we won't have the clout because only Angus has any seniority. Poor Aidan's hardly allowed to open his mouth. And they'll confine him to Mayberry to try to save his seat".

This was a bit desperate, as if she cared about Aide. But in her fury, she'd let the cat out of the bag, "If they go, he'll know he's next". So she and Angus have a plan, get Raphael to do the heavy lifting, win us a majority and then as soon as possible shunt off the Great Man and put Angus in his place. I looked at Aide but his face had become a mask, as it does when he's thinking dangerous thoughts.

Rupert came back for more. "Darling, you know that we all want this time to be different, but look how far we've got. Angus has the whole of our economic policy on his plate. We'll have lots of the new MPs on our side. And we need some time to grow into our jobs. Raphael won't want to stay forever. Then all this will be yours."

Aide stirred, "Well, Rashida's got a point. And I wouldn't bet he'll be moving on any time soon. They never do. There's an angry old man in Scotland who's just been turfed out of his job because he underestimated Rafs. Our great leader can be bloody ruthless, in his public and private lives".

Rashida, slightly calmer, rowing back, "I just want us to plan. And we won't even get the chance if we start off with drift and delay".

Angus had said nothing until now, but started to uncoil himself from a green chintzy armchair, looking more knackered than I'd ever seen him. "I'm tired, and I've got an early start. We know the problem, but we can't force him to move against Derek and the others if he won't."

"Well, how's this for a plan?" Rupert's never tired and loves proving how clever he is. "We keep up the pressure during the campaign. If we start getting any of the ex-ministers crawling out of the woodwork we savage them. But we stay just within the limits. Then come close of polls, 'pow!'" (this not spoken but exploded). "We hit them with everything, we pile on the pressure, and we make it clear we're pushing through the radical stuff straightaway. We make it impossible for them to cling on. And, you, Aide, you make sure he gives us the strategic jobs."

Aidan just said quietly, "perhaps I might remind you then that I won't be in a strategic job come the results. I won't have any fucking job at all".

"So you'll be completely free to apply the pressure in the way only you know how," - this from Rashida, the only time I've ever heard her make an arch comment; and quite funny in her sweet smiling innocent way. But no-one dared laugh for fear of provoking an explosion.

There was a long pause before Angus drew it all to a close, "OK, we grin and bear it. And for polling night we let slip the dogs of war. Rupert, you prepare a grid and send it round". (Angus sees everything in terms of grids and charts.) "We want a really hour-by-hour countdown for election night so that Raphael's got no let-out. We lay out a kind of 'manifesto plus' with each of us adding to it as the night goes on. By three that morning, Derek, Brian, Arthur and the others" (unspecified) "will be out."

After we'd split up, I sensed Aide wanted a de-brief of the de-brief so we slipped into number twelve where there's some proper refreshments. I said I didn't like Angus assuming too much about the future:

"Oh, she's just pushing him. The real question is does she want him to seize the thing himself, or is this the first stage in her own game plan?"

I hadn't thought of it like that. But it's not impossible. In public she holds back, never shows her hand, and seems more moderate. She's even friendly with Louise, who really shouldn't be in the party. Maybe she's pushing Angus so hard that when it comes to a succession, she seems the moderate alternative who's created no enemies.

Bloody hell!

BARRIE

This first week has been a nightmare. After Monday's cabinet I feel almost sick with fatigue. But I battle on, finally taking the completed version up to the No 10 flat. Both Raphael and Aidan looked through it, the latter chuffed to bits to find four typos and a split infinitive. Later in the week we're all off to Mayberry for the adoption meeting. Afterwards it's back here until Friday just governing and then it's the Brussels summit.

From then on we'll have less than two weeks for the campaign, and Bo has worked out the schedule from hell for the boss. It's seriously crazy stuff: nothing for a week and then a succession of monster events in all four quarters of the country, including the TV debate, for which he's built in no prep time, and a final day's campaign where he's left a blank, but which is obviously going to be a killer.

Cynthia informed Miranda and me almost gleefully that we are both on unpaid leave as from the end of the summit. So my career as head of policy for the Prime Minister will have lasted just ten days.

Rupert has organised the leader's debate for Wednesday week, just over a week before polling. He and Nigel have negotiated the rules most helpful for our guy: one debate, all three leaders, him in the middle, two and a half hours' debate, with three interviewers, one each from the main stations. Lots of Rottweilers vetoed, and not just by us. An invited audience, but no applause allowed. Nigel's more worried about the Liberal than the main challenger, "he'll play the outsider, plague on both your houses stuff".

Elaine will chair all the press conferences (Cynthia has curtailed her status as Prime Minister's spokesperson to just 5 days so Miranda and I are relatively lucky – but then Elaine doesn't need the money). And even Elaine didn't dare challenge the orders dished out by "Superbitch"- (Rupert's phrase, not mine). And Angus will lead at all of them, probably biting lumps out of lobby correspondents and dragging us further to the left with every utterance. He'll be doing the Chancellor's debate this Friday and I dread it, but we'll be in Brussels and it'll only be on Channel 4.

Nigel is getting us all worried about the polls. We're stuck at 8 or 9 points behind, and only a little better in the key marginals. Women put us at level pegging, men far behind. Kids love us but won't vote. Old people are afraid of us and will. Raphael's a bit ahead of the party, but we still trail the Tory on nearly all issues except the NHS where we coast on our reputation, with nothing new to say.

****

Everything's flat at the moment. The Tories are just waiting for our launch to pounce. Meanwhile Raphael is bored, pacing the cabinet room, sitting alone and doodling. He took Miranda out for dinner on Tuesday to some red-checked tablecloth bistro at the far end of the King's Road. He charmed her all over again. They had a really nice friendly chat, and allowed the waiters and other diners to take shots with their mobiles, just the boss out with his head of staff for a quiet evening meal and half a litre of house red. Of course it went viral, and was meant to. Only one paper did the utterly predictable, "A French restaurant of course".

NED

I ring up Aide in Brussels where he's taken the night off from the Council meeting, alternating with Lorna. It's all about preparing the summit and of course all they're worried about is removing any pitfalls from the conclusions, which for once will be put under the microscope when they're published.

He tells me he's staying at Jose's flat and sounds a bit plastered. I lecture him about behaving himself and being discreet. "Don't worry, Neddo, no clubbing, and it's early to bed so I'll be fresh as a daisy in the morning. And this very kind boy's actually made me a cod dish with sweet potatoes."

Oh dear!

BARRIE

Aidan of course has been in Brussels for his big Council of Ministers meeting, getting every camera to fall in love with him and putting all the Foreign Ministers in the shade. How they must love this diplomacy Richards-style! It had been arranged that he'd stay at a hotel, since Lorna was hogging it at the Residence. Raphael kept ringing the hotel to be told that he had yet to check in. Later, when we were still going through boxes in his flat, Raphael got a call on his mobile, and unusually took it in the kitchen. When he came back, his face looked bleak, "Aidan's only gone and stayed at Jose's flat in the city. He sounds drunk or worse, but at least Jose is sober. He says they're having a quiet meal and then they're not going out. They'll stay in and go to bed".

I refrained from asking about precise details of the dispositions of the rooms in the young man's flat which I remembered as being very small. All this cast a bit of a pall over the evening.

Another worry: Raphael's health. He's getting no exercise, and is puffed every time he walks up the stairs in No 10. And his back's playing up again. And of course he hates it that when he gets in or out of the car, people can see how he infirm he looks or draw comparisons with his younger rivals.

NED

Letter to Mart

Dear Bruv,

Thought I'd send this by your old-fashioned letter because it's worth the telling.

Yesterday we all went up to Mayberry - well down in my case - for the adoption meeting of all three candidates. They wanted me to do the warm-up and Rashida to introduce, as we'd both done ours the day before. Winning team stuff.

We arrived early, so we're just lolling about in the living room at Rafa's house. Me, beer in hand, prone on the sofa, Rupe in an armchair, and Aide at the table, with his laptop, fielding emails from Lorna about the summit. She wears the trousers at the office, so he takes it out on Rafa at home.

Any case in walks Rafa, a bit stiff in the joints I'd say but relaxed enough. An hour to go before the off. I shift up a bit on the sofa to make room for him, but he declines and sits on a dining-room chair at the table, "Better for the back". Rupe says something like, "I'd really like to play up your modest beginnings so people compare it with the toffs on the other side". A bit rich from our own little public school boy, but never mind.

Then Rafa starts, "Actually there's quite a story to tell. Both my parents came from broken homes between the wars. Dad's family was dirt poor, his father did a bunk in the 20s and his mum was on hand-outs for most of her life. She kept all the children together by taking in lodgers to their dingy little house in Clapham. In a way she was lucky not to have a husband, because all the fathers on the street went down the pub on Friday nights, coming home just to slap about their wives and beat up the kids. In fact the lodgers were a huge source of fun for my dad and his sisters. There was the sinister Mrs Danvers type, the kleptomaniac who stole the silver when they went for tea with the vicar, the woman who kept dozens of empty bottles of sherry under her bed, and the former West Ham player who took to drink. It's great to hear Dad talking about it. They had this pauperish existence but were really happy as a family. All of them did OK for themselves. One of the girls got a job on the local paper, another became a librarian and Dad did really well at school and after the war became a teacher.

"On mum's side, it was a lot grimmer. She was one of two in a quite wealthy family who lived in the South Riding. Well, my grandfather ups sticks and emigrates with his bipsy secretary. They head off to New Zealand in the late 1920s. My grandmother is destitute and gets no help from his family. With two kids, she has to choose. And it's not mum, but her elder sister, Aunt Agatha, who gets to stay on in a little flat in Leeds. So mum's then sent to some really grim church orphanage outside Huddersfield, and has a miserable time. She's just six when she's cast out. Her only release is books. She's still the best read person I know although her eyesight's failing now, of course. In the forties she holds down two jobs, and then starts teaching in a primary, and she meets dad at some NUT gathering in the early 50s. But even now she's never got over the expulsion into the darkness. The rejection.

"Aunt Agatha was some character. She went to Denmark just before World War 2 - to be with some bloke who later joined the resistance. She manages to survive all that. I guess the Germans were as afraid of her as everyone else. Then she gets a job as a manageress at quite a successful Danish underwear factory. And in the early sixties she's travelling the world with what she calls her "mannequins", showing off quality Danish underwear. One day when they're east of Suez she jumps ship and goes on to Christ Church, looking for her dad. No clues, except one. The bipsy was called Joan Roberts. So she starts the hunt for a Cedric Roberts, aged 70+. After much sleuthing she tracks him down to his homestead, just him, his wife and five kids, plus about a million sheep. Somewhere inland from Christ Church, about seventy miles I think. So she pitches up, rings the bell, an old man answers and she says, "Hello, father". He collapses, has a heart attack and dies three weeks later. When she told me the story, gloating wasn't in it. Talk about revenge served up cold."

We'd sat through all this riveted. Total silence, then Rupe pipes up, "This is great stuff. We've got to use it. It's a back story to die for. All these Etonians will be sick as parrots".

Aidan looks up from his computer for a moment and says, "Don't get too hung up on the details. If my Rafa is running to form, he's probably made half of it up".

****

The adoption meeting was great. Bo up to his old tricks. A room for 600 filled by more than a thousand. Hundreds outside. The stage great of *course with the 'walk of fame' gangway right out into the crowd. All the good old Insurgency tunes. I make them laugh. Angus then grinds the Tories to pulp. He gets more ferocious by the day.*

But the revelation was Aidan. He's now got his own following. His photos look more and more like that of the leader of a boy band in a fanzine. So he's always got lots of young men (and not just gays) and women who turn up and literally scream when he appears. Weird or not? His campaign is now overrun with volunteers; and Angus and Rafa have practically closed down their machines and shipped everyone off to try to save Aide's seat.

But it wasn't how he looked; it was what he said that had them on their feet, cheering themselves silly, "We've still some unfinished business from the wars. We've still got a day of reckoning for those who took us into this illegal, immoral war which cost hundreds of young lives. Needlessly. Only Labour will give you the immediate judicial inquiry into the wars; how and why we went to war; why we failed to plan; why we left these countries poorer, ruined, with corrupt criminals in power; with thousands upon thousands dead; who profited from the war? Which corporations? Linked to which politicians? The blood of our brave soldiers requires justice. Labour alone will give them justice. Wherever it leads. Whoever it indicts. Whatever the punishment. They'll pay. They'll pay for the criminal breach of faith with our troops, our country, and our world".

The crowd went pretty wild. At last someone had offered them blood, and, boy, did they love it.

Thank goodness it wasn't Raphael next. Rashida sensibly took her time to let things calm down. When Raphael started it was a change of mood, to put it mildly. It was the Statesman, at ease but in earnest. The old lines honed and brushed up, but still working. But lots of "I, Prime Minister, will do this...I, Prime Minister will do that", to add to the credibility of what still seemed incredible.

As a double act it's a bit Jekyll and Hyde. I do wonder if they've worked it all out. Aide and Angus whipping our people into hysteria so they'll all work 20 hours a day. Rafa then providing a modicum of reassurance for the centre ground.

HELEN

I could not attend the campaign launch in Mayberry but by the end of the meeting it felt as if I had been there the whole time. Half the cabinet rang up enraged by Aidan's outburst, which had led some of the bulletins to the detriment of Raphael's own rather powerful speech. It took a long conversation between Raphael and Derek to avoid the latter's immediate resignation. Rupert and Nigel found some words about, "Aidan Richards was giving vent to the anger that many people still feel about the war. He recognises that a Judicial Inquiry is the right way to proceed now and that the outcome must not be prejudged. Aidan remains very upset at the number of young lives lost in the war". This was put out as a party press release. The culprit himself seemed quite unmoved at the furore he had caused.

I had long taken the view that Angus and Aidan had it in their hands to bring us all down. I now began to think that perhaps this was precisely what Aidan wanted. He thought he was going to lose his seat and couldn't stomach the idea of all the rest of us in government jobs, while he had to hawk his CV around think tanks or lobbying firms. And Raphael put up with this because of his own unspoken but deep insecurities. He needed the love and adulation from this young cabal, and Aidan Richards understood this well and exploited it to the hilt.

On the phone, Rupert was soothing, after a fashion. "It's all good cop, bad cop stuff. We've got Aidan and Angus to keep up the Insurgency spirit and mobilise the kids' army. Raphael and the others can appeal more to the middle ground. Remember we're not after 50%. If we get 35%, just ahead of the Tories, we keep our majority, just like last time. But we need turnout. We've got to get our people out. That's why the Leftist stuff helps."

I interrupted the flow, "Rupert, that makes a kind of sense, but not if it pulls the cabinet apart in the process".

It was then he said, "Well that doesn't matter in a way because in two weeks, Raphael will purge the old guard. Then we can really get cracking".

BARRIE

This afternoon, Miranda and Cynthia were closeted with security for nearly an hour. There are literally hundreds of death threats daily, some with real credibility; some militant Islamist, some our own home-grown racists and homophobes, and one organisation called 'AttackLEFT' which they think may be funded from abroad.

Afterwards they insisted on speaking to Cynthia alone. But she is so embarrassed by the conversation that she confided in us. "They've done the usual vetting on all the new ministers. And only one hasn't been positively authorised for access to top secret documents. I'm afraid it's Aidan Richards, lifestyle issues naturally, including some escapades in - would you believe it? - North Korea, and some class A substance abuse. Of course the PM can overrule but he has to do that in writing. Will you handle this one, sweetie?" (to me, of course).

The Brussels trip should have been like a weekend break. A drop in at the socialist leaders' pre-summit lunch, an afternoon at the European Council on jobs and growth, a dinner (not too late) to discuss the top EU appointments coming up, and some foreign affairs stuff the next morning. We're all staying at the Permanent Representative's rather gloomy residence in the Rue Ducale, at least convenient. Aidan's proposal that he and Raphael stay at Jose's bedsit was knocked on the head straight away. (I'm not entirely sure he was joking!)

On the train, once security had shooed away journalists and camera men, we manage to do some work. Aidan and I checked the latest version of 'the Conclusions' and he worked out some tough anti-austerity language to put forward; he knows the other member states won't accept it but that's not the point. And he behaves like the playground bully to Helena Chandler, the Foreign Office girl who's Raphael's European adviser. She's not pretty, small, with her nose slightly too long for her face, which in any case is half covered by very large glasses that make her gawp like a fish in a bowl all the time. A gift to Aidan who delights in finding fault with her syntax and in rewriting a brief for the boss on the top appointments question. I've worked out that Aidan would be delighted if when the Foreign Policy Supremo post comes up, we push for Lorna, creating a convenient vacancy. Hence the permanent campaign to discredit Derek, who's been promised the post by Raphael. But does Aidan know that?

Raphael and I head off to the socialist leaders' lunch leaving Aidan to go to a Sherpas' lunch (for which he's too senior - but he doesn't trust the civil servants). Our do is on the first floor of a characterless hotel not far from the Berlaymont. When we enter the lobby downstairs we are met by Jose on greeter duty, escorting PMs and party leaders upstairs. He's looking very spruce, dressed not merely formally but almost severely as if to compensate for the exoticism of his last public appearance on the lawns in front of the Pavilion. He came up rather tentatively to Raphael and said, "Hello, Prime Minister". To general amazement Raphael put both arms round his neck, kissed him on both cheeks and whispered something in his ear, to the effect of wanting to see him soon. No-one could hear precisely but all could see this tender little attention and the effect on all the entourages loitering in the foyer was quite noticeable. Jose's reputation will be on the rise again after the Brighton humiliation!

Jose took us upstairs and helped us navigate round an extremely long table crowded with leaders of all the parties, large, small and miniscule which make up the European socialist family. By the time Raphael had greeted all the 'comrades' and sat down in a fairly prominent position, with me as usual perched on tip-up behind with no place for both papers and food, the 'debate' for want of a better word was underway. It's all fairly chaotic, people mumble, clanking plates and cutlery, and the interpretation in wooden booths in the room keeping up a constant cooing noise like pigeons on a very long window-sill.

Raphael bided his time, then made a brief statement of utter banality which is greeted like tablets coming down the mountain side (because to most in the room he is European Socialism's new rock star. A left-wing pro-European British socialist - 'du jamais vu'!).

Then he was off already, courtly excuses about meeting the President of France who would be chairing the Council meeting in the afternoon. As we went, he squeezed Jose's cheeks and mussed his hair, thus adding to the quality of the stardust transfer. The boy was blushing in ecstasy.

We then dropped off at the European Parliament building, which is so mammoth it could have been designed by the Ceausescus on an off day, and do a meet and greet with a mild-mannered but incomprehensible Slovenian who is the President. Then we get taken along a route so complex it can only be negotiated by hordes of guides and hangers-on. At the socialists' meeting room we were greeted by a shouty Dutchman who is the leader of the socialists in the EP and who tries to give Raphael a bit of a duffing-over, doubtless in revenge for the ill-treatment he had suffered at the hands of previous UK Labour Prime Ministers. We then greeted some staffers who had been inveigled to stay behind at the office on a wet Friday afternoon. Throughout, Raphael gave minimum service.

We were rather relieved when the Permanent Representative pitched up. He'd come along to a briefing at No 10 two days earlier and was affable if slightly too voluble in the short car ride to the pink grey bunker which is where the European Council meets - Brussels brutalism at its worst. We were met at the small 'protocol' entrance - where the media scrum was corralled - by a middle European who has clearly majored in obsequiousness. The Perm Rep, Sir Clarence, a big guy - twice my size, jovial, bumptious but I guess bright enough, took us up to the 'presidency floor' (the eightieth!) to the suite occupied for these six months by the President of 'la Grande nation'. They'd laid on coffee and biscuits and an interpreter but Raphael says charmingly to his French host in French, "would it be agreeable to you if we spoke French?"; the President feigned delight at what he called an "exquisite gesture" and shooed away the interpreter. In fact it was just Raphael showing off.

I got a presidential handshake but he didn't look me in the eye. His two advisers on the other hand gave me the once over: my suit (needs a dry clean and press); my tie (a bit loud but a present from Digby); my shoes (in need of a buffing), and gave metaphorical shrugs. Both Sir Clarence and I struggled a bit to keep up with Raphael's French. I notice for all his aura of entitlement and self-assurance the Ambassador's cup was shaking in his saucer as he placed it back on the table top.

Raphael and the President appeared to hit it off. The President who, like any politician, is fascinated by accounts of the coup d'état and how quickly the old PM had caved in, asked lots of questions. "Is he planning a comeback?" "Have you kept any of his ministers?" Then there was a bit of badinage about the elections, "So this is going to be your only summit", to which came the instant reply, "Could well be. So let me enjoy it. And as it happens I do have a couple of points". Neat.

On the top jobs, the Frenchman conceded that Raphael couldn't really negotiate ten days before an election, and noted that the British might have a candidate for the post of Foreign Policy chief but couldn't try to sneak it through now. Raphael then raised the wording he didn't like in the conclusions with the explicit emphasis on austerity and the absence of any credible plan for jobs and investment. The President shook his head sadly, and then started to point the finger at the Germans, a default EU gambit when for once the British couldn't be blamed.

"Try to talk to her. But she has her own problems at home. Her people won't accept helping Greeks who don't work and pay no tax." They talked through this for 15 minutes and the President agreed to speak to her again to get a few concessions. They then parted amicably but we're sure he wouldn't lift a finger to help.

There were a few more calls, including from the Commission President, who came with a small retinue of officials to our fiftieth (!) floor. They squeezed in as if their careers depended on being present at the scene. Raphael was cool and distant. When he got up from his chair there was a distinct crack not from the wooden frame but from his back and he winced with pain and went pale for a couple of seconds. It was then that Aidan breezed in, without knocking, went up to the Commission President and shook his hand as if he was just another staffer. He sat on the end of Raphael's desk like a straggler at an office party and turned to the Ambassador, "Well, Clarence, what does one have to do to get a coffee round here?". End of interview.

Aidan had on his slightly manic expression, hyper, eyes ablaze, and of course next to me who he once described as 'His Shabbiness' he was dressed to kill: a brilliant blue jacket, dark closely fitting trousers and, the shocker, tieless. The hair's brushed up and then back, the stubble under strict control. In other words, the total film idol. He knows bloody well that he's the real star of this summit, that all the cameras and some of the cameramen will love him, and he realises it's probably his last so he's going to make the most of it. Raphael looked totally bewitched.

A few minutes later we followed the labyrinthine corridors and took the lift back up to the floor where the European Council meets. Prime Ministers and ambassadors and staffers were milling around, introductions made, little bits of business transacted. Raphael had his 'pin' as a member of the Council. The Ambassador and I have red badges which means we could walk around outside the room, but Aidan had a special red badge which means he could go in and out of the room but not stay, unless the PM were to leave, in which case he could take his seat and represent his country. The scope for mischief is almost limitless!

I checked out the room. The UK was stuck between Portugal and Slovakia. I know there's a reason but I'd forgotten it and hoped Raphael wouldn't ask. But of course later he did. And what's worse he knew the answer so he was just teasing me. The best I could do was to retort, "What's this all about, the next Mayberry Labour pub quiz?"

On request the Ambassador steered us in the direction of the familiar figure of the German Chancellor, surrounded by a cluster of very German sycophants of varying degrees of seniority. She has very sharp blue eyes set in a pale, podgy, expressionless face. She was wearing her trade mark trouser suit (the colour changes daily but not the shape). She didn't try to charm Raphael and he certainly didn't charm her. In English of a high standard she congratulated him on becoming Prime Minister but said that he'd better make the most of it because the British people wouldn't like real socialism. He replied, "We're all hoping you come over to campaign...for the Opposition", which was halfway between cheeky and downright rude. But he's obviously calculated he has to show from the outset that he can give as good as he can take, and the courtiers duly laughed. He then took her to one side to lobby her on that part of the conclusions which seems to endorse austerity. She listened intently, and then just shook her head silently.

The bell sounded and Aidan walked side by side with his partner into the meeting room. I could barely peek over the heads of the massed photographers but could see that they are only interested in one thing. The new Prime Minister and his lover, sometimes leaning over his shoulder to rearrange papers or to whisper (probably some obscenity) in his ear, and strutting his stuff in front of the Portuguese Prime Minister on Raphael's right, widely rumoured to be 'one of the boys in the band.'

When Aidan finally emerged from the room, after the last cameras had been expelled he was at his most insufferable. "Well, Barriekins, everyone's got their photo for the front page and I've just been visually undressed by the Portuguese Prime Minister. Quite a coup if I get to sleep with two European heads of government, hey?"

I ignored him and we walked back to the UK Representation rooms back on the fiftieth, where he managed to offend practically all the staff and teased poor Helena Chandler beyond endurance. He is of course seriously clever and is the first to spot any possible snags in a draft but, boy, does he know it.

The afternoon dragged on and Aidan was delighted to get called back into the room to stand in while Raphael had to do the BBC afternoon news interview which Elaine had arranged. He was thrilled to be the UK sub in the Council, and came back after 45 minutes quite elated, "Carlos Eduardo's all over me like a rash. Got the invite to his private villa in Cascais after the election and his mobile number. I suppose I'll have to take Raphael along".

I was just about to choke but worse was to follow. Some keen young press officer from the representation, all pink and eager to please, came in to tell us that the German Chancellor had just done a press point saying that she had had talks with Raphael and that they'd disagreed on economic policy. When pushed she said she'd prefer the Tories to win the election even though she was not enamoured of their European policy. Aidan had that dangerous glint in his eyes but said nothing.

And we soon get called upstairs for a quick word with Raphael as the meeting was breaking up, the 'family photo' being set up, to be followed by the early working dinner. Raphael wanted to get back to the Residence in time for the 'Chancellor's debate' which would be going out at 9 on Channel 4, Brussels Empire Time. Aidan had instructed the blond gushing saccharine-stuffed wife of the Ambassador (who he calls Lady Penelope) how to get Channel 4 set up on their TV.

In the lift up to the 80th we were alone until, just before the lift doors closed, in stepped a young journalist from the Guardian's Brussels desk. A propos of nothing Aidan just purrs, "If she's endorsing the Tories someone should remind her that the last time her country tried to decide who ran Britain it didn't end well". The doors opened, he walked out, turned to the journalist and winked.

We were still helping ourselves to the puddings at the tutti quanti buffet on the floor beneath where the dinner was taking place, Aidan having rather ostentatiously chatted up a tall moustachioed waiter from the southern banks of the Mediterranean who kept our glasses filled, when Raphael appeared, looking irritated.

"Well, Aidan, I can see you've taken to this diplomacy thing like a duck to water. Your little comments about our German friends have certainly made some ripples. I've just had one plain, doughy-faced, middle-aged, blondish German woman come up to me not best pleased: "your friend does politics in a way we do not like. Stirring up the old feelings in Europe is not a good thing".

"I hadn't the faintest idea what she was talking about until one of her staff handed me a Reuters clip. So thanks for the really up-to-the minute briefing (he glares at me) and a big thanks to you too, Aidan. You've had a brilliant afternoon, putting yourself about for the photographers like some wannabe Page Three tart; then chatting up the leader of our oldest ally like a rent boy in the seediest bar in Porto; and now poisoning our relations with 'the most powerful woman in the world'. So good day's work, chaps. Now let's get back to the Walton's for some nice family show on the box."

All this was said in a subdued way, but you could tell he was both furious at my slacking and Aidan's irresponsibility and faintly amused at the same time. And he was obviously nervous about how Angus would perform in the debate.

So off we trooped to the Rue Ducale. We flopped down in the comfortable green armchairs in the drawing room; all except Raphael who sat bolt upright in a hard-backed chair. Elaine arrived just in time, having tried to put out the media firestorm about 'PM's lover at war with Germany'. The Ambassador, Lady P and one or two staffers took Aidan's heavy-handed hint that the Prime Minister would rather watch his young gladiator enter the ring in the exclusive company of political friends. Penelope (not what she's actually called of course; I forget her real name because Aidan's hit the nail on the head with his nickname) had arranged trays of drinks and thermoses of tea and coffee. She almost backed out of the room, saying, "I wish you a pleasant evening and hope you sleep well. We look forward to seeing you all at breakfast at around 8, if that suits".

I twiddled unsuccessfully with the remotes until Aidan snatches them from me, and within seconds we were watching the debate. When the programme started they were already standing at their lecterns; the Liberal small, grey, old and nervous; the Tory, pink like a plump chicken, hugely pleased with himself, a face just crying out to be smacked; and Angus, tallest of the three, centre-stage, hair swept back, slightly over his collar, tieless, wearing a pale blue shirt and grey suit, and thunderous; eyes ablaze like some young medieval preacher, about to have a fire and brimstone moment. Beautiful and frightening.

The aggression began from question one, which he answered after the Liberal who had tried to present himself as the sage who'd predicted the credit crunch. "No you didn't. You just followed the lead from Raphael Sinclair. Don't try to kid people. And you're lying about the crisis, trying to frighten people into accepting cutbacks which will just make the recession worse. Yeah, go on, kill off the recovery, and throw some more people out of work."

A couple of minutes later it was time to get the Tory, "Share the pain? What pain will you and your friends feel? Who's paying for your campaign? Who's paying for your office? Hedge funds. Personal equity. And you expect us to believe you'd bring in tough regulations to control the financial services. Who are you trying to kid? They pay you. They control you. You're just a puffed-up tailor's dummy who's there to do the bidding of his slick fat-cat paymasters".

When the Tory spluttered a comeback he got barracked by Angus in full flow, a beardless Jesus chastising the usurers and traders in the Temple. "How much exactly do the hedge funds give you each year? How much do they pay for your office? How much? How much?" When the others dared mentioned trades union money, Angus shouted back, "The unions represent hardworking families. Your backers just stand for greed, irresponsible gambling, and speculation. And in you, they've found their perfect glove puppet."

So it continued. The Glencoe massacre live on TV. When the interviewer asked a question about Labour's tax plans, he got a sharp nip at his ankle. "I know you're nervous about our plans. How much do you earn? If you tell me, I'll tell you how much tax we'll make you pay. You see, you've got the same vested interests as all your media buddies. All those hundreds of executives at the BBC who earn fortunes to put out third-rate trash every night, all at the public's expense. The billionaires who run our newspapers just to peddle lies. Who spy on us. Who bully helpless people. Of course they hate the idea of a government committed to social justice and a free press."

It just went on and on. Every timid interruption by his two now cowed rivals was greeted by this ferocious rabid dog primed to eviscerate any passing rabbit. His concluding remarks were comparatively mild, "So there you have it. The real choice. Gutless Tories stretching out a helping hand to their rich friends, shielding those who brought us to the brink of ruin. The Liberals with their pathetic pandering, jumping on the nearest passing bandwagon, meaningless platitudes as a substitute for policy. And Labour. On the side of the people. But angry as hell. Fighting mad. Determined to change Britain. Believe me (voice at full throttle, his eyes powerful, intimidating) we'll change this country. We'll give Britain back to its people".

When it finished, he walked off the stage not shaking hands with his opponents, straight into the arms of Rashida, who was treated to a full-on kiss on live TV.

BBC NEWS 10 p.m.

The political editor's commentary: "Angus Buchanan tonight was a raging bull on the rampage reducing his opponents to pulp. This was attack politics as we've never seen before. He has given us a fascinating view of himself, his beliefs, and his politics. Unknown just a few weeks ago, now number two in the government, he will have given heart to his dedicated followers. Others will be perplexed, even anxious. It will give the Prime Minister, who is in Brussels at the euro summit, something to think about. The Insurgency has proved it can generate excitement and stir passions unlike anything in recent politics. While Labour sympathisers will love the aggressive style and the radical programme, what will worry the Prime Minister is that his party still trails in the polls by between 9 and 10%. And this was before tonight's piece of 'theatre of cruelty'. There's less than two weeks to go and Mr Sinclair will be anxious to strike a different tone when his own campaign finally gets under way."

BARRIE

We sat there in silence. Aidan finally said, but unconvincingly, "The boy done good". And ten seconds later, while I fill the glasses, Rupert is on the phone putting his own gloss and spin on it, with a plea relayed to Raphael, "Don't be too hard on him. Give him a ring. He feels he may have gone a bit overboard".

For Elaine, this was the final straw. Her mouth set, her teeth clenched, she exploded, "A bit overboard. It was fucking lunatic. 'The boy done good'"(she imitates Aidan to a tee). "Don't be a cretin, Aidan. Whoever thought one could end up feeling sorry for the Tory? He totally lost it. We're reducing ourselves to a teenage sect, 'Brats for Britain.' Today's been a totally wasted day. It was your best crack at doing the statesmanship bit, hobnobbing with world leaders, influencing decisions. Just generally being Prime Minister and giving yourself a bit of urgently needed credibility in the role. But we've blown it. All everybody will remember from today is this ponce hogging all the publicity here and, like some teenage moron, insulting the Germans. And at home the Glaswegian maniac you've put in charge of the British economy goes on a killing spree. Great. Really well done. You lot don't need spin doctors. You need psychiatric help."

Raphael rose uncomfortably from his seat by the table. "Well, I'm off to bed. Tomorrow's another day. But we've got to turn things round. Aidan, unless Lady Penelope has put us in separate rooms, you can come now." "I want another drink", Aidan whined. "Come now", was the authoritative response from the Leader. And after a second's hesitation he did, not bothering to say goodnight. I poured Elaine and myself the largest malt whiskies I've ever seen.

NED

When Angus and Rashida get back to No 11 I'm waiting in their sitting room (the staff let me in and out of both the other houses on the street. PS Haven't found numbers 1 to 9 yet.) I suggest a drink and can tell the idea is about as welcome as red wine spilt on the newly laid white carpet. I did manage a "you could charm the birds out of the trees". I retreated before he slaps me. He's overdone it and he knows it. And whatever he says, it matters to him. Not the job so much. He really deeply cares about what Raphael thinks of him.

Late that night I get a visit from Rupe, not an everyday occurrence these days. He's in a funny mood. All the bounce and enthusiasm gone. We do the post-mortem on the debate, which maybe won't play as badly with the public as we fear. Perhaps people have had enough of bland. But Rupert thinks it's pretty catastrophic, and says "We're going to need something spectacular to turn this around". I say, "Don't worry. There's the tour starting on Monday. Bo's pretty optimistic about them. And then the debate which should more than level things up". And he just says, "No. I mean something spectacular. Really spectacular. I need a couple of days out to get my thoughts together". I don't like the way he stares at me when he says this.

Letter from the former Prime Minister to his sister Dr Anne Nugent, consultant gynaecologist at Minneapolis General

Dear Anne,

Thank you for your lovely letter. And for the fantastic bunch of crimson roses, which have still not wilted. We split them up into two vases, one in the living room, and the other in my little upstairs study. Things were very hard at first but gradually the gloom is lifting. In truth Sylvia hated the last couple of years, and worried what all the pressure was doing to us as a family and me in particular. Two weeks ago it became clear that I didn't have the support to carry on: half the cabinet was on the verge of defection and the Sinclair kids were running amok. Friends like Ted and Mary, as well as some of my staff, were all for trench warfare for a few months in the belief that the Sinclair bubble would burst but I didn't have the heart to run a campaign and fight the economic crisis at the same time. So we talked it over in our Brighton suite at the beginning of conference week, took our decision, and returned home.

Of course had we known earlier in the day about the incident with the ex-boyfriend spread-eagled on the grass in front of the Pavilions we might have been tempted to slug it out. But would it really have made us change our minds? And would it have made a difference?

But Sinclair can really thank me; the Prime Minister quitting was about the only thing big enough to relegate his 'lifestyle issues' to second place. And they had just enough breathing space to regroup and continue their onslaught. That woman from the TV who's his press spokesman is no slouch, and carried off the press conference with panache.

The Queen was really kind and we spent a good half an hour, talking mostly about the children, and Ayrshire. She didn't mention Sinclair but I could sense she was concerned about the future.

You ask me what I feel about Sinclair. I've known him for so many years, of course, and yet I feel I know him not at all. He got into the cabinet by fluke, when poor old Rory died. Without that I don't think he'd ever have made it. He was always not so much a dilettante but just not interested in subjects which ordinary people care about. I had quite good arguments with him about Europe, multilevel governance, the reform of the UN, and disarmament. But get him onto public services or the economy, and his eyes glaze over, and he retreats into, "well, if that's your view" niceties. And of course he was never on the left. He was as New Labour as anybody. It was only when he walked out that he suddenly became this great ideologue. Was this clever positioning? Or did he really have a change of heart? Or more likely was it this gang of young extremists from Oxford he took up with? I always hated that place.

I think they flattered him leftwards. It's a case of "who's using who?". He was their vehicle to leapfrog into prominence. He used them to build a formidable power base among young activists and sympathisers. But one day all these internal tensions will boil over and have to be resolved.

And 'ambiguous' is really the word I'd use about Sinclair, in his private life as well evidently.

And as to his being gay, I hadn't the faintest idea. But Sylvia always says I'm the last person to pick up on gossip, much to her disappointment. No, I'd assumed that he and Helen Mitchison were partners; and quite a few politicians dither about formalising things. I did, as you well remember. I couldn't care less about his proclivities; and contrary to what the press said, I didn't unleash Ted to make his silly remarks. And they did us a lot of harm. But what he said was almost prophetic. People can just about get to grips with a homosexual in a steady relationship being at the top level in politics. But the way he's been carrying on with a succession of young men like that, people won't accept it. And now of course the whole thing with Aidan Richards, who's the most obnoxious of his team, is just a time-bomb.

I'm most disappointed with Angus Buchanan. I'd marked him out as someone to watch. I'd read his articles about currency and growth theory, which for someone who was then just twenty-two were terribly impressive. When he became an MP I tried to encourage him, but all I got in return was my junior ministers being ripped to shreds in the Treasury committee. He is of course the master and commander of this hell-raising crew, and so far to the left that he'd have dismissed our 1983 manifesto as insipidly right-wing. He can't see an institution or a tradition without wanting to destroy it.

I saw him last night on the Chancellors' debate, where they bring the economic spokesmen of the parties together for a hustings. It's a kind of curtain-raiser for the leadership debate this coming Wednesday. What did I think of it? They used to accuse me of being brutal but I was a cuddly little hamster, and a declawed and toothless one at that, compared with this violent thuggery. For 90 minutes he dominated the debate so much you almost wondered whether he wouldn't burst through the screen and grab you by the throat. He was pitiless on both his opponents, to the extent I almost felt sorry for the Liberal, who of course I knew quite well at St Andrew's. The Tory had it coming to him anyway. Buchanan won the debate but lost the audience. It's not a question of being loveable. I wasn't liked, but I wasn't hated either, and I usually won respect.

Do I think they can win, and I find I do think of it now as "they" not "us"? I doubt it. I think people will have a last minute revulsion. They'll hold back, possibly even as they're in the booths. We've enjoyed the spectacle, we've been entertained, had all the thrills and spills, but then we'll sober up. I think the Tories will limp home, Sinclair will go off to some nice Spanish or French university and write books and carry on with his extramural activities. And his monsters will start tearing each other apart. I expect we'll be out of office for a generation. Believe me, Anne, this gives me not one iota of pleasure. We were on our way back. The economy was turning. A fourth term won in adversity would have really established us as the natural party of government. Now it's all chucked away because of one man's colossal vanity and a conspiracy of irresponsible students who refuse to grow up.

On a lighter note, even their juggernaut of a party machine is creaking. They've sent young commissars to all seats up and down the land. As I think I told you, with the boundary changes we are no longer living in my parliamentary seat, but just the other side in the neighbouring one. This lunchtime, a pretty young woman with a strong

Sassenach accent walks up the drive and rings the bell. "Hello", she says, "I'm Kate, I'm canvassing on behalf of your Labour candidate, and he was wondering if we could count on your support." I replied, "Well I usually vote Labour". "And is your wife a Labour supporter, too?" "Well, you'll have to ask her but she's out at the supermarket, I'm afraid." She continued blithely, "We don't have many supporters on this estate. I wondered whether you might put up a poster". I politely declined as I did the offer of help in getting to the polling station, and she went cheerfully on her way. To be forgotten, and by your own party supporters in ten days after ten years at the top of the tree, now that's good for the soul. This is indeed a fitting parable for these times of Insurgency.

It's great that you, Mark and the kids are coming over for Christmas. I hope I won't have been sent to a gulag by then.

Much love from your young brother

HELEN

We had really hit rock bottom that ghastly weekend. In the aftermath of the debate, there was some briefing from a 'very senior cabinet minister' (which usually meant Derek Jamieson) about "lunatics taking over the asylum". Some of the New Labour gang started to get their albeit anonymous voices back; there were at least two articles in the Sundays about a campaign "careering out of control".

We all met up at Raphael's old Putney flat. And I of course was the one who had to go over early with Marjorie Delaney to give the place a good old clean. We were all there, the old crowd, except for Aidan Richards, who in any case should have been in disgrace but who had decided to stay put in Mayberry for the rest of the campaign with his army of supporters, who were like members of some fanatical religious sect in a devoted trance worshipping a cult leader quite capable of doing a Jonestown on them.

Bill gave the usual gloom and doom report. We were still ten points behind[49] and had slipped back a notch in the marginals. There were some bright spots in this dark tableau: there was huge social media enthusiasm. Even the debate had been greeted in the blogosphere as a triumph; and the take-outs of Angus Buchanan mauling his opponents were a bit of a YouTube sensation. Aidan's anti-German crudity had caused a spike in support. There were record donations and almost too many volunteers. Even B-teamers (like me) were getting crowds at our meetings.

Then Bo laid out the plans for the next ten days, and the leader's tour. It was not a relaunch because we have yet to have the launch. But it was a staggeringly intense schedule: four or five big meetings per day, town centres, huge venues. The debate on Wednesday; a post-debate rally at Central Hall. A lot of universities on the tour to keep up the youth interest. Some ideas for spectacular backdrops. The posters, black and white with just Raphael's picture and the one word, "Transformation"; and a second one - an idyllic photo of an English village set in woods on the side of the hill, with a smiling Raphael and the slogan "Renewal". And then a sensational last week culminating in Wembley again, then Trafalgar Square and an eight-city marathon for eve of poll.

It was disappointing that after this impressive plan we allowed the tensions of the past few days to boil over. Everyone was fractious. Louise

---

[49] See for example the NOP poll in 'The Times', 4th October

Marchant and Rashida Hussein wanted more details about campaign costs. Then Hattie Reynolds, Paul Howkins, Maudie Hinton and I weighed in about the indiscipline of our young colleagues, the chaotic messages, the irrelevance of all the constitutional issues and the media bashing. Angus Buchanan was silent and sullen. The odd joke from Ned Warren fell flat.

But then two interventions changed things. Rupert Dennison interjected, "We've got to come out all guns blazing on 'Rip-off Britain' – start flinging the furniture round the room; the energy companies, the utilities, the supermarkets, the banks, the media, the food and drinks industry, the pharma economy: all ripping off their customers, all exploiting their workers, all selling investors short, all the bosses paying themselves the salaries of princes. Talk about the new economy and don't be afraid of saying 'the state' which is there for you. We'll protect you. We're on your side. Throw them the facts, the statistics. There's enough to shock people. You can't back-track now. You've got to attack, attack, attack."

All this said in that mellifluous piping voice: a voice you almost wanted to dance to.

Then came a bit of bathos - Bo Sampson - but he held our attention.

"Can I say something? People like it when you use the flag at meetings. Why don't you talk more about Britain at meetings? About what being British means…"

This we pondered until Raphael said, "I think I get it. I see it clearly. Thanks everyone and now for Rashida, Ned and me it's gorgeous downtown Croydon. Who'd be anywhere else on a wet Sunday afternoon in October?".

Insouciant, almost upbeat. Off he went.

NED

<-<-<-<-<-<-<-<-<-<-<-<-<-<-<-<

#@nedwar82

<-<-<-<-<-<-<-<-<-<-<-<-<-<-<-<

Down to Fairfield Halls. Huge crowd. Bo's done his stuff. The big launch. Overspill.

NED

<-<-<-<-<-<-<-<-<-<-<-<-<-<-<-<

#@nedwar82

<-<-<-<-<-<-<-<-<-<-<-<-<-<-<-<

I was funneeee. Shirt tail out. Rashida real pro. All that about girl of immigration. Parents worked hard. How Labour had given her hope.

NED

>>

From: ned.warren.1982@hotmail.com

To: martin.warren.78@hotmail.au

>>

Then on comes Rafa. In the car he's distracted and silent. Shifts around all the time as if he needs the loo. But it's his back which is agony for him when he gets in and out of the car.

But once he walks the plank he's transformed. And he uses the phrase "The Idea of Britain" for the first time, and talks of our history, our values, and our finest hour. This he compares with the brutal unfair materialistic place we've created before he launches into a blistering attack on "corporate greed, waste, inequality and injustice where we value traders more than nurses and teachers", all this with masses of figures, firing on all guns, "the betrayal of the British ideal".

The little bits of dross from Rupe and Bo he's spun into threads of gold (wow! Did I really write that?).

They love it. Brilliant. We have a message at last.

Back in the car, he asks the No 2 body, Kevin, (nice kid from up north, stick-out ears, pink face and tiny blue eyes; shy but with a sense of humour) "Where's Bud? Haven't seen him since we went off to Brussels".

"Oh he was owed a lot of leave, so he's taken it now to go and help Aide, er, Mr Richards, in the campaign. He's staying in the house in Mayberry."

Raphael just says, "How nice of him". And falls silent.

Christ almighty.

BARRIE

After the Croydon rally, in the early evening, I get summoned up to the flat above the shop. He'd just had a huge row with Aidan. "He ended up saying, 'Don't worry, he's in the spare room. All nice and proper. I didn't think it important enough to say anything. He's helping me out here till Wednesday then he'll be back keeping the leader of the people safe'."

And then comes the attack. "'You refuse to get me a good seat. I'm stuck here in fucking, boring old Mayberry. All my mates, all of them in safe seats, mind you - they're all out on the campaign trail having the time of their lives. You hardly ever bother to phone. So, yes, a bit of company helps to keep me sane. But don't let your sex-obsessed imagination make you even more paranoid than usual. There's nothing 'going on'. Not now. And there won't be.'"

So of course Raphael is worried.

HELEN

We began to feel we had turned the corner. The slogan, "The Idea of Britain", once Raphael had fleshed it out, really caught on. On Monday he did rallies in the North-East: open air in Newcastle, Durham and Easington. Then big late afternoon events in Leeds and Bradford, rounding off in York town hall. Rashida Hussein, who had become quite a star herself, and who was doing most of the warm-ups, said he was at the top of his game.

On Tuesday he went north of the border with Angus and some of the Scots crowd. He did six big city events before a rural rally in Fife. He struggled to find his feet a bit: the new slogan did not travel as well outside England. But when he started laying into the Nationalists he hit his stride.

Barrie Jones had by this time become almost frantic about the lack of time for debate preparation. Both the other party leaders had taken 24 hours out of their schedules to work on arguments, do mocks, and prepare key lines. But Raphael kept wading through his programme with a street rally in Wandsworth just two hours before the debate.

Like in the heyday of the leadership campaign, the crowds lifted him and he excited them. The adrenalin was pumping; he was euphoric, as if scared to let up lest the fatigue overcome him. Although he was exhausted, so much time out of doors kept replenishing his natural tan. And the crowds were becoming ever more boisterous: people grabbing, snatching, taking off buttons. Just six hours before the debate someone gave him a handshake with broken glass on his glove. It took some time for anyone to realise he'd been assaulted, but blood was soon pouring out of his palm; he was given a quick bandaging by someone from security who always carried a first aid kit. I suspected that he used the bandage as a stage prop for the debate.

And throughout those days there was the sound of distant drums: ever more pressing, specific and credible death threats, relayed from security by Cynthia Montcalm and Miranda Fawcett. Raphael, careless for his own safety, just carried on, ignoring pleas from most of us –perhaps more careful about our own - to take more precautions, to adapt his schedule, or to cancel the walkabouts. And of course Angus Buchanan and Bo Sampson were arguing from the other side - nothing must temper the "edginess" of the campaign. Rupert Dennison sends in the odd message but no-one had seen him since the Putney gathering.

On the eve of the debate, with one week of campaigning to go we were still an average eight or nine points behind the Tories[50].

---

[50] See, for example, MORI in 'The Guardian', 9 October

NED

Text to Mart

ooooooooooooooooooooooooooooooooooooooo

>On warm-up for Central Hall tonite. Just me and Hat. Debate on big screens in the Hall. Then it's us, and he should amble along after<

TRANSCRIPT FROM THE LEADERS' DEBATE:

THE HIGHLIGHTS

WEDNESDAY OCTOBER 10th

BBC, ITV & SKY

From Mr Sinclair's introduction: "First I'd like to thank the broadcasters for giving us the chance to discuss the issues of Britain's future. I know our minders have been overcautious in setting rules for the debate. They just want to protect us. That's their job. But I think we should use some common sense and have a real debate. It's a privilege to be here as the first British Prime Minister to be taking part in a leaders' televised debate. But I have to say, it's also a privilege to be sharing this occasion with my two colleagues, Tim and Andrew. They are both distinguished leaders of great parties. They represent the best of the parliamentary tradition of our country. They are both amply qualified to hold the highest office. They are both devoted to public service. My arguments with them are not personal. I admire and respect them as individuals. Let's concentrate tonight on the issues."

NED

Text to Mart

ooooooooooooooooooooooooooooooooooooooooo

>Just had a one word text from Aide: 'yuck'<

HELEN

I was on point duty in 'spin alley' with Brian Dawkins, the friendly faces of the new and old regimes. I was a little surprised that Rupert Dennison had fielded us and was not present himself but I think he at least has understood how dangerous the 'lunatics running the asylum' slur has become. Raphael started brilliantly, completely wrong-footing the others, being affable, apolitical and asking for flexible application of the rules he had asked Nigel Bolton to negotiate as strictly as possible. On immigration, he triangulated shamelessly.

EXTRACT

From Mr Sinclair, in answer to a question about immigration

"We've got a lot of common ground here. Immigration is an economic necessity and has given us some growth. Nearly everybody who comes here, comes to work. But it's been poorly managed. We underestimated the numbers and that was our fault. Now we have in place a points system which has worked elsewhere. If it doesn't work I'm prepared to look at Tim's proposal on an annual cap but frankly I'm not sure that would work. Businessmen tell me it would hamper their efforts to find the labour they need to grow. But if we're serious about stopping illegal immigration then the border police tell us we need ID cards but of course you two oppose that as well... ."

NED

<-<-<-<-<-<-<-<-<-<-<-<-<-<-<

#@nedwar82

<-<-<-<-<-<-<-<-<-<-<-<-<-<-<

Another score on the NHS. I make that 3-0.

EXTRACT

From Mr Sinclair on Europe

"Tim, you're not at Tory conference now. We all know our interests lie in Europe and that it'd be a disaster if we left. But you continue to make Eurosceptic noises. Let me tell the viewers something. If it's so important to you that Britain leaves Europe, don't vote for me. But don't vote for one of these two gentlemen either. We all have the same broad view about Europe. If you're seriously against the EU, you've now got a choice. It's called UKIP. They really believe it. If you vote UKIP, you vote to leave Europe. The real thing. So don't let Tim fool you that we differ on Europe."

NED

<-<-<-<-<-<-<-<-<-<-<-<-<-<-<

#@nedwar82

<-<-<-<-<-<-<-<-<-<-<-<-<-<-<

Wow. Brilliant goal, and on Europe. Watch Tim's face go puce.

HELEN

It had always been the economic segment of the debate which would be the real test. When Raphael spoke - after the two others - his demeanour had changed: deadly serious, passionate, and almost angry but in control.

EXTRACT

"Let's not rewrite history, Tim. The debt and the deficit are there because a worldwide credit crunch put the finances of every country in the world under strain. And that crisis was the result of the folly of your friends in the City. People like the boss of … who sold dodgy financial products to the banks and who has just contributed to your campaign. Just how much has he given you?"

"That's a smear."

"How much?"

"I'm not going to answer these… "

"How much? He won't tell you but I will. Two million pounds only last week from just one of the people who helped create the crisis which nearly destroyed our economy. People have been thrown out of their jobs because of the recklessness of your friends. You get more than 50% of your funds from these, your fellow travellers. Then there's the property developers who've just given you a million pounds so that you'll rip up all the controls that protect our wonderful countryside. Let's look at the bankers: Sir Stephen …one million pounds. Well, he can afford it: he's getting six million a year from the taxpayer. And then there's the tax dodgers. You're not a political party, you're the wholly owned subsidiary of every loan shark, every spiv, and every tax dodger in town. And you want us to trust you with our money. I don't think so."

NED

<-<-<-<-<-<-<-<-<-<-<-<-<-<-<

#@nedwar82

<-<-<-<-<-<-<-<-<-<-<-<-<-<-<

Tim's sweating and purple. Can hardly get the words out.

EXTRACT

Mr Sinclair

"Our plan is simple. Growth alone can get us out of this hole. We need responsible finance but it's job creation and investment which will cut the dole queues and the welfare bill. And that saves public money. Above all, our plan gives hope for future generations."

HELEN

By going on the attack on the economy as lethally as Angus but in a much more controlled way, he completely dominated the debate. He had spoken little at first and saved up time for the economic onslaught. When the winding up came, the other two seemed physically to have shrunk. Thanks to Nigel's negotiation, Raphael had the last word.

EXTRACT: Concluding Remarks by Mr Sinclair

"I want to use these last moments to give one simple message: vote. Vote for Tim's party. For Andrew's party. Or for mine. For the Greens. For the nationalists if you will. For UKIP if you really have to. But vote. Don't vote for the BNP of course because they are the purveyors of Hitler's message of hate. They oppose all that's best in Britain. But vote" (#@nedwar82 See the hand gestures. It's a command not a request). "Vote because it matters. Vote because we're not all the same. That's just a lazy cop-out. You've just seen the proof of our differences. Vote because people here once gave up their lives so that we can vote. Don't betray their sacrifice. Use your vote next week."

HELEN

His last message - "to use your vote" - was so simple, so clear, and so authoritative it was spell-binding. Brian Dawkins and I had a wonderful half hour in Spin Alley when it was all over. A scrum surrounded us as we tried not to sound triumphant. But we had won the debate hands down.

BBC NEWS 10 p.m.

Over to our political editor in Spin Alley:

"Experience from other countries shows us that leaders' debates don't win elections. But performing badly can lose them. Tonight only the most hardened opponent would deny the Prime Minister his triumph. He overwhelmed his young rivals by wrong-footing them at every turn. Consensual, courteous, generous when they seemed just partisan. Then when they were lulled into copying his back-slapping chumminess, he suddenly bites their heads off. Then the climax. He didn't bother with a riposte. He appealed head-on for people to do their civic duty. Masterclass stuff. But he will know that all he has done tonight is to make a fight of it."

NED

He comes in really late to Central Hall. Just saunters down the main aisle as if he's just dropped in for a few beers with some mates after a match. I get a hug; Rashida a long embrace. He talks to the thousands for just a few minutes, intimate, casual. How we must fight for the next few days. How we still need money and volunteers. The nature of the change we seek and his new rallying cry, "I can't do it on my own. I need your help. I need you". Off he goes, lots of us in tears, all shouting our heads off. Great life moment.

BARRIE

In the car the fatigue hit him. Head back on the head rest. Back twinges. Kevin, the other bodyguard, offered him a back massage. I laughed, and Raphael said, "Tempting, Kev. But better not". We all went up to the flat. Miranda stomped around the kitchen, making tea, pouring the whiskies (she can drink me under the table). He showed me a text, "My brilliant beautiful man. Proud. Love you more than ever. Come home to Mayberry tomorrow night, whatever time. Needing you. A, X"

His eyes moistened up. Hell!

NED

The next day He's in our neck of the words (He who I worship). Four dos in the East and West Midlands. The crowds are bigger than ever and in Coventry a fight breaks out with some of the EDL (sorry, bruv – English Defence League - our own home-grown fascists) people. He keeps hammering away at the banks and the utilities, it all seems autopilot stuff for some of us. But no matter, the crowds just grow, as if people want to see something that's a moment of history. The first polls after the debate call it for him 3 to 1. 22 million saw it live plus all the millions getting the YouTube take-outs. Social media awash, and Bo's booked bigger venues for next week.

EXTRACT FROM 'THE JC DUNNETT ANTHOLOGY (199- to 201-)'

Until yesterday's televised debate with the party leaders I was coming round to the view that history would soon look back on the short Sinclair premiership as a comet streaking across the night sky before burning itself out with a spectacular and deafening flash. With just over a week to polling the opinion polls have hardly shifted. All the considerable oratorical prowess of the Prime Minister, the zeal of his fanatical henchmen, the thousands of activists deployed in every corner of the land were simply highlighting a gulf which exists in Britain. There's the cosmopolitan Britain - progressive, liberal, internationalist, open to radical ideas for change, politically motivated and caught up in the excitement of a political campaign which has seen no precedent in a hundred years. They attend the monster rallies, they follow the outpourings of the Insurgency leadership on social media, and they are intoxicated with this heady brew of the profound change on offer and its glamorous purveyors. They are the groupies of this revolution.

And then there's the rest of Britain, outside the city centres, the campuses, the more prosperous suburbs, just wanting a government to understand them and to be a little bit more visibly on their side, to weather the economic storms, to restore a little 'normalcy' (to use the Calvin Coolidge word). They care little for politics and have scant faith in politicians. They are not for the most part bigots or xenophobes or reactionaries but on the whole they'd prefer a Prime Minister and his spouse who could make a decent attempt at pretending to live lives a little bit like their own, rather than living out episodes of the exotic soap opera currently showing in Downing Street. And this Britain represents the majority in our country.

But watching the debate on television last night I was struck by how cleverly Mr Sinclair is repositioning himself and his government. His tone was for the most part light and pleasant, complimentary about his rivals, eschewing adversarial partisanship, the mask only slipping when the discussion turned to bankers and the City, where his radicalism chimes with the popular view, and where he adopted the stern moral stance of his Finance Minister minus the psychopathic menace. For the rest he completely outmanoeuvred his Conservative and Liberal Democrat rivals, who seem in all their pink bland puppy flabbiness and clichéd technocratic politicians' language completely interchangeable and who both made the error of getting in their mediocre attacks on the Prime Minister too early in the proceedings. These two young challengers never fail to disappoint, and their campaigns have had all the excitement of partially reheated rice puddings.

But it was Mr Sinclair's clever footwork on Europe and on immigration that covered his opponents with fast-setting glue from which they were unable to free themselves. On immigration control, it was a case of saying to the Tories, "you may be right. If our new system doesn't work as we would wish we will look at your idea", as if the leader of her Majesty's Opposition was a tyro young think-tank researcher. And on Europe he pretended they all agreed, and invited all those who loathe the European Union to look elsewhere, and particularly to UKIP.

He did not so much win the debate, he took ownership of it. And with his final magisterial appeal for voters to exercise their rights, ignoring the rehashed partisan point-scoring of his jejune rivals, he transformed the event into a two-hour-long party political advertisement for himself, with all the nobility of a Roman Emperor, acting always in the public interest, cloaking himself in the flags and symbols of his people.

Both the understandable Labour triumphalism and the caveats of commentators after the event are misplaced. While the debate will not settle the election in Mr Sinclair's favour, because debates are rarely as decisive as the broadcasters would have us believe, it had its significance in the fact of opening up the contest, of displaying a masterclass politician at the peak of his game, and it gave him a potentially winning strategy for the last seven days, provided he speaks to the nation and not just to his fan base and keeps under lock and key those members of his team who terrify voters from middle England.

A resounding victory in the debate was a necessary pre-condition for remaining a contender. Victory requires something a little more. But I no longer rule out a great upset.

BARRIE

I stayed with them overnight after the big Midlands swing. Raphael was tired but needed to talk late to wind down. Aidan dragged him off to bed earlier than he wanted. I stayed down doing the dishes with Bud, who was subdued and uncommunicative, although he's usually chatty with me. He was sweating a lot, and looked pale. I asked him if he liked campaigning and he just said, "Interesting. Real hard work". "Was Aidan good on the street?", was my next gambit but all I got was a quiet, "yeah". So I gave up and we went up early to the spare rooms. All quiet.

And so begins the worst day of my life. I can hardly believe it even now I'm writing about it.

Aidan left early for the school run, mums gathering around in various states of ecstasy. We'd got a regional business coffee morning in a hotel outside the city at eleven before we headed off to God's country (mine) for four meetings including two monsters in Newport and Cardiff.

Raphael, Bud and I went out to the car at 10.30 a.m. I go to the other side to get in the back. There was the usual crowd of hacks, a few supporters and lots of curious bystanders: about four hundred I guess. The customary rigmarole: Bud stood between him and the cameras as he folds himself uncomfortably into the back seat. Then I heard a little crack from somewhere in the crowd, like a Xmas cracker. Instead of moving back to shut the door, Bud just stood there, and then suddenly buckled in slow motion. Raphael could see something wasn't right and held on to Bud's lapels to stop him falling backwards. But instead he fell forward on to Raphael's knees and lap. Someone shouted, "He's been shot". Then we saw the blood seeping out of Bud's dark suit. I just yelled to the police escort, and to our driver, "A & E. Now!"

A policeman helped fold him on the back seat, onto Raphael's lap, moving him as little as possible. He then jumped in the front. He asked, "Is he still breathing, sir?"

"Yes, I think so," Raphael replied, stroking Bud's head so gently, like a father with his son who's fallen over and hurt himself. It took eight minutes to get to Casualty; paramedics waiting; they eased him off Raphael's lap. Raphael, now covered in blood, follows instinctively - a bit shaky and stiff. The medics came immediately to ask if he was hurt. We were both given cups of tea. We both felt sick. We both then headed for the loo, and vomited simultaneously in adjacent stalls. And then we waited. For a while he held my hand, distractedly, while Bud was wheeled off to the operating theatre. I asked him what he wanted to do. He just said, snapping out of his trance, "We wait. Get Aidan here, and get the office to track down his parents. Campaign's off all day. Everywhere. No details. No statement now".

Aidan turned up just as I'm ringing him. He was completely out of it. He hugged and kissed Raphael so got a lot of drying blood on his shirt and jacket. Of course he wanted to see Bud, but wasn't allowed.

After two hours and four cups of tea each, all of us numbed and silent, our mobiles switched off to cocoon us from the world, the doctors came out. "We're going to lose him, I'm afraid. The bullet was lodged in the heart. Locked there because of the pocket revolver he was carrying in his inside pocket. Just a short time before he goes, I'm afraid."

Aidan got up and said, "I want to see him". The doctors look at Raphael and then conclude, "Well, no more harm, I suppose. You can all go in". But I didn't accompany them in to the room - it just didn't feel my place - and they stayed there for two hours until his parents arrived; a tiny, insignificant-looking little couple, Wilf and Doris, in quiet dignified distress.

When they emerged to give the parents some time alone with their boy, Aidan had obviously been crying. Raphael was calm, still covered in now dark caked blood, like a victim in a Hollywood disaster movie. A nurse came to offer to clean them up, but Aidan snapped at her, which I didn't understand. We sat there for another couple of hours while I started to plug into what passes for the real world. I soon learned that it was the global story, and for a time it was Sinclair who was dead, or at least shot. There was still confusion about the injuries; two young white men had been blown up, after trying to leave in a white van parked in the road which cuts across Raphael's street. All this was thanks to the CCTV cameras installed because of who lives there. Several messages from Nigel begging for a statement.

All campaigning had been stopped by all the main parties, despite some clumsy hesitation from the Liberals. And there'd been some remark from a leading Tory about Raphael's "lifestyle issues" possibly catching up with him. This had been immediately disowned by the Tory leadership, at least officially.

Rupert, who I'd not seen for a couple of days, had sent the same message to Aidan and me but I picked it up first. "Don't clean him up, whatever happens; when he leaves the hospital he's got to be blood-spattered. Get some ketchup or chicken blood if necessary. There's hundreds of TV crews and journalists camped outside the hospital, so play it to the hilt." Sometimes all this stuff just makes me so sick.

I went back, sat next to Aidan, and nudged him and for once he didn't spit at me. He reads Rupert's messages and says, "sick fucker" but I noticed neither he nor Raphael got cleaned up.

We waited another hour, saw the sun fall behind the elms which form a square round the hospital car park. Then Wilf and Doris came out with the same two doctors. One said, "It's over I'm afraid. Very peaceful". We all hugged Doris and Wilf, but Raphael couldn't speak. It was Aidan who found the words, "He was a wonderful son. You can be so proud of him. That's just what he did - serving his country".

At last Raphael asserted himself and said, "You can come and stay with us at home. Or we can put you up in the hotel nearby. Or get you driven home", very gently, very kindly.

"We'd rather go back home, Mr Sinclair, sir" said tiny Wilf, deference gaining the upper hand over his grief. "But thank you sir. He really admired you, both of you. I've never known him so settled, so happy. Thank you sir."

Marjorie had arranged everything of course and they left by a back passage to a car waiting to take them home to weep in private. We wandered slowly to the side room where the body lay, now partially cleaned up, face in peace if a little shrunken, but still beautiful in all its rough boyishness.

By this time I was crying uncontrollably, but Raphael just leant forward and kissed Bud's forehead, then left. Aidan kissed him on the lips and said, "I love you, kid". I touched his cold hand lying palm up above the sheets. We then left the room. Outside we thanked the staff. Raphael walked out of the hospital holding Aidan's hand. I followed, a few steps behind, still splattered with some blood, no-one having offered to clean me up.

Then a thousand cameras flashed or whirred or whatever. As a tearful Kevin opened the car door, there was a momentary pause to give them all the image of the year: the noble face of the bloodied leader, stoic, proud, unbowed. The picture the world craved, and which politics demanded.

We squeezed into the back but we didn't head home. Rupert had arranged we all go to a safe house, Angus's flat, to clean up, get some food, and talk it out. Just the four kids, Rashida, Helen and me. I felt outnumbered, isolated, and desperate to see Digby but I knew he wouldn't be welcome.

NED

Letter to Mart

So how was it for me, you ask? Effing awful. I was on a housing estate in Bolton around 10.30 when someone comes running up and says, "He's been shot". "It's the Prime Minister - they've shot him." I went frantic: we piled into some punter's house uninvited, and zapped between 'breaking news'. Then it seems he's not dead but a bodyguard is really badly injured. Then we hear Rafa's not been injured at all but rushed with the wounded guy to the local A&E. It turns out to be Bud who's hurt, not Kevin. Angus is first up on the box, looking really stricken, white as a sheet, "The Prime Minister is not wounded but is staying at the bedside of his wounded bodyguard until his parents can get there. Two people have been killed trying to make a getaway. Our prayers go out to Bud Mitchell and to his parents who we are bringing to the hospital. Out of respect all campaigning is cancelled until further notice."

I can't get through to Aide, Rupe or Angus of course but Rashida rings in around lunchtime, while we're still scrounging sandwiches in the house we'd invaded in Bolton: nice young couple, never voted before, but now really interested. Rashida says to come down to their place in Mayberry where we'll all meet up later. I'm at their flat by the end of the afternoon. I learn the kid's dead and of course the tears flow.

He was a great kid, a toughie, went a bit wild when he was in his teens but sorted himself out and got taken on by the police. Because he was tough, brave and not stupid they put him in Special Duties which is how he pitched up as protection for Rafa. And he really likes working for the Boss who always treats people well until he gets to know them: thoughtful, remembers family details, the real pro. So he starts becoming more than just the resident heavy, he does the cooking, the washing up, and goes jogging with Aide, starts to be part of the gang, likes the acceptance, goes and helps Aide on his days off. We - or at least Rupe and me - wonder whether this is not something more than a kid suddenly getting our religion, or whether Aide hasn't changed some orientation other than the purely political. Well, who cares? He was a good guy, and that's all that matters.

We wait for Rafa in the living room at Angus's flat; all minimalist furniture but maniac clean. I nip out and get some beers but the others are on tea. Rupe arrives hyper, no shred of grief and straight on to his mobile, texting the whole time. After 7 p.m. Rafa comes in followed by

Aide and Barrie. He looks like death, caked blood on his face, his jacket, his shirt, his trousers, everywhere. And it's in contrast to his face, drained of all colour. Unbelievable. Aide is quiet, and he's obviously been crying a lot. Little Barrie's also splattered with dark blood stains, and is pretty shaky.

Rashida says, "Come to the bathroom, Raphael, I'll help you clean up", but Aide snaps at her, "That's my job. Come on". And he leads Rafa through the bedroom into the bathroom, shutting both doors on the way, and we wait for ages before there's any sound of running water. Rashida fills the conversational gap with "I've left some clothes for him on the bed. Marjorie went round to the house to pick up a change of suit and tie. All that. Barrie, you'll need a shower when they, when Raphael, has taken his and I've put out on the bed an old tracksuit of Angus's as well. It may be a bit on the large size, I'm afraid". (A Rashida understatement but she uses "I'm afraid" in the very British middle-class way because in fact she's not afraid of anything.)

The two come out of the bedroom, Raphael in his change of clothes and the pair of them ten times better than they had been, but still drawn. It's Barrie's turn and after he's showered he comes out with track suit arms and legs flapping. "You look like a shrunken lime penguin," I say, which at least lightens the atmosphere.

We talk and drink while Angus tries with a little subtlety for once to steer us back to the campaign. Rafa's got a big rally planned for Southampton tomorrow night but says he doesn't know whether he'd be up to it so soon. It's then that Rupe explodes, "I know you're not going to like this. But face it, this is our Reichstag Fire Moment. We've got to milk it. This is the game-changer. You're due in Southampton tomorrow night, right? We get the whole cabinet down there. It'll all be 'hung be the heavens with black.' Sombre. No glitz. You make the big speech, start bleak and then build the 'They won't intimidate us. We're the British...' symphony. A big photo of Bud on stage, a black sash across it. We might even drag along the parents..."

There's a ghastly silence as we absorb this with the deep revulsion it deserves. Aide mutters, "You cynical little fuck". Instead of leaving it at that, Rupe says tartly, "Look, darling, I know you're upset; no more little playmate... " Before he can finish Aide's out of his chair like the dog at the rabbit and starts slapping Rupe around the head, really hard. Angus and I step in to separate them, Rupe in tears, clearly hurt in the assault.

There's an endless silence which is broken by Rafa, who has been quite unperturbed by Rupe's outrageous ideas and the ensuing scuffle. He says very slowly, "You know Rupert's got a point. What's happened to Bud is awful, and I'm really upset for his family. But even if we cancelled the whole campaign it won't bring him back. Let's do this for Bud". I start texting Bo, upgrading the event, changing the nature of it. The others start preparing when Aide and Rafa get up to leave, with Barrie literally tripping after them as his track suit bottoms get caught up with his shoes. Aide doesn't say a word, and Barrie's still shaken by everything the day has dumped on him. But Rafa's something of his old self. He says to me on his way out, "And tell Bo to be a little sensitive in his choice of music; I don't want the lovely Martha and 'Dancing in the fucking streets' tomorrow". I kip on Angus's sofa, but I'm too tired to sleep.

BARRIE

Eventually, we went back to their house and Kevin, who was pretty shaken himself, kindly offered to make us tea and a sandwich. But Aidan headed straight for the whisky bottle and Kevin took the hint and went back to the cars, parked around the cordoned off 'crime scene' which was by now deathly quiet.

Inside, after several minutes of silence, Raphael asked in a low voice, "What did Rupert mean by your 'little playmate'?"

Aidan replied, back to his sullen unpleasant self, "I don't want to talk about it now, and certainly not in front of him (murderous glance at me) although why not? You tell him everything anyway. I expect he gets off on all our spills and thrills".

I was just too tired to be hurt by all this venom, but he went on, "He was not my lover. I liked him. I wanted to help him. We were close. He was pretty confused about things. He turned to me and I was there for him".

"So, nothing happened?", Raphael persisted, not seeming to realise how desperately trivial all this was after what had happened to poor Bud.

"Nothing of any significance," (a telling piece of ambiguity from someone not given to reticence) "and now I'm going to bed, where I want you to hold me all night if you can bear to tear yourself away from the post-mortem of the post-mortem of the post-mortem with this ridiculous little gnome lost in his synthetic lime rompers" (and I love you too, Aidan).

He headed off to bed. Raphael on his way upstairs put his hand on my shoulder, kissed my cheek, and said, "Sorry, Barrie, it's been a horrible day for us all". I spoke to Digby on the phone and cried a lot.

HELEN

The waiting was awful. We had all had to cancel campaign activities until the Friday evening, giving the other parties no alternative but to follow suit. Then the whole cabinet was summoned to appear on stage in Southampton, again causing havoc in our schedules. Derek Jamieson was the only one who had sent in an excuse, making his dismissal after the election a certainty. I still had not managed to speak to Raphael although Barrie had given me a flavour of things as they happened, including apparently a sharp disagreement afterwards between his own Gang of Four as to how to pick up the pieces of the campaign.

During Friday the police released the names and photos of the two young men who died after the bodyguard had been murdered and the attempted assassination when their van had been blown up. Both were members of a breakaway sect of the EDL[51], both from Wolverhampton, rootless drop-outs, which caused questions to be asked about how two such people had managed to get so close to killing our Prime Minister, how they had been able to buy two very sophisticated firearms and how they had been able to pay for a white van, not hired but bought outright. So a flood of conspiracy theories surged on the Internet: everything from a dissident right-wing group in the security services; Americans alarmed at the election of a left-wing socialist in Britain; al-Qaeda of course; Islamic fundamentalists or fanatic believers of other faiths. And who had planted the explosive device which blew up their getaway van and conveniently removed any possibility of getting answers to these questions?

We had all been told to wear dark clothes as if we were going to a funeral and when I arrived at the hall everything was draped in black, with a plain stage, a couple of rows of chairs, and a huge photograph of Bud Mitchell, with a black sash across the left corner. The photo was of a young man with boyish features, those innocent blue eyes, the toughness and the fearfulness, the cropped hair, the strong jaw, a dark suit, white shirt and black tie. Just seeing it I wanted to cry and yet I had hardly known him.

The hall was full beyond reason; the event a global one. When we were all seated, there was a hush as Aidan was the last to take his seat, and every eye and every camera was trained on him. His hair looked ruffled, he was unshaven and wearing a sharp black suit, brilliant white shirt and shoelace thin black tie. They then played, 'Crying', the Roy Orbison/k.d.

---

[51] English Defence League, a far-right group

Laing version, and in fact a Raphael favourite which the young man had probably never heard, but which was the perfect dramatic mournful scene setter. Aidan walked forward to the platform in the silence which followed, only interrupted by the incessant clicking of cameras.

In his clear flat voice, with just that hint of the Essex where he came from, he simply said, "I got to know Bud Mitchell just a few weeks ago. A regular bloke, doing his job, professionally, protecting our democracy. A kid who a few years ago had gone off the rails. In with the wrong crowd. Drank too much. Dropped out. Then he turns his life around with the help and love of his parents, Wilf and Doris, who become so proud of their boy as he starts to serve his country.

"I got to know him, to like him, to laugh with him, to join in with being a bit cheeky to Raphael and to make him listen to my favourite music.

"I cannot express how much I feel this loss. But above all tonight I give my thanks to him. For saving the life of the man I love, the man who leads us, Raphael Sinclair."

There was a moment's hesitation as he returned to his seat and suddenly the silence was broken as the hall erupted with a fervour I had never before felt at any public event I had ever attended. As he and Raphael pass each other their hands brush for a second.

NED

Text to Mart

ooooooooooooooooooooooooooooooooooooooo

>As Aide comes back I start crying like everyone else except Rupe who whispers, "Bang goes your top spot on next year's NEC". Cynical bastard<

HELEN

And of course, Raphael was magnificent. The encomium was restrained and dignified but with a crescendo of defiance; "No Pasarán'; the betrayal and the wickedness of extremism and violence. Then he talked of the solidarity with all minorities, all those persecuted, and all those under threat. He appealed for national unity, standing together against terrorism whatever the source, and paid tribute to the other party leaders for upholding the standards of public decency in the face of this outrage. He concluded, "And now let's make this a week for democracy, dedicating our efforts to the memory of yet one more youngster who has given his life in its cause".

When he came back to embrace us he was crying; the first time I had seen him cry so openly. If, as some people later claimed, this was just theatre, then it was classy, great theatre.

NED

Rupe wakes me early, triumphant, vindicated. The polls show us just edging into the lead with Rafa's standing sky high. People are flooding in, volunteering, paying, which is just as well as Bo has gone crazy booking venues. We now spend nearly a million quid on each rally. As I lie in my bed trying to decide whether to get up or just turn over for another hour something makes me shiver, the memory of something which I can't quite call back but which frightens me. Really odd.

BARRIE

This bunch will manage to snatch defeat from the jaws of victory if anyone can. Just as we are romping ahead Angus starts upping the stakes. The Governor of the Bank of England issues a statement which endorses Tory spending cuts and hopes "Labour will give the same amount of attention to what is our number one problem". This was a provocation to be ignored but that's not Angus's way. At the press conference he goes ballistic, "The Governor of the Bank of England has just waddled" (that I like) "onto the political stage. And in so doing he's put his position on the line. I say this to him, if I'm in my job come Friday, then we start the public enquiry on day one. Who led us into the credit crunch? Who sat on his fat arse as deregulation was subverted into a criminal defrauding of the finances of Britain? Which rotund self-satisfied chump allowed this to happen, said nothing, and now lectures us on financial probity? Our future ex-Governor now faces the music. Why should he keep his bloated pension when others have lost their livelihoods? It was on your watch, Governor. We hold you responsible".

The press revels in it, and of course our people are thrilled, mobbing the hero of the Revolution, but you could almost hear the subsidence in our centre-ground support.

Raphael is furious at this exocet, about which he'd had no forewarning. Between three rallies during the day, he phoned from a pit-stop. "Your anger is becoming a problem, Angus. You go out there now and you explain that the difference between our deficit plan and theirs is that ours works and theirs wouldn't. And you spell it out line-by-line."

This is beyond appeal and Angus backs down. By the evening the headlines alternate between the breath-taking Sinclair rallies and the new 'iron Chancellor' with his firm hand on public spending.

NED

Text to Mart

∘∘∘

>Headline today, "Buchanan cuts". Every department gets new ceilings. Pension age up to 67- higher than the Tories<

HELEN

In those last days we managed to get back the momentum. And Raphael's tour was an astonishing piece of record-breaking bravura. People lined the streets, filled market squares. Every meeting had overspills. Yet people could still approach him as he refused all extra security or anything which would put distance between him and the crowds. He said to me, "If I can't be protected in my own street in my little leafy Mayberry suburb, then what's the point isolating me anywhere else?".

Hattie Reynolds telephoned late on Monday night in tears. In the car on the way back from a meeting in Leicester, he had just said to her in a very matter-of-fact voice, "Hattie, we're not going to discuss this now. I know it was you who leaked the campaign to Derek. I don't know whether I can keep you on after Thursday, but I'd like to hear you apologise. Now".

She had almost been as shocked by the calm in his voice as by the accusation. She had tried to explain that Derek had been a friend for a long time who had given her the first break by making her his parliamentary secretary. He had been conflicted in the wars but had stayed on. She could not not tell him. He had not broken her confidence, just warned against any attempt to stand for the leadership.

Raphael repeated, "We'll talk on Thursday night". And then he said nothing for the rest of the journey, which had really hurt her.

I told Hattie to leave it there. Because I liked her and could see easily how she had got herself into this position, which is the way some things just happen in politics, I promised her I would speak to Raphael before the day. I did not tell her of the pressure he was under from Angus Buchanan's gang to sack Derek and sweep out fellow travellers, capitalist running dogs and anyone who might stand in their way.

NED

Text to Mart

∘∘

>Slept really badly. Kind of anxiety attack. Something someone said to me like an omen. Getting worried<

BARRIE

Leicester was one of the really great rallies but it was late when Raphael got back to No 10. I had to break it to him that there was a Chief Inspector from the Met waiting for him in the Reception Room who wanted to brief him on the ongoing investigation into the assassination. This seriously annoyed him and punctured his buoyancy because it threatened a delay in getting some sleep. But he went into the room, snapping his fingers at me to follow, and offered neither seat let alone drink to the rather seedy-looking copper. "So, Chief Inspector, what's the news?"

"I thought you should know, sir", (the 'sir' just to underline a degree of insolence and contempt that some domestics used to show their masters before the War) "we've had a bit of a breakthrough. We've been following the money trail and an account in Switzerland. We now believe this is some international extremist network targeting leftists and political radicals."

If Raphael resented being lumped into this general category, he didn't show it. He asked, "And where did they get their money from?"

"Too early to say with any certainty, sir, but we believe it's possible this money come from some neoconservative groups the other side of the Atlantic. But I have to insist, sir, do not make any of this public or you'll undermine our enquiries."

"Thank you for briefing me, Inspector. I look forward to your conclusions. I also expect the police to keep this to themselves as well. Now, goodnight."

The Inspector found himself being guided to the door when he turned and said, "Just one other thing, sir", a look of malign triumph lighting up his face. "We did a blood test as part of the autopsy on the young man, Mr Mitchell. Standard practice. We found very high levels of class A drugs in his bloodstream."

There was a silent moment. Our little procession halted at the still shut door.

"And this is relevant how?"

"Well just to let you know that this may come out in the coroner's report. The pathologist tells us that such high levels of drugs stay in the bloodstream for about three or four days. I understand Mr Mitchell was in Mayberry for the days before his death. Taking a bit of leave. I think he was staying at your house, giving a hand to your boyfriend for his election."

Raphael was white with fury, but still very controlled. "I would hope for his parents' sake that this does not have to become public. It does not seem to me to be relevant to his murder, as he wasn't even the target."

"I'm sure we all have our reasons for hoping this doesn't become public, sir."

"Not least our valiant police and security services, Chief Inspector. This business doesn't reflect well on the reputation of the service, does it?" said Raphael, regaining his balance a little.

"Unfortunate business all round I'd say, sir," the Inspector having the last word and scarcely able to contain his glee.

We proceeded upstairs in silence. In the flat he turned to me and asked, "How long before this leaks?"

I said, "Well, before Thursday, I imagine".

"Then I think we change our itinerary tomorrow. We'll pass by the house at Mayberry first thing."

I tried to say, "But you've got…"

"Tomorrow morning we pass by Mayberry. I have to speak to Aidan in person. Until then we speak to no-one."

****

Sod's law operating to the full. Tuesday morning first thing, Aidan was at the BBC studio in Mayberry doing his one and only national radio interview in the campaign. It was on that station which has the schmoozy interviewer who lulls his guests into talking about their private lives and revealing more than they ought. Raphael had tried to kill this but had got lots of stroppy, "I'm never on the box. You can't switch on the fucking telly without seeing Angus or Rupe. I'm stuck here going out of my mind, knocking doors with moonstruck but deeply unfanciable kids, most of them fantasising about me". Thus the grateful candidate talks of his loyal foot soldiers.

We were on our way in the car to Mayberry, the schedule having been sewn together again with just a stop in Willesden cancelled; so we listened to Aidan as the snake oil salesman bowled him some gentle questions as starters.

"Who says he picked me up? I chose him, as a matter of fact." This in answer to an insidious question about when Raphael had pulled him. Then lots of affirmations of love and admiration for the Prime Minister.

As to the minefield of his well-documented republicanism, "The Royals? I met the Queen once. It was an honour; and we had to make the point about the way Britain has changed. She was very gracious. They know my views about the monarchy. But it's not an issue now. The British people prefer the monarchy to a presidential system and we have to respect that." So far, I had to admit, he had been perfect.

"You look a right fit young man. And you've knocked around a bit. Lots of clubbing I expect. There's been quite a bit of drugs, I guess." After last night's revelation this new line of attack sets off deafening alarm bells.

"I'm not a great one for clubs now. That's very much in the past."

"And the drugs? Are you still a user?"

"Like most of my generation, straight or gay, men and women, I've done recreational drugs."

"Do you still do them?" the interviewer persists.

"I've stopped. I've seen the harm it does."

"So we should keep the ban?"

Aidan almost relieved at the switch to policy even in an area where he didn't like the line, "That's a political decision. There isn't really a consensus on this. We certainly need to look at it because the old 'war on drugs' approach isn't really working."

Then the sirens started blaring again, "Just as a matter of interest, when did you last do a line?"

"Some time ago. Now I've developed a deep addiction to cups of milky tea and ham sandwiches, which is all you get to consume when you're campaigning." Good, move on, please.

"Some time ago? How long ago? Since you've been an MP? Since you've been a minister?"

"Some time ago." The answer which wasn't one was left hanging in the air.

Raphael told the driver to turn it off; he clutched the biro in his hand so hard, it snapped. When we arrived at the house, Aidan having already had time to come back, I offered to stay in the car, fearful of the explosion about to detonate.

"Come," he ordered.

We entered the house, Aidan, working away at his lap top. They kiss in a perfunctory manner. "And I see you've brought a little witness. Hi Barrie," he said almost civilly.

"Aidan. I had a visit from the police doing the Bud case yesterday. They think they were paid by some foreign group, possibly American neocons."

"I know. I had a visit this morning."

"So you know the kid had cocaine while he was staying here?"

"I'd rather be having this conversation without Fido, if you don't mind. Let's go upstairs."

I got up to leave, but Raphael said, "No. He stays".

"Very well. Look, one night after five hours canvassing in the sodding rain he and I come home. We were chatting about drink and drugs. We'd both had a skinful and he asked me what cocaine was like. I told him how it gives you a great lift. He then says he'd wished he could try. So I phone Trev, you know, the teacher from Mayberry Central, who runs one of my wards. We did some lines sometime back but I've given him a wide berth recently. And, no, he's not gay. So we go round to his place, do a couple of lines each. We come back here, end of story."

"So that's all, then?" asked Raphael, in mock relief. "The Minister of State and the Prime Minister's bodyguard doing class A drugs together. So no story there then. Just the little matter of the kid getting shot to death 36 hours later, with the stuff still in his bloodstream." All this was said pleasantly.

"He just wanted to try." I could tell how uncomfortable Aidan was becoming.

"And you obliged as a kindness. Because there was something else you wanted him to try." A savagery crept into Raphael's voice.

Aidan didn't even pretend not to understand what he was getting at. "He needed to know what he wanted. We were both off our heads. We ended up in bed. I just woke up in the morning and we were there together. I don't have the faintest idea what happened. And I don't think he did either. It was nothing..."

Raphael gave a false laugh. "No. Nothing. You take a young confused kid. Who just happens to be my security officer. You feed him drugs. You sleep with him. Then he gets shot and the pieces of the story of his last days start to be reassembled. Two days before the election. And just to make this perfect - for our enemies - you choose today to talk about your drug habit on national radio. Great timing there, kid."

Aidan snarled with aggression as the best form of defence, "I don't know what bothers you most, Rafa: a kid's life, the scandal of me having a bit of fun with him while I'm stuck here waiting for my career to end with you and all my mates getting ready to run the show for five years ... "

Raphael now beside himself, interrupted, "So you decide to wreck it all not just for yourself, for me, for your friends, for his reputation, for his parents' memories of him and, just by the by, for the party and the country. So that's the real Aidan".

"Barrie, please leave us," ("please", a first from the cornered little monster). Raphael tried to stop me but I got off out, into the pale morning sunshine, and walked around the street and chatted to Kev. And we waited. And we waited.

By now the programme of the day was in tatters again but by the time Raphael emerged from the house it was as if they have had a little tiff over who was doing the washing up or where to book for their next holiday. He only gave a few coded comments because the driver was new and Kevin had yet to enter the toxic vortex of this modern-day revival of 'Who's Afraid of Virginia Woolf?'.

"In a way, I get it," he whispered. "He does love me but he needs attention from me all the time. And he's frustrated stuck here. And I guess monogamy is a bit of a challenge for him."

I said nothing. But it really goes to show that all that cod psychology about relationships really just being another form of power play has some truth in it. And in this relationship, the younger one has the upper hand which he exploits mercilessly.

They had been speaking to Rupert who knew everything anyway. And immediately, Rupert had the answer because Rupert always has the answer. That's why we all put up with his ebullient insufferability. "I'll nose around," he said, "If we get the word that it's coming out, we trump it. 'US money behind plot to assassinate the PM', now that's what I call a headline."

NED

Text to Mart

ooooooooooooooooooooooooooooooooooooooooo

>Blimey. Just heard Aide on the news. I overslept and missed the interview. Drugs now the issue<

HELEN

Some people are just lucky. I thought the revelations from Aidan Richards on some morning radio show I had never heard of, just two days before the election, might sink us. And of course there was a spate of headlines, "the PM, his lover and the coke parties". But something else turned up which helped us out.

One of the inner circle of New Labour, a senior ex-minister, launched a frontal attack on Raphael, "the poisonous clique of young radical extremists with whom he has surrounded himself", and his "anti-business agenda of state control". Nothing could have been better designed to rally the troops. At a late afternoon rally Raphael calmly but lethally went onto the attack. "For a moment I felt inclined to expel him from the party but I found he hasn't paid his subs for years, not even when he was a minister. Such was his unstinting devotion to the cause of Labour." The media and the party loved this bitchiness although the effect on the wider public was uncertain.

According to Bill Sampson, who rang me that night, the momentum from last week had ground to a halt with us flat-lining just a couple of points ahead, "and within the margins of error". For ages Rupert Dennison had been telling us we had to talk up UKIP because they were fighting the Tories for their traditionalist supporters who didn't trust their leaders on Europe or immigrants. Raphael always discouraged this as "too clever by half" and as something which could channel Euroscepticism in a very dangerous direction. But that night in the press review[52] I saw that two papers were running with stories about "new UKIP threat to the Tories".

On Wednesday morning the markets threw a serious wobbly. They had been nervous throughout the leadership campaign, panicked when Raphael was elected, but steadied immediately the election was called. Then they nosedived after the debate and even more after the shooting, not because they were aghast at the attack on Raphael but at his survival. Since then, they had been jittery but calmer until the Wednesday morning - the day before the election - when they started to believe an outright Labour victory might still just be possible. During the morning nearly eight hundred points were lost on the FTSE 100[53].

In the early bulletins another story competed for attention. The last Labour Prime Minister but one had decided to break his silence. Writing

---

[52] Prepared daily by Labour Party staff during the campaign.
[53] The main stock exchange index

in the Telegraph, of all places, he said, "Raphael Sinclair has all the qualities needed to be a good Prime Minister. But he must end this flirtation with statist socialism and he should change his team. The enthusiasm and surface brilliance of some of the young radicals who have captured the Labour Party cannot constitute a serious government pursuing sensible polices to solve our serious economic problems. I simply urge Raphael Sinclair to change course."

It competed with various other bombshells for coverage and won. The morning was spent waiting to see how Raphael would respond. With his eight-city marathon and ten huge rallies there would be opportunities galore.

NED

Text to Mart

∘∘∘

>Market meltdown. Old regime attacking. Sex and drugs stuff everywhere, except for me, sadly. So all well<

BARRIE

We were stuck in this crummy hotel outside Newcastle waiting for the cars for the first rally (at 9 a.m. in an airport hangar - 9 a.m!). Nigel phoned in with the former PM's interview. Rupert was suggesting a robust counterattack. But Raphael hesitated, the serpentine former minister is one thing, the Great Helmsman another. Nigel got a bit short with him, "The press conference starts in thirty minutes. The press will only be interested in our response. Do we go for him or not?" Raphael was a little taken aback but said, "oh, alright," (yet again hardly masterful in a face-off of his young acolytes!).

After Newcastle and the helicopter trip to Glasgow, actually on time, we picked up the 11 a.m. bulletins. "Labour campaign spokesman and Culture Minister Rupert Dennison has made a strong personal attack on the former Prime Minister who this morning has criticised Mr Sinclair's team." There was then an excerpt from Rupert's remarks, "Our former Prime Minister has taken time out from his current duties such as representing the interests of companies which evade taxation and third countries where journalists and trade unionists get garrotted. His advice to us needs putting in context. If we win tomorrow he knows his own complicated financial arrangements will come under scrutiny. And of course there's the little matter of the judicial public enquiry we'll hold into his conduct of the wars. What was the evidence on which he based his decisions? What did he promise the Americans? What was the secret legal advice he was given? What plans did he make for the aftermath of the wars? Did he lie to Parliament?

"And you're surprised he now wants the Tories to win?"

HELEN

It was breath-taking, spoken with all his high octane verve. And of course it dominated all the lunchtime bulletins. The media was now reporting that Derek Jamieson had threatened to resign. Lots of former Labour ministers were demanding Rupert's dismissal.

BARRIE

Raphael got a text from Aidan, "If Rupe goes, so do I". This was followed by a call ten minutes later as we're at the heliport heading south after two rallies in the Scottish leg. "Go easy on Rupert."

Raphael replied tartly, "So you two have kissed and made up. No more hair pulling and spitting in the playground?"

"Yeah. He's here now. I'll pass you over."

Rupert at his wheedling best, "I just hate it when someone criticises you. I'm sorry. I really went overboard. If it helps, sack me. I'll go quietly. You know how much I worship you." This gushing self-serving crap never fails to work with Raphael, providing the one who's saying it is young and fetching.

"Don't worry, I'll find the words." Every stop we make journalists were shouting, "Are you going to sack Dennison," "Why are you protecting him?" "Do you agree with Dennison?"

HELEN

Finally at the fifth stop, in Leeds, at a huge event in the Theatre, uncontrollably boisterous, waiting for the signal, Raphael finally said something. There had been a kind of nervous breakdown in the political world, as he had deliberately piled on the suspense about his own reactions.

"I'm having a busy day", he started lightly, "but even so you get to hear what's going on. This morning I'm told I was gifted with some unsolicited advice from one of my predecessors. My spokesman is a flamboyant young man and he chimed in to give us the benefit of his considered reaction." (The hall fell completely silent) "Rupert Dennison doesn't do understatement" (a little resigned smile as if chastising a wayward hyperactive child) "and he responded in the heat of this frenzied day at the climax of a torrid campaign.

"But what he said is not the issue.

"I just say this to my old boss, the former Prime Minister. Inevitably if you leave politics and cash in on your past career, you've got to expect some flak. We in the Labour Party believe if you earn big money then you pay your taxes. If there are grey areas, you clear them up. Because when it comes to fiscal tolerance, tax loopholes, cosy arrangements with the Inland Revenue, offshore foundations, the party's over. We need the revenue from tax just as we need to save money by not paying out to welfare cheats. More, in fact, because tax avoidance and evasion cost the Treasury far more than fiddles on housing benefit or overpayment of invalidity allowances. Both are morally wrong. But not equally wrong."

His genius was on full show. He had made no direct accusation about the former Prime Minister but the lightly spread smear was toxic. He carried on, "On the war, what Rupert Dennison said was nothing new. I've been saying for the best part of ten years that we went to war on trumped-up evidence. We went to war against the best legal advice. We went to war ill-prepared for the aftermath. Now those who suffered, those who lost their loved ones, those who paid for this illegal war - they want to know why all this was done? They want answers to the questions that have been nagging them. My predecessor knows that if his former party..." (I gasped at the word "former") "...wins the election, there'll be a public judicial inquiry to find the answers. And then he will be held to account.

"This afternoon, though, let's concentrate on our plans to get the economy moving…" The master had laid it all to rest. He'd avoided sacking his favourites or resignations from the other side. But it seemed to me that his boys were now out of control and I came almost to the point of dreading winning.

NED

Text to Mart

ooooooooooooooooooooooooooooooooooooooo

>Polls neck and neck or us just ahead. Huge rallies everywhere<

BARRIE

In the car to the heliport, Rupert phoned in, "You're my hero. I'd die for you."

Sounding weary and irritated, "OK Rupert, get to the point. What's up?"

Rupert replied, now business-like, "In the Mail tomorrow. Headline on the front page, 'The Death of a Bodyguard; The Unanswered Questions.' Why do his post-mortem blood tests reveal large quantities of cocaine in his bloodstream? Why was he staying at the Prime Minister's house when the PM was in No 10? Where was the PM's lover? Did they take cocaine together? What was the nature of their relationship? Then pages on you, your ex-lovers and Aidan's 'racy life-style'".

"Anything new on Aidan or on me?" Raphael could have been asking about the prospects for Mayberry City's next match.

"Nothing I didn't know."

"You know it all, anyway, because Aidan blabs everything. Anything not yet public?"

"Well there's the usual gallery of your exes, including a really pretty one of Jose looking dreamy-eyed; and a bit about Aidan in North Korea and security risks."

"Right", he said, "Plan B. Give it to them."

"A pleasure."

NED

Wembley, his nth rally of the day. Arena full again. Bands. Great music. Huge. My warm-up hits the spot. Rashida's quite good, and He's just amazing. Socks it to them about Tory money, press corruption, the anti-Britishness of the media, the Tories' "dog-whistle racism", their chumminess with tax dodgers, their sense of entitlement, crude but brilliant. Then the appeal for "timeless British values" and of course, "I can't do it alone. I need your help. I need you."

HELEN

The story of Bud's Mitchell's murder and the US connections with a possible assassination plot led all the bulletins.

NED

We make it for the rally in Trafalgar Square. It's dark, so we just say there's a hundred thousand there, and tell the police to shut the fuck up about their (smaller) estimates. It's huge anyway and some luvvies dragged up by Rupe fill the time till we arrive. Then it's me, Rashida and 15 minutes of Rafa, who's losing his voice. But his croaks and all the pics fill the evening bulletins. The poor sod has then got to schlep it up the M1 to a Mayberry midnight vigil (Bo's last throw).

BARRIE

Midnight in Mayberry town square. Bo had built a podium jutting out from the local Co-op, so we can get on to it through the shop. We could only hear the crowd as we waited inside but there was obviously a fair number listening to 'Bo's Greatest Hits' interspersed with short speeches from Angus and Aidan.

Rodney had told me the day before when we going through the programme that Aidan has built up a real local power base. Every time he goes out on the streets he has about a thousand kids to accompany him. And they use a real "community method", they help people, they clean up litter, they'll mow your lawn. And he thinks Aidan can hold on to the seat even if there's a small swing against us because it's basically an inner city vote, and there's been some "suburban flight". All his escapades haven't dinted local enthusiasm for him one little bit. "He's the best street campaigner I've ever seen", was the verdict. Probably in love with him.

When Raphael got inside the shop, and held on to the counters to steady himself, I could see his back was killing him and he's almost catatonic. After a few minutes silence, while he was sitting on a cashier's chair that kept sliding on the tatty linoleum, he asked pathetically, "Do I have to do this? I'm starving. I'm near death with fatigue. I can hardly walk. Can't we just send someone out to apologise for me. They'll forgive me. And they've had my boys all evening."

Tom's reply had its own clarity, "Get the fuck out there, you ungrateful bugger."

So out he goes meekly on to the stage into the lights, sees the thousands who've waited for hours, and it's been chilly all night. He does something I've never seen before, like a School of Billy Graham preacher he starts calling people down to join him on the stage, Angus and Aidan of course, Tom and Rodney, then some local councillors he likes, some of the kids from the College of Further Education or just old friends. Then it's Elaine, Marjorie and me, each with a playful few words in a spiral of gushing sentimentality. "These are some of my friends. We made the journey together. They've kept me going. And this one here," (he raises my hand) "he and Marjorie have been with me since the dark days of the War. Ok, he's Welsh but we're broadminded" (totally unfunny, how they laughed) "and Tom here he bullies me all the time, and Rodney does all the work." This schmaltz continues for another ten minutes, when he finishes up with Aidan who he pulls centre stage, to the squeals and shrieks of his teenage groupies. "My partner for life, Aidan. And next month, my civil partner. And if we win, we push through gay marriage, and we're first in the queue. And you're all invited." He then gives Aidan a full-on kiss.

No speech is needed. Everyone delirious with pleasure. Well, nearly everyone.

NED

I wake up at three in the morning. I'm sitting up in bed. Bolt upright. Wide awake. It's come back to me: that phrase, "We need something spectacular to turn this around… something really spectacular". The phrase just keeps whirling around in my head. Rupe, just a week before the debate. And the way he said it, almost sinister. And then he disappears for three days. And I start to think, reject the idea, and come back to it again and again. I don't believe it. It's not possible. I can't imagine that even Rupert Dennison could have set it all up. I got out of bed and googled something I'd read for my French politics paper at Uni, Francois Mitterrand and the Observatory. Fifty years ago. It's all there. How a desperate politician on the slide tries to save himself with a fake assassination attempt. And this time too it went wrong, but here someone died. I feel sick and a few minutes later I am sick and go back to bed. In the morning I try to expel the whole thing from my mind. I'm febrile, overtired. We've got one more day to fight. And we're going to win.

BARRIE

When we finally got back to the house after this warm bath of sloppy sentimentality which was the last rally of the campaign, all I wanted was to hitch a lift back to Digby. But as we arrived at the garden gate, Kevin whispered to me, "Looks like we've got company, hombre". Sitting on the short flight of steps from the garden to the front door, chatting to a policeman, was the familiar figure with his chic dark red hold-all.

Raphael said something I didn't catch - an endearment in French, I guess - and the kid replied, "I want to be there for you on the big day, Raphael" (he manages to pronounce every syllable) "and Aidan says I can come" (Kevin had to stifle a giggle. He's got a bit of a taste for low-grade double-entendres).

"For moral support," says Aidan mischievously, "Come on in." Inside I looked at Jose, the dark suit and lime tie on a pale blue shirt, hair shorn really short, the groomed stubble, the large eyes always near to filling if he's upset yet also a little knowing, and those superbly full lips. He first gave Raphael "a right snog" as Digby would have called it; then it was Aidan's turn for the slightly shorter version. I get an impersonal manly hug, as did Kevin, who also got a peck on each cheek, as if he's receiving some continental military honour; the poor man went bright pink.

Raphael now headmasterly said, "Right. Bedtime. Kevin go and get some bed linen from the airing cupboard so he can kip down on the sofa".

Kevin replied, "Oh, I don't mind sir. He can have my bed", but then after this typical example of self-abasement he realised a possible ambiguity, turned even pinker and said, "I mean..." interrupted by Raphael who concluded this time-wasting with, "We know what you mean, Kevin; but you've got a job to do tomorrow unlike this political tourist here".

Jose didn't seem interested in following all the nuances of this exchange and asked for a shower, which he being a cleanliness freak was probably his fourth of the day. Aidan told him he couldn't monopolise the bathroom and added, "tomorrow, Chico, is a busy day for you too. Voting starts at 7 here".

I don't think anyone slept well that night except possibly Raphael, who is able to switch off in almost any circumstances and is a professional short napper. I on the other hand had to go down stairs at 3 in the morning for a refill of my water glass to find Jose wearing just shorts, sitting on his makeshift bed, legs crossed, texting. He followed me into the kitchen, "You think I should not be here, Barrie". (He pronounces my name to rhyme with 'sari' and as if it has at least four 'rs'.)

"I just remember how you left last time," I replied, "and every time you're around, things become more complicated between Aidan and Raphael."

"But they both want me here", he pleaded.

"That's part of the problem", I said as I turn off the light in the kitchen, followed him back to his sofa, resisting the temptation of giving his extraordinarily inviting and scantily clad backside a little slap by forcing myself to think of Digby. I went back to bed.

HELEN

Beyond tired, I had put on breakfast TV and took our mugs of tea to bed, Ted having had the same difficulty as I in getting up that morning. The top item of course was, "The Prime Minister pulled one last surprise at the last rally of the campaign. He announced that he and the Europe Minister, Aidan Richards, would get married as soon as the 'Marriage for All' legislation is passed". The cameras focused on the first proper public kiss between the two in front of the cheering crowds. As theatre, as a piece of defiance, it broke new ground but I could not help wondering what all this was doing to Middle England. Or did people not mind anymore?

Just as I had made some toast, Bill Sampson rang up with the last polling, "Too close to call, but turn-out projections are very good, and we're ahead in three out of five marginals".

The later bulletins featured a late foray into the campaign by the Prince of Wales who, in what he may well have thought was an off-camera remark, said he wished that "politicians wouldn't keep meddling with our constitution". He added, "the House of Lords has done good work keeping governments in check which is probably why they want to scrap it".

NED

<-<-<-<-<-<-<-<-<-<-<-<-<-<-<

#@nedwar82

<-<-<-<-<-<-<-<-<-<-<-<-<-<-<

I'll tell him what we'll meddle in. The Civil List for starters.

HELEN

Ned's tweet preceded the general message from Barrie Jones by five seconds, "strict instructions from the Boss: 'do not repeat not react to the Prince'". So we now had the Royal Family more or less backing the Tories and one of our number starting to blackmail them with cuts to their state allowances. An inauspicious start to the day.

NED

Text to Mart

ooooooooooooooooooooooooooooooooooooooooo

>Oh well, too fast out of the traps. Get a bollocking from HQ. Still on edge from my bad dreams, nervous and wondering how the boss will react when he finds out what Angus himself has planned for later<

BBC NEWS 8 a.m.

Polling is underway in today's general election. Our political editor gives his assessment of the campaign.

"All election campaigns seem momentous to the candidates who fight them. This one became a global sensation from the moment that an openly gay politician launched a successful putsch against a sitting Prime Minister and then, against all conventional wisdom, called a snap election. Defying all the rules of the game, he drags the whole political debate to the left, to the obvious discomfort of some of his senior ministers. In the biggest Whitehall shake-up since the First World War, he brings into government a brilliant but youthful team of supporters which constantly gets him into hot water. His young Finance Minister subjects his rivals from the other parties to a savaging the ferocity of which has rarely been seen before the watershed. He also announces his intention to sack the 'independent' Governor of the Bank of England.

"The new leader's own debate puts on show his ability to defenestrate his opponents with a silky smile. All this takes place as unprecedented crowds gather to hear him at his barnstorming rallies, as the financial markets slump to their lowest point in twenty years and as violence simmers below the surface. Mr Sinclair receives literally hundreds of death threats every day. And then just over a week before polling day, there's an assassination attempt which costs the life of his young bodyguard, who had become a family friend and who is now the totemic martyr for the last days of the campaign, despite the subsequent allegations of substance abuse. His death is being attributed to right-wing extremists financed from US sources.

"The New Labour icons turn on the Prime Minister's team, which reacts with vicious zeal, seeming to brandish the prospect of prosecutions over the conduct of the Middle East wars. Lifestyle issues surround the Prime Minister's lover and threaten to engulf the Labour campaign until the Prime Minister announces that the couple will be the first to avail themselves of the promised 'Marriage for All' act. Even this morning's royal criticism of Labour's plan to abolish the House of Lords is met with threats to slash the Civil List. This is 'mano a mano' politics with no rules of combat.

"I'd just ask two questions; where's the opposition been? Day after day of the campaign the only story has been Mr Sinclair, his programme, his team, his style. Broadcasters like us have been stretched to find anything at all newsworthy in the Opposition's activities to allow us to respect the *balance in air-time our Charter requires. They have found that playing safe can't compete for coverage with life on the edge. But perhaps that's just good political calculation.*

"For the other political question, and the big one, is: these hundreds of thousands of supporters at the rallies, flooding the constituencies, raising the huge funds to mount this extravaganza - who do they represent? Are they 'the beating heart of a new and vibrant Britain', to quote a phrase from Mr Dennison, who has been described as the Goebbels of Team Sinclair? Or is the silent majority of Middle England about to call time on this experiment in white-knuckle-ride government? The answer - in fourteen hours' time."

BARRIE

Aidan bounded downstairs at 7 fully dressed, grabbed a coffee and a piece of toast made by Kevin, and said to a pale, bleary-eyed Jose, "Come on, sleepy head, I want you on the campaign trail to see what a real election's like."

Too late. "No, you don't," said Raphael coming downstairs. He's my 'moral support' remember. I know what you've got planned for him. You dump him all day at a polling station in your safest Tory ward, only sustained by some ageing Tory crone who pities him and gives him the occasional tea from her thermos, until someone back at your HQ remembers he's still alive, hauls him back in and then sends him somewhere else for another five hours. He has a choice: he can have nine holes of golf with me, if my back will stand it, then a spot of lunch in a pub, and then he can join your campaign bus."

Jose looked a little peevishly at both and said in French, "I come with you, Raphael. Can we get some golf clubs for me? Aidan, I am sorry. I want to help you in the campaign. But I want to be there for le chef". Aidan's eyes darkened but he beat a strategic retreat.

He did however summon up just about enough grace to go with his partner to the local polling station where they are both registered, both presumably voting for Raphael since it's his seat, although I wouldn't bet my life on where Aidan put his cross. Thus they soak up all the publicity but mercifully didn't do too much hand-in-hand newly-betrothed stuff. Raphael then did a lightning tour of the polling stations in his constituency to thank the staff before coming back to pick up Jose for a few holes at the Royal Mayberry, thankfully deserted midweek. I hear from Kevin that apart from one or two photographers they were left in peace for a bit of fresh air on this fine, mid-October morning.

I preferred staying back at the house planning things as it was - for once - blissfully quiet. I didn't even put the radio on for the one o'clock news. Just before 2, Bo arrived, looking his usual inscrutable self, wearing a black polo-necked jumper, black trousers and a discreet grey check blazer, a major concession to the solemnity of the moment.

"Everything OK for tonight?" I asked Bo, who had planned the end of poll festivities at the same venue as the one constructed for the eve of poll, a rare sense of economy having prevailed.

"Yeah, it's ok" (Bo at his monosyllabic best). After he pause, he asked "Is the boss around?"

"No, believe it or not he's playing golf and having lunch at the course. Won't be back until 4-ish, I'd say."

"I need a word."

"Well, you'll have to make do with me."

"There's been a lot of traffic." I look puzzled, it did seem a bit early for rush-hour. After a bit he continued, "Emails, texts". I still looked blank. "Between the boys."

"Bo, I'm still not getting this."

"I think Rashida, Angus and the lads are planning something for tonight. I think they're going to force him to do things he may not want to do."

This began to sound alarming. "What sort of things?"

"Like sacking a lot of the others and getting all of themselves the top jobs. It's Rashida who's been pushing most."

"And so, Bo, what makes you think this?"

"All their emails and texts are encrypted as Rupe ordered. But I do the encrypting. And I give them their pin numbers and passwords because they change all the time and they keep forgetting them. So they need someone who knows."

"So you listen in on them? "I asked, trying not to let my voice rise too much.

"Yeah, it's easy enough", he said, as if he is about to give me a level-one lesson in hacking.

"Maybe, but it's against the law."

He's not fazed at all by this rebuke. "Dunno. We pays for the gear? Anyway, the boss knows. That's how I found out about Hat."

"Jesus", I replied, "Just you forget this conversation ever happened. Or anything like it."

"But you'll tell the boss?"

"I decide what I tell him," I said, with an attempt to sound firm. But I think he realised that meant a "yes".

Raphael returned just after 4, the Indian summer having done wonders for his colour; and his young sidekick was chirpier than I'd ever seen him. Jose started gabbling, "I practise every week. I beat him on every hole, though he cheats, makes mistakes with score and he places ball nearer the hole".

Raphael, stern, "Now go and change upstairs. Someone will drop you off at Aidan's campaign office so you can make yourself useful and I can head off a row." As Jose bounded upstairs already starting to strip off, Raphael whispered to me, "Making amends".

Raphael tried to sound nonchalant, "Any messages?"

"All I've heard from Bill and Angus is that polling's brisk with record highs in some areas. No hard evidence on trends yet. Oh, and Bo called in on the off chance."

"Everything OK for tonight?"

"Apparently. I suppose you know he's been bugging all your boys?"

The tell-tale pause. "Well I guess it's his equipment."

"Oh really, that's a new one. I get a mobile phone at work and that gives the office the right to bug me? Come on, Raphael, you can do better than that."

"Why on earth did he tell you?"

"Because in his words, he's 'picked up some traffic between the boys'. In English this means that your young heroes are planning something tonight which is a bit livelier than the usual beers and the odd line of coke." Raphael winced at that one (result!). "Yup. It seems Angus and co are going to force you to sack Derek and some of the others, so they get the pick of the top jobs. Home Office for Rupert is my guess, and Aidan for the Foreign Office. Then they push us all to the left, and if you don't go along with it, who knows?" I invented this last bit to make him take it all seriously.

"Well I did promise I'd sack Derek", he whined.

"Promise who?", I spat back.

"Well, Angus."

"So he can now extract promises from you on who you appoint as your Justice Minister. Why don't you just ask him to write the whole fucking list?" By this point I was totally furious.

"Well thanks for your advice, Barrie" - his way of putting me in my place. "I'll play it by ear. Now who have we here? God's gift to the Royal Mayberry Golf Club." Jose after shower number three of the day (and I'm just counting the ones I know about) had come downstairs looking rather too elegant to be spending time outside some godforsaken polling station in the remoter parts of the borough.

"Now have a cup of tea" (Raphael all maternal, as if speaking to a slightly simple eight-year-old nephew) "and do try a real English speciality straight from our local supermarket. It's a piece of Battenberg - German name for an English treat: Kevin bought it specially. Then someone will drive you over to Team Richards."

Jose twitched his delightful little nose and carefully placed the offending pink and yellow cake to one side of his plate. He said, "I'd much rather stay with you," - putting on a look of maximum soulfulness.

"No you wouldn't Jose, believe me. Go out on the stump or we'll both get a full hurricane blast Aidan tantrum."

Off he went and I hit the phones; the markets now in freefall. Angus said we must close the stock exchange. Raphael just shrugged his shoulders and went back to watching 'The Weakest Link' on the box, shouting out the right answers with tediously appalling regularity. I phoned Cynthia and told her to convene the Privy Council at 9.30 p.m. to close the stock exchange and to impose credit controls until Monday night; the announcement to be made after the close of polls. Marsha to lead as "it's just a formality". Quite exciting, really.

NED

<-<-<-<-<-<-<-<-<-<-<-<-<-<-<

#@nedwar82

<-<-<-<-<-<-<-<-<-<-<-<-<-<-<

Queues round block. PEOPLE WANT TO VOTE. Not raining yet.

HELEN

By 9 p.m. we had run out of names to be "knocked up"[54]. All our people felt it was the highest turnout ever, without understanding what it might mean. Had our excitement so enthused people or was this Middle England fighting back?

Bill Sampson telephoned just after 9 p.m. with less than an hour to go before the close of polling, but I guessed he had spoken to Raphael much earlier. "Looks like we're in, and big. I'm off to Mayberry now. Get yourself there as soon as you decently can after your declaration. Bo's planning one great party." The justifiably proud father.

---

[54] In elections, the political parties – where resources permit – station activists at polling stations to 'take the numbers' of voters: i.e. their unique reference number on the electoral register: this enables them to contact ('knock up') electors who have promised to vote for their candidate but who have not yet done so.

BARRIE

When polls closed we gather round the set, just Raphael, Marjorie, Elaine, Kev and me. The BBC graphics told the story of the exit polls. The cut-outs of the three party leaders started to walk together up Downing Street, heading to the door of No 10. The Liberal stops in his tracks just a few steps after the gate. Raphael's figure and the Tory carried on walking. Halfway up the street the Tory stops; and Raphael just carries on, gets to the door, turns round, looks at us (in what can only be described as a leer) and walks inside. We started hugging each other, Kev included. The anchor, no friend of Labour's, looked sick.

BBC 10.05 p.m.

"Our exit polls tell us that Labour has won with a landslide. Now they're only exit polls of course. And we don't expect the first real result for a good hour. So what do we make of it?"

The political editor takes over, "What we do know is we've got a record turn-out. 82%, the highest ever recorded. And the exit polls - and you're right to make the usual caveat – well, they give Raphael Sinclair's Labour Party a huge majority. But this is interesting - the popular vote result looks like being a lot closer: the Tories at 33%, a bit higher than last time, and Labour quite a bit below 40%. But these Tory votes are squandered with huge majorities in their really safe seats, and our polls show them losing perhaps 100 seats overall. And here's another clue. Our polling shows UKIP at around 5% nationally, roughly what the opinion polls were telling us before the election. But in the key Tory marginals, the UKIP vote shoots up to over 10%, and because it's at the Tories' expense, Labour gets in. This looks to me like a very sophisticated tactical vote for UKIP."

BARRIE

Raphael just said, "I don't get it," and shook his head. By now Elaine was opening the first of many bottles of champagne - "the Widow, of course", she trumpets. And then Bill walked in - gone the hangdog expression of a harassed 1950s bank clerk: he's like the man who's won the Euro millions jackpot. But Raphael punctured the elation with a faintly sneering, "Well done, Bill. Now tell me how come the UKIP voters have suddenly become so clever that they mete out such deliciously selective punishment to the Tories".

Bill knew he couldn't dissemble, "Well, you see, we worked out where the Tories would be most vulnerable to a UKIP surge and slipped their local parties a bit of cash. Angus and I have been chatting them up for weeks". If he was expecting a pat on the back, he was soon disabused. Raphael said, blackly, "Well done. So we've created a new fourth party which stands for everything we hate. And we don't bother to worry our leader with such trifles. My God, you lot take the biscuit sometimes". He took a massive swig of champagne, not enjoying himself at all; it looked as though he was terrified of what might be coming next.

As if to make matters worse, Angus then appeared, sleeker than usual, with a look of pent-up ferocity in his eyes. He gave Raphael an affection-free embrace and Raphael almost freezes. He walked straight into the kitchen, holding the door open by way of command to Angus to follow. The door shuts and we hear muffled sounds of some hell of a row going on.

When they came out, Angus told Marjorie, "Get Derek and then Brian Dawkins on the phone for Raphael" (no "please" of course). But Raphael countermands this with a "Not until after their counts, please, Marjorie" (with the "please" underlined, the last hurrah of passing civilities). Then in came Aidan, followed by Jose at his most obedient. Aidan's eyes were on fire (after, I would guess, a short visit to his unlicensed pharmacist), Jose also in an advanced state of excitement.

Raphael got big full-on kisses from both, and Aidan went upstairs, saying, "I'll just have my shower, then a couple of slugs of champagne, and I guess it'll be my turn to go to the count". Jose followed - as if on an invisible lead. Tom rang me up from the count at 11, with the TV showing the first Labour wins flooding in. "We'll need Aidan here in 45 minutes, then Angus at 12 and the Boss at 12.30. They're counting Aidan's boxes now and the turnout's phenomenal. And God there's some excitement here, I can tell you." We then watched some real declarations.

BBC 11.15 p.m.

"And now we're going over to Portsmouth for a result (flash to Ned's seat two hundred miles away from Pompey, the anchor had clearly lost the plot!), "...and I declare the above-mentioned Mr Ned Warren duly elected..." (The rest was drowned in cheers as the commentator added needlessly that Ned Warren was one of the mainstays of the Sinclair Insurgency. He was moist-eyed but had smartened himself up for the occasion: for the first time I can remember his shirt appeared to be safely tucked into his trousers. He came forward to speak, "and above all I'd like to thank the man who has been my inspiration and I'm proud to think of as my friend, Raphael Sinclair, our Prime Minister, who'll now make the big changes we need".

HELEN

The early results were even better than the exit polls. And there were some gratifying bonuses as Tory front-benchers started falling like ninepins.

BBC 11.35 p.m.

"And now we're going back up north because we can have a word with Mr Ned Warren, the Government's business manager and a close associate of the Prime Minister. Congratulations, Mr Warren. And precisely what business has the government planned for the next few days?"

"We'll want to set a cracking pace for radical change. So Parliament's recalled for Monday. We'll announce the programme. Then we'll push through the Emergency Economic Powers Act to get the British economy moving again. And we'll start the work on a proper Constitution for Britain."

"You had some tough words for the Prince of Wales this morning. Is the Constitutional Convention going to look at the future of the Monarchy as well?"

"I don't see how we can avoid it. They put themselves in the political arena today. They may have behaved stupidly, but they did it. So we've got to see whether now might be the time to start a debate about a republic. If your constitutional monarchy's not quite so constitutional after all, it makes sense to ask some questions."

"Well, thank you, Mr Warren, and now we're going over to the count at Rupert Dennison's seat, the very controversial Mr Dennison…"

HELEN

Ted and I watched the live broadcast on the small portable in the corner of the hall where my count was proceeding. Ned Warren's outburst seemed to me at the time so uncharacteristic, even the way he spoke and addressed the camera, almost as if he had been brainwashed. I clutched at the thought that the exuberance of the evening had just gone to his head, but it sounded more premeditated than that. We then saw the beautiful form of Rupert Dennison, gleaming with deep self-love, as he made a gracious little acceptance speech, full of respectful praise for "our truly inspirational Prime Minister" seconds after the tripling of his majority had been announced. But within minutes the pattern was confirmed as he stepped up for his BBC interview.

BBC 11.45 p.m.

"Mr Dennison, has this result given you a mandate for radical change?"

"Well, it's a very clear result. If the Prime Minister confirms me in my current role, I'll press on with the Press Freedom Bill, to break up the media monopolies and to give the public proper protection against press intrusion. In the meantime the courts will be busy with journalists from the Murdoch press.

"And it's time for big changes at the BBC. I expect a clear-out of senior management and the BBC Trust. The national broadcaster has become bloated and lost sight of its mission to educate and inform. I'll see the outgoing Director-General of the BBC and the Chair of the Trust on Saturday morning."

"Thank you, Mr Dennison. So that's clear. The Culture Minister's calling in the BBC's Chair and Director-General to hand in their cards; and all this live on television."

HELEN

I managed to speak to Raphael before midnight and he was outraged. "They've gone berserk, young fools! It's all been planned you know. I've a good mind to sack them both." But then he became distracted as the cameras switched to a close-up of the demonically beautiful face of his lover, standing on the platform in Mayberry Town Hall, his expression giving nothing away. And I knew there'd be no sackings, at least not of them.

BBC midnight

"And now the result everyone's been waiting for. Just look at the hundreds of media people and the crowded gallery in Mayberry Town Hall. Mr Aidan Richards, the Prime Minister's fiancé - is that what we call him nowadays? - so controversial a figure in his own right, so detested by grandees in his own party, and whose defeat has been slated since the beginning of the campaign. Will this be the first reverse of the Sinclair Insurgency?"

"I therefore declare the aforementioned Mr Aidan Richards duly elected as Member of Parliament for Mayberry, Central" (the rest lost in cheers).

(From the studio) "I make that a swing to Labour of more than 10%. A wafer-thin majority has now become rock-solid."

HELEN

After a gracious little acceptance speech, Aidan did the interview with the BBC, six other stations vying to catch a word from this new power in the land, the teen idol of the putsch, relaxed, cold, and tieless.

"About NATO, we'll have to think whether it makes sense staying in. I'd rather go for a European defence organisation. There's always the risk that the Americans land us in the shit again, with their serial adventurism. And from now on, I expect our friends the Americans to start acting like friends, to stop spying on us and to stop their citizens trying to assassinate our prime minister."

BARRIE

As we drove to his count, Raphael was in graveyard humour mood, "I don't really see what's left for Angus to announce. The massacre of the first born? Boiling bankers in oil? The nationalisation of all corner shops?" He then added, "By the way, tell Marjorie to cancel those calls. I want the whole cabinet here in Mayberry tomorrow at 3 p.m.".

I ventured, "But you promised them you'd sack Derek".

"Sack Derek? Never. Good chap, Derek. Bit of ballast. Feet on the ground. I'm going to get seriously close to Derek."

BBC 12.10 a.m.

"There's the Prime Minister arriving at the Town Hall in Mayberry, the whole plaza lit up with a thousand lights and teeming with supporters, more arriving all the time to hear the victory speech, which we are expecting in just over an hour, now that the other party leaders have conceded. He's looking very relaxed, difficult to read what he's thinking, as usual. He's followed by Barrie Jones, his long-time aide; by Nigel Bolton, another of his old staffers, now head of communications of the government; by Miranda Fawcett, the tall lady in crimson, his head of staff; his spokesperson, our old colleague, Elaine Chayter; and another young gentleman of continental origins, I'd say, looking around him as if he wonders where he is. They disappear up the steps of the Town Hall, this monument to Victorian splendour which survived the blitz. Hope they don't decide to pull it down..."

BARRIE

He headed straight to his count to avoid meeting up with Angus and Aidan, already installed in the mayoral parlour. Tom briefed him on his own count, majority up to 31,000 - incredible. On Rodney's laptop he watches the interview with the remaining member of the Gang of Four.

"I want the Emergency Powers Bill on the Statute Book by Monday evening so we waste no time in restructuring British business and the economy. I'm closing the Stock Exchange next week and all capital movements will be frozen until Monday week. I've notified Brussels that we are clamping down on a deliberate organised attempt to undermine our economy. I have tonight fired the Governor of the Bank of England and the Chair of the Financial Services Agency, who have failed Britain so miserably. I'll name their replacements tomorrow."

Not even the slightest genuflection in the direction of his boss, nor any doubt as to his entitlement to stay in post and to wield all this patronage personally.

The BBC seemed almost too petrified to break away for Raphael's own declaration and his words of thanks to the Returning Officer and his staff.

Afterwards, on our way out to speak to the masses, the parlour door opened and Aidan almost physically dragged Raphael inside, where he'd been waiting alone with Angus. As I took a step to follow, Aidan said in a loud voice, "Fuck off, Barrie. Or better still, stand outside and mind the door".

Then Raphael really shouted, "No, Barrie, in here. You need to hear what I have to say to these two". He faced Aidan down, and I am allowed in, but alone, leaving Miranda to guard the door, more credibly than I could, but from outside.

Angus opened fire, "Well, have you sacked them yet?"

"Back away, Angus, I don't like you that close. And this'll be quick because I'm not going to disappoint my public." ("My public!" like some operatic diva) "We've twenty thousand people out there who deserve to share in the celebration of the day we made history. And no, Angus, I'm not going to sack Derek or Arthur or Bradley or Brian or Lorna; and despite all your noisome behaviour I'm not even going to sack you."

"You bastard. You swore you'd do it," Angus now again invading Raphael's personal space and making him flinch.

He finally asserted himself, "I would have been frank with you but when I heard about your little games, your pathetic plot to push us to the extremes, to get anyone who might not toe the line sacked, like some playground Trotskyites, I decided I didn't owe you the loyalty you were denying me.

"You've been going behind my back for weeks. First with this boosting of UKIP, a little ploy which is just going to come back and bite us in the backside. Then, what, fly the Republican flag? Put some journalists in jail? Purge the BBC? Walk out of NATO and add in some juvenile anti-Americanism? Sack the Bank's Governor? The siege economy? You're out of your minds.

"We manage 38% in a turn-out of 80%. A hell of a lot better than expected, but still barely a third of the people who really back us. And this is as good as it gets; our opponents were pathetic, people wanted to give us a chance, and then we get the boost from what Rupert so tastefully describes as our 'Reichstag Fire Moment'."

Aidan tried to play against type, the sweet reasoning conciliator, "Rafs, don't you see that just makes our point. This is our chance, perhaps our only chance. For the next year or two, not more, we've got the levers in our hands. People are listening to us. We're in control. We can make real changes now or never. The tone is always set by what you do in the first days or hours. Later things get sticky, anyway. By-elections. Cock-ups. The media. Or do you just want to be another Harold Wilson? Some well-meaning half-measures, a little bit of progress, but everything frittered away as weaving and trimming become your hallmark and then your only lasting legacy".

This made Raphael even crosser, perhaps because his lover's points had really struck home. "You've forgotten which country you're dealing with. Even Marx gave up on the UK as a serious revolutionary prospect. Besides, I need a wider support basis. I don't really trust you four, so the others stay where they are as my insurance policy.

"And try to remember just one thing. You owe me everything you've got: your seats, your position, your power. Whatever little cult followings you've created won't sustain you if I withdraw my love. So now we go out there, we make an effort, we put on a good show. Angus, you smile. Aidan, you hold my hand. We manage a little kiss. And tomorrow, the 'broad church', which is what the 'Great Movement of Ours' is, will do as we always do. We'll do some good things, we'll try to help people, make a bit of a difference at the margins. We'll muddle through.

"Angus, you're more intelligent than all of us, the brightest guy I know; but clever people can also be unbelievably stupid. I've tried to teach you some politics but you really don't get it, do you?"

Then he did something really weird, "Aidan, come here," he drew him up close with one hand and pulled his hair back tight with the other, then kissed him so aggressively hard on the lips that they start to bleed." Aidan yelped, said "crazy fucker" but stayed in his grip. Raphael said softly, "Yeah, crazy enough to love you, against all reason".

Aidan took his outstretched hand, and they walk out together, followed by Angus who really had no choice but to follow. As we went down the steps, Miranda whispered, "What the fuck was all that about?" I just managed to mouth the words, "Tell you later", as all conversation was drowned by the Betty Everett anthem and the roars of the crowd, accompanied by the flashes of a thousand cameras. The leader of all the progressives of the world, the repository of all our hopes, walked out on to the rostrum, but alone.

HELEN

The BBC was the first news outlet to pick up on the squalid backstairs deal with UKIP. Some of our people were horrified, others lost in admiration at the superhuman political qualities he had demonstrated, and none but a few in the inner circle knew that he was entirely ignorant of the low politics his clique had engineered.

NED

Text to Mart

ooooooooooooooooooooooooooooooooooooooooo

>As he walks past me to the rostrum, we embrace, but he has kept one hand free to squeeze my balls really hard. "Remember," he whispers, "I have these in my pocket. So behave".<

BARRIE

He wanted to get home as soon as possible after the rally but knew he had to make a token appearance at the cavernous Labour Club, which is in a bit of wasteland surrounded by bushes, strewn with litter and condoms and pasted with dog shit. He did one more victory lap and headed off out as soon as he decently could. These are his people - they're forgiving because they can see how exhausted and distracted he was. He travelled back alone with Kevin riding shotgun. I followed in the next car, but only after I'd yanked Jose off the dance floor. The last thing we want is a repeat of "the incident of the Portuguese pinioned in among the shrubs".

NED

(a letter never sent to his brother Mart in Adelaide)

My privates are still a bit sore after their earlier manhandling. And for once I don't really want a drink. We won but I don't feel celebratory. It's this 'Bud' business I can't get out of my head. I can't believe even Rupe, who can be a bit of a wild fucker when he wants - not even Rupe - would pull a stunt like this; but I know I've got to speak to him. He arrives at about two, surrounded by a whole busload of worshippers, and it takes me a few minutes to manhandle him into the bushes, which are sinister and stink of dog crap and very human emissions of various kinds, as well as rotting vegetation and wet ivy leaves, soaked after the first shower for several days.

"I never knew you cared," he says, typical Rupe.

"Sorry but you've got to tell me. It's doing my head in. Our own little 'Reichstag Fire', the shooting, did you plan it, you know, for some little October surprise, help us in the polls?" I couldn't believe I was asking this of one of my best mates.

My worst fears, he pauses, as if to compose an answer, "I never intended for anyone to get hurt of course, and certainly never Raphael or Bud. I just had the idea, found some people who arrange these things. Not rubbing people out, but who can set things up. We were so careful about the money trail, the intermediaries, and the choice of the guys. There's no way they could ever trace it back to us. And they never will. I've seen to that.

"All brilliantly planned, but then that poor sap Bud darts in front of the door to shield our vain

sovereign, who won't be seen creaking like some octogenarian. The suddenness of his movement threw the two blokes and they fire at him, instead of at the car floor. But don't worry, they knew nothing and of course are now in no position to tell tales. They really thought they were working for some 'sinister US organisation operating in the shadows'. And the van was detonated by serious professionals from abroad - a totally different outfit - who've been well paid off, and think they are getting their money from some American neocon crazies."

I don't know whether it's the horror of the story or the nonchalance of its telling but I'm overcome. I throw up, and then immediately start pummelling his head. And of course who should appear then but Aidan?

"A lovers' tiff?" he smart-asses. He doesn't know. Rupert says nothing and walks off, trying to clean himself up. I don't want to say anything, but when Aidan puts his arms around me I start to blub, and then to blab. I think he's going to go back in the Club and kill Rupe.

But to my surprise he just walks off in the drizzle, coatless into the night.

BARRIE

In the car home Jose said, "I don't understand. Raphael, he is not happy. And where is Aidan?" We sat in the car outside the house as I unburdened myself and recounted the story of the plot, the bullying and Raphael's resistance. The biggest shock for Jose is of course Aidan's apostasy, which to me is the least surprising part of the whole story.

When we got to the Mayberry home, Kevin told us that Raphael had already disappeared upstairs, so Jose trotted in his footsteps and after a quick call to Digby I followed, sensing that this would be a bad time for the two of them to be on their own. Jose, who had stripped down to his shorts in record time, was sitting on the side of the bed holding Raphael now in his pyjamas, and whispering, "I'm here for you," "I will look after you", "I won't let them harm you". They held each other tenderly and me, well, I'm truly *de trop*. As my presence was becoming oppressive and as even Raphael didn't dare ask me to leave, they each drew back just a little. To say something I announced that I'd asked Kevin to make some cocoa, which is hugely perplexing for Jose who must think that our pink jug-eared bodyguard is now official supplier to the household.

But to my surprise it was a bedraggled Aidan who came bounding up the stairs, looking soaked to the skin and seriously unhinged. "Well this is a touching sight of domestic tranquillity. Now you two, out. I need to speak to Rafs alone. And, you," he prodded Jose in his bare chest, "you need to be up early and then wearing some clothes because it's the first train back to the Gare du Midi tomorrow."

"No, actually, you're not leaving tomorrow," said Raphael. "I spoke to your boss in Brussels earlier and said it would be terribly helpful for me and the government to have someone here as a permanent link to our comrades on the continent. Good for them too to have some connection to a successful socialist party, so you'll be on secondment. You'll work in No 10, and while you're looking for your own place, you'll be very welcome to stay at Downing Street." Jose just looked ridiculously pleased and kept repeating, "I am really happy". Aidan didn't react to what I guess was unwelcome news (he likes to decide when the Portuguese comes and goes) but showed us to the door not too roughly, saying "I've got a few questions to ask Rafs so, gentlemen, downstairs please, now". He shut the door and I heard a quiet, "What did you know?" and nothing more so they must have been speaking in whispers for ages. Happy chappy and I watched the news for an hour, beginning to measure the size of our victory. We had two more cups of cocoa (living the real highlife!), I patted him on his head, he smiles and I go up to my room. There's still a light under their bedroom door, but no sound. A bit later Raphael knocked at my door, put his head round, his jaw set, and just said, "Barrie, I'll need to speak to Lorna first thing, preferably before she gets here".

No explanations, none needed. With Raphael Sinclair, there's no emotional strife which cannot be resolved by political negotiation.

JC DUNNETT'S ESSAY IN 'ENCOUNTER'

Thursday of the following week

"Some political leaders fixate on deciles. For Hitler it was 'the thousand year Reich'. Kennedy had his 'thousand days' but there the limits were set independently of his wishes. Others have their 'hundred days of dynamic action'. In the high-octane world of Raphael Sinclair a hundred hours has been sufficient to leave an indelible mark on Britain, its institutions, its politics and perhaps its people.

"We will never quite know what happened late at night the day of the election when the scale of his majority became clear. I say 'majority' rather than 'victory', for this was a tainted triumph. It is now clear that Labour High Command, flushed with funds, overrun by enthusiastic supporters, quite simply purchased another party, put it in fighting order, and sent it out on a mission to obliterate Conservatives. In the now much maligned world of finance this kind of activity is better known as 'personal equity restructuring'. The Conservatives were seen off in some fifty Labour marginals and lost fifty of their own because the notorious 'Gang of Four' which now controls the Labour machine sent in UKIP like a mercenary army to defenestrate her Majesty's Opposition.

But all was not well in Labour's ruling clique. From the first declarations of result Mr Sinclair's cubs turned into savage carnivores. First up was Mr Ned Warren, the apparently jovial runt of the group, to declare for a Republic. He was followed in short order by the Culture Secretary, Mr Rupert Dennison, who announces in his native Goebbels-speak that he will press on with 'the Free Press Bill'- designed to silence systematically all press criticism of the regime. On live television he fires the Chairman and the Director-General of the BBC, who had shown some qualms about infusing the Corporation with the journalistic standards of North Korean television. Then up pops the current paramour of the Prime Minister himself - a respite from the parade of pretty Mediterranean boys who had previously been court favourites. Mr Aidan Richards was at that moment a mere minister of state at the Foreign Office, not even in the cabinet. But it is left to this supposedly junior member of the team to inform us we are to leave NATO, our Special Relationship with the United States is to end and the relics of our military might subsumed in a new multinational army run from Brussels.

"By comparison, the utterances of Mr Angus Buchanan, who runs our economy, bordered on the mild. True, the Governor of the Bank of England was sacked for his gross impertinence in suggesting that governments might on occasion think about balancing the books. And of course with a delightful double lèse-majesté he announces that our beloved Queen will be wheeled out for a farrago of a State Opening of Parliament on the Monday; and that the first measure out of the traps would be the Emergency Economic Powers Bill, which he ordains will have to be passed on the same day and which will enable him to nationalise anything which moves.

While 20,000 Insurgency storm troopers massed in Mayberry Plaza at two in the morning, a little drama is said to have been played out in the plush setting of the Mayor's Parlour in the Town Hall. Words are spoken between the new Caesar, his tempestuous lieutenant, and this year's lover. We are led to believe that the putsch is quelled. The two young men had made the classic error of believing what Mr Sinclair had told them, that in the flush of victory he would dispatch the last remnants of New Labour and promote to the highest of offices those of his retinue who had not yet been rewarded. Mr Derek Jamieson's head on a platter was the ultimate prize that had been pledged by the conqueror.

In a series of 'deep off' briefings (the traditional niceties of the 'old politics' being respected) there was talk of "a furious row", "a dressing-down", and "a lecture about staying on the centre ground" (a terrain long since abandoned in the view of most observers). All the standard-bearers of Labour's tribes would be present at the cabinet table. Mr Jamieson would be staying on, perhaps promoted or given a fancy title. Mr Dennison would have to content himself with the arduous chores of stifling the media. Mr Warren would be confined to his quarters in No 12, Downing Street, and concentrate on his mundane duties of intimidating Parliament and supervising the political business of the emergent one-party state. And the official Lover would not after all be joining the cabinet, stuck with the status of 'Minister in Attendance', although we understand that he intervenes in cabinet discussions more often than most of its full members, provided he is not in one of his legendary and awesome sulks.

So Mr Sinclair finally addresses the multitudes gathered in the square of his home town, emphasising in his address the plenitude of his responsibilities, the leadership he will display and the "reconciliation of all progressives round our banner held aloft of peace, social justice and freedom". Peace is thus restored to this unruly Camelot.

But within hours, the compact in the Parlour has started to unravel. While Mr Jamieson is indeed given the courtesy title of First Secretary and bumped up the meaningless protocol order in cabinet, he is not given a new job. But it is the doughty figure of Baroness Lorna Horrocks who is the collateral damage. This Tory grandee was Sinclair's September signal of his willingness to reach out beyond his clans to people of good-will and talent. She boards an early train from London as Foreign Secretary. She is bundled off it at Watford, having received a call from the Supreme Leader informing her not merely that she is dispensable but that she has indeed been dispensed. She is fobbed off with a promise that she will be Britain's nominee for the new Foreign Policy job in Brussels, but which is one item of patronage not yet in the gift of the Sinclair Insurgency.

When the cabinet meets later that day in Mayberry, which like Oxford in the last Civil War has become a transient alternative capital city for our great nation, the seat reserved for the Foreign Secretary is occupied by none other than the young athletic figure with the dark brooding handsome features, Mr Aidan Richards. There has been a codicil to the Parlour Compact, a sort of Pillow Compromise, negotiated by the two protagonists in the bedroom of the Mayberry Residence in the middle of the night.

The real terms of the historic settlement become clearer as the days pass. Mr Buchanan, still reigning from Mayberry, summons the press in the late afternoon of Friday. He has in tow a small Chinese lady, a Mrs Bai Lishan, apparently a certainty for the Nobel Prize in Economics because of her ground-breaking work on currency and monetary economics in which as a postdoctoral student he assisted her, and of gratifyingly leftist persuasion. The press release of MINFINEC, as we must now call it, helpfully explains that her Chinese name means 'Beautiful White Coral'. She is our new Governor of the Bank of England. Inscrutable, even bemused, throughout the proceedings, she convinces few that she will defend the independence of the Bank against a marauding Mr Buchanan on the rampage, so strappingly athletic in comparison to the slight tiny figure at his side. The Financial Services Authority, a New Labour contraption which whitewashed banks whenever they dreamt up dodgy scams to make their managers millionaires, is quite simply scrapped.

On Saturday Mr Buchanan abolishes our currency, but with subtlety. "For the sake of our export the value of the pound is locked in parity with the euro", which is one way of presenting a 22% devaluation. And henceforth the euro will be legal currency everywhere in the Kingdom, if we are still allowed to use that term. Neatly done, and no need for a referendum of course. I searched in vain the pages of Labour's 'Manifesto for Change' for any hint of this particular bombshell.

On Sunday he takes charge of a tame television interview, the days of confrontational interrogations of government ministers having ended abruptly at 10 p.m. on Thursday October 18th when Mr Dennison's subjugation of broadcasting took full effect. Our Finance Minister shares with us the details of his Emergency Economic Powers Bill: the 'golden share' the state will have on the boards of all the privatised utilities, which means that for one euro per company it's the government which will take control. To some it's public ownership by the backdoor, free of charge; 'confiscation' is the other term for it. He informs us he will take over any failing company with potential which his hand-picked 'Business Council' (a bunch of tame business executives and self-styled academics who have seen which way the political winds are blowing) will have identified.

But for Mr Buchanan, this was just the start. On Monday we are treated to the post-pageantry State Opening of Parliament orchestrated by the Junta's 'events organiser'. The Queen arrives by car not carriage. She is hustled into the Lords, gives a quick blessing on a poorly attended occasion, with, from the Labour ranks, only the Prime Minister and his ever game deputy, Mrs Worthington, in attendance in the gallery. The Monarch is then shooed out, while the real action in the Commons gets underway.

The Prime Minister presents there his own programme, the House entirely intimidated by the young, snarling Jacobins who constitute its new majority. Far from watered down, its radicalism is ratcheted up. The Emergency Powers Bill is to be passed that day, under the guillotine provisions of the Parliament Act, to "calm the markets" (Dennisonspeak at its best). The Constitutional Convention will begin its work of demolition of our institutions in the next few days, packed with house-trained academics whose disrespect for our traditions is matched only by their obedience to the New Order. But the abolition of the Lords is to be fast-tracked first, before the great thinkers in the Convention have had time to design any replacement. Some might think this was putting the cart before the horse, but the aristos are even now being allotted space on the tumbrils. That other venerable institution, the Church of England, has already been dispatched by the simple of expediency of the government withholding all funding and by our militantly atheistic Prime Minister refusing to nominate bishops. The beyond irony 'Press Freedom Bill' should indeed be on the statute book before Christmas.

On Tuesday the demonically active Mr Buchanan is at the despatch box presenting a budget which slashes defence spending and cuts the budgets of all departments by 5%, something of a surprise to any gullible elector who attached any credence to announcements made by the same government before the elections and the tiresome repetition throughout the election campaign of the anti-austerity mantra. An immediate freeze on all energy prices, water charges and public transport travel will last indefinitely, but sumptuary taxation (how attached are our young radicals to this anachronistic terminology provided it obfuscates their intent!) will rise by 25% forthwith; or to use the language of the soon-to-be-out-of-business tabloids, booze and fags are being priced beyond reach.

But our young Lochinvar is not done yet. In the same speech he has two more poisoned arrows in his quiver. Supertax returns at the eye-watering rate of 75%. Non-domiciled British citizens will pay it or lose their passports. Those with properties in the UK will all pay a new wealth tax at the highest rates in Europe. But the biggest bombshell is left to last. The state will withdraw all guarantees for deposits in private banks before Christmas. But a new state Investment Bank, which will give total cover for all monies deposited, whatever the amounts, is created by ministerial fiat under the catch-all Emergency Act. As the rest of our centuries-old banking system goes to the wall, an entirely state-run bank will ensure public investment in manufacturing selected by government and de facto run by government.

While the people's Finance Minister, the Glaswegian Gladiator, labours in the field, another young colleague has been active. It is not uncommon for overweight people to be quick on their feet once they take to the dance floor. Such is the case of Mr Ned Warren: before the election the flabby mascot who served as Court Jester by appointment, now a fully-fledged Insurgency Rottweiler. At 10 p.m. on the same day our increasingly supine media announce that an amicable agreement has been reached with the peers of the realm. They will pass the Democratic Reform Bill (another classy Dennisonianism) before the end of the week, abolishing the Lords and replacing it with the Council of State, which will advise the government on any matter ("chosen by the government") and with the identical composition, premises and allowances currently enjoyed by their lordships. Better still, they will be able to retain their courtesy titles. Thus the honourable members of the Upper House have been won over by a mixture of menace (the threat to swamp them with a thousand Insurgents ennobled for the sole purpose of voting for their extinction) and usury; and so they act as willing accessories in this latest piece of constitutional vandalism. Mr Warren waits until after the final stages of the Bill have been completed in thirty minutes flat to announce in his much-admired estuary tones, and relayed by Twitter of course, the medium of choice of the new Bolsheviks, "When the Lords pop off, they won't be replaced. So more money saved". An elegant epitaph for one of the last ramparts of our civil liberties.

Yesterday our Prime Minister and a large part of the new revolutionary aristocracy attended the funeral of the young man who quite literally took the bullet for him a few days before the election. I do not subscribe to the speculation doing the rounds on Twitter and Facebook, as yet beyond the control of his Culture Secretary, that parts of the ruling clique mounted a fake assassination attempt on the life of our leader to create sympathy for him at a delicate moment in the campaign, and that the plot went awry; or, more intriguingly, that some of the same clique had planned the elimination of Mr Sinclair himself for the benefit of his ambitious second-in-command so that he could take over all the reins of power. But there remain unanswered questions about the poor bodyguard, his relationship with the Prime Minister's intended spouse, and their shared predilections. The death of any young man is always an event attended by great sadness, and for Mr Dennison and others a serious media opportunity not to go unexploited.

For myself, my own grief is for our past, our traditions, and our former glories. The cornerstones of 'the Idea of Britain' to use the Prime Minister's own sophisticated semantics, were liberty, the rule of law, respect for institutions, checks and balances on executive power, freedom of the press, and a fiercely competitive private sector. All of this has been swept away in just one hundred hours.

Many of us look at Britain's future with nothing but the greatest foreboding. But I clutch at one straw. The Jacobins swept all before them, butchered all their enemies at home and defeated those abroad. But then at the apogee of their power they turned against each other, in the end suffering the same fate of all tyrants who forget that the fundamental laws of gravity apply without distinction of rank, power and place.

******** THE END... FOR NOW ********

ABOUT THE AUTHOR

Julian Priestley is a former Secretary-General of the European Parliament.

He was brought up in Plymouth and graduated from Balliol Oxford in 1972. He is a past President of the Oxford Union.

His non-fiction writings include 'Six Battles that Shaped the European Parliament', John Harper Publishing, 2008, 'The European Parliament: Places, People, Politics' (with Stephen Clark) John Harper Publishing, 2012, 'The making of a European President' (with Nereo Peñalver Garcia) Palgrave 2015; he edited 'Our Europe, Not Theirs' (with Glyn Ford) Lawrence and Wishart 2013, new edition 2016.

He is a commentator and writer on European and British current affairs, a member of the board of the Jacques Delors Institute in Paris and a visiting professor at the College of Europe in Bruges.

He lives in Luxembourg with his partner, Jean Schons.

He was knighted in 2007.

Printed in Germany
by Amazon Distribution
GmbH, Leipzig